PRAISE FOR THE WRITING
OF GWEN BRISTOW

Jubilee Trail

"Miss Bristow has the true gift of storytelling."

—*Chicago Tribune*

"This absorbing story giving a thrilling picture of the foundation on which our West was built is heartily recommended."

—*Library Journal*

Celia Garth

"An exciting tale of love and war in the tradition of *Gone with the Wind* . . . The kind of story that keeps readers tingling."

—*Chicago Tribune*

"Absorbing and swift-paced, well written . . . The situations are historically authentic, the characterizations rigorous, well formed and definite. The 'you-are-thereness' is complete."

—*The Christian Science Monitor*

"Historical romance with all the thrills [and] a vivid sense of the historical personages and events of the time."

—*New York Herald Tribune*

Deep Summer

"A grand job of storytelling, a story of enthralling swiftness."

—*The New York Times*

The Handsome Road

"Miss Bristow belongs among those Southern novelists who are trying to interpret the South and its past in critical terms. It may be that historians will alter some of the details of her picture. But no doubt life in a small river town in Louisiana during the years 1859-1885 was like the life revealed in *The Handsome Road*."

—*The New York Times*

DEEP SUMMER

DEEP SUMMER

PLANTATION TRILOGY

GWEN BRISTOW

OPEN ROAD
INTEGRATED MEDIA
NEW YORK

Cover design by Connie Gabbert

ISBN 978-1-4804-8535-8

This edition published in 2014 by Open Road Integrated Media, Inc.
345 Hudson Street
New York, NY 10014
www.openroadmedia.com

For Jeannette Deutsch

DEEP
SUMMER

PART ONE

CHAPTER ONE

The river was silky in the late sun. On shore the light pierced the live-oaks with golden spikes, and the wind in the long gray moss made a soft undertone to the shouts of the boatmen.

While the men tied up the flatboat Judith leaned over the side washing some kerchiefs and a pair of her father's nankeen breeches. It was hard to get clothes clean in the river. No matter how hard one scrubbed they had a yellowish tinge when they got dry. What a relief it would be to get done traveling and settle down again like civilized people, with a well of clear water and a big convenient fireplace for cooking. The men made the boat fast with ropes flung around a tree, and Judith's brother started a fire on the bank. Her father sent the boatmen to look for game.

The flatboat bounced on the current. Judith spread the breeches and kerchiefs on deck to dry and began making herself tidy for supper. She combed out her hair—it was tawny like the river, and like the river unruly—and when she had pinned up her braids she got out a fresh kerchief and knotted it around her shoulders. Her mother had already gone ashore with the tripod and was setting it up over the fire. Judith picked up the cooking-pots and followed.

The men had brought out the dried corn and beans and jerked venison. Judith mixed a pot of succotash. As she slung the pot over the tripod she heard a voice call from the river.

"Good evening, my fellow-travelers!"

Judith started and looked up. Another flatboat was approaching the bend, and as the strange boatmen pushed down the current the owner of the boat waved toward the bank. He was tall and broad-shouldered, with a face ruddily tanned except where a scar cut a white line across his left cheek. His coat was of claret satin and there were silver buckles at his knees and on his shoes, and the sun glinting down his legs caught the shimmer of silk stockings. Judith stared. They had met other settlers on their way down the Mississippi, but never one who journeyed in such splendor as this.

"Good evening, sir," Judith's father called from the bank. He bowed with perfunctory courtesy, evidently having no great opinion of a man who would attack a wilderness in the jubilant audacity of satin.

The stranger grinned in return, unabashed. The sun caught red-gold lights in his hair, which was long and tied back with a black silk ribbon. "You are settling in Louisiana?" he called.

"Yes."

"Good. So am I. Permit me to present myself. Philip Larne, sir, at your service."

"My compliments, Mr. Larne. My name is Mark Sheramy. These are my wife, my son Caleb and my daughter Judith."

"My respects to you all. I trust we shall meet again."

Mark Sheramy bowed. Young Mr. Larne touched his forehead as if meaning to doff his hat, but since he wore none the gesture had the effect of a jaunty dismissal. His flatboat had reached the bend, where a canebrake jutted into the river. Mr. Larne turned to look at Judith and he smiled again. His eyes did not leave her till the canebrake was between them.

Judith felt a tremor run down her back. She glanced uneasily at her parents lest they had observed this impudent attention, but her father was piling sticks on the fire and her mother was busy cleaning the grouse the boatmen had brought in. Judith fetched a pot of water, wondering if Mr. Larne had looked at her like that because he thought she was pretty. She was fifteen, old enough to want to be pretty, but her father said she was too young to be concerned with adornment and as she had never seen a mirror larger than six inches by eight it was hard to form much opinion of her looks. She knew she had eyes that were brownish gold like her hair, and her complexion was all right except for being sunburned, but glancing down at her gray cotton gown and her plain kerchief she found it hard to believe that a gentleman in satin and silver could notice her with admiration. Judith looked disapprovingly at the nut-colored garments of Caleb and her father. They had seemed very tidy and proper back home in Connecticut. But at home all decent farmers dressed like that, except when they rode to meeting, or to market on holidays. She wondered where Mr. Larne came from.

"Mother," she said suddenly.

Mrs. Sheramy looked up from the grouse. "Yes, child?"

"That Mr. Larne," said Judith. "He—he's traveling all by himself, and maybe he spoke to us because he was lonesome. He's tied up his boat just the other side of the canebrake. Don't you think it might be nice if we asked him to have supper with us?"

"Why—yes," said Mrs. Sheramy after an instant's hesitation. She turned to her husband. "What do you think, Mark?"

Mark leaned on his gun.

"I hardly know," he returned slowly. "He doesn't look like very good company to me."

"Why, father!" cried Judith. "He looks like a lord!"

Mark smiled slightly. "More like a good-for-nothing dandy. I've seen his kind. Cluttering up the colonies and making trouble for thrifty folk trying to establish homesteads and live in fear of the Lord."

Judith jabbed a spoon into the succotash. "It's positively unchristian of you to think hard of a gentleman just because he's all dressed up."

"Judith!" said her father.

"I'm sorry, sir." She bit her lip. But she was gladly surprised to hear her mother say:

"After all, Mark, if the poor man has had nobody but those rough boatmen to cook for him all the way down the river he must be starved for a woman's hand about his food. Why shouldn't we ask him to supper?"

Mark shrugged. "Very well. Go ask him over, Judith."

"Yes sir." Judith hurried to push a path through the canes. The sun was slanting rapidly, but the stalks had a faint sparkle as she shoved them away. On the other side of the brake she stopped, quivery with sudden shyness. Philip Larne was sitting on the knotted root of a tree. His gun across his knees, he was watching the sky for game while his boatmen built a fire. Judith felt tongue-tied. He was not their sort; asking him to supper seemed a feat requiring intimacy with courts and ballrooms. She might have fled in silence if he had not at that moment caught sight of her and sprung to his feet, laying his gun against a tree.

"My charming semi-acquaintance!" he greeted her.

He came up and kissed her hand. Nobody had ever kissed her hand before. Judith curtseyed in a flutter of embarrassment.

"I—I beg your pardon, sir. But my mother—my mother sends her compliments, and wants to know if you'll have supper with us tonight."

Philip Larne's blue eyes swept her up and down, and though his answer was all grace his lips twitched with amusement.

"I am honored, ma'am."

"Then—then you'll come, Mr. Larne?" she asked tremulously, pushing back against the canes again.

He began to laugh. "Wait a minute," he exclaimed, taking her arm to make sure that she did so. "You are positively trembling, Miss Sheramy! Do you think I'm an Indian hankering for your scalp?"

"Of course not—but—" She hesitated, but he was so warmly friendly that before she knew it she was laughing too. "I'm not very used to strangers," she confessed.

"Then it's high time you got used to them," he retorted. "Aren't you moving into a brand-new country? Come sit down and talk to me."

Judith drew back. "But I thought you were coming with me!"

"I'd love to. But—" The late sunshine skittered over his claret shoulders as he turned to look toward the river, where his boat lay moored. It was larger than most flatboats—nearly sixty feet long—with a narrow deck and an enormous cabin that had all its tiny windows shut tight. He must have a quantity of household goods to need so much space for storing them, which was odd, for you hardly expected a man to acquire household goods before he had a household. And evidently he had no family on the flatboat. "I can't possibly leave my boat unguarded," he was saying to her.

"But your boatmen, sir!" Judith protested. "They have guns."

His blue eyes twinkled upon her. "They're loyal enough as long as I'm watching them. But I wouldn't trust any crew on the river with a costly cargo."

"A costly cargo?" she repeated. "Then you're a trader? Bringing down merchandise?"

He started slightly and his hand on her arm tightened. "What did you think I was bringing?"

"Why—plows and chairs and spinning-wheels, like us," she returned in surprise, but as he did not release her she felt a flash of irritation. "I never thought about it at all," she snapped. "And I'll thank you to quit holding me like a constable!"

"Forgive me. I didn't realize I was holding you." He smiled as he let her go. "I must confess I don't own a plow nor a chair, nor even a spinning-wheel. I have only—" he hesitated a fraction of a second, and ended—"merchandise."

Judith looked down, abashed at having spoken so rudely, though she wondered why he had answered evasively instead of saying flax or whiskey or whatever it was. He was speaking again with an enticing eagerness.

"I simply don't dare leave my boat. But I've been so lonely on this everlasting river—why don't you stay and have supper with me?" He caught her hands, drawing her toward the fire. "Yes, you must stay."

"But I can't!" She stopped halfway. "What on earth would I tell my father?"

"Tell him—" Philip chuckled. "Tell him I offered you cakes made with honey and rice-meal, and oranges soaked in syrup of cinnamon, and dried figs from the gullah coast—"

Judith found herself sitting on the knotted root of the tree. "The gullah coast—where in the world is that?"

"It's the lower edge of South Carolina."

"Is that where you came from?"

He nodded, stretching on the grass at her feet and raising himself on an elbow to ask:

"And you? New England?"

"Why yes. Connecticut. How did you know?"

Instead of answering, he said, "Did anybody ever tell you your eyes were the color of champagne?"

Judith felt herself blushing. "Certainly not. What is champagne?"

"It's a sparkly wine they make in France."

"Have you been to France?" she asked in astonishment.

"Yes. Don't they ever drink champagne in Connecticut?"

"I don't know. Not up our way, anyhow. You've never been to Connecticut?"

"Once, for a very little while. During the French and Indian War."

"Oh, you were in the war?" she exclaimed gratefully, glad he was a soldier of the king. Now maybe her father would think better of him, for Mark had also been in the war.

"Most assuredly," returned Philip, "under General Braddock and young Mr. Washington of Virginia." There was a trickle of laughter under his voice.

"Then you are coming down with a royal grant?" she asked, delighted to discover he was a responsible citizen and not as her father thought an elegant ne'er-do-well.

He laughed aloud. "Surely. Want to see it?"

From inside his frilled shirt he drew a great document with a seal, informing all who cared to know that His Majesty George the Third had bestowed upon his subject Philip Larne, as reward for his service in the colonial war against the French, three thousand acres on the east bank of the Mississippi River in the country of Louisiana, in the sub-province West Florida that had been ceded to England by the treaty that ended the war. Done by the king's emissaries in the town of Charleston in the colony of South Carolina January 12 in the year of grace 1772.

She gave the paper back, saying, "Yes, my father has one of these. Father waited till long after the war before asking for it. He didn't want to leave New England."

Philip sat up, wrapping his arms about his knees. "I wonder he left at all. He doesn't look like the footloose sort."

"He isn't. Not a bit. But our crops failed three times, and there was such bitter cold last year half our cows died. And everybody was talking about this new English settlement in Louisiana. Men who hadn't been in the war told father they envied him his chance to get free land here. And he got a letter from a young man who left our township five years ago with a royal grant—Mr. Walter Purcell. Mr. Purcell said Louisiana was such a fertile country that from its best land a man could get four crops a year."

"Do you think you're going to like it?" Philip asked smiling.

"I—guess so," she said doubtfully, looking around at the forest and the lazy river purpling in the twilight. "But it's so strange. Weird, don't you think, with the palms and the moss like curtains on the trees, and so flat. Maybe it doesn't seem so

13

strange to you," she added shyly. "You're a traveled man. But I—well, I'd never been out of our township till we left for good last winter."

"And you thought the whole world looked like New England?" Philip asked gently.

"I don't rightly know what I thought. Only now I know better. I feel—"

"What?" he asked when she hesitated.

"Ever so much older than before I left. Didn't you feel that way when you went to France?"

Philip chuckled softly, and she started in surprise at herself, talking so confidentially to a stranger. But he had seemed so interested. Philip knelt in front of her, putting his hands on hers.

"You're the most delectable child I ever saw in my life. But you aren't really a child, are you?"

"I'm fifteen. Father always calls me a child."

"But you aren't, you know. You're a very beguiling young lady."

She caught her breath, and Philip asked,

"Didn't any other man ever tell you that?"

Judith looked down at his hands covering hers in her lap. It had abruptly grown so dark she could hardly see them.

"You're going to think I'm a dreadful yokel," she said. "But I've never been alone with a young gentleman before in my life."

"Heavens above," said Philip in a low voice.

"And I'm sure my father is coming to get me almost any minute," said Judith, "and I think I'd better go—"

There was a yelp from the forest.

It was short and horrible. Judith sprang up with a cry as Philip grabbed his gun. The boatmen dropped the pots and snatched their own guns, rushing toward the forest, where she saw two eyes staring at her from the gloom under the trees. They were greenish eyes gleaming like a cat's, only much larger, and they shone out of the dark as though they belonged to a bodiless spirit. She heard a shot and then another, and the eyes vanished as she felt Philip's arm around her shoulders and heard him say:

"Don't be afraid! It's all right!"

"What—what was that?" she gasped.

"A panther. They'll attend to it."

"Are you sure it's dead?"

"Yes, yes," he assured her, but she did not hear what else he said. She had wheeled around toward the river, dizzy with a new alarm.

His cargo had come to life. From the cabin of his boat were yells and beating noises that might have been those of wild animals fighting the walls of their prison. Exclaiming "Stay where you are!" Philip rushed down to his boat, but she ran after him, terrified at being left alone. He sprang to the deck and pulled open one of the windows, and she saw stout wooden bars inside it and a dim light beyond them.

Philip was shouting through the bars demanding quiet. He slammed the shutter as she reached him, but not soon enough to keep her from seeing his cargo. She cried out in amazement.

He turned to her. They were so close together that in the

dwindling daylight she could see his smile, impudent and placating at once. He asked:

"Are you so astonished that I should trade in slaves?"

Judith twisted the end of her kerchief. "Why no," she answered dubiously. "We've seen several slave-traders on the river."

But she was walking away from him, toward the plank that led from the deck to the shore. He came after her and caught her shoulder.

"Then why are you leaving me like this? Aren't there any slaves in Connecticut?"

She paused. "Yes, of course there are. Not many—they are no good in winter—we never had any." But she was still confused. Other slave-traders she had seen didn't keep their blacks locked up like that. There was something wrong about that boat. Then with a flash of horror she knew what it was.

She jerked back. "Let me go!" she cried. "You're a smuggler—a pirate—let me go!"

He smiled at her astuteness. "Do you think," he asked her, "that I look like a pirate?"

"I don't know what pirates look like," Judith retorted. "But if you hadn't stolen those slaves you'd have purchase papers, and if you had papers you wouldn't be so almighty careful not to let anybody see what's on this boat. Let me *go*, I tell you!"

She began to cry. She had heard hair-raising tales of how smugglers on the Mississippi cut men's throats for the sake of their cargoes, but she was crying less in fear than in disappointment. He had been so suave and charming.

"Don't be absurd," said Philip, but Judith covered her face with her hands and choked helplessly. Suddenly she heard her father's voice from the bank.

"Judith! Mr. Larne! What were those guns?"

Judith pressed back against the cabin wall, drying her eyes on her kerchief. Philip went down to the bank.

"I'm sorry you were disturbed, Mr. Sheramy," she heard him say, as smoothly as if he had not just proved himself a blackguard. "The men have just killed a panther. The young lady was frightened and ran to the boat. One moment—I'll help her down."

He came back, saying clearly as he took her arm, "It will be quite safe for you to go through the brake with your father, Miss Sheramy." But as they started toward the plank he added under his breath, "Stop crying, you little puritan blockhead. Do you want to get me hanged?"

Judith halted. The night had grown quite black. Her father's figure was only a cloudy outline on the bank, and Philip was real and warm beside her. She looked up, and he was smiling again, that smile of his that was so teasing and yet so tender.

"I'm not crying," she whispered. "And I won't tell. I promise."

"Thank you," said Philip, in a voice so low she could hardly hear him.

There was no time to say more. He led her to where her father was waiting, and bowed low.

"Present my compliments to your lady, sir," said Philip, "and tell her how sorry I am that the necessities of travel prevent my accepting her invitation. Good night."

He gave Judith's hand a warm little squeeze as he released it.

The sun flashed on the golden river, and on both banks the orange groves were blossoming with such luxuriance that it looked as if miles of white lace had been thrown over the trees. The air was heavy with sweetness. Judith sat by Philip at the edge of the water, listening. Seven days had passed since their first conversation, and every time the boats had stopped since then Philip had found means to speak to her. At first she said she would not talk to a slave-smuggler, but Philip pled with that singularly sweet smile of his and it was so hard to tell him no to anything. She listened now conscience-plagued but enchanted.

"So up came Bonylegs, climbing the mast with a knife between his teeth and two pistols in his belt, and I thought my luck was over. I can see that knife now, double-edged, and a gap above the blade where one of his teeth was out—"

"Yes—then what happened?"

"I fired my last bullet, Judith, and the Lord's hand put it right into his chest, for my own hand was shaking so I could hardly hold the gun, and down went Bonylegs like a falling star!"

"Like Lucifer!" she cried.

"Who?"

18

"In the Bible."

"Oh yes, yes, of course.—And after that the crew was easy. So we had his ship, with her hold full of slaves, and bales of silks and silver he had taken off the English vessels—"

"What did you do with them?" she gasped.

"Why, we took them, my dear, and it's my share of slaves and treasure I'm bringing down on my flatboat."

"But Philip," she protested in a shocked little voice, "they didn't belong to you!"

"Why no, honey, but they didn't belong to Bonylegs either." He laughed under his breath. "By getting rid of him we did clear the sea for coastwise boats, and don't you think we deserved some reward for that?"

"But isn't there a law about pirate ships? That the booty goes to the royal governor, and he gives a reward?"

"I'm sure I don't know," Philip answered merrily. "But the royal governor didn't risk that knife between his ribs. Don't you understand?" he exclaimed. "I wanted to come to Louisiana, and I couldn't come with only my two hands to clear the jungle!"

"I—suppose not," Judith owned doubtfully. She got up, holding in her apron the sticks she had been gathering. "They'll be missing me, Philip. I've simply got to go."

"Why don't your folks invite me over again?" Philip asked as he stood up. "If I knew in advance I could tie up close to you, and we could eat in sight of both boats."

"Well—" She peeled a bit of bark off a stick. "I'm afraid my father doesn't think very much of you, Philip. He told mother not to ask you again. He—he said you wouldn't be a good influence on Caleb and me."

Philip chuckled. "I couldn't possibly influence a stony young man like your brother. And as for you, my dear—"

"I've got to go," said Judith again. She ran off through the grove.

As she mended the fire she thought of Philip's last interrupted phrase. Oh, he was influencing her, dangerously. She was defying her father's wishes and listening secretly with less and less horror to yarns of plunder and blood—if somebody had told her a week ago that she would be entranced with such wickedness! Though she suspected that even yet Philip had not told her all about his dreadful past, already she knew he was a sinful man unconcerned about the bliss of heaven or the pains of hell, and she was not reminding him. For when she was with him she forgot that men and women were put on earth to prepare their immortal souls for eternity. She forgot everything except how handsome he was in spite of the scar on his face and how dull her life had been until she met him. Judith took the venison off the fire and called to the men that dinner was ready. Her father filled his bowl and beckoned her.

"Daughter," he said as she sat on the grass, "were you talking to that Mr. Larne awhile ago?"

Judith dropped her eyes. "Yes sir."

"I thought I heard your voices," said Mark gravely. "Judith, you must not allow him to speak to you when you are alone. We know nothing of him."

"But we do!" Judith protested. "I mean—he told me his father was a rice planter on the Carolina coast."

Mark shrugged. "They're a giddy lot, I understand. Reading atheistic French books and doubting the word of God."

"He said he went to school in England," Judith went on defensively, "and after that they sent him to Paris to learn polite conversation—"

"Hm," said Mark. "Young gentlemen are likely to learn a good deal in Paris besides polite conversation."

Mrs. Sheramy interposed. "Mark! The child is only fifteen!"

He did not answer and they ate in silence. Judith watched the glittering water, wondering what he had meant. She didn't know, unless it was something else about atheistic literature.

When the boatmen had finished their dinner she went to wash the pots in a pool made by a projecting arm of the river. While she was dipping them in the water something cold trickled across her neck and inside her kerchief.

The pot fell with a splash. By the bushes at her elbow stood Philip, smiling his naughty, teasing, provocative smile. "I'm sorry I frightened you," he said, and bent to rescue the pot.

Judith sat back on her heels, her hands twisting together. "Please go away. My father said I mustn't talk to you."

"I thought he would." Philip coolly sat down beside her.

Judith glanced over her shoulder, but the bushes hid her from the others. "What did you put into my kerchief?" she asked, feeling it lying shamefully hidden between her breasts.

"A little present I've wanted to give you since I saw you first. See if you like it."

She took it out, a thin gold chain set with jewels. "Oh Philip," she cried, "how beautiful! What are they?"

"Topazes. You're the only girl I ever saw who had eyes the color of topazes."

Judith watched the sun flash through the stones, finding it hard to believe her eyes were as golden as that. But after a moment her conscience struck a blow at her heart and she demanded:

"Philip, did you come by this honestly?"

"I'm afraid not, now that you ask me," he returned laughing, "but it's no less beautiful for that, is it? Please take it, Judith! I'll never trouble a ship again as long as I live. I'll be as honest a planter as ever came to Louisiana—"

Then all of a sudden he was holding her in an embrace so tight it hurt, and was covering her lips with his. Judith had wondered sometimes what it was like to be kissed by a man, and had thought it would be embarrassing. But she found it quite the most glorious thing that had ever happened to her, though after a moment's yielding she pushed herself away from him.

"Don't do that!" she cried. "You're a pirate—a thief—a murderer—"

Philip moved back as though to keep himself from touching her again. His smile was no longer amused, but very tender and sweet. "Yes," he said. "But you'll never find anybody else who loves you as much as I do."

Tears were rushing into her eyes. "You dear girl," said Philip. He took her hands in his, tangling the topaz chain through her fingers. "Don't you love me too?" he asked in a low voice.

"I don't know," she returned brokenly. "Only I know—if I do it's wrong. You've done such dreadful things—you must have broken all the Ten Commandments—"

"Every single one," said Philip promptly, "and I'll break them all again for your sake, or keep them for your sake, which is harder. Won't you let me tell you from the beginning, Judith?"

They sat down together on the grass. Judith was thinking that if the Lord could create anything as splendid as Philip Larne and then send him to hell it would be a sad waste.

"Dearest," said Philip, "I want to marry you. Funny—I never thought I'd want to marry anybody. May I go on?"

She nodded. Philip wrapped his arms around his knees.

"Judith, I'm a good-for-nothing younger son. But if one is a younger son on the gullah coast it's hard to be anything but good-for-nothing. For there are only the church, the army and the law, and if you won't have one of those you're condemned to idleness. Ever since I can remember I've wanted to be a planter, but the plantation went to my oldest brother. After my father died my brother and I were always quarreling, for having nothing to do I drank too much and gambled too much and made a general nuisance of myself, so he finally bought me a commission in the army and packed me off to fight the French."

Judith looked at the river. The water was dark gold like the topazes in her hand. Philip went on.

"I liked the war at first, but I got bored with that too, so when it ended I came back to Carolina. One evening when I had drunk too much I quarreled with a cousin of mine about a lady who mattered not two pins to either of us, and the next day we met and he slashed my face with a rapier—"

"You got that scar in a *duel*, Philip?" she asked reproachfully.

"Yes, honey child, and if I'd only slashed his face I don't suppose I'd be on the river now, but I'm afraid I must confess to you that I ripped him open from his belly to his collarbone—"

"*Philip!*"

"He died three days later in a great deal of agony, and after that I simply had to leave. So when I heard King George was rewarding soldiers of the French war with grants of land in Louisiana I asked for mine. It's on the Dalroy bluff—"

"The Dalroy bluff? That's where my father's grant is too."

"We're both fortunate. It's choice land. But how could I go to it without plows or slaves or money to buy them?"

"So you—" She paused questioningly.

"So I went out and got what I had to have," he said, "from ships bringing to the houses of older sons on the Carolina coast things they had bought but didn't need. Then we got Bonylegs' treasure and I quit the sea. I stole everything I've got, but it's only about as much as my patrimony might have been were I not punished for the crime of having been born later than my brother." He leaned over and looked at her searchingly. "Do you think I'm hopelessly wicked, Judith?"

She put her forehead on her hands. "I don't know! I always

thought people should do their duty in the state to which God had called them. I'm all mixed up."

"Look," said Philip. He was spreading a map on her knees, and the lace at his wrist covered New England as his finger pointed to Louisiana. "Here is the river, and here, four days' journey above New Orleans, is the Dalroy bluff. Three thousand acres of the richest land on this continent are waiting there for you and me. Such a home we will have!—orange groves and fields of indigo, and its name will be Ardeith Plantation—all the way down I've thought of what I would name it. Do you like that?"

"It's beautiful," said Judith, and thought feebly of her immortal soul.

"We'll build a manor," Philip went on, "and have a city of slaves in the cabins behind it. Our house will be made of clay and this gray Spanish moss plastered over cypress lathes. Clay is more durable than wood and keeps out the heat. We'll have a double line of oaks leading to the door, and before we're old they'll be vast and spreading like these in the forest, with long draperies of moss brushing our shoulders as we ride underneath. You'll be a great lady, Judith. We'll found a dynasty, you and I, and a hundred years from now the rulers of Ardeith will be proud to remember us, first of the house, who came down the river together."

Judith stood up slowly, catching her hands across her breast. She looked around at the oranges and palmettoes, the dark pomegranate trees and the creeping seductive river, as though she were seeing them for the first time. With a protesting movement she put her hands over her eyes, seeing too the little white house among the hills of corn and herself a little girl on the doorstep working a sampler that said "Thou God Seest Me, Judith Sheramy, July 4, 1768," three letters in red cross-stitch every morning before she could go out to play. She remembered the cruel beauty of storms and trees etched as though in ink against the bitter sky, and knew with sudden nostalgia that she would never see snowdrifts again, nor icicles a yard long hanging from the eaves, nor the parson giving thanks for the coming of a cold timid April on the hills. Slowly she took her hands off her eyes and looked at Philip, recalling through an enormous distance the words of the royal governor that the king's soldiers were going to found another New England on the river.

Philip, who had stood watching her, seemed to understand what she was thinking. He took her hands in his and came very close, saying simply:

"Tomorrow if the boatmen are right we should come to the port that the English call New Richmond and the French Baton Rouge. Your father is going to tie up there several days to give his boatmen a rest. I had planned to rest there too, but I won't. I'll press down to Dalroy. And when you come I'll find you."

She said tremulously, "Yes."

"But until then," Philip went on gently, "you'll be with your own people, to do all the thinking you like."

She said again, "Yes."

"You darling," said Philip. He drew her to him, and this

time she did not resist nor even try to make herself do so. She put her arms around him and held him close in a surge of adoration that thrust out of her everything but the awareness that Philip loved her. How long they held each other there she did not know, but suddenly a stern hand caught her shoulder and flung her back. She staggered and nearly fell, but as she caught her balance she saw that her father was there, speaking furiously to Philip. Judith thrust the topaz chain into her bosom and heard Philip answer:

"Very well, Mr. Sheramy. But I haven't hurt her."

Mark held his gun at his side. "Mr. Larne," he said, hardly opening his lips, "if you touch my daughter again I shall kill you."

Philip bowed. "Mr. Sheramy, it has been my intention for some time to ask your permission to marry your daughter. I trust you will do me the honor of granting it." He smiled at Judith as though to assure her that her father's answer would not matter very much.

Judith felt the chain cold on her breast as her father returned:

"Under no circumstances, Mr. Larne, would I consent to such a marriage. Good evening."

"Good evening," said Philip, and went off through the wood.

Mark came up to Judith and put his arm around her. "Come with me, daughter," he said gently. He did not seem angry with her, only grave and very sad, and it made her feel more guilty than any reproaches could have done. They walked along in silence, but when they came in sight of the campfire he asked:

"Do you want to wait here awhile before we join the others?"

"Yes sir," said Judith, and her voice broke and she began to sob. He made her sit by him on a fallen tree, holding her like a child and stroking her hair. After awhile she managed to ask:

"Why did you say you would kill him?"

"Because I will if he touches you again." There was a pause, then Mark added, "I love you too dearly, Judith, to give you to a man like that."

"Like what?" she demanded rebelliously. "He hasn't told *you* anything about himself!"

"No, he doesn't need to. Dear child, can't you see that he's godless, improvident, untrustworthy—that he'd neglect you, and put his own love of pleasure before your need of protection? No, Judith. You are not to see him again."

Judith held to a broken branch jutting out of the trunk. "He says he loves me very much, father."

"Daughter, trust me," said Mark. He moved his hand along the bark until it rested on hers. "You would be cruelly unhappy with such a husband. More unhappy than I can tell you. You're too young to understand. When a worthy young man comes courting you, I'll be as glad as you. I want you to have a husband. But a good husband, Judith."

Judith was silent. A week ago she would have marveled that any girl could dare to doubt her own father. But in seven days Philip had shaken all her standards, though his values were still so new that she had no words with which to explain them. Mark said:

"Marriage isn't a moment's desire, Judith. It's a holy sacrament that lasts a lifetime."

"Yes sir," said Judith. And then, because he seemed so troubled, she added, "I want to do right, father."

"I know you do," he said, and pressed her hand.

Caleb called them. The men were untying the boat for the afternoon journey.

"What on earth were you and Judith doing off in the woods?" Mrs. Sheramy asked as they came near the fire.

"Just talking," said Mark. "We'll have to get along if we want to reach Baton Rouge tomorrow."

It was not until they were under way that Judith remembered she had left two good cooking-pots by the pool. Her mother scolded her for being so careless, but Mark said, "Don't be too stern with her, Catherine. She's more biddable than most girls her age."

Judith walked away and sat down on deck, watching Philip's boat rounding the curves a long way ahead. Evidently her father was not going to say any more to her about Philip. He was taking it for granted that she would obey him now as she had done all her life. A pirogue from Illinois came alongside, the traders singing a lusty French song as they pushed ahead. Behind it came a canoe piled with beads and blankets, paddled by Indians who took the swirls with silent ex-pertness. After awhile she heard her father responding to greetings from another flatboat belonging to a family named St. Clair from Pennsylvania. She caught sight of Philip's boat again, further ahead now. He was keeping his word and leaving her as fast as he could.

Judith clasped her hands around her knee and leaned back against the cabin wall. No matter what her father said or did, Philip would find her. And what was she going to say to him?

She wanted him so! Knowing he would not be there when the boat tied up tonight gave her a sense of dreadful vacancy. She wanted him there, talking to her of pirate fights or duels or anything he felt like talking about, telling her again that he loved her and holding her in an embrace that would not have to be interrupted. She was aware of a new, unconfessable need of him that was no less real for being beyond her own comprehension. Judith began to wonder again what it was men wanted of women. It was something beautiful or terrible or perhaps both—strange that though she knew so little about it she could be sure it was something beautiful now that she knew Philip Lame wanted it of her.

She felt a vague urge to cry. Idling like this was wrong. One should be always doing something useful—or was that only another of the New England rules that had no meaning under the river sun?

She went into the cabin and got out a kerchief she was hemming. How mousy her clothes were by Philip's blue and claret satins. And if she obeyed her father how mousy her whole life would be. Until they built a house of their own they were going to be guests of Walter Purcell, son of her father's oldest friend. Walter Purcell was an industrious young man with all the virtues. Judith puckered her mouth distastefully as she sewed. No doubt his house would be crisp and staid, where she would be expected to be a sober young person in a cap and kerchief sitting at her spinning-wheel until another sober young person in a fustian coat and nankeen breeches came to woo her into a sober marriage. Oh, she didn't want any of that! Why should God create this delirious landscape but for frivolity and laughter and men like Philip Larne?

At last they came to the Dalroy bluff.

Below Baton Rouge the river banks had been low and soft, but suddenly the east bank went up in a hump and a bluff hung like a shelf over the water. At the lower end was the wharf, so wild with flatboats and keels and pirogues that the Sheramys thought their boatmen would never land at all. But by what looked like a creation of space they tied up the boat. Judith scrambled ashore after her father.

They stood together on the swarming wharf while the men shoved their boxes ashore. Judith was suddenly frightened to think that this wild place was where she was going to live. This confusion of shouting flatboatmen, Negroes rolling hogsheads down the planks, Indians singing to the incoming boats and catching the melons and coins their hearers flung to them, this muddle of wagons and wheelbarrows and fruit-crates—this was the town of Dalroy in the province of West Florida in the country of Louisiana. This was home. Philip would like it. Philip would laugh at her for being scared. She looked around, wondering if he was here, but all she could see was a mob of strangers and merchandise. Of course he was not here. He was back in the forest, and it might be days before he even knew she had arrived.

Then, jumping over hogsheads and ordering Negroes out of the way, came a figure that she recognized with amazement as that of staid-minded Walter Purcell of Connecticut. But Mr. Purcell was burnt brown as an Indian and his coat was of apple-green satin and his breeches were buckled with silver. He shouted and waved to them, leaping over a wheelbarrow to grasp Mark Sheramy's hand with delighted welcome.

Judith took a step backward and stared at him with sudden secret glee. It was really true, then. Nobody could bring New England to Louisiana. Somewhere on the river they all crossed a dividing line, and Philip belonged on this side of it.

The wagon bounced along a trail through the woods, here and there passing an indigo clearing with a cabin or sometimes a more pretentious house of pink clay-and-moss plaster, till they came to the home of Walter Purcell. The estate, he said, was called Lynhaven. His house was bright pink, built with a passage down the middle and five rooms on each side, and in front a white wooden porch that Mr. Purcell called a gallery, explaining when they asked him that the Creole word was galérie and in Louisiana the English language was enriching itself with a great many Anglicized Creole words. Mark asked dubiously if one had much association with the Creoles. But certainly, said Mr. Purcell. He himself had a wife from New Orleans. Charming people, these colonial French.

Half a dozen Negroes ran out of the house to meet them, and while they jabbered and unloaded the boxes a small black-haired girl came out on the gallery. She looked like a doll with her gown of pink dimity and little curls dancing on her neck, and so young that Judith was surprised when Mr. Purcell said, "My wife, ladies and gentlemen. Gervaise, my friends from Connecticut."

Gervaise smiled and curtseyed, her little hands holding back her panniers. "You are so welcome," she said in a soft exotic accent, and with as little fluttering as if receiving four guests was the most ordinary of occurrences. "Every day for a week my husband has looked for you at the wharfs." She gestured toward the bowing Negro man holding back the door. "You will step inside?"

As she followed her mother indoors Judith glanced sideways at Gervaise. She had never seen any girl who looked so self-possessed and cityfied. Judith wondered if she wore those curls and ruffles every day. She must; there was no way for her to have known in advance when the Sheramys were coming and so be dressed up in their honor. Gervaise was speaking to her husband.

"Walter, the chambers at the left back are for monsieur and madame and the young gentleman. I will conduct the young lady." She tucked her hand into Judith's, paused to give orders half in French and half in English to a cluster of black attendants, and led Judith into a pink-walled room with long windows reaching to the floor and a high narrow bed draped with a mosquito bar. A Negro girl whom Gervaise called Titine came after them carrying a wooden tub and a jug of hot water.

"You're being very nice to us," Judith ventured as she untied the strings of her sunbonnet. "I hope we aren't going to be a lot of trouble."

"But certainly not." Gervaise laughed a little as though in surprise. "I like having guests. Walter is out half the day, and one gets bored with only servants and a baby for company."

"Have you really got a baby?" Judith exclaimed.

"Yes, a little girl. Her name is Babette. What makes you so astonished?"

"Why—you look like such a little girl yourself."

Gervaise laughed again. "Because I'm so tiny, I suppose. But I'm seventeen. I've been married three years." She put her hand on the latch. "If you'll excuse me I'll tell the girls to put on the extra plates for supper. Ask Titine for anything you want, and please don't feel shy. We want you to be comfortable." She curtseyed and closed the door, leaving Judith looking after her while Titine uncorded the box holding her clothes. Judith was conscious of a sense of awe. Such a casual, self-confident little person Gervaise was, as though she had never had a disturbing moment in her life. It must be women like her Philip had known on the gullah coast, women who knew how to meet strangers and supervise slaves and wear exquisite gowns, and move always with an air of smiling sophistication. Judith tossed her bonnet on the bed with dissatisfied vehemence. She was sophisticated about things like mutton-pies and chilblains. She felt out of place.

"Young miss ready for de bath?" said a soft voice behind her.

Judith turned around. Titine was standing respectfully by the wooden tub. She was slim and black, in a dress of blue calico and a yellow kerchief wrapped around her head.

"Why yes," said Judith, "as soon as I undress."

She wished Titine would go away. She was not used to taking off her clothes before strangers. But Titine came up to her and unpinned her dress and with deft hands began loosening the drawstrings of her petticoats. Judith smothered her astonishment. Evidently this was the custom of the country, though it was very odd to stand up stark naked in front of a slave-girl and then to be bathed like a baby. But after her first shock she found that though it might be immodest it was very convenient. She had always had trouble washing her back. Being a helpless female was really quite nice. This must be what Philip meant when he said he would make her a great lady.

"Miss wear dis here to supper?" Titine inquired.

She was holding up Judith's best gown, a blue muslin that her father had said was too frail to bring into a jungle, but which seemed very sturdy beside the flimsy elegance of Gervaise. "Oh yes," said Judith, noticing that Titine had laid fresh stockings and underwear in a neat line across the bed. Placing the blue muslin by them, Titine held out a chemise Judith had washed three days ago in a bayou. Judith stepped into it obediently, and sat down while Titine fetched her stockings. It was hard to see how anybody could put on anybody else's stockings, pulling backwards, but Titine evidently took it for granted that no white lady could be expected to perform such a task for herself, and she knelt and drew the stockings up with expert speed.

It was all strange, but surprisingly easy to get used to.

Then Titine brought curling irons and a lighted candle in a wire frame and a pink jar holding scented pomade. She put the irons on the frame to heat, and combed Judith's hair high over strips of cotton. Little ringlets were patted over her forehead with pomade, and the irons set curls to bouncing on her neck. When everything was done Titine set a mirror on the chest of drawers and Judith turned around slowly.

The mirror was narrow, but long enough for her to see herself halfway down. Her head felt as if she were carrying a basket balanced on it and her stays were laced so tight she could hardly breathe, but she gave a little gasp of joy at her reflection. Nobody had ever told her how gracefully her shoulders sloped or how small her waistline was. She looked fragile, delicate, crushable—she looked—Judith leaned over the drawers and stared at herself—she looked like the kind of girl Philip was used to. If everything else was as easy as this—?

There was a tap on the door and Gervaise came in.

"If you are ready, shall we go to the dining-room?" Then she stopped. "But how different you are, now that you're dressed! It's such a relief, isn't it, to end a hard journey and get back to civilized living!"

"Why—yes," said Judith.

She hesitated, looking at the mirror and then back at Gervaise, wondering if she dared confess how unused she was to what Gervaise called civilized living, but she did not quite have the courage.

Still she did consider the possibility of telling Gervaise about Philip. Gervaise was young and she must know what it was like to be in love, for she was married.

But she did not do that either. Everything about the house was romantic—the rice and crabs they ate, the soft-footed servants, the little black boy who pulled the fan of turkey feathers above the table—but Gervaise herself was so tranquilly matter-of-fact that Judith could not imagine her having any experience of ecstatic recklessness. Gervaise did not talk much, except when she answered Mrs. Sheramy's questions about housekeeping in Louisiana, and she was as polite to her husband as if he and she had just been introduced. Walter and Mark and Caleb talked about crops and wharf business. Her father did not comment on Judith's tight lacing or her extravagant coiffure; she concluded he had resolved to be lenient about minor matters to repay her for giving up Philip. Which she had not promised to do, Judith told herself fiercely, though she was realizing it was something she must decide all alone. There was nobody she could talk to. She felt remote from the others, and was glad when it was time to go to bed.

After Titine had undressed her and retired Judith stood by the window in her bedgown, looking at the trees and the quiet moonlit fields of indigo. Somewhere out there was Philip, Philip who loved her, Philip whom she loved in spite of all her father could say. "You would be cruelly unhappy with such a husband . . . you are too young to understand." She could almost hear him say it, sitting on that fallen tree by the river, so stern and yet so gentle that it hurt her to think how it would hurt him if she chose Philip in defiance of his wishes. He was so much older and wiser than she, and so good—but Judith re-remembered how Philip had kissed her by the pool and wondered if anything he could do to her could be as dreadful as living without him. She blew out her candle and tumbled into bed, lying with her face buried and her arms around the pillow. Wasn't there anybody who understood? Was she the only girl in the world who had been swept into a whirlpool of stars and fire because a man had kissed her?

It was so quiet. Everybody must be asleep but her.

"Judith! Judith, my darling!"

She sat upright. It had been a whisper hardly louder than the rustle of the wind in the palms outside, but she knew it was Philip, and in the moonlight she saw him step over the low sill of the window. Judith pressed the back of her hand against her mouth.

Philip pushed back the mosquito bar and dropped on his knees by the bed.

"Sweetheart, is it really you?"

"Philip," she gasped trembling, "they'll kill you if they find you in here! Go away!"

"Judith," he said as though he had not heard her, "come with me. I have a house—a log cabin my slaves pegged together, but it will do until we can build a moss house like this—I can't wait for you any longer! I've a horse outside, and the clergyman from St. Margaret's chapel is at the cabin waiting to marry us—"

"Not tonight, Philip!" she protested in a frightened whisper. "Not all of a sudden like this—not tonight!"

Philip sat on the bed and slipped his arms around her. "Dearest, it will have to be like this. They'll never give you to me. You know that. Don't you love me enough to come with me now?"

He kissed her lips and eyes and throat, and the ghosts of her grandfathers who had come to America to save their souls melted into the moonlight. Judith reached up and felt his hair, and the scar that crossed his face invisibly in the dark.

"I love you so much, Philip. I'll go with you."

He took her hands in his and kissed the palms. After a moment she raised up. "Go outside till I can put on a dress."

"Hurry," said Philip softly. "And don't make any noise."

When he had slipped through the window Judith got out of bed. In the moonlight she groped for her clothes. But she could not put up her hair as the slave-girl had done and she was unwilling to pin it in somber braids again, so she stepped across the window-sill with it blowing loose on her shoulders.

"Philip!" she whispered.

He caught her in his arms. "How lovely you are with your hair down! I never knew you had such hair."

Before she could look back she felt herself put on a horse and Philip was leaping up behind her. He thrust a gun into her hands.

"You hold it ready, Judith. There may be Indians in the forest."

The horse started. Without speaking again they rode into a wood that closed darkly around them as they went. Judith held the gun in her left hand and put her arm around his neck. They went down a weird trail between the oaks, and they were still riding when the moon set on the other side of the forest. Judith could see nothing but the black trees and hear nothing but the clatter of the horse's hoofs, and she wondered where he was taking her, but as she felt the support of Philip's arm around her waist and his cheek against hers she knew he could not possibly take her anywhere that she would not want to go.

CHAPTER TWO

Black Tibby knelt before the fireplace, reaching into the pot with a long-handled iron spoon. She brought up a dip of gumbo and examined it.

"Dinner nigh about done, young miss."

The odor filled the cabin, rich with suggestions of shrimp and chicken, okra and bay leaf and thyme. Judith sat on the edge of the bed pretending to mend a rent in a shirt of Philip's, but her hands were so damp that the cloth clung to them and her seam was crooked as a little girl's. The sun poked fingers of hot light through the chinks between the logs and poured through the windows to make blinding splotches on the floor. In the fireplace the flames licked around the pot, scorching Judith's face although she had huddled herself on the farthest corner of the bed. She felt sick and dizzy with the heat; a dull ache throbbed at the back of her head and she could feel perspiration trickling down her thighs.

She held her under lip between her teeth and bit on it hard. The pain gave her something beside the heat to think about. She was repeating to herself, over and over, "I am not going to faint. I am not going to faint. If I start fainting in June I will probably die in August. I am not going to faint."

Why hadn't somebody told her it was going to be like this? Six weeks it had been now since she reached Louisiana, and for five of them the sky had been like a cup of brass turned down over the forest that Philip proudly called "the plantation." The sun came up with a blistering glory so beautiful that sometimes for a little while one could forget its intensity, but it moved across the sky with a torrent of fire which there was no escaping. Then when evening came the sun tumbled down again into the river, leaving streaks of purple and red to be blotted out by the dark. But even at night the heat still pressed down with a weight that made the covering of a sheet unbearable, and she tossed about until the moss mattress under her was wet and she fell asleep from sheer exhaustion, to be wakened again by that pitiless sun pushing between the logs.

Even when it rained the coolness was brief and one paid for it afterward, for when the sun came out again the ground began to steam and the air was so thick one could hardly breathe. Sometimes when she remembered the gentle summers of Connecticut Judith cried with homesickness. But she tried not to let Philip know. Philip was so splendid and adoring; it would hurt him if he knew she cried. Philip minded the heat no more than he minded the grasshoppers that leaped away as the trees of the Ardeith forest fell under the strokes of the axes, and Judith knew he would find it impossible to believe that sometimes she really thought the heat was killing her.

"Tibby," she exclaimed, "if you make that fire any hotter I am going to scream!"

"Ma'am?" said Tibby. She stood questioningly, another log in her hands. "Gumbo gotta bile, Miss Judith."

Judith sighed helplessly. She couldn't understand half Tibby said, but Tibby was a good cook and Judith supposed she knew what she was doing. She was the only house-woman Philip had found among the slaves he took off the pirate boat, so he had given her to Judith and put the others to work clearing the forest. If there was only another room, Judith thought despairingly, where she could go to escape the fire. But the cabin was only four walls with a door and a couple of holes for windows, and outdoors it was worse. Judith looked out at the slaves setting up cypress lathes on the foundations of the new dwelling. It was going to be a big house like the one where Gervaise and Walter Purcell had welcomed her and from which she had run away that first night. Sometimes she wished she had not run away. Philip might have waited for her till he had a house fit for a woman to live in. But she stopped herself with remorse. He had loved her too much to wait, and had not dreamed how horrible the summer would seem to a girl from Connecticut. He did not mind living in a log hovel or seeing ants creep between the cracks in the floor, and he laughed about the bugs in the cornmeal. None of this troubled him, for he was clearing his own land and planting his indigo.

Judith dropped the shirt into her lap and put her hands to her aching head.

"Oh, all right," she said to Tibby. "Make up the fire. Make it so hot I cook like a shrimp in the gumbo. I don't care. Maybe I'll die sooner."

"Now, young miss." Tibby stuck the log under the pot and came over to the bed. "What ails you, honey child?"

Tibby's black face sparkled as the sun struck the drops of perspiration on it. She put her arms around Judith and patted her.

"Don't you get yo'sef upset, honey. I 'spects you miss yo' mamma, don't you now?"

Judith hid her face on Tibby's deep bosom and nodded. She wondered how her mother was enduring this inferno. Judith had seen her mother only two or three times in these weeks; the Sheramy grant joined that of Philip Larne, but between this cabin and that of the Sheramys was the forest, so thick that the space might almost have been a hundred miles. She asked:

"Does the heat ever kill people, Tibby?"

"Lawsy mussy me, young miss! 'Fo' long you gets like me— you don't pay it no mind at all. Ain't dey got no summertime where you come from, honey?"

"Not—not like this." Judith had not lifted her head. It was a comfort to have somebody holding her so tenderly, even a black slave.

"Well, jes' you be patient now, sugarplum, twell Mr. Philip

get you dat air big new house put up out yonder, and you'll be so nice and cool—"

Judith doubted it. But she was too exhausted to argue. She pushed her damp hair off her forehead and stood up.

"I think I'll go out," she said. The smell of that bubbling gumbo was making her sicker every minute. How could anybody eat anything rich and hot like that in such weather?

"Yassum. You c'n call Mr. Philip in."

"Dinner's ready?"

"Yassum, sho. Shum deh?" Tibby covered her hand with a rag and took the lid off the pot.

The odor of shrimp and hot spices rose thickly. Judith ran out of the cabin. She was angry with heaven for devising this heat to torture her, and with Philip for coming in at noon hungry enough to eat that spicy mess, and with Tibby for using gullah talk nobody from Connecticut could be expected to understand. Leaning against the side of the cabin she covered her face with her hands and hated everything and everybody. A mosquito lit on her neck; Judith slapped at it and walked back toward the woods.

The axes were ringing against the trees where the slaves were clearing a field for indigo. The air out here was fresher, but the sun was pounding on her head. Her sleeves felt prickly on her arms. The cuffs were too tight for her to roll them up, and it didn't seem quite respectable to be going about with bare arms anyway. There was a smell of food out here too. The slave-women Philip had brought with him were cooking greens and side-meat in pots slung from tripods over fires outdoors. The earth clung to Judith's shoes and weeds slapped her skirts as she made her way among the stumps, around the foundations of the new house.

The slaves were working to the rhythm of a droning song. The words were a mingling of the half-forgotten tongue of the jungle and the patter of the gullah coast, and the song as they sang it, lifting their axes in slow time, was grewsome like a savage chant in some far lost wilderness where no Christian had ever set foot. Through the pressing heat she felt a chill run down her back as she stopped to watch them. The sun glanced on the bare backs of the Negroes, for they were naked to the waist, and the muscles of their shoulders knotted as they raised their axes. Overhead the branches of the trees met in a green tangle. Here and there a vine climbed up, hugging the moss close to the branches and hanging purple and scarlet flowers like lights in the forest dimness.

Little showers of bark and splinters gushed from the trees as the axes struck. Judith watched, half frightened and half fascinated. She wondered what Negroes were like, really. The parsons argued about whether or not the blacks had souls like white people—how could they, the rector of St. Margaret's had asked, when they roamed like animals in the African jungles and boiled each other in pots for dinner? But then, Tibby who was cooking the gumbo, she really seemed human.

One of the Negroes pointed to Judith and called out. Judith started and stared; he shouted again, and then they all turned and saw her and began to yell, and Judith caught her kerchief over her breast with both hands and wanted to run, but her knees were shaking so she could not. Visions of being boiled in a pot rushed into her head. She opened her mouth and tried to scream for Philip, but her voice stuck in her throat, and at that instant the Negroes dropped their axes with a unanimous gesture and rushed toward her. She found herself stumbling under an avalanche of bodies, and as the black cascade went over her terror opened her throat and she began to scream. But though she cried out and struggled she felt herself picked up, and the Negro carrying her stumbled on a root and fell and another Negro snatched her and dragged her over the ground. Her skirt ripped on the shrubs and palmetto fronds scraped her face and tore through her hair. There was a thundering crash behind her and then as the Negroes stopped she saw Philip. He shoved the slaves out of his way and knelt down, gathering her into his arms.

"Are you all right, Judith?"

She clung to him, feeling a trickle of blood run down her cheek.

"Philip!" she gasped. "Philip, what were they doing to me?"

The Negroes were standing around, grinning and jabbering.

"Philip," she cried again, "what were they doing?"

He laughed aloud. "Judith, honey, haven't I told you to stay out of the woods? Didn't they tell you to run?"

He was sitting on the ground, holding her like a baby. Judith choked.

"They all started howling at me at once. I—I thought they were going to eat me up."

Philip was still laughing. "Honey child, that tree was coming down on your head. They called and you didn't run and there wasn't anything to do but knock you down and drag you out of the way. I reckon they're due for an extra ration of sidemeat."

"Stop laughing at me," snapped Judith. She got to her feet. Philip was brushing mold and dead leaves from his legs. His shirt had big wet streaks across the shoulders and his thick light hair, tied back with a ribbon, was wet for two inches on either side of the parting. Judith started back toward the cabin, feeling little and worthless and cross at Philip for laughing at her.

Philip caught up with her and laid his arm across her shoulders.

"I'm hungry as a mountain lion. I hope Tibby has lots to eat."

"Gumbo," said Judith, "with shrimp and rice."

"Perfect," said Philip. "It's hungry work, clearing. Look, Judith, how much they've done on the house today. If I could spare more of them from the fields we could move in before winter."

He was not walking very fast, but she found it hard to keep up with his long strides. Her skirts clung damply to her legs and the heat was making her dizzy again.

"This time next year," Philip was saying, "there'll be indigo back there where they're cutting those trees, and then a tobacco field. We ought to have it all clear in a few years. Indigo is the best crop, but we'll have rice too, and oranges, and we might put a few acres into cotton."

He isn't concerned about a single thing but his crops, she thought rebelliously. He doesn't even notice how miserable I am. He just takes me for granted like Tibby—

She put her head against the cabin wall and burst into tears.

Philip stopped short. He took her in his arms. His voice when he spoke was low with troubled astonishment.

"Judith, darling, what on earth is the trouble?"

All her resolutions seemed to have gone down at once. She hid her face on his breast and sobbed.

"I—I can't help it!" she choked out. "The heat and everything—and I can't breathe and my head hurts all the time and I'm sick all over and I think I'm going to die."

Philip held her close to him. She felt his kisses on her cheeks where the tears were.

"You poor dear child," he was saying. "It's the first deep summer you've ever seen, isn't it? Come inside."

"By that fire?" she protested, but apparently he did not hear her, for he drew her indoors. With a great effort Judith swallowed her sobs. Philip made her sit down on a box in the corner away from the fire.

"Bring her some water, Tibby," he said.

Tibby was scooping the gumbo into big bowls and setting them on the table. "She ain't been feelin' so peart, young miss ain't," she said. She dipped a gourd into the bucket of water on the shelf. "Heah you is, honey lamb."

Judith tried to drink it. She had grown used to river water on the flatboat, but suddenly she thought she had never tasted anything so vile in her life. It was lukewarm and felt gritty on her tongue. The rich odor of the gumbo steamed up toward her. She felt herself get cold with loathing, and then the heat rushed over her again and her stomach turned inside of her and her head began to spin. With an abrupt movement she rushed out of the cabin. By the time Philip reached her she was down on her knees among the weeds, holding herself up with her arm around a palm-tree, retching.

Philip helped her up and led her to the step by the cabin door, where it was shady. He sat down by her.

"I'm so terribly sorry, Philip," she murmured.

Philip put his arm around her and drew her head down on his shoulder. He began asking her questions. Judith drew back and caught her breath.

"Do you mean I'm going to have a baby, Philip?"

"Darling," he said gently, "didn't you know?"

Judith shook her head.

After a moment she said, "I guess I don't know anything. You must think I'm an awful fool, Philip."

Philip was gathering up weeds in his hand and breaking them off near the ground.

"No," he said, "but I think maybe I am."

Judith rolled up the edges of a tear the palm-fronds had made in her dress. "Philip," she asked, "does it hurt very much?"

He nodded. "They say it does."

"Tell me what it's like, Philip."

He lifted his head. "I can't, honey. I don't know anything about it."

Her eyes widened with surprise that there should be anything Philip did not know.

"But Philip—"

"I really don't, sweetheart. I never thought about it before." He smiled a little. "I'm sorry, Judith."

"Oh, I'm not," she exclaimed. Her first thought had been that she mustn't let Philip start feeling remorseful on her account. Not when he had so much to do. "My mother can tell me. She'll make it all right. And we really couldn't start that dynasty you were talking about unless I had babies, could we?"

He laughed and pulled her over to him and kissed her. "I reckon we couldn't. You dear little soldier. Yes, first thing tomorrow morning I'll get out the cart and take you over to see your mother."

"Will you really? She'll be awfully glad to have us come to see her."

"She'll probably want to wring my neck," said Philip dryly. He took her hands. "Judith, you do love me, don't you? You aren't sorry you ran away with me?"

"Oh, of course I'm not! I love you so much." She smiled up at him, relieved to discover that she had a legitimate reason for feeling sick and that it didn't mean she was unfit to stand the hardships of pioneering. It was exciting to have a baby, particularly a beautiful baby who would look like Philip, and to know you were starting a great house in a wilderness you were going to turn into an empire.

There was a noise under the trees. Judith turned around.

"Why look! Is that a wagon coming down the trail?"

"It certainly is. Now what on earth—?" Philip got his gun out of the holster at his belt. "You'd better go in, Judith."

She stood up, but before she could obey him the wagon had reached the cleared place in front of the cabin. Judith exclaimed:

"Why, it's my brother Caleb."

Philip put up his gun and went toward the wagon, calling a greeting. Judith came after him, wondering what Caleb could want that was important enough to bring him on this long ride.

Caleb got out of the wagon and approached them timidly. He was a tall, bony lad with a stern face like his father's. Caleb had always been more taciturn than Judith, and more amenable to the rigid discipline of their house, but though he had slight patience with her impulsive ways they were very fond of each other.

He glanced down, kicking his toe in the dust, and said:

"Judith—it's mother. She's pretty sick. I guess you'd better come."

"Mother sick?" Judith echoed in astonishment. How strange. Her mother had always been so healthy. "Is she taken bad, Caleb?"

"I guess so." Caleb kicked at the dirt. Though he was taller than she was he seemed all of a sudden like a little boy. "She's not been right well since we got here, the heat and all, and now she's come down with some kind of fever. Father said it looked like there wasn't anybody to do for her."

Judith looked up at Philip. There was a troubled frown between his eyes. "Do you want to go to her, Judith?" he asked.

"Oh yes! Please let me go, Philip."

"But you aren't well yourself. Haven't you got any house Negroes?" he asked Caleb impatiently.

Caleb bashfully shook his head. "All we've bought are gumbo French from New Orleans and they're just field-hands. Mother didn't want any for the house. She's not used to them."

"Oh Philip, please let me go!" Judith repeated. "Wait, Caleb." She pulled Philip inside. "You've got to let me go. I was going over anyway tomorrow. And I was a bad girl to run off like that with you. I guess she's been worrying about me all these weeks. She wouldn't say anything but I'm sure she's been worrying. I'll just go and tell her I'm doing all right, and put her mind easy."

"Very well," he agreed doubtfully. "I'll tell Caleb you're coming."

"Give him dinner while I'm putting some things in a bundle. You can come for me tomorrow."

Philip went out to speak to Caleb while Judith wrapped up a bedgown and a clean dress. She was ashamed to own to Philip how eager she was to see her mother.

"This isn't much of a place that man makes you live in," said Caleb suddenly, as the wagon rumbled along the trail.

"It's perfectly all right," retorted Judith. "We live mighty tidy there. And I have a nigger slave to do for me, too."

"Mother says they're all right for the fields but not messing around the food. How can you tell if they're clean, she says, when they're so black?"

Judith would not admit that at first she had felt the same qualms about Tibby. "They can be clean as white folks," she said stoutly. "The black don't mean they're dirty. Philip's had slaves all his life and he knows."

Caleb clucked at the mules. Judith was holding the seat on both sides of her to keep from being jolted out. The sun was scorching her head through her sunbonnet, but she would not say so to Caleb; it seemed to her that in defending Philip to her family she should defend too this country he loved so much. After awhile Caleb cleared his throat and asked:

"Judith—you're doing all right, are you?"

"Why of course I am."

"Well, mother—she's been kind of afraid you weren't. She got upset the day she rode over and saw that cabin. Don't the rain come in?"

"Not unless it's raining very hard."

"And Philip—he's good to you?"

"He's wonderful to me."

"He don't make you work too much?"

Judith laughed. "He won't let me work at all. I asked him to get me a spinning-wheel and he said he wouldn't till he could get a house-girl to do the spinning. Back where he comes from ladies of quality let slaves do all their work."

"Well," said Caleb, "we never let on to be quality."

"But we will be, Caleb!" she cried. "All of us. With plantations from the king and indigo growing so easy. Look how the Purcells live."

"Father says he don't know what's come over Mr. Purcell, putting on such airs. Must be that French wife of his."

"Gervaise? She's nice, just a little bit quiet. I don't believe she means to be uppity."

"Anyway, you set mother's mind easy about you," said Caleb. "She's not been doing a bit well."

Judith smiled. She would tell her mother how splendid Philip was, and then she would ask about her own problem. Tonight they would send the menfolks out and they would have a long private talk. Judith gave a sidelong pitying glance at Caleb. He was four years older than she was, and yet he was just a boy, while she who was only fifteen was a married woman about to have a child who would be the heir to Ardeith Plantation.

The Sheramys' grant of land had been named Silverwood. Caleb had suggested the name, for though it was buried deeper than Judith's he too had a streak of romance in him, and the white trunks of the cypresses had set him to thinking of a musical word that would fit the land where they grew. He and his parents had stayed with the Purcells while Mark Sheramy's slaves put up a house snug enough to live in a year or two, until the land was clear and the slaves could be spared to build a moss manor. The house was a log cabin with four rooms, strong and tight. No wonder they had looked askance at the shack Philip and his Negroes had knocked together in a week. But he had built it in a week because he couldn't live without her any longer, Judith remembered proudly as she scrambled out of the wagon and ran indoors.

Her father came across the front room to meet her, walking slowly.

"It was good of you to come," he said. "I was sorry to take you away from your husband."

Judith's conscience struck her, for he was so gentle and unrebuking.

"But I wanted to come, father," she assured him.

"I'm glad you could leave. Caleb and I, we don't know much about nursing."

"Where is mother?"

"In the bedroom. Walk easy."

Judith crossed to the side door. What a cool house this was, and so clean, with a separate room for the cooking and no mud in the cracks. She went softly into her mother's room, feeling a pang at the sight of the spinning-wheel that had stood by the hearth at home, and the rag rugs she had helped braid. Her mother was on the bed. The mosquito bar blurred Judith's eyesight, already dim after the glare outside. Mrs. Sheramy lifted her head a little way from the pillow.

"Judith?" she said faintly. "My dear little girl."

Judith lifted the mosquito bar and took her mother in her arms and kissed her. But when she felt how slowly her mother's arms went around her and how hot her mother's cheek was under her kiss, Judith knew she wasn't going back to Ardeith tomorrow, and she knew too with a feeling of sudden terror that it would be a long time before she could ask any questions.

CHAPTER THREE

They did not tell her Catherine Sheramy had troubled herself into her bed, but Judith told herself so. Walter and Gervaise Purcell rode over, bringing gruel and good advice, and Gervaise, her ruffled fragility more incongruous than ever among the rag rugs and crazy-quilts, touched Catherine's forehead with cool presses and said it was the sort of fever that crept up from the swamps and struck people who weren't used to the summers, but Judith could not help believing that her mother might have stood the fever if she had been easy in her mind. She tried to imagine what her parents must have thought when they woke up that morning and found Philip's boy Josh waiting with a letter to tell them Judith had run away.

The letter they had sent back had been so simple that until now Judith had never tried to think what it might have cost to write it.

My dear daughter Judith:

While we would wish that you had dealt with us differently, your mother and I desire nothing but your happiness. Since as you say Mr. Philip Larne has been joined to you in honorable marriage, we offer our prayers that you may be to him a dutiful and obedient wife, and he to you a kind husband. May the Lord ever keep you, nor permit you to depart from his just precepts.

Your devoted father,
Mark Sheramy.

"There now!" she had exclaimed jubilantly to Philip. "I knew they wouldn't mind when I told them how much I loved you."

"Of course they don't mind," said Philip laughing. "And I really wouldn't care if they did."

Now that her mother was ill they still made no reproaches. Catherine murmured that she was sorry to be such a bother, and Mark asked, almost timidly, "You have been happy with your husband, Judith?" When Judith answered, "Why of course, father!"—Mark said, "I am glad he is good to you, daughter." But he never reminded her that he had been, and might still be, afraid for her.

Judith did the best she could. But there was so much to

be done. There were meals to be cooked and the house to be cleaned, and soup and gruel to be prepared for her mother, who did not seem to rally no matter what was done for her. Philip came over, protesting, "But Judith, you can't work like this. Do you feel quite well?" She insisted that she did, though cooking at the fire made her so ill that sometimes she wanted to crawl into bed by her mother. Philip sent Tibby over to help her, and he ate what the field-Negroes cooked in the tents at Ardeith.

Sometimes Catherine would have chills, and even in the breathless heat she would lie shaking, her teeth chattering with cold, and all the blankets they had brought from Connecticut failed to warm her. Then the fever would return. There were days when she seemed better, with the chills and fever alike gone out of her, and Judith would hope that now her mother would be well and she herself could ask for advice about her baby, but before Catherine had gained any strength the fever would be back and Judith did not dare ask her anything. She tried not to worry. Nearly all women had children and most of them seemed to get along all right. She remembered that now and then her mother had sent her with jelly or flowers to the home of some friend with a new baby, and the women always seemed happy and proud, but occasionally there were women in Connecticut who had died having children. She did not know what it was that killed them. Probably they hadn't been well to begin with, and that ought not to bother her, for she had hardly ever been ill in her life. But it did bother her just the same. If Gervaise would only come back she could ask her about it. But Gervaise did not come again. Walter Purcell came often, riding a horse over the forest trails, and one day he called Judith into the front room and asked if there was anything she needed that Gervaise could send. Judith shook her head. "But I should like to see her," she said.

"I'm sorry she can't come to you," said Mr. Purcell. "She asked me to tell you, because you might think she did not care about your mother's being so ill. But she is in her third month, and it takes three hours over these trails and longer if it has been raining. I won't let her come. The jolting might kill her."

Judith nodded. "It's all right. Thank you for being so good to us."

But as she watched him go she felt alone and frightened. She envied Gervaise in her big house thronged with servants. And Gervaise had had a child before so she knew what to expect. Judith envied her that too.

Tibby asked her one day, "Miss Judith, is you standin' behind a baby?"

It was a moment before Judith grasped what she meant, and when she did she exclaimed, "Don't you say anything like that to my father. He's got enough to worry him."

Tibby said: "Yassum," and went off mumbling, but the next time Philip came over she said to him, "Mr. Philip, you got business to take dat young un home and ease her bones."

But Judith would not go. By this time it was August, and she suspected her mother could not hold out much longer.

Catherine was tossing and talking in broken words, and her father wandered about the house and fields, so worn and silent that Judith found his grief harder to bear than her mother's delirium. There was little she could do beyond smoothing the pillows and trying to cool the fever with wet cloths on Catherine's forehead, but even this was of little use, for it was still deep summer and there was no really cold water to be had. Before the end she sent a field-boy for Philip and asked him to stay at Silverwood with her. He stayed, but he seemed strangely inadequate for such a time. Philip was pained and bewildered, like a child, before a crisis against which his own vitality was helpless.

Just before she died the wild fever look went out of Catherine's eyes and she asked for Mark. Judith brought him, and waited in the front room with Philip and Caleb. After a little while Mark came out, closing the door softly behind him. He said nothing, but went out to the gallery, walking heavily, and Judith thought for the first time that he looked like an old man. She knew it was over, though he had not said so. She wondered what he and her mother had said to each other in those last minutes, and knew she would never be told; already she had learned that after two persons had been husband and wife there was something between them that nobody could violate. After a moment she put her hand in Philip's and they went together out to the gallery. Caleb followed them and stood in the doorway.

Mark sat on the step, his forehead resting on his hands. Judith went up to him softly, laying her hand on his head, and feeling how strong and stiff the hairs were under her fingers. Mark did not look up. He only said:

"In this soft country there's not even a stone to mark her grave."

Judith's breath caught in her throat. Philip put an arm around her. She thought how strange it was that though tears usually came to her so easily when there was only slight reason for them she could not cry now.

The slaves pegged together a coffin of cypress wood, and the next day the rector of St. Margaret's came for the funeral. Walter Purcell came, and several other friends her father had made, bringing gardenias and white roses to lay on the coffin. Judith looked around for Philip. She had been so occupied during the day that she had lost sight of him, but she thought he was somewhere about the place. But he was not here, and she hoped her father in his grief had not noticed it. Caleb had, for he whispered a query to her. She could only shake her head and say she did not know.

The rector came and stood by the coffin. He began to read.

"I am the resurrection and the life; he that believeth on me, though he were dead, yet shall he live, and he that liveth and believeth on me shall never die."

The slaves carried the coffin out and put it on a cart. Judith got into the wagon with the others, and they followed the coffin down the long uneven trail to the yard of the little log chapel. The sun was setting, throwing long thin shadows across the grave as the slaves lowered the coffin and the rector flung in the first handful of earth. Mark stood by the grave, his head lowered, so still that Judith and Caleb did not dare speak to him, even when the coffin was covered. The darkness rushed up. It was very quiet.

There was a sharp noise in the silence, the sound of a cart creaking over the shaky road. They turned and tried to see, for there were not many people out after dark. The wagon came straight into the churchyard with noisy irreverence, but not until it was almost upon them did Judith see that Philip was driving, with his boy Josh by him on the seat. She dropped Caleb's arm and ran to him, but Philip hardly noticed her; he was busy helping Josh unload something from the back of the wagon. They set it on the ground, and Philip went up to Mark.

"Here it is, sir," said Philip.

Mark started. He alone of them all had paid little attention to Philip's arrival.

"What?" he asked after an instant, as though only just realizing that he had been spoken to.

"A stone, sir," Philip said.

With an exclamation Mark dropped to his knees and felt of the dark lump on the ground. The rector's servant was holding a lantern. Judith took it from him. She had not seen a stone since she came to Louisiana. But this was a stone, unevenly rectangular, and cut into its side were crude letters that in spite of their irregularity could be read.

"Catherine, wife of Mark Sheramy. Died August 21, 1774."

She flung her arms around Philip and began to sob. The tears that had refused to come yesterday and today poured out of her, bringing a curiously tender relief, because Philip had not forsaken them, but had somehow managed to bring the single material consolation that could have eased her father's sorrow.

It was days before he would confess to Judith where he had got the stone and then only on her promise that she would never tell her father. He had stolen it, he said. The French and Spanish ships that came to New Orleans to buy raw materials brought very little merchandise with them, for there were not many families who could afford to buy manufactured goods from Europe, so the larger ships filled their holds with rocks for ballast on the outgoing trip. The rocks they discarded on the wharfs of New Orleans, not realizing their value in a country made of mud, and the city government took possession and used them for cobbling the marshy streets.

Only a day or two ago Philip had heard that a rich planter near Baton Rouge had ordered for a great price a few of these French stones to pave a walk from his gate to his house, and the stone-laden boat was docked at Dalroy. So Philip went down to find the boat, adroitly made the boatmen drunk and helped himself to a stone. Judith, who still believed thievery a deadly sin, could not help forgiving him.

Philip took her back to Ardeith the first week in September. Mark came out to the wagon to tell her goodbye. Philip had told him she was with child, and Mark said he was sorry he had not known it before her mother died.

"I should have thought of that before I asked you to come here and do so much," he added.

"It was all right," Judith answered, though all she could think of was that now at last he knew what she had been going through this summer and understood why she had not done as much for them as she might have done. "I'm sorry to be leaving, sir. There won't be anybody to do for you."

"Philip says he'll send back that black woman of his," said Mark. "Don't you worry about us. We'll manage fine."

He put his arm around her and gave her awkward little pats on the shoulder. Judith remembered that her father had had a great deal of sorrow in his life. There had been four children older than herself and Caleb, who had died of smallpox the year before Caleb was born. And now her mother was dead too, and she who might have stood by while he had to work so hard in this forest hadn't brought him anything but more concern.

She said, "Father, I'm sorry I ran away with Philip without telling you. I won't ever do anything to worry you again."

"You were always a good girl, Judith," said Mark.

Philip came out of the house and greeted them both. "Ready?" he asked Judith. He lifted her into the wagon and shook hands with Mark. "I'll send Tibby back tomorrow. I wouldn't be taking her off now, but I've bought a new girl for Judith and Tibby'll have to show her around. Good day, sir."

He sprang into the wagon and clucked at the mules. Judith glanced up at him as they started. Philip was so different from the men of her family. How wonderful it must be to have a temperament like his. Philip was sincerely sorry when her mother died, but now that it was over it was over—he seemed blithely incapable of concerning himself with any demands but those of the day he was living in. Judith caught at the seat on both sides of her to keep from being jolted out. "Don't let them go so fast!" she exclaimed.

"I'm sorry, honey." He pulled back on the reins and smiled down at her. "Now then, we won't bump so. It's going to be good to have you back," he added. "Every time I came over I missed you more when I went home."

She smiled at him, wondering what had happened to the cabin while she was away. Probably the ants had taken possession entirely. It had been hard enough to keep them out of her father's kitchen, though it was built so tight.

How hot it still was, though it was already September. The trees in Connecticut would be turning red and gold before long, and the mornings would have a frosty nip. The men were gathering the harvest and the women spinning wool and knitting warm stockings against the winter—wool and heavy stockings! The thought made her legs get crusty with goosebumps.

"With this good weather," said Philip, "we ought to get in a lot of indigo."

"Is this good weather for indigo?" Judith asked.

"Oh yes. We'll put in a little cotton too, next spring. Most planters won't put in cotton. They say it costs as much as they get for it to have the slaves pick out the seeds. But we'll set the children to that. It's easy work."

"I—suppose so," said Judith. She held tight to the seat. With this jolting her bones would be thrown out of place and her baby shaken to death. No wonder Mr. Purcell made Gervaise stay at home when she was carrying a child. Philip took one hand from the reins and steadied her.

"Did you hear me tell your father I'd bought you a new girl?"

She nodded. "That was good of you. Then I won't have to do the work myself?"

"I wouldn't let you. You're white about the eyes now from working too hard. She's a nice girl from New Orleans. Her master was a man named Peyroux, and when he died they sent some of his Negroes up the river to settle the estate. Her name is Angelique."

Judith glanced back to where Tibby sat on the floor of the wagon. She had hated to think of doing without Tibby.

"Angelique," she said. "It's a pretty name. Is she a French Negro?"

"Oh yes. You'll have to teach her English."

The wagon creaked over a fallen log. Judith bounced and caught at Philip to keep from falling. He was telling her how planters brewed indigo in vats to get the dye. She wished he'd stop talking about his wretched indigo and pay some attention to her. Couldn't he understand she was aching all over, and dreading to be left alone with a servant girl who couldn't speak English, and scared about her baby? There was nobody to help her solve her problems but Philip and he was too merrily self-assured to know a problem when he saw one.

"Yassum," said Tibby hastily. She brushed off her apron. " 'Scusin' de respeck I owe you, young miss."

Angelique was listening with amusement. Evidently she was too well acquainted with the dislike of black slaves for bright ones to need any language to comprehend it. Now and then she flashed a little secret smile at Judith and Judith smiled back.

"Bright-skin niggers," said Tibby contemptuously. "All time tryin' to be white folks."

Judith laughed and told Tibby to take a bowl of okra out to Mr. Philip. Relieved of Tibby's resentful presence, she ran about touching objects in the cabin, teaching Angelique their English names. Angelique learned quickly and they laughed together over her mispronunciations. Angelique didn't seem like a slave. She was just another girl who wanted to be friends. She was astonishingly pretty too—prettier than Judith had thought any colored girl could be. Judith put her hands to her own face thoughtfully and wondered if Philip still thought her pretty. The only looking-glass in the cabin was a little square one Philip used for shaving.

That night she asked him if he would get her a big mirror when he went to town.

"The first one I can find on the wharfs," he promised, and he drew her to him and kissed her.

Her head lay back on his shoulder so that she was looking up. Between two of the logs that roofed the cabin she saw a star.

"Philip, the roof is warping," she exclaimed. "Next time it rains we'll get wet."

"I'll have the men mend it," he said, glancing up. "It leaked during that rain last week and I meant to have them put on a patch. I'm glad you reminded me."

Judith pulled back from him. Every joint in her body was aching from her ride, and his casual way of telling her the hole had been there a week cracked open her resolve not to complain.

"A fine husband you are!" she cried. "Why didn't you mend it before you brought me back from father's?"

"But honey, it's not raining now!" he exclaimed in astonishment. "I'll have it fixed. I told you I forgot about it."

He tried to put his arms around her again, but she caught the bedpost.

"You let me alone! You say you love me and you're going to make me a great lady and you put me in a hovel not fit for a pig. Father told me I'd be miserable. You and your grand vaporings! I never pretended to be elegant but before I married you I could always get out of the rain."

"But my precious child," Philip protested, "it's not raining. What on earth are you shouting about?"

"How did you know it wouldn't be raining tonight?" Her voice broke in her throat. She began to sob. "I've done the best I could. I've smothered and choked in this horrible weather and I've fished bugs out of the gumbo before I could eat it and I nursed my mother till she died and I've never told you how scared I was because I don't know anything about having a baby and there's nobody to tell me, but I can't stand not having a roof over my head!"

She was sobbing so violently that her last words were like screams. As she flung them out Philip picked her up like a child and laid her on the bed. He held her in his arms and leaned over her as she sobbed into the mattress.

"Judith," she heard him say.

"You stop trying to talk to me. You get me into all this trouble and all you can think about is indigo."

"My poor dear girl." He was holding her tight. "I'm sorry about the roof. But you aren't going to make yourself feel any better by behaving like this."

Judith caught a short breath. After a silence Philip spoke again.

"Judith, I do love you, and you've got to believe it. I reckon this is what a man gets when he loves a woman too much to be reasonable and wait for her. I didn't know I'd get you with child so soon and I did think this cabin would hold together a year—please, sweetheart, say you love me in spite of it! You must love me or you wouldn't have come with me that night."

She was crying quietly, without any sobs. "Oh Philip, I do love you! But I haven't had any peace since I saw you. It's all been heat and mosquitoes and rats and being sick and having my ankles swell up—"

"I know it, dearest. Isn't there anything I can do to prove I'm sorry?"

"Yes. Get some plaster and stop up the holes in this cabin."

He laughed under his breath. "All right. The next time I go to town. Honey, I did try to tell you how trifling I was."

"You aren't trifling." Judith reached up and put her arms

around his neck. "Hold me tight, like that. Do you really love me as much as you said you did?"

"I didn't know you were listening."

"I wasn't. But I heard you. Philip, I love you so much. I don't care what happens to me as long as I've got you."

"You aren't scared any more about the baby?"

"I'm not scared a bit. I hope I have a dozen and that they all look like you."

She held him close and he kissed her, and that night she was not scared.

CHAPTER FOUR

But the next day, and the next and the next, she was scared, and though she did not tell Philip, she grew more frightened as the time passed.

There was nobody she could ask, and even if there had been she did not know what questions to put. Gervaise sent a servant over one day with some lengths of delicate muslin, and a funny little misspelt note, for Gervaise spoke English better than she wrote it. Another day a lady came by and gave Judith some flannel for the baby's petticoats. She spoke with a French accent. "I am Sylvie Durham. My husband is American, a builder of flatboats. When your trouble is over you will come to see us, yes?"

Judith said yes, thank you. Everybody in Dalroy seemed to know Philip and to know his wife was with child. But she could not question these strange women. And in the meantime she could feel her child moving within her, and that was very curious, but she did not know what the rest would be like. Philip said when it happened it would be February. Maybe Angelique knew. But Angelique's English was still not good enough for her to converse much.

Still, it was comforting to have Angelique. For Angelique had been a lady's maid, and she could comb Judith's hair into a dozen exciting coiffures, and sew with stitches so tiny as to be almost invisible. She helped Judith make up the muslin and flannel into garments for the baby. Judith taught her how to make the letters of the alphabet as she herself had been taught to make them in the dame-school when she was a little girl. They had some merry times as the winter fogs drew in and Judith was more inclined to sit by the cabin fire than to go outdoors. She was more glad every day that Philip had bought Angelique to be with her through these worrisome months.

But her terror of what lay ahead increased as the time passed. One misty day in December while Angelique was washing clothes in the space behind the cabin, Judith went out for a walk. As she neared the tents where the Negroes lived she began to hear groans as of some one in dreadful pain. She stopped where she was, aghast, and a moment later the groans turned into terrible cries like those of an animal being ripped to pieces by the jaws of a trap. Judith rushed toward the fires where the women were cooking. They seemed to be working placidly, too deaf to hear that some one was being tormented to death in the tents, and she ran up breathless.

"What's happening in there?" she cried, her words coming in panting little gasps.

The woman nearest lifted her head. "Ma'am?"

"Can't you hear me?" Judith demanded furiously. "What's happening?"

The woman glanced back, shrugged and shook her head. "Oh, don't you bodder, miss. She jes' gettin' a baby."

Judith put her hands over her ears and stumbled away from the screams, back toward the cabin. When she reached it she flung herself across the bed, her hands still over her ears. But she could hear the screams, faint but unmistakable, and she was listening in a panic when Angelique came in.

Angelique hurried over to her, speaking anxiously in a jumble of French and English. She sat on the bed and gathered Judith into her arms, still talking, though it was some time before Judith could grasp what she said. But Angelique said it over and over, and at last Judith made it out.

"I get baby one time, miss. I be here to help when it comes your time."

Judith raised her head. Angelique said again, "I help you, miss."

"Oh," said Judith. "You had a baby?"

Angelique nodded.

"What happened to your baby, Angelique?"

"It die, miss. We not let your baby die."

"And you'll take care of me?"

Angelique smiled and nodded. Judith put her arms around Angelique and hid her face. Angelique held her tight, stroking

her hair tenderly, and began to sing to her as though she were
singing a child to sleep.

Yé halé li la cyprier
So bras yé 'tassé par derrier,
Ye 'tasse so la main divant. ...

Judith could not understand the words, and neither could
Philip when he came in and Angelique was still singing. He
told her it was the French of the Congo slaves spun into a
folksong. But Angelique's voice was so low and rich and her
caresses so tender that Judith did not need any words to make
her feel less alone.

In spite of the big fire the cabin was cold these days. Judith
had thought it would not be cold in Louisiana. But the winter
had come with a strange damp chill and such clouds of fog
that nobody could get warm. Philip had set his Negroes to
mending the roof, but it was still not secure against the heavy
winter rains, and the wet came through the chinks between
the logs. Philip promised to get some more plaster when he
went to town, but he forgot it again, for the indigo was being
planted and his precious cleared acres crowded the cabin out
of his mind.

In January the fogs cleared and the days were cold and
bright, and Judith began to feel better. Then, all of a sudden, it
was February.

Nobody had told her to expect February, except as the
name of a month. But she woke up one morning to a day so

blue and gold and glorious that she leaped out of bed and leaned her arms on the window-sill, wishing her body was not so heavy because she felt like dancing. The sun was blazing on the oaks and magnolias, brilliant as summer though the air was still cold. The days went by and the glory was still there. Even though Judith felt sometimes so heavy her legs were inadequate to carry her from one side of the cabin to the other, her spirit was on wings. What a strange splendid country, in which February was the peak of beauty. The name sounded like snow and ice, but here the earth was heaving and putting forth green shoots, and the live-oaks were turning up the tips of their branches with eager new leaves that pushed the old ones to the ground, and there were long dark buds on the magnolias. The moss that had been gray on the trees was a shadowy green, and there was life everywhere, life new and stirring and magnificent.

Why hadn't somebody told her, Judith wondered, last summer when she had been nearly prostrate with the heat, that February would be like this? Oh, she was sorry for the folk she had left behind in New England, who could not open their shutters every morning to such miracles of gold and sapphire. There would be summer again, and the sky would be like a cup of brass turned down by a pitiless God, but this year she would not mind because she would know the world was turning and soon there would be another February. Maybe those poor souls who first came to New England had felt the same way about the long white winter, because there had been nobody to tell them that in June there would be daisies and the queen's lace over the fields. What a marvel that first June must have been to them, just as this first February was to her. There should be some way to know beforehand that June in Connecticut was worth the winter, and February in Louisiana was worth the summer and the fogs.

But maybe it was better just to have it happen. For when it came like this you were thrilled to such ecstasy with the surprise of it. Here there were no daisies, but there were great red blooms for which she had no name, and purple flowers bursting on the dead-looking sticks in the bayous; and soon this trouble she was so afraid of would be over and she would be light on her feet again. Even now it was splendid to feel a child moving in her body and know it was the first of a dynasty that was to rule this glorious country. She was proud to be having a child so soon.

Philip came in unexpectedly one mid-morning.

"I'm going into town to get the plows mended, Judith. What shall I bring you?"

She smiled up at him.

"Some plaster to chink up the cabin, *please*!"

"I will, dear, really. I won't forget this time. And that looking-glass?"

"Do you still think I'm pretty?" she asked wistfully.

"You have the loveliest eyes I ever saw. Dark gold like the sun on the river."

"Anyway," said Judith, "I feel perfectly wonderful."

"So do I. I hate to take time out for sleeping." He kissed her. "Goodbye, honey, and I'll be back as soon as I can."

She stood in the doorway and waved at him as he climbed into the wagon and drove away. The wind ruffled her hair. Judith stretched out her arms and took a deep breath. In the west, over the river, some clouds were piling up very white against the deep blue of the sky. She did hope it wouldn't rain before Philip came back with the plaster.

By afternoon when Philip returned the clouds in the west were black, and the sun behind them made purple ridges in the pile. Judith went to the door, watching as Philip and Josh unloaded things from the wagon. Philip ran in eagerly.

"Look what I've brought you, darling! A boat came up from New Orleans yesterday and they were having a sale of merchandise on the Purcell wharfs. Look at this."

He shook out a bolt of silk gauze, so fine and thin one could almost read printing through it. "From Paris, Judith. There'll be mighty few ladies on the bluff who can have a gown like this. Angelique can make it for you—Angelique! Regardez!"

"Oh Philip, how beautiful!" Judith and Angelique together gathered the gauze into their hands. It was vaguely rose-colored, with little clusters of blue flowers printed on it. She thanked him, though she was wondering what on earth she was going to do with a gauze dress in a log cabin.

"And look at this. Rose-colored ribbons to trim it, silk both sides. And here's a jar of pomade to set the curls in your hair, made in New Orleans with crushed jasmine flowers."

"And what's in this package?"

"That's a couple of French romances."

"Oh, I see. I can't read them."

"I'll read them to you. See this—a girdle of plum-colored velvet."

"It's perfectly beautiful, but—but really, I can't get it on!"

"Keep it till you can. These flasks are wine from Burgundy. And now, this is the finest present of all. Just what you wanted."

He brought in a big covered object, taller than a spinning-wheel.

"What's that, Philip?"

"Uncover it and see."

Judith reached out eagerly and pulled off the cloth. She started and her jaw dropped and she moved a step backward. For an instant she was silent, then she began to cry.

"Judith, honey, what is it?"

Judith turned around and put her hand over her eyes to keep back the tears.

"Oh my Lord, Philip, is *that* what I look like?"

Philip stood quite still. He glanced at Angelique and she shook her head. He looked at Judith, crying with her back to the mirror.

"Cover it up!" she said angrily.

Philip slowly reached down and replaced the cloth over the glass. "Maybe you're right," he said after a moment. "I'm sorry I brought it now."

Judith was drying her eyes on the end of her kerchief. She ran impulsively to him and put her arms around him.

"Oh Philip, I'm so sorry. You were sweet to bring it. I do like it, really I do. But I was so—shocked!"

Philip smiled at her tenderly. "It's all right, honey. We'll keep it covered till you're pretty again."

"No we won't. I'm just behaving like a little girl. I don't know how you put up with me at all." Judith pulled the cloth down. "I think you're a dear to bring me such pretty things."

"You do like them, don't you?"

"Why Philip, I love them. We must put that beautiful silk in the bottom of the chest where it won't get wet if it rains tonight. I think you'd better have Josh start filling up the worst cracks now. Those clouds look awfully threatening."

Philip's arms dropped from around her. "Judith, I forgot about the plaster."

"Oh Philip! Again?"

He nodded. "I reminded myself all the way in to bring it, then when I got to the wharfs I was having such fun buying things for you that it pushed everything else out of my head."

Judith took a long breath. She walked away from him. Then she wheeled around.

"Oh, you're *such* a fool!" she cried. "I can't go to town because shaking over the trails would kill me and I haven't anybody to depend on but you, and all you get me is clothes I can't wear and French books I can't read and a mirror to show me how ugly I am! All I ever asked you for was something to keep the rain off and I can't trust you even for that. I'm tired of living in a chicken-coop!"

Philip turned around on his heel and walked out. Judith ran to the door and saw him getting back into the wagon.

"Where are you going?" she cried.

"To town to get that plaster," he called without turning.

"Not now, Philip! It'll be night before you can get back!"

"Josh will take care of you. It's easier driving at night than staying in the house with your temper."

He struck the mules. The wagon started with a jerk. Philip was standing up, and Judith guessed by the way he was slashing the mules that he wished it was herself instead of them he was punishing. Josh, standing by the cabin step, looked up.

"I reckon I better hang around, young miss?"

Judith said yes. She went back inside. Angelique came toward her timidly.

"Dis glass?" she said, the covering cloth in her hand.

"Oh, leave it alone will you?" said Judith curtly. She went and sat by the window. The clouds were too thick to leave a vestige of sun, and Judith was too unhappy to care.

Presently Angelique came and touched her arm, and Judith saw that she had set out some cornbread and cold meat on the table. Judith shook her head. She sat watching the trees bow to the rising wind, not thinking about anything in particular but dully miserable. Angelique sat down on a chest in a corner to eat her own supper.

All of a sudden Judith felt a thunderclap of pain in the middle of her. She jerked, catching her breath, and Angelique sprang up.

"Qu'est-ce que c'est, madame?"

"I—I don't know," said Judith shakily, for the pain had gone as abruptly as it had come. Angelique went back to her supper and Judith sat down again, but before she had time to relax the pain struck at her again. She grabbed the back of the chair behind her and cried "Angelique!"

Angelique came to her. Judith was white, less with pain than with bewilderment, for now that the pain had passed she felt almost well. Angelique spoke to her soothingly; Judith did not catch the words, but she smiled to show she understood the tone. Angelique stood with an arm around her, and when the next pain came Judith caught her hands and held them till it was gone. "I feel all right now," she said.

Angelique began to be very busy about the cabin, getting things out of chests and hanging a kettle of water on the crane in the fireplace. She called Josh to bring in some wood. Judith stayed where she was. The pains came curiously, like two hands tearing her apart in the middle, but there were long spaces between when nothing hurt her at all. She wished Philip would get back. She could tell him she really believed their baby was about to be born, and she would like to have the chance before it was born to say she was sorry she had been so foolish about the looking-glass and scolded him like that for forgetting the plaster. Yes, she must be hard to live with. She did try to hold her tongue, but when it got the better of her she could say things that were pretty nasty.

The pain grabbed at her and Judith held the window-sill with both hands. Josh came in and piled up the wood. When he had gone out she began to think maybe she ought to go to bed. Women who had babies had them in bed. She asked Angelique to bring her a bedgown, and Angelique undressed her, stopping to let Judith hold to her shoulders when the pains came. But when Judith tried to climb into bed Angelique held her back.

"No, no," she said. "No. Walk."

That was strange. But she walked up and down obediently. Angelique was gentle and sympathetic, and she kept murmuring soft things in French, incomprehensible but comforting.

Judith began to think it really wasn't so awful to have a baby. The pains were getting rather bad, but they weren't unbearable.

But as it got dark, Philip did not come back and the pains got worse and worse and worse. They came so close together that she could hardly catch her breath between them, and while they were wrenching at her she couldn't breathe at all, but only hold on to Angelique and make little tormented gasps in her throat. Angelique was so dear and gentle. But Judith wished for Philip. He should be back by now. She could lean on him as hard as she wanted to, and sometimes Angelique stumbled when Judith caught at her. Besides, it did take a good deal of pain to have a baby and Philip ought to be here to appreciate it. Then maybe he'd forgive her for being so quicktempered.

Angelique said, "You hold de bed, young miss. De fire, he go out for more wood."

Judith held to the bedpost while Angelique put logs on the fire. The pains came faster and harder. Judith bit on her fingers. She held the bedpost tight and would not scream. Angelique looked up and said, "You good brave lady, young miss."

It occurred to Judith that this was quite a lot of pain. It

was dark outside and it must have been several hours since the first one struck her. A lot of curious things were going on in her body that she hadn't expected at all, though Angelique didn't seem surprised. But the baby ought to be getting itself born by now.

"How much longer does this last, Angelique?" she inquired unsteadily.

Angelique looked up from the fire. "Ma'am?"

"I said—" Judith stopped, for the pain had caught her again and she wrapped both arms around the bedpost and found herself clamping her teeth on the wood to stiffen her through it. As it passed she managed to jerk out, "I said—how much longer—does this go on?"

Angelique stopped tending the fire. She stood up slowly. "Pauvre petite," she said gently and she came over and took Judith in her arms and kissed her forehead. She did not say anything else. But Judith understood that this was not the end. The pain began clawing at her again. By this time it was agony pure and simple and Judith thought if this wasn't the last she would rather die now than have the baby born at all. But nothing happened. Angelique tried to make her walk again when Judith's relaxing muscles told her this one was passing, but Judith fell down when she tried to take a step. As Angelique bent to help her up she managed to gasp out:

"Please let me lie down, Angelique! Please!"

Angelique let her go to bed then. Avalanches of torment came over her, so fast she thought she was going to split in two and she bit her arms till blood seeped through the prints of her teeth. She remembered how the woman in the quarters had screamed and didn't blame her. Angelique sat by her and wiped her forehead.

She could see everything so clearly, the broken cabin walls and the leaning roof, and the clothes hanging on pegs and the boxes standing around because there was no place to put the things that were in them, and the bag of cornmeal with a cockroach crawling over it, and a line of ants winding over the floor, and the firelight making everything look red. She had jerked up the coverlet in a spasm of agony, but though she had had a vague sensation of something stinging her ankles she had paid no attention till now, when she saw them and cried out:

"There's ants all over me, Angelique!"

Her voice trailed off. Angelique saw the ants and rushed to get them off her, but there were hundreds of them and a moment later Judith knew why they were so thick.

A raindrop splashed on her arm, and a fine spray coming through a break in the wall peppered her forehead. She remembered that she had heard it raining for some time but had hardly noticed. But now in the moments between the pains she began to understand that the rain was coming down in a torrent, tearing up the flimsy patches in the roof and washing the mud from between the logs of the wall. The ants on the floor were circling a puddle. The ants in the bed were stinging her arms and legs. The rain was dripping on her, and this time of year there was not even a mosquito bar over the bed to keep some of it off. She was jerking with torture, and Philip was out in the forest. A cockroach with wings crept through a chink in the wall and then, terrified at the sudden firelight, flew up and struck her in the face.

She screamed then. She shrieked over and over, calling Philip, and begging Angelique to help her. Angelique shoved at the bed to move it from under the leak. She brought wet cloths and tried to wash the ants off Judith's legs. Pulling out the sheets, she emptied the ants into the fire, but there were more of them than she could fight. The rain poured in through the roof and ran out again through the cracks in the floor. The flying cockroaches buzzed around the bed. Sometimes one of them plopped against the wall and fell down. Judith shrieked for Philip, but it was daybreak when Philip returned, wet, cold, conscience-stricken and slightly drunk, for he had sat in a tavern till long after dark and the rain had bogged the trail so that it had taken him seven hours to make the journey home.

He heard Judith's screams above the beat of the rain. At the cabin door he leaped out of the wagon and rattled the bolt, calling who he was. Angelique slipped the bolt and he went in, dripping. Judith raised halfway up from the bed, crying out, "Philip! Get these things off me!" But for a moment he could not move.

The bed was in the middle of the room. Angelique had torn holes in the corners of a blanket and tied it over the bedposts to make a shelter, for the rain was coming in through a dozen places in the roof of the cabin.

He went over to the bed. In the firelight Judith's face was yellow with agony. The sheets were off and there were damp spots on the moss mattress. The quilt Angelique had put over her was tossed to one side, lined with ants, and there were streaks of ants crawling over Judith's arms and legs. She looked up at him and through her clenched teeth he heard her say, "Please get them off me, Philip!"

"I'll take care of you," said Philip. He scraped the ants off her with his hands and threw the quilt on the puddled floor. "Judith," he exclaimed as he worked over her, "can you understand me? Do you forgive me for leaving you like this?"

She nodded. Philip lifted her up and brushed the ants off her. He picked up a cockroach from the mattress and crushed it between his fingers. Angelique had not been strong enough to raise the legs of the bed, but Philip held them up one by one and made her set each leg in a pot of water to prevent any more ants crawling up from the floor. He picked them off Judith's arms and legs as fast as he could. At last he sat by her and wiped the lines of sweat off her face, helplessly watching the muscles of her neck knot like ropes.

Judith smothered a cry in her throat and felt for his hands. She held them tight, straining at them as the pains went through her. He saw red splotches on her legs where the ants had bitten her, and Angelique crushing with her fingers other ants that had hidden in the creases of the mattress. Streaks of wet gray light pushed between tile chinks, showing him a huddle of rats gnawing the sack of potatoes in a corner. It was the first time Philip had ever felt like the good-for-nothing fool everybody on the Carolina coast had told him he was; he remembered his father's warning that one day something would happen to make him know it. He wondered if Judith would ever believe he loved her, and resolved bitterly that after this he was going to be so tender with her that she would be compelled to understand it.

"Judith," he said, "dear sweetheart, I'm so sorry for everything! Please tell me you know what I'm saying!"

She made some noises in her throat. He could not tell whether she was answering or not.

Philip tried to speak to her again, but at that instant she jerked herself up with a shriek and sank back with such gray exhaustion on her face that he thought she was dead. He sprang up and bent over her, and saw her chest move as she caught her breath, and behind him Angelique said:

"Mais il est beau, 'Sieur Philip!"

Philip leaned over Judith again. "Dearest girl, it's all over. You have been delivered of a son."

She lay still, her arm over her eyes. By the time Angelique brought the baby to lay it by her, wrapped in a calico apron which was the only dry garment she could find in the cabin, Judith was asleep.

Philip covered her with a fur-lined velvet cloak he had bought in Marseille.

CHAPTER FIVE

Philip said she must have a white dress for her churching, and Judith had Angelique make it out of a roll of ivory silk Gervaise had sent over when she heard Judith's son was born. Philip named the baby David for his father. "To remind me of something," he said, and though she did not know what he meant she had acquiesced. One name was as good as another as long as she had the baby like a new present to see every morning. He was fat and healthy, and now that she was well the night he was born seemed remote like a bad dream.

The Sunday she was churched Judith went to Lynhaven to stay with Gervaise until the moss house at Ardeith was ready. She was reluctant to go, for the cabin was not so bad now that the cracks had been plastered. But since the night David was born Philip for the first time seemed to find the place intoler-

able. He detested the cracks and the ants and having to sleep
and cook in one room, and often said he didn't see how she
endured it at all. So though she hated the idea of leaving him
she yielded, and climbed with Gervaise into the beautiful carriage Walter Purcell had just received from New Orleans.
Gervaise was but recently up from her own confinement.

Angelique rode behind in a cart with the nurse Philip had
brought from the quarters for David. Judith whispered to
Gervaise that at first it had shocked her to see her little pink
baby nursing at the breast of a black woman, in spite of Philip's assurances that women who had slaves never troubled to
nurse their own children. Gervaise chuckled softly and whispered back that she too had had a problem about her children—both of them had been baptized here at St. Margaret's
chapel, for though she was Catholic, George the Third permitted no Catholic churches in English Louisiana, but she had
rebaptized them herself in private, just to be sure. After this
exchange of confidences they laughed intimately and felt like
good friends.

Philip came to Lynhaven every Saturday and stayed till
Sunday evening. Though she missed him between times,
Judith enjoyed being there. Gervaise was an impeccable host-
ess and housekeeper, though she was quite unable to do any
work herself and marveled at Judith's ability to cook and sew
fine seams. Judith found it delightful to lie in bed every morning until Angelique brought her coffee, and to spend the day
riding or gossiping or being fitted for new gowns according to
fashion dolls from Paris. On his weekly visits Philip told her

she was changing. She could feel it, vaguely; it was as though the rhythms of her body were adapting themselves to the indolent rhythm of the river by which she lived. And the working of her mind too—it was so easy here to be casual.

But she would never, thought Judith, learn to be as casual as Gervaise; never learn to regard life with detachment as though it were only an amusing spectacle. Sometimes she envied Gervaise and sometimes pitied her for this. It was a very protective attitude, but it shielded her from ecstasy as well as pain. In spite of her success at making her home-life pleasant, Judith could not help wondering if Gervaise really loved any one as she herself loved Philip. Certainly not her husband, though she liked him very well and they never quarreled.

She told Judith about her marriage in a matter-of-fact way. It was evident that she regarded Philip as a charming scamp and Judith's elopement a piece of puzzling recklessness. When Gervaise was fourteen Walter Purcell had come to New Orleans to buy slaves from her father, an importer of blacks from Sainte Domingue. Her father was a hard-headed Creole burdened with several daughters whose need for dowries was keeping him in debt. Gervaise was pretty, and the young American from up the river with his royal grant in his pocket was potentially rich. Moreover, Monsieur Durand was happy to discover that Americans were not as insistent about dowries as Creoles, an inducement sufficient to let him overlook Mr. Purcell's British heresy in the matter of religion. Walter Purcell wanted a wife, and women of good breeding were scarce in the rude settlements of West Florida. So Gervaise was offered almost empty-handed and thus accepted, and each of the two gentlemen considered that he had driven a good bargain. Gervaise was then informed that she had been happily disposed of. She did not complain, for Walter Purcell seemed to her a personable young man, though his barbarous language made acquaintance difficult; to tell the truth, she considered herself fortunate. An epidemic aboard one of her father's ships had carried off half a cargo of good Negroes and she had been wondering where her dowry was to come from. If her suitor was willing to accept her with but a handful of sous to her name Gervaise decided he must be smitten indeed with her charms.

Oh yes, Gervaise was happy enough. Walter was fond of her and treated her like a pet kitten, and as Gervaise never manifested any desire to control her own destiny things went smoothly at Lynhaven. But when Philip came on his weekly visits Judith compared the flaming love between them to the carefully nurtured pleasantness of the Purcells and knew she would not have exchanged a minute of her life with Gervaise, not even the cabin and the bugs.

Philip arranged to buy part of Walter Purcell's uncleared land, for Walter had built docks on his riverfront property and was more concerned with wharf development than planting. Gervaise remarked that she couldn't see what Philip wanted with more forest when it was going to take him years to clear what he had, but Judith understood; her vision of the future, like his, included a realm of indigo far out-reaching the three thousand acres he had from the king. Philip sold his first crop at a profit, and gave Judith money for shopping. She and Gervaise rode down to the wharfs, with Angelique and Gervaise's maid following them, for she had found that here ladies did not venture out of doors unattended. They boarded the boats from New Orleans, and Judith bought muslins and shoes, and a French rattle for David made of thin wood painted with animals. She got blue calico and plaid tignons for Angelique, partly to show gratitude for her tenderness the night David was born and partly because Angelique was so pretty it was a joy to dress her up. Angelique was so grateful Judith was surprised, and exclaimed impulsively:

"But Angelique, I'd like to get you something really nice. Tell me what you want."

Angelique said, "I got mighty little want, young miss." She was silent a moment, and added in a low voice, "No white lady been good to me like you."

Judith watched her thoughtfully. Angelique was embroidering a dress for David. Her golden hands moved deftly over the muslin. Judith wondered what her life had been like before they brought her up the river to be sold.

"Weren't they good to you, Angelique, at Mr. Peyroux's house?" she asked.

Angelique did not lift her eyes. "Dey was arright. We get plenty to eat and not too much work. But dey don't make talk to us like you, young miss."

"Maybe," ventured Judith, "you never had a chance to show them how good you could be. I'd really like to give you something, Angelique, just to prove I haven't forgotten."

Angelique looked up, hesitated, and dropped her eyes again.

"I don't need something bought," she said. "But I could make wish—"

"What?"

"Dat you not ever sell me away from you."

Judith sprang up. "Why Angelique! Did you think I ever would?"

Angelique shrugged fatalistically. "Sais pas," she said.

"But I wouldn't, Angelique!" Judith put her arms around her. "I don't know what I did before I had you. You're my very best friend. Not for a thousand pounds. Not if the king and queen came from London to buy you. Not ever, ever, ever."

Angelique's black eyes were bright with tears as she raised them again. "You say for true, Miss Judith?"

Judith nodded vehemently.

"You are good lady," said Angelique.

Judith sat down on the floor and rested her arms on Angelique's lap. "Listen. I want you to promise me something."

"Yes, ma'am?"

"Don't ever tell anybody about the night I was delivered. About the rain coming in or the ants or Mr. Philip's leaving me alone."

Angelique smiled. "I don't tell, young miss."

Their eyes met in comprehension.

Gervaise came in, and told Judith Philip was outside. Judith ran out, for it was not Saturday and she wondered if something was wrong. But Philip was evidently in high spirits, and he looked more elegant than ever in a blue coat with a cascade of pleated linen falling from the stock around his neck. Judith adored the courtly way he bent to kiss Gervaise's hand and murmured, "You grow more beautiful every day, madam."

He put his hands on Judith's waist and lifted her to sit on his crossed arms like a baby, while he asked her about David. Then he told her he had come to take her home. The moss house at Ardeith was done, yes, and furnished too. "Not a castle," said Philip, his blue eyes crinkling with a teasing pride, "but fit to live in."

Judith hugged him in delight. "Let me down. I do want to see it so!"

Philip spoke to Gervaise as he set Judith on her feet. "Where's Walter?"

"Indoors," said Gervaise. "Why?"

"I have great news for him. A boat came down this morning with some English despatches. They say the seaboard colonies are rebelling against the king."

Judith caught her breath. "But how dreadful!"

"What are they quarreling about?" asked Gervaise, more for politeness' sake than because she wanted to know, for the seaboard colonies were as remote from her reckoning as England itself.

"Oh, trade and taxes, and they want to send representatives to Parliament."

"There was a lot of talk about the taxes before I left Connecticut," said Judith, who like Philip saw the Atlantic coastline as a vivid reality. "In Boston they threw a whole cargo of tea overboard. Father said that was a good gesture—"

"And so it was," agreed Philip. "But a rebellion against the king's majesty—that's mighty drastic."

"Are they fighting?" Judith asked.

"Yes, there've been several clashes between colonial troops and the royal garrisons." He chuckled. "It almost makes me wish I was back home."

"Why Philip! You wouldn't bear arms against the king! What about the oath you swore when you got your grant in Louisiana?"

"I wouldn't keep my promises if he didn't keep his, honey. A good hearty rebellion might teach them a lesson in London. The colonials aren't claiming to be anything but subjects of the king even now—nobody has asked for independence."

"Independence? I think that's ridiculous. I was born English and I hope I'll die English." Judith stopped and glanced at Gervaise, afraid she had been tactless since Gervaise had not had the good fortune to be born a subject of George the Third. But Gervaise was laughing.

"Chère," she said, "I have changed my country three times already and I am but eighteen years old. New Orleans was French when I was born, then King Louis gave us to Spain and they put up new flags in the Place d'Armes and after that I married and came up here to live, so now I am English, and what I shall be before I die I don't know, but I know this—"

"What, Gervaise?" Philip asked when she paused. He was laughing too.

"That in Louisiana, Mr. Philip Larne, you are asking a great deal when you ask to die in the same country you were born in. Is that treason?"

"It's food for philosophy, ma'am."

"And now I will send you coffee." She went into the house.

Philip smiled down at Judith. "Are you glad you're finally coming home?"

She nodded. "I've missed you so terribly."

"I've missed you too, honey." He grinned mischievously. "Your father and brother are going to meet us at Ardeith. Maybe now they'll be persuaded I didn't utterly ruin your life by taking you away from them."

Judith rubbed her cheek against his satin sleeve. "I don't care what they think. Let's go in and tell Angelique to pack my things."

Judith was bubbling with eagerness. But she had not expected such a house as he took her to that day.

She saw it behind the oaks as the carriage shook over the Ardeith trail. Even before she got close to it she realized triumphantly that her house was bigger and grander than the Purcells'. It was shining, bright pink behind its white gallery, and she saw that it had three entrances instead of one, for it had three halls lengthwise and one crosswise and two rooms front and back between the arms of the crosses, making sixteen rooms in all, not counting the slave-quarters built sideways at the back. Judith stepped over the threshold of the main entrance, followed by the nurse carrying her baby, and after her came her father and Caleb, and after them the Purcells. She gasped, unprepared for such splendor of space and pink walls and cunningly devised crosscurrents of air. Through the open doors she could see slave-made furniture with turned legs and cane bottoms. For a moment she stood speechless, a sob of joy rising within her as she thought of the cabin that had stood here last year, and she turned and looked at her father's astonished face and the envying admiration of Gervaise, and Philip proud as a king showing off his realm. Her voice choked as she exclaimed :

"Oh Philip, Philip darling, I never expected real glass in the windows!"

Philip tucked an arm around her as he turned to the others. "Come see the rest of it."

He showed them the master bedroom, where there stood a bed so big four people could have slept on it as comfortably as two. Across the hall was the nursery, with a cot for the nurse and a cradle made of woven canes. "And look," said Philip, leading them back to the bedroom. Over the bed hung a cord that ran across the ceiling under a series of loops, and through the wall to a bell hanging in Angelique's room. "So you can call her for coffee in the morning without getting up," he said.

Judith glanced at her father, who was dumb before such luxury. "There's another bell in the parlor and another in the dining-room," said Philip, "to save you running about for the servants."

He led them to the dining-room, where there was a table big enough for twenty or thirty diners, with a fan of turkey feathers hanging over it from the ceiling. Outdoors was the kitchen-house, with a fireplace twelve feet wide and four cranes for pots and kettles.

Judith couldn't say anything. She wanted to cry. Her father took her hands gravely.

"You must pray the Lord to save you from pride, daughter," he said, "living in such opulence as this."

Judith was hurting all over with too much happiness. She could see herself mistress of this house, summoning her slaves with bells and queening it at that great table. That she could have come from the flatboat via the log cabin to this was too much to be borne. She snatched her baby out of the nurse's arms and ran to the master bedroom and dropped on her knees by the bed. David was so soft and sweet in her arms; Philip had promised that her child would be lord of a kingdom, but she hadn't been able to imagine anything like this. She tried without success to smother the sobs in her throat, and began to pray in broken little whispers.

"Please, God, help me to be good. Make me good enough to deserve everything—the big kitchen and slave-bells and glass in the windows. Make David a good boy and kind to poor people who haven't got a palace like this to live in."

Then she saw, crawling over the cypress floor as though they had as much right here as she did, a thin wavy line of ants. She shuddered and sprang up, and a grasshopper leaped out of a corner and watched her. She added another prayer.

"And please, Lord, help me not to call Louisiana a bug-hole where Philip can hear me."

Before she had been in her new house a month Judith agreed with the proverb that the mistress of a plantation was the biggest slave on it.

She had to supervise the spinning, weaving and sewing, plan a flower-garden in front, and give dinners that were veritable banquets. Philip loved to entertain and by this time the circle of his friends had grown to include most of the important planters and business men on the Dalroy bluff. Judith had nine house-servants including Angelique, but they were never finished with what had to be done. Besides, the new ones spoke nothing but gumbo French and though she had picked up some French from Gervaise she was thankful to have Angelique as inter-preter. But for Angelique, Judith wondered how she would ever have run her house. Angelique knew everything; how to dry bay leaves in the shade to make the powdered filé that sea-soned okra gumbo, how to extract oil from pine to take out the sting of mosquito bites, and how to pile Judith's hair over a frame to make the castle-like structures fashionable these days. Angelique showed her where to put piles of arsenic on the galleries to lessen the plague of grasshoppers attracted by the indigo around the house. It was Angelique too who advised that the beds be taken apart twice a year and the cracks painted with quicksilver beaten up with the white of egg.

"What's that for?" Judith inquired.

"Bedbugs," said Angelique succinctly.

"Oh my God," said Judith. She wondered impatiently why decent people should try to live at all in Louisiana, which looked like such a paradise and wasn't really a paradise for anything but bugs of one sort or another. But she painted the beds with frantic conscientiousness after that, and made the slaves in the quarters paint theirs so often that Philip said she was going to pauperize him with so much buying of quick-silver. The stuff was expensive, didn't she know that—for it had to be imported from Europe, and since the American war started imports had doubled and tripled in price. To which Judith retorted tartly that if he'd stop spending so much money on French wines he'd have more to spend on keeping the house clean—did he want to wake up some morning and find vermin in David's cradle? Philip asked if she wanted to serve nothing but domestic orange wine at her dinners, and nice people didn't have bedbugs anyway, and Judith said that was because nice people took pains to keep them out, and Philip exclaimed that she was getting a little bit insane on the subject of bugs.

Judith, who was thoroughly angry by this time, snapped at him that if he had ever spent a night enduring not only child-birth but the added frightfulness of being eaten by ants and cockroaches he might be a little bit insane too. Philip went out and banged the door. She looked after him with a certain indignant satisfaction. That was a weapon she could always use against him. At that instant she was glad she had it.

But in the fall, when she found she was going to have another child, she remembered her first delivery with such horror that it was hard to make any pretense of bravery about facing another. She thought Philip was quite unsympathetic to be so frankly glad of it when she told him.

"What makes you so cross?" he asked her. "You don't want to spend your life clucking over one baby, do you?"

They were in their room getting ready for supper. Judith

twirled a little china snuff-box on the bureau with such force that she spilt some of the snuff. It blew up her nose and made her sneeze.

"I think you might at least say you're sorry," she retorted when she could speak again.

"But my dear sweetheart," Philip exclaimed, "I'm not. I'm sorry having children is such a miserable business, but not half as sorry as I'd be if you were barren."

"Oh, all right," said Judith shortly. She replaced the cover of the snuff-box and added without looking up, "At least when this one is born I'll have a roof over me."

There was a pause. "Any time you decide to stop talking about that," said Philip, "I'll be grateful."

She turned around impulsively and went to him. "I'm sorry, darling. I really am. Philip, I'm truly not as horrid as I sound."

"I know it," he said, and laughed down at her. "You're—let me see, how old are you?"

"Seventeen in November."

"Do you think you can learn to hold your tongue by the time you're twenty?"

She nodded seriously. "I'll try."

After that she made up her mind to keep her temper and pretend to be tranquil, though she did not always succeed. She had so much to do! Besides attending to her own house and getting clothes made for the baby she tried to keep a supervising eye on housekeeping arrangements at Silverwood. She knew her father and Caleb appreciated her interest, but when the winter rains came and turned the roads into streaks of marsh she was afraid to travel, and had to send Angelique in her place. Angelique reported that Mark and Caleb were living comfortably, and were talking of building a moss house as soon as the worst rains were over.

"I wish to heaven Caleb would get married," said Judith. "There ought to be a woman at Silverwood."

Angelique chuckled. "Mr. Caleb will get married when he's good and ready and not before. If I were you I shouldn't be trying to give him any advice." Angelique's English was improving fast, and she was careful to avoid the dialect of most of the slaves.

David's mammy brought him in, and Judith pulled him to her and kissed the top of his golden head. "Do you suppose I can possibly have another baby as beautiful as this one?"

"That'll be the Lord's doing, Miss Judith." Angelique reached into her dress and took out a rabbit's foot. "One of the girls at Silverwood sent you this. It's the left hind foot of a rabbit killed in a graveyard on a Friday midnight. She says put it under the mattress after the pains start and you'll come to a good delivery."

"Thanks." Judith laughed in spite of herself as she took it. "Angelique, do you believe that?"

"Why, I don't know. It doesn't hurt any to try it. She says you should wear it inside your clothes till the time comes."

"Very well." Judith tucked the rabbit's foot into the bosom of her dress. "But don't tell Mr. Philip on me. He doesn't believe in anything he can't prove."

But Philip would have let her drape herself with a hundred

charms if she had wanted to. He was occupied with affairs of his own.

Everybody had been talking that year about the rebellion on the seacoast, wondering how long it would last and if it would make much difference in Louisiana. The first echo of the rebellion sounded when the Spanish governor of New Orleans, frankly American in his sympathies, decided to annoy the Tories up the river by curtailing their trade. He announced that increased port duties would be demanded of boats from the English plantations.

The order roused a storm among Creoles and Tories alike. Being patriotic was one thing, as Gervaise's brother Michel wrote her from New Orleans, but conducting trade was something else again, and since Spain and England were technically at peace Governor Unzaga was a blockhead to try to put New Orleans and West Florida into a state of war. The Creole traders could not live without Tory merchandise and equally the planters could not survive without a market, and neither of them would submit to having commerce choked by taxes. Let the boats come down as usual and if the governor interfered he'd have a little private war of his own to deal with.

Philip observed that this line of reasoning was too obvious to require comment. But when he loaded seven boats with indigo and said he was going to smuggle them to New Orleans himself, Judith could not help protesting.

"Suppose you're caught?" she exclaimed.

"I've taken worse risks than this, honey," Philip reminded her. "You attend to your own business."

GWEN BRISTOW

He came back from New Orleans triumphant. Judith received him in tearful relief.

"What happened?" she demanded.

"Nothing," said Philip. "We unloaded the boats at night and got the stuff into the warehouses before daybreak. It will go out in duty-free Spanish vessels. Governor Unzaga's a lame-brain. We didn't even pay the regular wharf duty. By the end of spring there'll be so much smuggling down the river he won't even collect enough to keep the wharfs in repair." Philip grinned. "It was rather fun."

Judith shook her head and sighed. Philip found everything fun, particularly if there was danger in it, and possible consequences to herself and David if he had got himself hanged for smuggling had not entered his happy head. She was thankful, however, that Philip's recklessness had brought him enough money to pay for the land he had bought from Walter Purcell. She insisted on this, though Philip wanted to let Walter wait while he used the money to buy her some extra house-slaves. But Judith had been taught debts were shameful and should not be allowed to run.

He was right about trade; before spring was over everybody was smuggling and Governor Unzaga was in despair. Philip made three more trips to New Orleans, smuggling his produce gleefully, and Judith managed to pretend a calmness she did not feel. She reminded herself grimly that if she had wanted a stiff-minded husband like her father or her brother Caleb she could have had one, and the glittering carelessness of Philip's that exasperated her was the same quality that made her love him.

Whether it was the rabbit's foot or not her second confinement was surprisingly easy. She asked Philip if he would let her name the baby Christopher Columbus. "I feel like Columbus," she said. "Finding out a lot of new things in a new world."

Philip said no son of his was going to be named Columbus, but she could call him Christopher if she wanted to. He wasn't sure what she meant when she said marrying him was like voyaging into a new world, but when she asked if she might name the baby he had been afraid she was about to suggest Melchisedek or some other Scriptural atrocity handed down in her family, and he was glad to make a compromise. The profits on his smuggled indigo had outdistanced his expectations and he was so pleased with his skill at evading the Spanish taxes that he would have given Judith almost any concession she had asked.

CHAPTER SIX

Though Mark Sheramy said smuggling was dishonest and refused to engage in it, he calculated his costs so nicely that he was able to squeeze out a narrow profit in spite of the wharf duties, and he built a small but comfortable moss-plaster house at Silverwood. In the second spring of the rebellion, when Christopher was nearly a year old, Caleb told Judith he wanted to go down to New Orleans to buy another consignment of slaves. Philip arranged passage for him on a boat belonging to his friend Alan Durham, an American settler who instead of planting his land had become a boatbuilder and sold the river traders flatboats and pirogues made of timber cut from his grant of royal forest. Alan went down to extend his market to New Orleans via the good graces of his French father-in-law.

Caleb wandered through New Orleans in half bewildered fascination. Such an enticing town it was, with the river at its front and at its back a palisade to keep out Indians—not of much use now, with most of the neighboring tribes either bribed or coerced into harmlessness, but the wall had been put there sixty years before when New Orleans was a timid huddle of huts. Caleb liked the muddy streets that seemed never to get dry—for mud crept up even between the cobble-stones; and he liked to watch the mantilla'd ladies stepping from their sedan-chairs upon the cathedral threshold so the mud would not soil their shoes; and the carriages flaunting armorial ciphers on their mud-splashed doors. He liked the slave-market with its medley of languages, the shops where French wines and muslins crowded for space against belts of wampum and uncured furs from the trapping country to the southwest, and even with his stern Protestant soul he could not help liking the cathedral with its bells ringing over the Place d'Armes the call to prayer. Alan Durham laughed at him for preferring the streets to the taprooms, but Alan did not understand that Caleb was already drunk enough with the sights and smells and noises of the town.

On the third morning after his arrival while Alan was sleeping off his merrymaking of the night before, Caleb stood leaning against a date-palm in the Place d'Armes, watching the sun come up and pinken the boats beyond the levee. The cathedral bells were ringing, and he fancied that even in the square he caught a drift of incense, though it was probably nothing but perfume from a thick-blooming magnolia tree. Over the levee top he could see boats from foreign parts in quest of indigo. The sun tipped them with red and gold, and shimmered over the water to light the forest mass on the other bank.

Behind him in the cathedral there was music, and pious folk passed him on the way to mass, fruit-women from the market on foot and great ladies and gentlemen in carriages, or sedan-chairs carried by slaves. A girl ran past him with a flutter of white skirts. A moment later he saw her climbing the levee.

She stopped by a lemon tree in flower and pulled off the printed silk shawl she had worn over her head. Her back to him, she stretched out both arms and took a long breath, the sun twinkling along the silk fringe of the shawl. She had black hair piled up under a high comb, and the wind rushing from the river showed him a slim-waisted corsage above billows of white muslin. She spread her shawl on the damp grass of the levee and flung herself upon it where the lemon tree shaded her from the sun. Caleb started toward her and began climbing the levee slope.

If he had stopped for ten seconds to think he would probably never have done it, he realized later, for Creole gentlemen sharpened their rapiers for men who spoke to their sisters and daughters without proper introductions. At the moment, however, he had forgotten everything but how enchanting was the sight of a woman under a lemon tree. Not until she saw him and started up did he remember that he had no right to address her.

At the same time he recalled that he had no words with

which to do it. He had picked up a smattering of French for trading purposes, but her mantilla suggested that she was Spanish. So he simply stood there, smiling his admiration.

The girl did not seem to be frightened. She supported herself with one hand while she regarded him with puzzled astonishment in her dark eyes. He observed that her narrow black eyebrows almost met over her nose, which was not beautiful, because it was dished and turned up a little at the end, but her mouth was warm and red like a strawberry and her complexion as flawless as a baby's. Caleb caught himself wondering why when these Creoles were so careful to guard their women they let them wear dresses cut so provocatively low.

He said, "I beg your pardon, ma'am," but he made no move to go.

The puzzlement did not leave her face, but she ventured hesitantly, "You—make—Angleesh, señor?"

"Why yes!" Caleb exclaimed in delight. "You speak English?" He sat down by her on the grass.

"Not so much good," she said. She moved away an inch or two. "Who are you?" she asked.

"My name's Caleb Sheramy." He moved closer. "Honestly, I'm not going to bother you. But you were just so everlasting pretty—I couldn't help speaking to you!"

She began to laugh. "Gracias. I mean thank you."

"Please, can't I stay just a couple of minutes and talk to you?" Caleb exclaimed. "I mean—well, I don't live here, and I don't know a soul in New Orleans."

She laughed with more amusement than before, and looked

him up and down appraisingly. Caleb was glad he had on his best black coat and a fluted linen stock. "You are so funny, you English," she said. Her foreign accent was heavy but adorable, and when she laughed she puckered her mouth on one side so that all the laugh came out the other.

"We're not funny really, not after you get used to us. Haven't you ever known any English?"

"A few."

"I'm not really English. I'm American. I come from Connecticut."

"Where's that?" she inquired. "Over the ocean?"

"No, up North."

She turned her dark little head and looked, as though trying to see Connecticut along the current, and he observed that she was looking not up the river, but down.

"Not that way," he said. "North."

"But that's North." Then she laughed again. "You make like all strangers. They think we are crazy when we say the river goes the wrong way by New Orleans. It turns around."

"It what? You mean it goes backwards?"

"No—so." She made a mark with her finger in the folds of her shawl. "It makes—how you say—a bend."

"Tell me what your name is," said Caleb.

She looked down, playing with the fringe of her shawl.

"Dolores Bondio."

"Spanish?"

"I was get born in Cuba."

"You live here now?"

114

Dolores was braiding the strands of the fringe. "I live here since my mother and father die. I live with my aunt Juanita."

"Is she strict? Would she get mad if she saw us talking?"

Dolores looked up. "She is most very strict," she said confidingly. "She make me all the time stay by her. This morning I—I ran away. She is at mass. She think I am there too. I slip out. The morning is so beautiful and I do not like to be always go to church like a nun."

Caleb scowled. "Do Catholics go to church every day?"

"The most pious Catholics. You are not Catholic?"

"No."

"Who are you? Tell me about you. Where is Con—Con—I can't say it."

"It's a long way off. It takes six or eight months to get there. But I don't live there now. I live in West Florida."

"Where is that?"

"It's English Louisiana, on the east bank of the river above New Orleans. My father and I have a plantation."

"Oh." She smiled, the funny little puckery smile that put her mouth all on one side. "One of the English that got a piece of land from the king?"

He nodded.

"What makes you come to New Orleans? You are in this new American war?"

"No, I came down to get slaves. We haven't enough to get the land clear." He turned over on the grass, resting on his elbows and looking up at her piquant Spanish face. "Now tell me about you."

There was a pause. Dolores turned up her hands with an eloquent Latin shrug.

"But I got so little to tell." She looked down again, her lower lip thrust out ever so slightly, and it gave her face a petulant sadness. "I just live here—with my aunt and all my cousins."

Her look of vague unhappiness made him suddenly sorry for her. "But aren't they good to you, Miss Bondio?"

"They—Oh yes, they make good enough." She laced her fingers in her lap and looked away from him, over the river.

Caleb impulsively covered her clasped hands with his. Dolores started and sprang up.

"I must go," she said.

"No!" he cried. "Not yet!"

"Yes. My aunt will lock me up if she finds I was not at mass. Let me go. Please let me go," she begged, for he was still holding her hands. "I must make a quick pass over the square and to the church to be there when she is done praying."

He protested, but Dolores was drawing him down the slope. She had pulled one of her hands out of his and gathered up the shawl. "Please, señor, I must go!"

"But wait." He held her at the foot of the levee. "I want to see you again. When can I see you again?"

"You must not." She gave an apprehensive glance at the cathedral.

"You've got to let me see you again. Can't you slip out? Tonight maybe?"

"Oh no! I can't. Please—"

"Yes, say you can slip out. I like you so much—they can't keep you locked up all the time."

Dolores stopped trying to get away. She looked at the cathedral spires and back at him. "Would American girl do that?" she asked fearfully.

"Oh yes," said Caleb with assurance.

"At sunset," she whispered. "I will try to come for evening prayer. By the cathedral steps. Now let me go."

She broke away from him and ran across the Place d'Armes, throwing her shawl over her head. Caleb watched her till she had disappeared in the shadows beyond the font of holy water.

He was waiting for her there long before sunset. She took so long to come he was afraid her aunt had looked back from prayers that morning to see them together on the levee, but as the last rays struck the spires he saw her come out of the alley between the cathedral and the Cabildo house where the government assembly met. Dolores came slowly, looking around as if she were afraid somebody she knew would see her. She was holding a black lace mantilla close as though to hide her face. Out of the alley behind her came a black woman in a red plaid dress.

He rushed to meet her. She turned and spoke to her attendant in Spanish and the woman went inside the church. Dolores looked up at Caleb, her eyes shaded by her mantilla.

"What do we make do now?"

"Can't we go over to the square?" He took her arm. With her other hand she pulled the lace over her mouth and chin.

GWEN BRISTOW

"No, no," she whispered through it. "It is still light—if a friend of my uncle's saw me in the Place d'Armes alone with a man—" she drew him back, under the arches of the Cabildo. "Here. Now we can make talk."

They sat down on a wrought-iron bench by one of the gates to the building. The heavy columned arches hung over them, shutting out the sunset. Dolores let her black lace fall. In the dusk her face was pale like old ivory.

"Concepcion—she will make stay in the slave seats in yonder a long time—she is good," Dolores whispered. She giggled. "My aunt Juanita, she say for why am I so pious all of a sudden like. I say I feel troubled about my sins."

Caleb gave a little laugh. He held both her hands.

"I don't believe you ever committed a sin in your life."

"Oh, but I have," she assured him. "Envy of my cousins with good dowries, rebellion in the heart against the good God for taking my father into heaven and leaving me poor, rebellion against my uncle for think he have found me a right husband—"

"A husband?" Caleb was unreasonably frightened. "Are you going to be married?"

Dolores nodded. "I must make marry or go in a convent. You see they got in me an extra girl."

"A what?"

"It mean—well, my uncle and aunt got daughters, too many to make a dowry for me. So they find me a husband who will take me with small dowry—and I do not want him! He is old—he have bury three wife and he have already eight chil-

118

dren but my uncle say he will be good to me and I will have a carriage. But I—" her voice had a little catch in it. "I do not want to make marry with old man that have three dead wife and eight live children!" Her words tumbled out fast, and her accent was so thick he could hardly understand her. "But I never make talk by myself with young man before this morning—or maybe you think I am not good girl because I run out on the levee with no duenna?"

And all of a sudden, as the sun vanished and the dark rushed up under the Cabildo pillars, Caleb found that he was holding her in his arms and kissing her, to his own delightful amazement. Dolores yielded for an instant, then she pushed herself out of his arms and sprang up, holding her mantilla tight with both hands.

"Madre de Dios! I should know what you would think—I am not like that!"

She had started to run away from him, but he caught her and held her.

"Dolores, you poor darling, I didn't think anything of the sort! It's just that you're so lovely and so unhappy—please come back and tell me everything. Didn't anybody ever kiss you before?"

She looked down. "No," she said in a low voice.

"Please come back and sit down. Concepcion or whatever her name is, she won't tell on us."

After a moment she returned to the wrought-iron bench. For awhile she had very little to say, and though she was so luscious in the dark that he ached to kiss her again he did not dare. But at last she began to talk as though she trusted him. She told him her father had been sent to Havana by the king of Spain before she was born. They lived in a big house where they entertained diplomats from the three countries that were perpetually quarreling about the river valley and the islands beyond, and it was from them she had learned English and French besides her native Spanish. "But they say my English is much bad," she apologized smiling.

"It's adorable," said Caleb. "Go on."

Her father had died, she said, three years ago, and she had been sent to New Orleans where her uncle was a member of the Spanish Cabildo. He thought he was doing right by marrying her to an old man who would be kind to her, for what else could be expected for a poverty-stricken girl unless she went to the Ursulines?

"And they say," said Dolores, "I would be very bad nun."

He agreed with her, though he knew very little about what was required of nuns beyond perpetual virginity. But that would be catastrophe enough for Dolores, who seemed no less enticing even after he noticed that she had had the misfortune to lose a tooth from one side of her upper row. So that was why she had that little puckery smile, to hide the gap, and very successful it was too. She saw him looking at it, and put up her hand to the side of her face.

"I fell off a horse once, in Havana," she said.

"It doesn't matter a bit," Caleb told her.

"It's a goddamn nuisance," said Dolores.

"What?" Caleb exclaimed.

She started. "What did I make say?"

"You said—" he laughed. Her English was so faulty anyway that he was sorry he had been startled; now he had to explain. "Nice girls who speak English don't say goddamn," he said.

"Oh. I am sorry. The gentlemen who came to my papa's house said it."

"I daresay they did. Don't bother about it."

"It's a bad word?" she asked.

"Yes."

"I am so sorry. I don't make say it any more."

He was about to tell her again that it didn't matter when he saw Concepcion crossing the alley between the cathedral and the Cabildo. Dolores went to meet her. Caleb waited through their Spanish dialogue, and Dolores turned back to him.

"She say time for evening prayer is over and I must go home. I am stay too long anyway."

"Tomorrow you'll run out from mass again?" he asked her eagerly.

She smiled over her shoulder. "Yes."

Caleb saw her every day after that. He bought all the slaves he had intended to buy and arranged to have them shipped up to Silverwood. Alan Durham finished arranging his market for flatboats and was ready to go home. But Caleb lingered. He told Alan about Dolores, and one evening he took Alan to meet her, outside the gateway to a hidden courtyard on Toulouse Street. Neither Gervaise's family nor the relatives of Alan's wife knew anybody named Bondio, they said, but then they were French and had not as yet reached the place of accepting the Spanish sufficiently for much social intercourse. But Dolores was vividly real. Alan agreed with Caleb that she was charming.

"But you can't stay here forever, meeting her in alleyways," said Alan. "At least, I can't stay here forever. And if I take the boat upriver how will you get home?"

Caleb had already made up his mind that he would not leave New Orleans without Dolores. He had never been so happy in his life. He was too happy to wonder what his father would think when he returned to Silverwood with this flashing Creole in her low-cut gowns and heathenish mantillas, or how Dolores would fit into plantation life. He was in love.

In the alley by the Cabildo he held her close to him and told her he loved her and wanted to take her back to the plantation. He felt her slim body stiffen in his arms and she dropped her head on his shoulder with a little sob.

"You will take me home with you? You mean it? Oh, you mean true?"

"Of course I mean it, darling. If you'll come with me."

"But—but you don't even know me."

"I know you're lovely and sweet and a dear and that I want you and I'm going to stay here until you'll promise to come." He smiled in the dark. "You don't know me either, Dolores."

"Oh yes but I do!" Her hands reached up and felt his face. "You are good. I know all you've told me is right. I just know, Caleb." She drew back from him. "You are going to make marry with me?"

"Of course, sweetheart. But—"

"Yes?"

"If your uncle is an officer of the Cabildo there's not a priest in Spanish Louisiana who would marry us without his consent. Should I run the risk of asking him?"

"Asking him!" she echoed. "You—English Protestant—he would as soon have me marry a heathen. He would send me to the Ursulines tomorrow. Oh, Caleb, don't ask him! Can't we marry without asking?"

"Yes, dear, if you'll trust me enough to come across the English line."

"Trust you—I would make journey anywhere with you. Oh—" her voice broke. "I didn't know you really loved me so much!"

He held her tight again. "Dolores, can you get out tomorrow morning at time for mass? I'll meet you here by the cathedral and we'll go to my boat. We can be married as soon as we cross the line."

"Where will that be?"

"Manchac. We'll tie up there. If the current isn't too strong we should get there the next day."

"Yes. I'll come. Caleb—I can't make to bring any clothes. Maybe I can get put on two of everything and be fat."

"That's all right. You're about my sister's size. She'll lend you whatever you need till you can have some clothes made. You'll meet me then, darling?"

"Yes. Yes." She flung her arms around him. "Oh, I was never be so happy. Silverwood—it's a big plantation?"

"It will be when it's cleared. You'll like it."

"I'll love it. Caleb, I will be such good wife to you. I will learn more English and do everything you want."

He kissed her again. "You darling. Oh, I hope you're going to be happy."

"Now I must go," she said. "Concepcion is in the church."

"Do you want to bring Concepcion with you? Maybe you could smuggle her out."

"No, no. I want to bring nothing. I want to have all your people my people. Tomorrow morning I will see you. Wait by the church."

She ran off to the cathedral and he saw her go down the alley with Concepcion after her.

Then at last it was morning, and Dolores was on the flatboat going upriver with him, Dolores in two pairs of stockings and with a bedgown rolled up under her panniers. She sat with him on deck, watching the plantation country pass as the boatmen strained against the current. After awhile she began to sing.

O Zeneral La Florio!
C'est vrai yé pas capab' pran moin!

"What does it mean?" he asked her. "It's not Spanish, is it?"

"No, my darling, it's Creole French. About a runaway slave. He sing to M. Fleuriau, who was for be high sheriff of the Cabildo. He say 'They cannot make for catch me, Zénéral!'" She laughed and squeezed his hand. "It is how I feel. They cannot make for catch me, I have run away. C'est vrai yé pas capab' pran moin!"

He had been afraid she would be homesick, maybe frightened, as the flatboat pushed out of sight of New Orleans up toward the English country she had never seen. But Dolores seemed twinkly with triumphant delight. "I am so glad for go with you!" she whispered.

The next day they were married at Manchac.

CHAPTER SEVEN

Judith was playing with her babies in the Ardeith garden when her father rode up with the news that Caleb had come back from New Orleans with a Creole wife.

"From Cuba," he said, "and very odd in her ways. Her talk is so strange sometimes I can't make out what she's saying. Anyway, she's got hardly a stitch of clothes to her name, and Caleb said you'd let her have some."

Judith was glad Caleb had married, but she was astonished that his stern young heart had been conquered by the sultry charms of a Creole. Mark told her briefly that Dolores was the daughter of some kind of Spanish grandee and had run away from home.

"What is she like?" Judith asked.

Her father hesitated. "It's hard to say, Judith. She's not like

126

any women of the sort we've known. But Caleb takes such delight in her as I never saw, and she'd be rather pretty except that when she laughs too much you can see she's got a tooth out. But it's not often she laughs so hearty you notice it."

Judith was dubious. She did not know much about Spanish Creoles, but she had heard reports of the vagaries of their temperaments that made her wonder about the wisdom of putting one of them under the roof with Caleb and his father. Tolerance of what they did not comprehend was not one of the Sheramy virtues. But she said nothing of this to Mark, who by the look of him was doubtful enough already. She said she was glad Caleb had found a wife, and rode back to Silverwood to welcome her, followed by Angelique with a collection of essential garments.

Dolores came timidly down the steps of the Silverwood house in a rather bedraggled pink dress with a flowered overskirt, but her hair was piled up splendidly against a Spanish comb. She wore two roses over her left ear.

"And you are Judith?" she said. "You make me so happy by coming!"

She spoke eagerly, as if she had feared that Caleb's family would not receive her at all. Judith gave her a kiss of welcome. Dolores glanced enviously at Judith's riding habit with its bright fringed sash and cutaway coat, and then down at herself. "You will forgive me?" she murmured hesitantly. "But it is only this gown I have."

"Of course," Judith said. "Father told me how it was you couldn't bring any clothes with you. I've brought you a few."

Dolores squeezed her hand. "Thank you. Such pretty gowns. You can spare these?"

"Oh yes. Which is your room, Dolores?"

"In here."

"Take them in, Angelique. Miss Dolores can look them over and see if I've brought everything she needs." Judith smiled as Caleb approached her and Dolores went into the bedroom with Angelique. "She's very sweet, Caleb."

"Isn't she?" He looked after her adoringly, and Judith's trepidation about his marriage began to thin. If he was as much in love as this he wouldn't be affected by his father's mistrust of foreigners. "Let me help her get used to us, Caleb," she whispered.

"Will you? I think she's badly frightened of all of you up here."

"Poor child," said Judith. She went into the bedroom. Angelique was laying out the clothes, which Dolores was admiring in a flood of rapid French. She stopped talking as she saw Judith, and waited for her to speak, almost respectfully. Judith put an arm around Dolores' little waist. Good heavens, she thought, the girl was laced to a wisp.

"Dolores, if there's anything I can help you with—you know, American housekeeping and all that, you'll ask me?"

"Oh—will you let me?" Dolores exclaimed. "I did not know how much they make to learn."

"Certainly. I'll show you how everything is done."

"Thank you. Your father—" Dolores cocked her black eyes toward the door. "He does not like me. But he will. I will make him." Her eyes flashed up with bright assurance. It was not hard to understand how Caleb had fallen in love with her. She had a sparkle that made her like a torch in this somber house. Judith kissed her impulsively.

"Dolores, you're a darling!"

Dolores returned her embrace with an ardor surprising even for a lonesome girl in a strange country. "You will really make like me, Judith?"

"Of course. I already do."

"You are good," said Dolores softly. She drew Judith over to sit on the bed. It was covered with a quilt Judith and Catherine had pieced from scraps left from their sewing the last summer they had lived in Connecticut. "Judith, I do so want to make me a good wife to Caleb, so he will not be sorry he make a marriage with me. You will tell me—

"What?" Judith asked when she hesitated.

Dolores chuckled. "How to make those things he and the old gentleman like to eat."

"Come to Ardeith any day you like," said Judith laughing, "and I'll tell you. My husband doesn't like New England eating but I think I remember how it's done."

"Tomorrow maybe?"

"All right. I'll write the directions."

Dolores shook her head. "I cannot read them."

"Can't you read?"

"Only Spanish. French and English I learned from hearing them spoke."

"Then I'll say it and you can say it back to me. Don't worry about my father, Dolores. He never did talk much, and he's been more silent than ever since my mother died. But he's very good."

"Too good." Dolores gave a little shiver. Then she smiled. "The old gentleman he will like me," said Dolores, "when I make a baby. I hope I make a baby soon. You got two, Caleb said."

"Yes, two little boys. David is two years old and Christopher will be a year old in June. You must see them. David is tow-headed and very bad, and Christopher is black-headed and very good. He's good even now, though he's cutting his teeth."

Dolores' hand went instinctively to her mouth.

"I wouldn't bother about that," said Judith gently. "It's not very obvious."

"Two gentlemen fought a duel in our courtyard in Havana. I heard noise of rapiers and ran out and I was so scared I fell down, against the courtyard wall—"

"Dear child, don't trouble yourself about it! It's much less noticeable than you think. With a complexion like yours you can stand a lot of defects."

"You think so honest?" Dolores asked wistfully.

Judith liked her. She was so pathetically eager for approval that it came almost as though in response to a demand.

Before many weeks had gone by it was evident that Dolores was winning her way even into Mark Sheramy's grudging affection. For Mark had to admit that she was less objectionable than he had thought a foreign woman would be. The men of his family were not used to marrying girls who came to the table with gardenias in their hair and gowns that exposed their bosoms to such a shameless degree; but it seemed less scandalous when he was engrossed with the meat-pies and sawdust puddings she served him. Caleb and Judith praised her for having gone so far toward gaining Mark's good opinion, but Dolores only lifted her black eyes demurely and puckered her mouth and replied, "My dears, where I lived we had a saying that a man always likes better a woman who gives him what he wants to eat."

Her English improved that first summer as to grammar, though her accent remained as heavy as ever. But it was a piquant English, and she was somewhat of a darling when she talked, with that pout hiding the gap in her teeth. She had acquired the habit of pouting all the time, which made her look as if she were always about to kiss somebody. Men liked it without often guessing its cause, and Judith could not help admiring Dolores for turning into an asset what would have spoilt the looks of a less resourceful girl.

Dolores was amusing too, after she got over her shyness. She told them about the heel-clicking statesmen who used to dine at her father's house in Havana, and the dignitaries who escorted her on horseback rides through the parks. Dolores could ride superbly; there wasn't a horse on the plantation she couldn't manage. "Odd, when she can ride so well, she should have fallen and knocked her tooth out," Caleb said.

"I didn't know she was on a horse when she fell," said Judith. "She told me two men got into a fight in the courtyard and frightened her. Strange she should have been riding a horse in the courtyard."

"Maybe the patios in Havana are bigger than they are in New Orleans," Caleb suggested.

Judith still thought it surprising and said so to Philip one day in August when they were riding over the plantation. Dolores had been four months at Silverwood. Philip, who liked virtually everybody, had accepted her with easy grace, but he tilted his eyebrows when Judith asked him if the courtyards in Havana were so big one could ride horses around them. "I suspect," said Philip, "that she's a shameless little liar."

"Philip!"

"My dear Judith, I don't know how she lost her tooth and I don't care. It's not important."

"I can't understand," said Judith, "why she should be so uncertain about the etiquette of entertaining. But it may just be ignorance of all our customs."

Philip gave her a level look. "She's all right," he said. "Mind your own business."

"She didn't even know about cups with two saucers," Judith persisted. "I thought they were in every good china service. But I had to explain to her that when the coffee was poured into the deep saucer to cool the cup was set in the shallow saucer so it wouldn't make a ring on the tablecloth. Maybe they don't have double saucer services in Cuba."

"Maybe," said Philip coolly, "you knew all about double saucer services when you came down from Connecticut."

"Oh Philip, we never made any pretenses to elegance! We were just ordinary farmers."

Philip did not answer directly. He made some remark

about his indigo and rode ahead to tell the overseer to put some Congo Negroes in among the Iboes, because the Congoes were amenable and the Iboes were likely to make trouble if there were too many of them in one place.

"David will have an easy time when he grows up and takes over the plantation," he said to Judith when he rejoined her. "By that time he can have all American-born Negroes. Africans are hard to control. You never can tell when you're buying one who used to be a king."

She saw that he was not inclined to discuss Dolores further, so she said nothing more about her for some time. But she noticed that Angelique, though she made no comment, had small regard for Caleb's Creole wife, and one day in the fall when she was getting dressed to go to dinner at Silverwood Judith asked Angelique what she thought of Miss Dolores.

"She has always been very kind to me," said Angelique. She was on her knees putting on Judith's stockings.

"That's not an answer."

Angelique smoothed the stocking over Judith's leg. "Well— she talks pretty big. Miss Judith, you should have let me polish these shoe-buckles."

"If they're tarnished it's too late now. You've barely time to do my hair. I want it very high with those silk birds on top. What do you mean by saying she talks big?"

"I don't like to be making remarks about white people," said Angelique, getting up from the floor.

"You've got more sense than most white people and you know it. Comb it over the frame and use lots of pomade so I won't have to take it down in a hurry. You mean you think she sometimes just tells yarns?"

Angelique laughed over Judith's head into the mirror. "Miss Judith, I reckon she talks big because Mr. Caleb likes to hear it. He thinks she's wonderful."

"Yes," said Judith moodily, "he certainly does."

She watched in the mirror as Angelique combed her hair up. Dolores still wore Spanish combs instead of silk figures in her hair. The combs were very becoming to her, particularly when she found a real silk mantilla at the market and draped it over the comb. "You want the birds, Miss Judith?" said Angelique. "Not the battleships?"

"No, everybody's wearing battleships these days on account of the American war. I want two birds and a nest between with eggs in it. You know the set."

"Yes ma'am."

When it was finished Judith picked up the hand mirror and turned around. "Nice. Eleven inches?"

"About," said Angelique.

"They say that in Paris the ladies are wearing their coiffures so high they have to kneel down in their carriages so the decorations won't be knocked off."

Angelique laughed as she put away the combs. "I reckon eleven inches is pretty good for the colonies, Miss Judith."

Judith still had an uncomfortable feeling about Dolores. But when their carriage arrived at Silverwood and Dolores came scampering across the gallery with more exuberance than dignity she found her apprehensions stilled again. The girl was really attractive—attractive enough to mollify Caleb's homespun ideas about the need for strict honesty. And to be sure, her fibs were harmless. If she wanted to put on a few extra plumes to impress her husband's family it wasn't a major fault.

Judith watched Gervaise, cool and remote across the table, and wondered if she too thought Dolores did not ring true. When they were leaving for home she got into the Purcell carriage with Gervaise, as Walter and Philip had some business to talk over and were riding together until their roads divided. When the carriage had started Judith asked abruptly,

"Gervaise, what do you think of my sister-in-law?"

Gervaise tilted a shoulder under her cloak. "She is very lovely as long as she keeps her mouth shut."

"That's not what I meant."

"Yes it is." Gervaise gave an ironic little smile. "I wish she would speak to me in English. Her French is shocking."

Judith owned she had a hard time understanding it. But then her own French was not very good.

"She speaks nigger-French," said Gervaise briefly. "And such language! I don't know where she picked up some of the words she uses."

Judith reminded her that Caleb sometimes had to stop Dolores from using swear-words in English. "She doesn't know what they are, Gervaise."

Gervaise repeated her little shrug. "I am afraid she thinks we are simple folk up here and makes herself too grand." She put her hand over Judith's. "But she is very sweet and don't you tell my husband I made unkind remarks about her. He thinks she is excessively charming."

Judith had observed before now that men liked Dolores more than women did. She decided to make Philip tell her definitely what he thought.

After she had kissed the children good night she told Philip what Gervaise had said about Dolores' French. They were together in the dining-room over the wine and biscuits that served them for supper after a company dinner in the afternoon. Philip listened with an odd smile. For a moment he was silent, as he refilled her wineglass and his own, then he said:

"Judith, why are you so concerned about Dolores?"

"Oh, because she's really a dear in her way, Philip, and she strikes me as the sort of person who'd be helpless in a disaster—"

"What sort of disaster?"

"The sort a pair of puritans like my father and Caleb could turn loose if they felt righteously indignant about anything."

Philip moved the candlestick aside so he could look more directly at her. "Judith," he said, "it's none of my business. But if that girl's the daughter of a Spanish grandee I'm a watermoccasin."

"Philip! Are you sure?"

"I think I know trash when I see it," said Philip.

Judith's biscuit dropped out of her hand into the plate. Philip's conviction crystallized everything she had feared.

"Who is she, then?" she ventured.

"I haven't the faintest idea." After a moment he asked, "Haven't you ever noticed how she sniffles when she dips snuff?"

Judith bit her lip. "I've noticed various things."

"Dolores is clever," said Philip, "and she's picking up the ways of mannerly people. But I think she's made an absolute fool out of your brother."

"But Philip," she exclaimed, "if you're so sure, why don't you tell him?"

"Why should I?"

"But for heaven's sake—"

"For heaven's sake what, Judith? He's perfectly happy as long as he doesn't know it, and she's doing the best she can. Maybe they decided between them to say she came of great folk so as to make your father more reconciled to a foreign marriage."

"Caleb wouldn't be equal to that," she objected. "He's so honest it hardly ever occurs to him that people lie. But he's dreadfully fond of her."

"So he is. That's why I tell you to leave them alone. Maybe Caleb enjoys deluding himself, maybe he's not deluded, maybe on the other hand I'm mistaken and she's genuine. At any rate it's not my affair and don't you try to make it yours."

Judith pushed back from the table and went over to the window, where she stood a moment looking at a clump of banana trees, pale in the autumn moonlight. "But how could he have been so foolish, Philip?"

"Oh honey child, it's so easy to be a fool when one falls in love." He came up to her and put his arm across her shoulders. "Didn't everybody say you were a fool when you fell in love with me?"

"Yes—but that was so different!"

"Was it? Thanks." He drew her head back on his shoulder. "Anyway, as long as Caleb and Dolores seem content as they are you're positively not to make any trouble. Understand?"

Judith promised not to make trouble, but she could not help feeling that trouble was made and ready to explode. So far Caleb seemed to have no suspicion that Dolores might not be all she professed. He adored her blindly. As for Mark, he rarely mentioned Dolores at all and Judith was never sure what he thought. When Dolores rode proudly over one day in March to tell them she was with child Judith found it hard to seem pleased. She had begun to hope Dolores was barren, since she had been married nearly a year without any expectation of motherhood. This new complication increased Judith's foreboding.

The climax came when other concerns had thrust themselves to the front so forcefully that the problem of Dolores became subordinate. Governor Galvez had replaced Governor Unzaga in New Orleans, but though the new governor took pains to keep amicable relations with the Tories of West Florida his own interest in lessening the power of his British rivals prompted him to offer supplies to the rebellious Americans. Gunboats bearing the striped flag of the rebels passed the Dalroy docks more and more frequently on their way to New Orleans. Most of the West Floridians regarded the rebel boats with indignant disdain, and were prevented from molesting them only by fear of having their own passage to New Orleans blocked off, but Philip wanted to know what was going on. He had no quarrel with either the British or Americans, he told Judith, but if he had stayed in Carolina he'd probably be into the rebellion up to his neck by now; besides, having a rebel emissary to dinner now and then provided enlightening conversation. When Mr. Thistlethwaite stopped at Dalroy on his way up the river with a suspicious-looking boat from New Orleans, Philip met him on the wharf and brought him to Ardeith for dinner.

Mr. Thistlethwaite came from Delaware. He was a big fellow with an ample paunch, a face like a beefsteak and a vocabulary that sent Angelique running out to the gallery to grab the children and send them into the back yard to play.

The Sheramys had been invited to dinner that same day, and Mark and Caleb were in the parlor. Philip brought them out to the gallery and introduced Mr. Thistlethwaite. "Mrs. Larne will be here in a moment," Philip told him. "She's working her flowers."

"Love to see a lady among the flowers," boomed Mr. Thistlethwaite. "Something so sweet and suitable about a lady among flowers."

Philip chuckled. So did Caleb.

"My wife used to be smart with a garden," Mr. Thistlethwaite told them, his beefy face creasing with a reminiscent grin. "Grew foxgloves. Foxgloves all over the place. Not much chance for gardening these times, with the damn redcoats tearing up the earth. Quite a time we're having, Mr. Larne, quite a time. All the men who want to fight want to be generals, and can't nobody make 'em all generals, you understand."

Mark Sheramy observed that he had been in the French war, and that the same rivalry had been noticeable then.

"Yes sir," foghorned Mr. Thistlethwaite, "always the trouble. Want to be big fellows no matter what it does to the country. Unselfish patriotism rare thing these days. But we right-thinking Americans can keep our men in line. Tell you, sir, day of crowns is passing. All men free and equal—"

Indoors, Judith heard him as she went into the bedroom to change her dress. "Can't Philip pick up the most astounding people?" she whispered to Dolores, who had been working in the garden with her.

"Who is he?" Dolores asked.

"One of those violent Americans you see sometimes on the wharfs. He's probably going to drink the house dry. I wonder if he'd like orange wine? It's awfully hot for whiskey."

"Shall I tell them get out the orange wine?" Dolores asked. "I have made dressed."

"Will you? Have one of the boys take it to the gallery."

As Judith stepped into the hall she saw Dolores pass, followed by a servant with a tray of wineglasses. Dolores was prettier than ever in a gown of buttercup dimity that set off her dark coloring. Nobody would have guessed that she was carrying a child.

Dolores hesitated a moment in the doorway. Mr. Thistlethwaite was booming, and the other three men, laughing at his yarn, did not see her. But Mr. Thistlethwaite did, and he slapped his knee with hearty recognition.

"Well, well, bless my soul if it ain't Dolores! What you doing up here?"

Dolores recoiled ever so slightly. Judith, who had come out after her, saw Philip and the others get to their feet as Philip said:

"Permit me—"

"Don't need a bit of introduction!" cried Mr. Thistlethwaite. He took a glass off the tray. "Seems like old times, I swear it does, taking a drink with Dolores!"

"You know each other?" Caleb asked in astonishment.

Dolores found her voice. She spoke through tight lips. "I was never see this gentleman before in my life."

Mr. Thistlethwaite's beefy jowls got a shade redder. He cleared his throat. "Well—ahem—I guess—"

"I think you are mistaken, Mr. Thistlethwaite," Philip said quietly. "The lady you are addressing is Mrs. Caleb Sheramy. And may I present my wife? Mr. Thistlethwaite."

"Howdy do, ma'am." Mr. Thistlethwaite gave an exaggerated bow and a chuckle. "Well now, ain't that just the funniest thing! Mrs. Sheramy, ma'am, I beg your pardon, and yours too, Mr. Sheramy, but I'll be damned—begging your pardon, ladies—if this lady don't look enough like a girl I used to know in New Orleans to be her twin sister. Spittin' image, I declare. Ain't that the funniest thing, now!"

He slapped his thigh and laughed. Nobody laughed with him and nobody said anything. "Tell you, her name was Dolores Bondio, and she come up from Cuby to serve drinks at Miss Juanita's place. Right pretty too, or would have been except she had a tooth out, but you could know her for a month and not see it, her having a funny little way of laughing out one side of

141

her mouth. Mrs. Sheramy, I swear I beg your pardon for thinking it was you."

Dolores' mouth was quivering. Caleb's face had gone as white as it was possible for the face of a sunburnt planter to be. His father was holding a chair so tight the muscles stood out on the backs of his hands. Philip said:

"Since you were mistaken, sir, I am sure Mrs. Sheramy accepts your apology. What was that you were telling us about the encounter at Bunker Hill?"

Dolores had been standing rigid, holding her wineglass tight. As Philip ceased speaking she threw the glass into Mr. Thistlethwaite's face. "You goddamn bastard!" she cried, and before he could blink the wine out of his eyes she was hurling at him a volley of invective. Philip gripped her wrists with a swift, "Dolores, stop that!" but as he said it Caleb jerked her from him.

"Let me attend to this," he said. He hardly seemed to move his lips when he said it. "I'll take her home. Be good enough to order the horses."

CHAPTER EIGHT

Go on," said Caleb. "What did your father do in Havana?"

"He worked in a livery stable," said Dolores sullenly.

"How long were you in New Orleans?"

"Three or four years. I disremember exactly."

"What did you do in that tavern besides serve drinks?"

"Oh, shut *up*!" cried Dolores. She held her hands to her temples. "I never meant to start any goings-on that morning you spoke to me on the levee! Always I tell men silly stories about me and they like it. Then you said you had a plantation up the river—"

He stood up. His eyes were narrowed. "And you saw I'd be easy to make a fool of, didn't you?"

Dolores caught fire. "Oh, you were *such* a yokel! You were

going to get trouble in that town anyway—you better thank God on your knees you got nothing worse than me!" She walked to the other end of the room and back again, beating her fists on each other. At last she held out her hands to him and began to plead. "Caleb, I did not think it was so awful. I did so bad want to be quality. Aunt Juanita beat me when she got drunk because she said I try to be too uppity. I had no place to go. I could not make a marriage with anybody except maybe some tipsy sailor that wanted a woman to cook for him. Then you came and it was so easy. You was believe everything I said—"

"Where did you get that nigger woman that went about with you?"

"I hired her. She was not speak English so it was all right. I was having fun even if you didn't marry me. But when you said you were in love with me I was so happy I could die, and I swore on the cross I would make you a good wife. And I did, didn't I? You liked me yesterday! I am the same as I was then!"

"Oh, go to bed," said Caleb. He felt as if there were sand in his eyes and he ached all over. This had lasted hours and had got nowhere. He couldn't bear any more of it.

"Yes," said Dolores. She went to their bedroom, hesitated on the threshold a moment looking back at him, then shut the door. Caleb sent a servant in for what clothes he needed and slept in another chamber at the back.

The days after that were worse and worse. His father said, "I am very sorry, son. She's not worth all this." But Caleb could not keep from talking to her. Sometimes Dolores pled, almost meekly; at others she was a screaming little vixen, lashing him with profanity until he ordered her into her room. When she came to the table she rarely said anything at all, but sat in a stubborn silence that killed his appetite.

Philip sent over a brief note, saying only. "I deeply regret the unfortunate scene on the Ardeith gallery Monday. If you feel in need of counsel or assistance, pray let me be of service. I remain, sir, your obedient servant, Philip Larne." Caleb blessed him for keeping away.

Philip would have kept away indefinitely, having an almost religious abhorrence for meddling in other people's affairs, but Judith was not so impersonal. Ten days after Mr. Thistlethwaite's unhappy visit Judith went to Silverwood with the avowed purpose of rescuing Dolores and bringing her to Ardeith. She did so over Philip's protests. Not only did he feel that Caleb and Dolores should be let alone to solve a situation primarily concerning only themselves, but he reminded Judith that Dolores' behavior had been pretty cheap and Caleb couldn't be blamed if he felt aggrieved.

But Judith insisted, eloquent with pity. She knew the men of her family better than he did. The Sheramys were descendants of the old puritans who had had women put into stocks for laughing in the street on Sunday.

"Philip Larne," she exclaimed finally, "you don't know how cruel a good man can be."

Philip shrugged.

"Anyway," Judith persisted, "aren't there any respectable barmaids?"

He cocked an eyebrow. "I never heard of any."

"Is that why you don't want her here?"

"No, dearest, I'd like to be kind to her. But she'll get in the way, you'll wish you hadn't done it, and Caleb won't thank you for interfering. However, if you've got your mind made up, go ahead and don't blame me if she brings trouble."

Caleb and his father were in the fields when Judith got to Silverwood, and though Dolores was not cordial Judith was glad she had come. Dolores looked thinner and there were hollows under her eyes. Her dress was crumpled as if it had been worn yesterday and the day before, and for the first time it was apparent that she was going to have a child, for her usually erect little figure had slumped wearily. She listened without a sign of gratitude when Judith said she wanted to bring her to Ardeith until she felt stronger.

"I feel all right," said Dolores coldly.

But she yielded and climbed to the pillion on Judith's saddle as though it was easier to do what she was told than to initiate her own actions. They rode to Ardeith, Angelique riding behind with a box holding Dolores' clothes. Judith took her into one of the spare bedrooms and gave her a girl named Christine to wait on her.

She drew Angelique into her room. "Get this riding skirt off me and put me into something fit to wear to dinner. Angelique, what am I going to do with Miss Dolores now she's here?"

Angelique laughed confidingly. "Give her something to do. Let her help sew for the children, maybe."

"With the servants? I can't do that."

"It will make her feel useful," said Angelique. "If you let her sit with her hands in her lap she'll just mope and be unhappy."

"Maybe you're right," Judith said slowly, after a moment's consideration.

Angelique was holding up a sprigged dimity dress Judith usually saved for church. "Why don't you wear this pretty gown to dinner? You'll want to look very nice when you tell Mr. Philip she's here. And let me get some roses. He likes you with flowers in your hair."

"Oh dear," said Judith. "You're so clever. Tell Josh to get out the English port too."

Philip, however, heard the news with fairly good grace. He only said, "With two children and twenty servants you want to take on more responsibility! All right. But if she starts throwing things at any more of my guests—"

"She won't. Anyhow, I don't blame her for throwing wine at Mr. Thistlethwaite. We can tell people Dolores hasn't been well since she got with child and we brought her here so I could look after her. Nobody will believe it, but it will sound passable."

Philip chuckled indulgently.

The next day Caleb rode over on his way to the wharfs to supervise the loading of an indigo boat. Judith, who was on the gallery teaching David to build a house with a set of cypress blocks, went down the steps to meet him.

"Where is Dolores?" Caleb asked shortly, without dismounting.

"She's indoors." Judith added eagerly, "Won't you let her stay here awhile?"

"How long does she plan to stay?"

"Till after her confinement."

Caleb bent his riding whip in two. His face had a look of adamant self-control, like the expression years of disappointment had stamped on her father, but softened by none of Mark's gentleness.

"How is she?" he asked finally.

"Well. May I keep her, Caleb?"

"Yes. See that she's taken care of. And whatever she needs—clothes for the child, or anything for herself—get it and have the bills sent to me."

"Very well. Caleb—" as he started to turn his horse—"don't you want to see her?"

"No," said Caleb. He rode away.

Judith wondered if she would have stiffened like him if she had not married Philip so young. David was pulling at her skirts, clamoring for completion of his block-house. She sat down on the step and drew him to her, glad he resembled his father. He had the Larne beauty and the Larne winsomeness; she could not imagine his growing up to be ruthless toward anybody.

She did her best to make Dolores feel welcome, but having her in the house proved to be not the pleasantest situation on earth. Though she evidently tried not to, Dolores did get in the way. When there was a stranger on the other side of the candle Judith and Philip couldn't exchange scraps of loving nonsense as they used to, or talk over the thousand details of their life together that were too tender for anybody else's ears. She was as cordial as she could be to Dolores, and told her how sweet it was of her to help with the children's sewing, but she could not help wishing her gone. Dolores was very quiet except when she played with the children. Then she laughed merrily, teaching them folk-songs in gumbo Spanish and inventing funny little games. Judith asked her sometimes if they weren't a bother. "Mammy can take care of them," she urged. But Dolores shook her head eagerly. "Please let them play with me! I love children, Judith!" So Judith left them with her.

Except with the children, she rarely showed much of the sparkle that had attracted Judith when Dolores first came to Silverwood, and she hardly talked about herself at all. But Judith had no cause to be really irritated with her until an afternoon in November when she had a group of her women friends in to dinner and they played cards afterward. Gervaise was there and Sylvie Durham, and half a dozen others. Dolores was expecting her child in a week or two, but she insisted she felt well and that she liked cards. There had been no cards at Silverwood, and Judith recalled her own qualms when she discovered that in Louisiana everybody played for money, but she had found that she liked it.

Dolores was in good spirits, though at first she played badly and lost. But she laughed at herself, and kept everybody chuckling with her remarks. Judith had not seen her so jolly since she came to Ardeith, and she rebuked herself for not discovering sooner how much Dolores liked cards, for they could have done this often. Even Sylvie Durham, whom Judith had never liked very much because she was so arrogantly Creole and so vociferously convinced of the superiority of everything Creole to everything English, unbent and had a hilarious time. Dolores began to win, but she won as graciously as she had lost. It occurred to Judith that she might have been a social asset if Mr. Thistlethwaite had waited another year to put in an appearance, and she regretted his coming for her own sake, for society on the bluff was not so varied that one could afford to dispense with anybody who was entertaining in company. Maybe Caleb might be propitiated and in the course of time people would forget everything. By the time the others rose to go home Dolores had won all the stakes and everybody seemed to be glad of it. Sylvie Durham exclaimed as they left the table:

"My dear, I don't know when I've had such an amusing time! Dolores, as soon as you're going about again you must come to see us."

"I will be most pleased," said Dolores. "Shall I go with you to get your hat?"

"Yes, do. You know I'm Creole too—you speak French, don't you?"

They drifted off, arm in arm. Judith walked out to Gervaise's horse with her. Gervaise smiled down at her as she mounted.

"We had a lovely time, chère." She glanced around and added in a lower voice, "Do you need any help?"

"No, thank you. She's all right."

"Yes, she is." Gervaise pressed her hand. "I hope, chère, your brother stops being a fool, but it is easier to be a fool about marriage than anything else, isn't it?"

"Do you think so?"

"Yes. So few people seem to have judgment enough to accept what heaven sends."

Dolores came out with Sylvie and they made affectionate farewells. As the guests rode away Dolores linked her arm in Judith's and they went back up the steps. "It was nice, wasn't it?" said Dolores.

"A lot of fun. Are you tired?"

"No, not a bit. I am not an invalid." She glanced at the sky. "The sun is nearly going down. If they do not hurry they will be riding in the dark."

Judith gave orders to light the candles and began gathering up the scattered cards. She glanced up as Philip came in. "Dolores won all the money," she told him.

"Good. You like cards, Dolores?"

"I always did," said Dolores. Mammy brought in David and Christopher to say good night. Dolores gathered up her winnings in both hands and ran to them.

"Good night, darlings."

"Good night, Aunt Dolores," they said together. They did not share grown folks' prejudices and adored her.

"Here. I have something for you. Look. Tomorrow you make go to town with mammy, and you can buy something pretty. A present from Aunt Dolores. Half for you, David, and half for Christopher—"

"Dolores!" Philip exclaimed. "Don't give it to the children!"

"Please don't," protested Judith.

"Oh, but that's why I wanted to win. They are so sweet!"

She was so eager neither of them had the heart to stop her. David and Christopher, who hardly knew what money was, were nevertheless speechless with delight at the pretty coins.

"Ain't you got no manners?" mammy was scolding them. "Li'l gennulmen says thanky when they gets presents."

"Thanky, Aunt Dolores," said David. "Chris, you say thanky too."

Christopher mumbled his thanks. Though Judith still doubted the wisdom of their having so much money all at once she could not bring herself to spoil Dolores' pleasure. She only said, as they went out, "That was very sweet of you, Dolores."

"But I wanted to." Dolores smiled at the moths fluttering about the candle on the table. "You have been most good to me—I like to do something for the children. I would like," she added softly, "to do something for you."

Philip, always embarrassed by gratitude of any sort, said, "I wish you could teach me to play cards as well as you do."

"Oh." Dolores took up the pack. "I show you. I do not know much. But look."

She shuffled the cards and began to deal. Judith caught her breath and put her hand over her mouth. Philip came close and looked over her shoulder.

Dolores flipped the cards so fast one could hardly watch her fingers. She dealt hands all of one color and hands where the two colors alternated. She whisked the cards back together and dealt hands containing all high cards and other hands containing only low ones, giggling softly as she did so.

Philip said, "Christ, is that what you've been doing in my house?"

"But yes," said Dolores. "I will show you. A gentleman who played on the boats taught me. Much of his tricks I cannot learn; I am too stupid. But these are simple. At first I had forgotten. Then I remembered—it is very easy if you know."

Philip gathered up the cards in his hand and threw them into the fire. He said nothing.

But Judith had found her voice.

"You—nasty—little—sneak," she said.

Dolores pushed back her chair with a gasp. "Why—Judith!"

Judith could feel herself getting hot and then cold. "Oh Dolores, Dolores," she said slowly, "how could you!"

"Be quiet, Judith!" said Philip.

Dolores was standing up, holding the mantelpiece. Philip took her arm gently. "Don't you want to go to your room, Dolores? We can't help being shocked, but we know you didn't understand how we'd feel about it."

"Let me alone!" She shook herself free. "You can be good. It takes money to be good on. You try sometimes taking charity. Knowing every time you eat a bite of rice it's somebody's else's rice. I hope I die and my baby dies and you will be rid of us. Damn your souls."

"Cheating my friends," Judith said half under her breath. "You do belong in a tavern."

"Judith," said Philip, "will you for the love of God hold your tongue?"

He led Dolores into her room. She flung a couple of ugly epithets at Judith as she went out. Philip closed the door after her and told the servants to take her supper on a tray. Judith was sitting in the parlor with her head on her hands.

"I hope," said Philip, "you enjoyed that diatribe."

"Oh, I'm sorry," she murmured. "I shouldn't have talked like that. I know I shouldn't. But why does she have to be so unspeakably common?"

"You brought her here, you know," said Philip.

"I know it! And she's knocked my home into a shambles. Why do you have to remind me—"

"Because I'm as tired of her as you are. But since you can't send her away now, you might practice keeping quiet while she's here. Lord, how you can talk!"

"Yes, yes, yes, I've heard that before. What am I going to do with that money she gave the children? I can't let them keep it."

"Why not?"

"It's hardly decent."

"Then give it to the church. But whatever you do, don't mention this again to Dolores."

Judith did not, but Dolores' white face and resentful silence told her it was no use to pretend to have forgotten it. She tried to take the money from David and Christopher, but they put up such a howl her stringy nerves gave way and she decided they might as well spend it, since they didn't understand the moral implications of cheating at cards anyway.

Dolores' baby, a boy, was born the following week. Judith was as congratulatory as she could be, and gave Dolores an embroidered baby-dress that had come from France, but she found it hard to conceal her thankfulness that this much at least was over, and now there was less reason why Dolores should not remove her annoying presence from Ardeith. She wrote Caleb a note telling him the baby had been born and Dolores was doing well.

Mark came over at once, though without Caleb. He looked so stern and forbidding that Judith forebore asking him if Caleb was not interested enough in his child to want to see it. She took him into the nursery. Mark bent over the cradle, and she saw a flicker of tenderness on his worn face.

"A fine healthy child," he said softly. "We will name him Roger."

"Roger?" she said doubtfully. "Was any of our family named that?"

He shook his head, letting the baby's hand curl around his finger. "In memory of Roger Williams of Rhode Island. Leader of heretics, but a man of great courage."

"Is that what Caleb wants him named?" Judith asked after a moment's hesitation.

"Caleb has said nothing of it to me," said Mark. Then he asked, "Is Dolores well enough to see me?"

"Why yes. She's in the next room."

Her father withdrew his finger from the baby's clasp and came with her to the door. "It is good of you to give her shelter, daughter," he said fumblingly. "If your mother had been alive it might not have been so hard for her at Silverwood."

Judith wondered. But she said nothing. She went to Dolores' bedside and said, "Dolores, father is here. He wants to see you."

Mark came in and stood a moment by the bed. Dolores looked up at him with black eyes very steady in her tired face.

"We are happy that you have borne so beautiful a son, Dolores," he said.

"Are you?" Dolores asked without moving.

"Why yes, to be sure we are. I have named him Roger, for a great clergyman."

"All right," said Dolores.

Mark wet his lips. He put his hands into the pockets of his coat. He rarely wore a wig, but he had one on now as though in honor of the occasion, and he wrinkled his forehead as if it was making his head uncomfortable.

"Caleb will come over shortly to see you," said Mark.

Dolores turned her face halfway into the pillow and began to cry quietly, without any sobs.

"Please go away," she murmured. "You old vinegar bottle."

Mark took one hand out of his pocket and began twisting a button of his coat. Judith stroked Dolores' hair gently.

"We'd better go, father," she whispered.

Mark took her arm and they went out. In the hall he said, "I guess I'll be getting back."

"Won't you have dinner here? It's nearly ready."

"No, I'll be going. You—" he hesitated. "You've been very kind to her."

"No I haven't," said Judith. "I've been horrid. I've done the best I could and I've still been horrid."

"I calculate," said Mark, "we don't understand folks like her very good." He sighed and went out.

The baby was six days old when Caleb came to Ardeith.

Caleb wanted violently to see his child, but an equally violent dread of seeing Dolores held him back. The Sunday after the baby was born he let his father go alone to church while he rode his horse along the bluff road. He had had no idea he would feel like this until he got Judith's note, but since that day the fact of Roger Sheramy's existence had been the one detail of the world that had occupied his attention.

He watched a wraithish fog blow across the river and hated Dolores. She had lied to him, cheated him, tricked him into marrying her because she wanted what he could give her. Caleb was careful and straight-thinking. He simply had not thought of questioning Dolores' romantic yarns and now that they were brought home to him he had a disgusting sense of having been *used*, which hurt his pride as much as his heart. He had been made a fool of, and everybody was talking about it with a pitying amusement. Caleb had never before in his healthy life had the sensation of being either pitied or laughed at and he found it intolerable. He felt a blazing desire to do something that would hurt her as much as she had hurt him, and to do it publicly, so those who had seen his humiliation would see his revenge and would have to understand that Caleb Sheramy was not the sort to yield supinely to such scheming. He pulled abruptly on the bridle and turned the horse toward Ardeith.

He did not want an argument with Philip and Judith, and was glad they would be at church this time of day. Josh, who was lounging on the steps, got up with a stare of round-eyed curiosity as Caleb approached. Evidently his affairs had been gossiped about in the quarters; this irritated Caleb afresh.

"Where is Mrs. Sheramy?" he asked curtly.

"She in her room, Massa Caleb."

"Tell the nurse to bring the baby out here."

"Yassah." Josh was still staring at him.

"Get on in the house and do what I told you."

He spoke so sharply that Josh jumped as though dodging a stick aimed at his shoulders. Caleb stood where he was on the gallery as Josh slunk indoors. A moment later a Negro girl appeared with die baby in her arms.

She stopped just over the threshold and curtseyed as though afraid to come nearer. Caleb went up to her.

"Let me have him."

She hesitated, then held out the baby, a tiny reddish bundle in a blanket. Caleb took him awkwardly, surprised to find that the baby was so light and so incredibly little. Roger was asleep, but as he was changed from his nurse's arms to his father's he wriggled and gave a little cry. Caleb turned around and started for the steps.

"Massa Caleb! Where you goin'?" the girl cried. She ran after him.

"Stay where you are," said Caleb over his shoulder.

She was running down the walk with Josh shambling after her. Caleb went with long strides toward his horse and sprang to the saddle. The nurse rushed up panting.

"Massa Caleb, please sir don't take away de baby!" Her voice was shrill with fright.

"Hush your black mouth," said Caleb. "And let go of the stirrup."

"But Massa Caleb, I darsn't let you have him! I's Massa Philip's nigger—he ain't told me to give de baby to you!"

"Be quiet," ordered Caleb. "And you," he added to Josh, "do you want to get this whip on your back? Get away from here." He jerked the stirrup from the nurse and started the horse. She was sobbing. In Caleb's arm Roger woke and began to cry. Caleb did not look behind him.

Philip and Judith came to Silverwood that afternoon, but Caleb was unyielding.

"I think if you could see her," Philip said at last, "you'd be more merciful."

Caleb did not answer.

"Do you know," said Judith vehemently, "you've nearly killed her? When you took the baby she got out of bed and tried to go after you, and Angelique found her lying in the hall. She was too weak to walk, and she had fainted."

"Will you both please get out and let me be?" Caleb cried. "He's my child and she's not going to bring him up to be like her. Now will you go?"

Judith picked up her gloves, but Philip interposed.

"Just a minute, Caleb. May I ask what you intend doing about Dolores? After all, she is your wife."

Caleb fingered a splint of the cane cradle in which the baby was lying. "Yes. I wanted to talk to you about that. You've been very kind to keep her so long."

"I suppose your taking the child in this fashion means you don't intend to live with her again?" Philip asked.

"Don't think I'm going to leave her on your hands, Philip. I married her and I'll do my duty by her. My plan was to get her a house, in Dalroy or in New Orleans if she'd rather live there, and make her a quarterly allowance. She can have the house as soon as she's well enough to leave Ardeith."

Philip shrugged. "All right," he said shortly.

"Caleb," said Judith, "you're a self-righteous prig."

She and Philip went out together.

Caleb hovered over the baby with ferocious tenderness. He had never loved many persons, but those few he had loved very dearly, and now it seemed to him that all the fondness he had ever felt had been channeled into a passionate devotion for his child. He felt such possessive adoration that he wished he could forget Dolores' part in giving the baby life. But he could not forget Dolores, and involuntarily he remembered the lovable girl he had brought to Silverwood instead of the little alley-cat she had turned to in their last days. This made him indignant, hardening his resolve to prove that he had conquered her power over him.

By the end of the second week he scarcely remembered the house as it had been before Roger came. As he watched the nurse get the baby ready for bed on his fourteenth night at Silverwood Caleb smiled with happy devotion. This was the moment he had learned to look forward to all day. He took Roger in his arms and cuddled him to sleep, "jes' sweet as any lady would," the nurse said as she put her own black baby into its cradle in the corner. Caleb tucked Roger under the covers, whispered good night and tiptoed across the hall to his own room.

The house was very quiet, so quiet that he fancied he could hear his father snoring faintly in the room next door. Suddenly Caleb sat up, realizing that he had been asleep and something had pierced his consciousness. It was the sound of a baby yelling from across the hall. He shrugged and started to lie down again; it was evidently the black baby, for Roger could not cry as loud as that yet. As he lay down he heard a voice from the nursery. His heart began to pound. It had been a guarded voice, but louder perhaps than the speaker had realized, and by the time Caleb had coherently formed the thought that there couldn't be two women on earth who talked like that he was out of bed and running barefoot across the hall. He flung open the nursery door.

Against the starlight beyond the window he could see only a silhouette which he might not have recognized if he had known her less well. She had the baby in her left arm and a gun in her right hand. The gun was pointed at the nurse, who was flattened in terror against the wall, and the black child, roused by the excitement, was crying with all his might. Roger was whimpering.

"Put that child down!" Caleb exclaimed furiously, and made a dive toward the window. Dolores wheeled to turn her gun on him, holding the baby frantically to her breast. There was a shot. The figures in the darkness swam an instant before him as he felt a crash of pain in his side.

Though he was not quite unconscious his tongue refused to form any words, and he had a vague impression that Dolores was scrambling out of the window with Roger in her arms and the nurse was too paralyzed with terror to stop her. As he tried to get up and found that he could not, there were more voices raised in the house and another figure rushed into the nursery. His father's voice said, "Get out of here, you shameless woman!" and as he saw Mark Sheramy tear the baby out of Dolores' arms a wave of pain and nausea swept over him, and Caleb fainted.

After four days of walking up and down the Ardeith hall, half frantic lest Caleb die of his wound and vowing that Dolores should never set foot in her home again, Judith relented suddenly with a flood of remorseful tears and begged Philip to go down to the guardhouse and bring her back. Philip had wanted to do this before, for the guardhouse was a filthy hole. But he knew how fond Judith was of her brother in spite of their differences, and with Caleb's life in danger he would not force her to accept as a guest the woman who might have killed him.

Dolores did not have the grace to thank either of them. Her only request was for a bath. She stayed at Ardeith like a quiet little ghost, and spent most of her time playing with David and Christopher. Caleb recovered, and he and Philip took expensive and extralegal steps to prevent Dolores' going to trial; Judith was not sure whether Caleb did that from feeling for Dolores or because he wished as little added scandal as possible. She hardly knew Caleb any more, and could only shake her head when Philip exclaimed one day that he must be made of those New England rocks they talked about. Caleb said again he was ready to build a house for Dolores whenever she was ready, but he had instituted proceedings for complete custody of his child and until that was decided Judith could not suggest that Dolores leave.

Six months later the king's court in His Majesty's beloved colony of West Florida presented a decision written on seven sheets of paper, to the effect that the woman Dolores Sheramy, having attempted murder on the person of her lawful husband Caleb Sheramy, after having induced him to marry her by means of representations false and deceitful, was hereby declared outcast from the king's grace; and moreover, her criminal attempt on the life of her husband demonstrating her unfitness to be a guardian of the young, her rights over the offspring born to herself and the said Caleb Sheramy were declared void and the person of Roger Sheramy was consigned to his father that the said Roger Sheramy might be trained in the true religion of the Church of England and the proper conduct of a subject of the king.

Judith was waiting on the gallery when Philip came in from the court. He dismounted and walked slowly up the steps.

"What happened?" she demanded.

He took out a copy of the paper and handed it to her. "It's what we feared."

Judith leaned back against the gallery rail. "Do I have to tell her, Philip?"

"I think you'd better. What's she going to do now?"

"I don't know. This will be dreadful for her. She's kept persuading herself they were going to decide differently."

Philip struck the post of the railing with his riding-whip. "After all, honey, if it's any consolation to you, she brought this on her own head when she nearly killed Caleb. And you've done all you could."

Dolores came out on the gallery. She stopped and looked with ardent questioning at the paper in Judith's hand.

"What did they do?" she asked after a moment.

Judith handed her the folded paper. Dolores opened it and turned over the pages. She gave it back.

"You know I was never read English!" she exclaimed.

"Oh, I forgot." Judith steadied herself and put the sheets in order. "It says, 'Know all men by these presents: In the name of his Majesty George the Third, by grace of God King . . . .' Oh Philip, you read it, please!"

Dolores had put her hands behind her against the side-panel of the door and stood leaning against it. She did not turn around. Philip read the words as fast as he could, stumbling sometimes over the long sentences and the flourishes of the clerkly script. ". . . Done at the town of Dalroy in the country of Louisiana this third day of July Anno Domini 1779."

Dolores had not moved. Both Philip and Judith had expected some sort of outcry, sobs or perhaps a torrent of profanity. But Dolores for a moment did not do anything at all. She stood where she was, as though he were still reading, then she held out her hand, saying in a low voice, "You will give that to me?"

"Yes. Here it is." He added impulsively, "Lord, Dolores, I'm sorry!"

She said, "Thank you," and went inside. They heard her go into her room and shut the door.

"Shall I go to her, Philip?" Judith asked.

"I wouldn't. We'd better have supper and let her be."

"Very well. If you want to wash up I'll send some hot water."

She went in, numb with pity. Maybe Dolores deserved what she was getting, but Judith was mutinously sure that nobody could ever make her want to be responsible for so much anguish. As she passed Dolores' door she heard her sobbing, deep dry sobs that tore out of her body with a retching noise like nausea.

Dolores did not come out of her room that night, and Judith would not let the servants disturb her with their well-meant offers of food and coffee. Philip suggested, after they had gone to their room, that Dolores was probably drunk. "She's been taking whiskey and brandy out of the closet now and then, when the suspense got too much for her to stand," he said.

"I don't care," Judith returned. If Philip had said Dolores was taking opium she would not have stopped her tonight. When Philip came to bed she put her arms around him tight, wondering what she had ever done to deserve so much peace and good fortune. It seemed to her that the Lord had dropped all these things into her lap, a fine house and a retinue of slaves, beautiful children and a husband who adored her, and before she went to sleep Judith offered a little prayer that God would make her good enough to deserve them, and that he would forgive Caleb, who really didn't understand what he was doing.

Philip rode out to the indigo early the next morning, but when he came in at noon Judith was waiting for him anxiously.

"She hasn't come out of her room yet, Philip. Don't you think I ought to go in?"

"Just crack the door open and see if she's awake. It's possible she couldn't sleep all night and dropped off this morning. But if she's just staying in there crying some sympathy might be good for her."

"I thought so too." Judith went down the hall to the door of Dolores' room. "Dolores?" she called softly.

There was no answer. Judith lifted the latch carefully so as to make no sound, noticing that the bolt had not been shot into place. She cried out in alarm.

"Philip! Philip, come here!"

He came hurrying down the hall. "What is it?"

"She's gone, Philip! And she's taken *everything*."

Philip came into the room behind her. The bed had not been turned down, but the quilt was rumpled and the pillow was wadded into a shapeless mass as if it had been hugged and pounded and hugged again. The whole place was disordered as though from a hurried departure. A stocking and some pieces of lace and ribbon were on the floor. Drawers were pulled out and emptied, and the candle on the table had burned down into the candlestick before the wick had sputtered out. Philip glanced at the window. The shutters were wide open. The house was low, and to drop a box out and climb after it would have been simple for anyone as young and agile as Dolores. Judith caught his arm.

"Do you suppose she's gone to Silverwood?"

"I don't know. Wait a minute." He went out. Judith noticed an overturned bottle lying on the floor in a pool of liquor. In a few minutes Philip came back.

"My guns are all where they belong. But I told Josh to take a horse and go to Silverwood, to ask if they'd seen anything of her." He gave an ironic smile. "I don't think that's where she is, though."

"Why not?"

"She took all the money that was in the drawer of that desk in the gun-room."

"Oh my soul. Was it very much?"

"Four or five pounds. Enough to get her back to New Orleans."

"She took that silver pomade-jar too," Judith exclaimed indignantly. "I daresay she's gone off with everything worth selling she could carry."

"Poor girl," said Philip, "poor girl."

"I don't understand her at all," Judith said hotly. "This is what you get for trying to be kind. If she'd asked you for passage to New Orleans you'd have given it to her—she might have known that."

"Don't you suppose," suggested Philip, "she found it easier to steal than to ask for any more charity?"

"Oh, I don't know," said Judith. "I don't know. I wonder what's going to become of her now."

"My notion is," said Philip, "that she'll like us better if we don't try to find out."

Josh returned from Silverwood with the news that they had seen nothing there of Dolores. By that time Judith was in a state of wrathful exasperation. Dolores had taken Judith's purse with her shopping money, three gold-lined silver goblets belonging to a set brought at great expense from France, some gold toothpicks from the dining-room, and various other articles of less value. Judith exclaimed to Philip that it was a judgment on him for founding his fortune with stolen treasure from a pirate boat, and he said maybe it was.

CHAPTER NINE

The keels and flatboats were crowded against the wharf and big-muscled slaves were loading them with produce of the plantations. Negroes and white men lounged about on the bales piled up near the waterfront, with here and there groups of soldiers who were shooting dice or basking in the sunshine. Dolores stopped and set down her box. Already the sun was hot and she was very tired. The box was heavier than she had thought it would be and her arms ached from carrying it; if she had not met that wagon on its way to the wharf with a load of indigo she didn't believe she could possibly have brought her things all the way here. It must be six or eight miles from Ardeith to the wharf, or maybe further, though she had been so tired and unhappy by the time she got a ride on the wagon that she hadn't taken much notice of the distance. She had asked the driver about boats to New Orleans, but he was a field-slave who didn't know anything about boats.

A girl was walking about selling fruit. Remembering that she hadn't had anything to eat since dinner yesterday, Dolores beckoned the girl and bought a banana and a bunch of grapes. She had put a few coins into a little knitted purse and tucked it into the bosom of her dress. The rest of the money she had taken from Ardeith she had tied into a bag and hung under her petticoats, cross that there was not more of it. The Larnes lived in such luxury that they must have a lot of money about somewhere, but she hadn't known where to look for it last night. At any rate, this would be enough to take her to New Orleans, away from these people who had made her so miserable. She hated them all—Caleb, who had taken away her baby when it was six days old, and Caleb's stern old father who thought she was an abandoned woman, and the Purcells with their constrained politeness, and Philip and Judith who had been so kind they had made her feel like a stray cat. Sometimes she had wished they would put her to work in the fields, or anything, if they would only stop being kind. She would have run off before now except that as long as there had been any chance of getting her baby back she couldn't leave. But now that they had taken him completely she could not bear the sight of the Dalroy bluff any longer, nor any of those people who could go to see her baby whenever they wanted to. It had been six months now, and even if she saw Roger she wouldn't know him.

She had heard Philip's reading of the court order with despair. It could not be that anything so awful could happen in the world, and yet here it was happening. Her English was not inclusive enough to grasp the long words, but she understood that Caleb had dismissed her from his house and was never, never going to let her see her own baby again. The first she had expected, and by this time she did not mind very much, though she had been fond enough of Caleb in the beginning, but that any bunch of judges with wigs on their heads could fail to know that her baby belonged to her as surely as her own hands and feet—that was impossible, yet it was happening. And here she was, a healthy woman who could walk and talk and go anywhere she pleased, and yet she was helpless to make them stop doing this to her. Even when she had taken a horse out of Philip's stable and had tried to get her baby, all that had happened was that she had put a bullet into Caleb's side and they had carried her off to the guardhouse. If she had just seen that damn little nigger in the dark she could have put a pillow over him so they wouldn't hear him cry and held the nurse back with her gun until she had got away with Roger. She hadn't really meant to try to kill anybody. But when she saw Caleb it had all rushed over her that he was going to take the baby again and that she hated him like the devil and when she fired she did want to kill him.

Probably, Dolores reflected as she bit the grapes, she ought to be grateful they hadn't had her hanged for that, but she wasn't; they might as well break her neck as kick her around like this. And probably if they found her here on the wharf with all these things she had taken from Ardeith they'd have her hanged anyway. But the Larnes could get plenty more where these came from, and she had felt so defenseless. Possessions provided a sense of safety when one was alone, and she had to get away. It would have been too horrible to wake up one more morning in the room where Roger was born.

And as for Caleb's saying he would support her—could he possibly think she was going to take his charity? Maybe he would like to hear people say how good he was to keep his worthless wife from starving. Like folks who boasted complacently of how kind they were to nigger slaves too old to work. Holy Mary mother! She'd steal or live on the docks, but she wouldn't give that crew any more chance to be kind.

Her legs ached, and her back too. A man dawdled past and spoke to her. "Oh, hush your mouth," said Dolores wearily. She looked around the swarming wharf and called a Negro boy who was idling on a fruit-crate. He had a badge on his shirt, which meant his master had sent him down to the docks to pick up odd jobs, having no use for him at home today. Dolores told him to watch her box while she went to ask about boats. Did he know of any going down to New Orleans?

The boy rolled his eyes around and told her it wasn't so easy to get to New Orleans these times on account of the American war. Dolores rubbed the toe of her shoe over a knot in the board floor of the wharf.

"Oh Lord," she said, "don't that be over yet?"

No ma'am, it wasn't, the colored boy told her, and the boats were being used mostly to carry soldiers. But there was a boat down the river a piece, the Cienega, that was going down to New Orleans tomorrow.

Dolores wandered along the wharf looking for the Cienega. She had a hard time finding it, for the wharf was so cluttered with boxes of freight and soldiers and stevedores and Indians selling furs that it was hard to walk around at all. There weren't very many women about, and she heard herself being accosted in all the three languages she understood and one or two strange ones. Sometimes she didn't answer and sometimes she turned around and swore in whatever language came first into her head.

At last she found the Cienega, a big flatboat being loaded with indigo, tobacco and furs. A lady and gentleman were talking to the captain, arranging passage for themselves and four slaves. Dolores waited till they finished and asked the captain if he would take her too. He told her curtly that he didn't give passage to ladies traveling alone.

She protested eagerly that she could pay for a bunk. He returned, "You heard what I said. I don't run that kind of boat."

"Damn you," said Dolores, but he wasn't listening to her; he had turned and was giving orders to one of the crew. Dolores turned away helplessly, watching the lady and gentleman who had just been arranging for the trip. The lady was being assisted by her husband into a carriage that waited above the wharf. Dolores sighed. That was what you had to have, a male protector with you, or at least a couple of genteel-looking slaves, and if you didn't have either you got nothing but trouble. The more you needed protection the more folks kicked you around. She tried another boat, but it was going upriver toward Baton Rouge, where there was an English garrison. The next boats were dirty things laden with furs and bear-grease from Illinois, and didn't take passengers. After that she passed boats with guns and soldiers. They were busy with the war and didn't want women around, not as passengers anyway. There was a Spanish boat heavily gunned, staying close to another gunboat flying a curious but very pretty flag with red and white stripes and one upper corner blue with white stars on it. Dolores wondered where it came from. Some foreign country. A soldier in a nut-colored shirt was coming down the plank, and she asked him what kind of boat it was. He said it came from the Free and Equal United States of America, whatever that was, and they were bringing some important diplomats down for a conference with their friends in New Orleans, and the Spanish boat was escorting them past English Louisiana lest the Tories here make nuisances of themselves.

"Can you take me to New Orleans?" asked Dolores.

He looked her up and down, grinning. "Well ma'am, I sure would like to say yes, but it ain't allowed, ma'am."

"I don't go making any trouble," she urged desperately. She was so tired she was almost ready to take any kind of boat under any conditions, if only they would let her lie down in a bunk and get some rest. She had slept only an hour or two the night before and wouldn't have slept even that if she hadn't drunk such a lot, and this morning she had pled with captains and crews until she was dizzy. The sun was blazing on the river and her head felt big and heavy. "Please take me to New Orleans!" she begged.

He chuckled and took her by the arm. "No woman ain't allowed up that there plank, lady, but let's you and me get over to the King's Tavern or whatever they call it and we can get a drink."

She shook her arm out of his grasp. "Oh, let me alone, can't you?"

"Hey," he said, "who started talking, me or you?"

"Go to hell," said Dolores. She turned around and ran, and tripped on her skirt and fell down. Two or three Negroes laughed at her as she got up. The sun was making her blind and her throat was blistered with thirst because of the liquor she had drunk last night. She was afraid if she didn't lie down soon in a cool dark room she might faint and then only the good God knew what would happen. Any room, any place, if she could find the Negro boy who was supposed to be keeping an eye on her box, if only he hadn't gone off with it. The wharf was so crowded that it took her a long time to find the place where she had left him. The boy was still there, sitting on the ground ogling a black girl who was waiting with a coffle of slaves to be led from the riverfront to the slave-market.

"You come with me," said Dolores.

The boy got up lazily. "You want de box, miss?"

"No, you tote it," said Dolores, feeling if she had to carry anything besides her own aching head it would be enough to kill her.

"Yassum. Where we goin'?"

"I got to get me a room to stay," she murmured. "The—the King's Tavern."

It was the only place she could think of and she didn't know where it was, but apparently he did, for he ambled off, lugging the box, and she followed him, praying the Lord she'd hold out till they got there.

Caleb would never have dreamed of letting her come down to these places on the riverfront, but from her recollections of New Orleans Dolores knew what the King's Tavern would be like. It made her want to giggle with hysterical triumph to think how bewildered Judith and Gervaise would be in a tavern like this and how sure she was of what to do. The front room was low and big, with kegs of ale and beer around, and long tables with benches by them. A man with pock-marks on his face was behind the counter with a slatternly fat woman, and behind them were shelves holding bottles of liquor and plates of bread and cheese and meat. Flies buzzed around the food and the splashes of liquor on the counter. Groups of men sat about drinking, one or two of them with girls. There were not many here now, but it wasn't noon yet. By night the tap-room would be packed.

Dolores went to the counter and rested her elbows on it.

"I want a room," she announced to the fat woman. "Tonight, but I move in now."

"Huh?" said the fat woman.

Dolores heard a man's voice speaking to her from behind her back, but she didn't pay any attention. He was saying, "Hey, pretty thing."

the bed, then at last she took off her shoes and dress and stays and lay down, pillowing her head on her crossed arms; but she remembered she had left the window open, and anybody who wanted to could slip in and take the bag of money or the silver goblets. Relaxation was so delicious that it took all her will-power to get up and close the shutters, but she managed to do it, and tumbled across the bed again.

She was too tired even to cry. Vaguely, in disconnected pictures, she saw the manor at Silverwood and the long dinners of spiced meats and European wines and herself facing Caleb across the table, and she remembered the gardens of Ardeith and the fields of tobacco and indigo as she had seen them through the windows of the room where her baby was born, and her tiny little baby lying in the crook of her arm. But they seemed hazy, like some remembered pleasure of childhood, too remote to cause anything but a nostalgic pain. How misunderstanding those people had been, turning that period into the sneering triumph of a wanton instead of an interlude granted by a happy-tempered God. But she couldn't think vehemently enough now even to hate them, or to tell one sensation from another; she felt like nothing but a huddle of misery and aching bones. But she was too tired even to feel like that long. It was only a few minutes before she went to sleep.

When she awoke it was nearly dark. She drew a long breath and turned over on her back. For awhile she lay where she was, her eyes following a crack in the plaster wall, while she wondered what was going to become of her. She could get back to New Orleans eventually, no doubt, but when she got there what? Aunt Juanita might let her serve in the tavern again, and heaven knew it was a better place than this, or again Aunt Juanita might not; the chances were she'd say Dolores was a bad ungrateful girl for running away. Or she might try selling fruit on the docks, but anybody with half a head on his shoulders could foretell where you ended if you started hawking things on the docks, unless you were an ugly old hag sailors bought from out of pity. She could always jump in the river, if she went down below the wharfs where there weren't any well-meaning folks to fish her out. And she might as well be dead as have a baby she wasn't allowed even to look at, or try to go on living among this cruel human race that hadn't let her have any peace since the day she was born.

Oh, she did want to be decent, Dolores told herself bitterly, but everything she tried to do was wrong and got her into trouble, and whether it was her own fault or other people's she was too fuddled with unhappiness to decide. And in the meantime it was beginning to be night, and she couldn't stay in this hole without a candle. She got up shivering, thinking it must be going to rain soon. There was some water left in the bucket so she took another drink and washed herself as well as she could. She had no soap, and she had to use a chemise out of her box for a towel, but cold water on her face and arms was refreshing. When she had washed her face she took off her stockings and sat with her feet in the water, for they were aching with so much walking on the road last night and on that sun-baked wharf this morning. At last, when she put on fresh stockings and another pair of shoes, and dressed and combed her hair as well as she could without a mirror, she felt almost well. Not having a glass was annoying until she remembered sardonically that it was safer here not to look attractive. She wrapped her discarded clothes around the pieces of silver she had taken from Ardeith, made sure her bag of money was safely tied under her petticoats with only a few necessary coins in the purse, re-corded the box and went out, locking the door behind her.

The taproom was full of men now, eating and drinking. A few of them were getting rowdy already. One soldier with a Cuban accent pulled her by the arm and tried to make her sit on the bench by him; Dolores laughed stupidly and pretended she didn't speak Spanish and didn't know what he wanted. She made her way to the counter and told the waiting-woman she wanted candles. Now that she had slept she felt well enough to chaffer about the price, and got three for what the woman wanted her to pay for one. Some kind of row was going on by the door. The words were English. Dolores turned around and looked, leaning back with her arms stretched along the counter, and reflecting that it was fortunate she had been asleep all afternoon, for it was a good thing not to need much sleep tonight; she'd have to be alert if those tipsy fools found out there was a woman alone in a room behind the bar.

The pock-faced bartender was throwing out a man who couldn't pay for what he had ordered.

"Hey you, listen," the man exclaimed. "Is it my fault I ain't had a job of work all day? Them folks don't want nothing but nigger slaves on the docks."

"I said for you to get out," the bartender repeated loudly. "Ain't I been trusting you three days for all you done et?"

"I said I'd pay for it soon's I got a piece of work to do! Look here, I ain't had a bite since this morning. How can I get work to pay you if I don't get nothing in my belly?"

Two or three customers, amused by the argument, had come closer to listen. They were apparently hoping for a fight, and it did look as if there might be one. The man from outside would have the advantage, for he was muscular and healthy-looking, and Dolores thought a blow on the jaw might be good for the bartender, but she didn't want to get caught in a general fracas. She wheeled around and faced the waiting-woman, who was looking on with her under lip stuck out contemptuously.

"Give me a plate of supper," said Dolores. "Hurry up."

"What you want?" The query was reluctant; the argument really did look on the verge of a fight, and the woman was loth to return to business.

"Whatever you got. And beer."

The woman stuck under her nose a plate on which was a pile of rice and another pile of river-shrimp with some greasy sort of gravy poured over both, and a piece of bread. Dolores picked up the plate in one hand and the beer-mug in the other and made her way toward the door.

"Here, mister," she said. Here's your supper. Don't jiggle my arm, you—" this to another man in the group looking on— "do you want to make me spill it?"

The stranger was looking down at her, a slow grin spreading on his face. "What you mean, lady?"

"I mean it's your supper." She jerked her head toward the bartender. "You can quit growling. It's paid for. This here gentleman is a friend of mine."

The bartender raised his voice. "Say, Lucy, this woman pay for supper?"

"Yeah. Why?"

"All right. I wouldn't pay him no mind if I was you, lady. He ain't got a penny."

Dolores set the plate on the end of the nearest table and pulled at the man's sleeve.

"You better eat it, mister."

He was eying the food hungrily. But as he sat down he hesitated, glancing up at her. "Say, ma'am, do I know you?"

"No. But you go on and eat. Be my company."

He tasted the beer, wiped his mouth on the back of his hand and reached up to catch her wrist as she started off.

"Ain't you gonta stay?"

"Take your hands off me, can't you?" said Dolores.

He obeyed. "Sorry, ma'am. I just thought—"

"Well, you made a mistake."

He dug his spoon into the rice and looked up to smile at her again. It wasn't a leering smile, but a pleasant grateful curiosity. She felt herself smiling back at him.

"I just meant you're right nice, ma'am, bringing supper to a fellow you ain't never laid eyes on before, and I sure am thankful. It's hungry work tramping them docks, specially when you can't find nothing to do. Just sit down a spell. I ain't meaning no harm."

Dolores sat down on the bench opposite, resting her chin

on her hands. He was eating so fast that for a few moments he didn't say anything else. She watched him. He had a big arched nose and a cleft chin, and a broad mouth with beautiful teeth. His hair was brown, bleached on top by the sun. His shirt had once been blue, but the color had faded out except at the seams, and it was torn in two places at the shoulder. She had noticed another tear in his stocking just below the knee. Evidently he didn't have any woman to attend to him.

He looked up from his plate. His eyes were blue, under thick eyebrows sun-bleached so light that they looked almost white on his tanned face.

"How'd you happen to get me supper, lady?"

"Oh, I don't know," she murmured. "I reckon you looked kind of lonesome."

"You had your supper?"

She shook her head. It was the first time she had remembered that she had eaten nothing all day but a banana and a bunch of grapes.

"You better have some."

"I don't want any. That's yours."

"You better have some. Look here." He dipped the bread into the beer and passed it across. "You just eat that. It's good when you ain't got no appetite."

She took it, and began to eat. It did taste good.

"Like it?" he asked.

She nodded.

"Them candles you got stuck in your bosom is gonta melt if you don't take 'em out," he said.

Dolores laughed and laid the candles on the table. "I was forget about them."

"What makes you talk so funny?" he inquired.

"I don't be English."

"Creole?"

"Yes. Spanish. New Orleans."

"Been up here long?"

"Not so very."

"What's your name?"

"Dolores." She stopped. Sheramy she dared not say; Bondio caught behind her tongue.

"I'm named Thad Upjohn." He hesitated, then asked, "What you doing here, Miss Dolores?"

"I just dropped in."

This did not seem to satisfy him. "Your husband here too?" he asked.

Dolores bit her lip. "I haven't got a husband."

"Then how come you wear a wedding ring?"

"Why don't you use your mouth for eating?" she snapped.

Thad Upjohn dropped his eyes. "Excuse me, ma'am. I didn't go to start no argument."

Dolores put her forehead down on her hands and pushed her fingers through her hair. "Oh, I don't be cross on purpose. But I've got such a misery in the heart it makes me mean."

"Sure, sure," he said to her gently. "It don't matter. I'm sorry you feel bad."

She did not answer or look up. After awhile he said to her,

"Look here, Miss Dolores. I ain't got nothing to buy it for you, but you'll feel better if you eat a little something."

"You reckon?"

"I sure do. You look mighty peaked."

Dolores reached down into her dress and took out her purse. "All right. You get it. But not that mess of shrimp."

He came back with some bread and cheese and a mug of beer. "Now you eat this here, ma'am. You'll feel better."

She bit into it. "Don't you want some more beer for yourself?"

"I don't like letting you buy it, Miss Dolores."

"I wish you would. I mean—well, as long as you stay here by me nobody pesters me."

He crossed his arms around his empty plate. "I can sit around without no beer, lady."

"Lord, but you're decent," she said in a tired little voice. "You're the first man I've met today that hasn't treated me like trash."

Thad Upjohn shrugged. "Well, you was right nice to me. It made me feel better."

"Did you feel as bad as that?" she asked.

"I felt kind of bad. It ain't so easy getting along these times."

"I didn't think," said Dolores, "that men had such trouble getting along."

"They do when there ain't no work for 'em, like now."

"Why ain't there no work?"

"Well, it's hard to say. Some says it's the war, and not so many boats needing to be loaded as there used to be. Then all the folks with work to be done is buying niggers. There was plenty work when I first came down, but they buys so many niggers these days it ain't so easy for a white man to find it."

Dolores frowned thoughtfully at her bread and cheese. Food really was making her feel better. Perhaps she'd been hungry without knowing it.

"But if you're English," she ventured, "how come your king didn't give you some land? Or wasn't you come down before the rebellion?"

"Oh yes, I been down hereabouts quite a spell," said Thad Upjohn. "But the king wasn't giving away no land except to them as had been in that French and Indian War, and I wasn't in it. I wasn't but a shaver then—about seventeen, and I didn't see no call for me to go fighting Indians up in Virginia or Pennsylvania or wherever they was fighting."

"Where you come from?" she asked with interest.

"Georgia."

"That on the ocean?"

"Well, yes ma'am, part of it. Only I ain't never seen the ocean. I come from the back country."

"I see," said Dolores, though she didn't, having never before heard of a geographical item called Georgia. But it was relieving to talk about somebody else's troubles. It helped her forget her own. And this Mr. Thad Upjohn, though so different from the fine gentlemen she had met on the bluff, was nice. He was friendly without being a pest, and he gave no evidence of the puzzled gentleness that had humiliated her so at Ardeith. To him she was just a girl who for some reason or other was having a misery in the heart and he wasn't either prying or sooth-ing. He was just letting her alone, and Dolores realized with wordless gratitude that this was the sum total of all she was asking right now of the human race. He wasn't very clean or very good-looking, though he might look better if he combed his hair and got a shave and if he had a woman to mend his clothes.

A girl standing on the other end of the long table was sing-ing a dirty song, swishing her skirts and shaking her hips while a group of half-tipsy soldiers stamped their feet to keep time. She was singing in Creole French. Thad Upjohn glanced at her now and then, and back at Dolores.

"You talk French?" she asked him, hoping he didn't.

"Lord no, Miss Dolores, I don't talk nothing but what I'm talking. Do you?"

"Some."

"Is it French that fancy female's bawling over yonder?"

She nodded.

"Say," he said with admiration, "you're educated, ain't you?"

"Not so much. It's easy to pick up different ways of talking in New Orleans."

"I bet you can read good, and all like that."

"I can read Spanish all right. Not French or English. Can't you read?"

His wide mouth spread in a grin. "No ma'am. I wish I could."

"I wish you'd get yourself some more beer," said Dolores.

"Say, Miss Dolores, it ain't right for me to be making away with your money."

"Oh, go on, do. I said you was be my company at supper."

He laughed, and went off for another mug of beer. Dolores was glad of it. She had eaten all her bread and cheese, but she liked to keep on sitting there talking. A patter on the windows told her the rain had started outside.

"They have many niggers where you come from?" she inquired when he came back.

"Not in the back country, they don't. There's heaps of them on the coast, around Savannah, but I ain't never been there. I seen powerful few niggers before I got to Louisiana."

"What made you come down if you didn't have some land?" she asked.

"Well ma'am, things wasn't so good around home. Cut-worms got in the corn, and that always makes a bad year. Folks said this here was a new country with lots of easy work for everybody and all like that, so me and my wife just figured we'd pick up and come along."

"Oh, you got a wife?" She was surprised. His wife didn't seem to look after him very well.

"No ma'am, not now. She had a baby and died, year after we got here."

"Where's the baby?" Dolores asked eagerly.

"It died too, Miss Dolores. Me, I don't know much about looking out for babies."

"That's bad. I'm sorry."

"Yes ma'am, cut me up, I don't mind saying."

189

Dolores fingered the candles lying by her empty plate. "I got a baby," she said in a low voice.

"Sure enough? Little girl?"

"No, a little boy."

"Mine was a little girl," he said. She did not look up. After a moment he asked, "Your little boy die too?"

"N-no. No, he's all right. My husband's got him."

"But I thought you said—excuse me, Miss Dolores."

Dolores felt tears coming into her eyes. She bit her lip hard and swallowed. Thad said, "I didn't mean to make you feel bad, ma'am."

Dolores put her elbows on the table and pressed her fists into her eyes. Somebody down at the other end of the table had started another song and a lot of them were singing it, a nasty song full of words you weren't a lady if you understood. Dolores felt her tears drying up. She had already cried so much there didn't seem to be many tears left behind her eyes. She looked up again. Thad Upjohn was watching her with a sober pity.

"You didn't make me feel bad," said Dolores. "I just felt bad anyway. I can't help it. I did have a husband," she added impulsively, "but he throwed me out. I wasn't good enough for him."

"Oh."

"I wasn't good enough for him," said Dolores, "but my baby was good enough for him. That's how it is. Maybe you've heard of him. He's named Sheramy."

Thad's mouth opened with astonishment. "Lordy mercy. You mean them Sheramys that lives at Silverwood Plantation?"

She nodded.

"Well, well, well," said Thad.

Apparently that was all he could think of to say just then. But after a moment he added, "Say, Miss Dolores, that's just too bad." He shook his head.

Suddenly she found herself telling him all about it. She told it without any embellishments, and it was a relief to be talking about herself with complete honesty. As she went on she realized what a strain it had been to live in a cloud of romances and try to remember if what she was saying today fitted what she had said yesterday. Thad listened in silence. Now and then he reached over and patted her hand.

"That's all," said Dolores finally. "I stole the money out of the desk and I stole some silver things I thought maybe I could sell. I don't know why I did it. Maybe I was a little bit crazy last night."

There was a pause. "I reckon you had a pretty good right to be crazy, honey," said Thad slowly.

"What can I do now?" she asked him.

He shook his head. "Blest if I know, Miss Dolores."

Dolores twisted her hands together in her lap. It was late. The taproom was close with candle-smoke and tobacco and the fumes of liquor. Two men had started a fight at the other end of the room and everybody else was cheering and taking sides.

"I expect you ought to get out of here, ma'am," said Thad.

"I guess so." She stood up and lit a candle from one burning in a bottle on the table.

He got up too. "I reckon I ought to be getting along. I don't want to get messed up in no fight and get my head broke."

She picked up her candles and started out. "You got a place to stay?" Thad asked her.

"I got a room behind this. It's kind of a hole, but I can lock the door."

Thad hesitated. "Mind if I come around tomorrow and see how you're making out?"

"I wish you would." They were out in the hall. "Where you live?" asked Dolores.

He laughed. "Lord, lady, I don't live no place. Mostly I sleep on the docks these days. I reckon I can find me a shed to keep the rain off."

Dolores stopped at her door and reached down into her dress for her key. She looked up at him.

"Mr. Upjohn, you believe in God?"

"Ma'am? Why sure, Miss Dolores, I believe in God. What makes you ask?"

She took a long breath. "If you'll swear before God to let me alone you can stay in here with me." She unlocked the door. "It's pretty awful but at least it's got a roof. You'll catch your death in this rain."

Thad stopped her as she pushed the door open. "Miss Dolores, I ain't going to bother you. I'll swear it and mean it, but you got no business believing it. You don't know me from nobody else."

Dolores turned to face him. "Oh, I'll risk it. I want so bad to just once see somebody that's decent. Come on."

She went inside. When he came in she was kneeling on the floor, holding the candle sideways to make a pool of soft grease that would support the end.

"You ain't using that there quilt and pillow on the floor?" Thad Upjohn asked.

"No," said Dolores without looking up. "They were too dirty."

"I've slept on worse than them. And you better let me fix that candle. You're gonta set the house afire."

She handed him the candle silently. When he had stuck it firmly on the floor she offered him the key.

"Will you catch a bucket of water so I'll have something to wash in in the morning?" she asked shyly.

"Sure, Miss Dolores," said Thad. He took the key and went out.

Dolores started to undress. Maybe, she reflected, she ought not to undress, but she had worn these clothes so long they felt sticky. She got a bedgown out of her box and put it on, lying down on the bed and covering herself with a wide quilted petticoat. Thad came in with the water.

"You got everything you need?" he inquired as he locked the door.

"Yes."

"All right, ma'am. Now just go on to sleep. I ain't gonta let nobody pester you."

He spread the quilt on the floor across the doorway and knelt to blow out the candle. "Miss Dolores," he said, "it's right nice of you to let me stay in here out of the rain."

"Oh, I don't mind," said Dolores.

Thad sat back on his haunches. "Well ma'am, I mean I been kind of having misery in the heart too, like you said. Ever since my wife and baby died, and me having trouble getting work and not having no friends around hereabouts and all. It was nice meeting you."

"Go on to sleep," she said.

He blew out the candle. Dolores heard him wrap up in the quilt. After awhile she could hear him snoring gently. She felt a grateful surprise. It was comforting not to be alone.

Thad waked her. It was barely daylight, and the rain had ceased.

Dolores sat up, holding the petticoat close under her chin.

"What you want?"

"Well ma'am," said Thad, "I thought I better tell you I was getting along, and give you the key. They start loading the boats right early."

"Goodbye," she said.

Thad started out and paused. He came back.

"Miss Dolores, where you gonta be? I mean, well, I mean I don't like leaving you with nobody to look out for you."

Dolores glanced around at the ugly room, gray in the dawn.

"I'm not used to having anybody look out for me," she said faintly.

"Well ma'am, you ought to have." Thad sat down on the bed by her. "You start running around by yourself and you'll get in all kinds of a mess. I ain't much of a one to be talking, but all the same—"

Dolores' eyes widened. At least he was a man, and that was what she needed. If she had a man with her maybe she could get to New Orleans. There was enough money in her bag for two passages. She caught his wrist.

"You mean you'll let me stay around with you awhile?"

Thad cleared his throat. "Well, I been kind of lonesome, like. It 'ud be nice having somebody to keep an eye on."

Dolores laughed softly. "Say, would you like to come down to New Orleans with me? You could make work there easy, I bet. It's a grand big town."

"New Orleans?" Thad was dubious.

She nodded. "I hate this place."

"How'd you get that tooth outen your head?" Thad asked suddenly.

"Oh, some sailors in the tavern where I worked had a fight and one of them chunked a chair and it hit me by mistake. That was a long time ago before I knew how to look out for myself."

Thad shook his head slowly. "Say, Miss Dolores, you don't know no more about looking out for yourself than if you was just born yesterday. You just go around scraping up trouble. If you go down to that crazy town you'll pick up more trouble than ever."

"But I'm not going by myself! You coming with me."

He stood up. "No ma'am, I ain't got no call to go to New Orleans. Don't nobody down there even talk English. And they got more niggers than they got up here. Fine chance I'd have making a living. No ma'am."

"You—you won't come?" Dolores sighed. Again she had been too impulsive. If she had stayed with him awhile he might have got to like her so much he'd go anywhere she wanted to. But here she'd let him go and get his mind made up.

"You're mighty right I won't," said Thad. "If you want to go there I ain't got no way to stop you. And if you want to wind up like one of them females lying drunk in the taproom back yonder I reckon I ain't got no way to stop you doing that neither. Because that's where you'd get if you went back to New Orleans, ain't it?" He stuck his hands in his pockets and shook his head. "Well ma'am, I reckon I better be going."

As he started off Dolores gasped and put the back of her hand to her mouth. He really was leaving. He meant it this time. And with him was going her only possible chance of safety. She had a sickening vision of herself walking the docks again today and sleeping in a place like this again tonight, and doing it over and over till her money was gone. With a terrified little jerk she flung the petticoat back and sprang out of bed, running barefoot after him.

"Please come back!" she cried at the door. "Please, please! You didn't understand me—please sir don't go!"

Thad turned around and came slowly back. "What's the matter, honey?"

Dolores pulled him back into the room and shut the door. She was panting with fright.

"Don't leave me!" she begged again. "Let me stay with you. I don't be that kind of woman. Honest. I don't be always an angel but not like what you said. Please let me stay with you."

He looked down at her, laughing a little. "Oh, you poor young un," he said, "you're all mixed up, ain't you?"

Dolores held him with both hands. Her thoughts clicked sharply. She didn't want to spend her life scrubbing and patching for a dock-laborer, but for the present it seemed the best she could do. He didn't have a job and he wasn't very bright and he couldn't read his own name, but he was good-natured and he didn't look as if he'd beat her or lie around drunk all the time. And when they got done with this war and the boats were running regular again she could get to New Orleans.

"Look here," she exclaimed, "if you don't want to go to New Orleans I don't mind. I'll stay here in Dalroy. I've got enough money to get us a room somewhere and we can make out on what I've got till you can get some work. Let me stay with you. I'll mend your clothes so you'll look better and I can cook pretty good, honest. Don't leave me by myself!"

Thad grinned and laid an arm around her shoulders. "Sure. Come on. I reckon we'll make out all right."

"We sure will," said Dolores. "Wait for me. I've got to get dressed. I won't be long."

CHAPTER TEN

That same Summer, Spain declared war on England.

The people of the river country heard this piece of news with mingled consternation and amusement. It meant that the Creoles of New Orleans and the Tories of West Florida were technically enemies, but ordering the city to wage war with the richest district of its hinterland was so exorbitant a demand that they could not help wondering if their kings by the grace of God had gone hazy in the head. It was the first time they had realized how enormous the Atlantic Ocean was and how little the rulers on the other side knew about America. The Louisiana Creoles had always been favorably inclined toward the American rebellion—they were mostly of French descent and France was sending soldiers to the aid of the general nebulously known to them as Mister Vasinton—but neither they nor the upriver Tories felt patriotic enough to cut the throats of their best customers.

"For my part," said Philip Larne to Walter Purcell, "I hadn't any quarrel with King George. But if he thinks I'm going to fight a war with my only outlet to the sea—"

Walter Purcell laughed and asked how the American rebellion had happened to turn into a world war. Philip replied that he had no idea, but by letting it turn into a world war a certain Hanover with the mentality of a turnip had deprived himself of West Florida and probably the thirteen other English colonies on the seacoast.

"But seriously," Judith asked, "what's going to happen to us?"

"Nothing to worry about, I'll warrant," Philip assured her. "It all depends on Governor Galvez in New Orleans, and he's no fool. Who ever got the idea of putting the Mississippi River into two countries anyhow?"

He curtailed her shopping trips, telling her there was too much excitement on the wharfs to make visits there advisable for a lady. But except for such precautions, most of the settlers of the Dalroy bluff agreed that the idea of a war with New Orleans was more funny than serious. A week after the news of war arrived, a servant from Lynhaven brought Judith one of Gervaise's characteristic notes.

"I understand that I am now yr allien ennemie, being myself a Creole. If it is so that you and Philippe can disregarde this I shall esteme it an honneur if you will come to dinner thursday at 3 o'clock. I do not kno why the warre is

199

and Walter says I woulde not understand if he tried to tell me. I suspecque he does not kno either but do not tell him I said so. Have you heard yr frend Mrs. Ste. Claire from Pensilvanie has been delivaired of twinn girls. That makes seven dauters in that house and unless they are savin for dowries already I do not envie them what they will go thro when the time comes to marrie them off. I have only Babette till yet but our fate is in Gods handes. Have you heard from Dolores? Yrs, Gervaise."

Judith wrote back that she would be happy to come to dinner, that she too found the war incomprehensible and that she had not heard anything of Dolores.

Everybody talked about the war, but nobody seemed to think anything was going to be done about it until one day in September they got reports that Spanish troops under Governor Galvez were marching up the west bank of the river. Philip observed coolly that since the west bank belonged to Spain the governor had a perfect right to deploy soldiers there, but Judith went into a panic. She made mammy bring the children to sleep in the bed with herself and Philip and lay awake half that night expecting to hear guns from the opposite shore, although Philip slept peacefully after assuring her again that Señor Galvez was too wise to blow up the indigo plantations. By morning the soldiers had gone quietly out of sight and Philip was proved correct. It was days before they knew what had become of them. Philip brought the news on a Sunday morning when Judith was dressing for church. She had on a new gown of blue silk lustring over a striped petticoat, and was surveying herself in the mirror when Philip walked in. He had ridden out early to ask for news.

"You'd better hurry and get dressed," Judith said. "I had Angelique lay out your clothes, and that wig you had recurled. We'll be late."

He squeezed her shoulders with both hands and turned her around. "Great news! No church."

"No church? What are you talking about?" Judith poked out her lower lip. Philip had evidently been into a tavern and had a drink or so too many.

"Let's go over to Lynhaven. Gervaise can teach us to say aves. We aren't English any more. We are Spanish—Catholics—heathens—nobody knows what we are, for the orders are put up in Spanish and there's not three men in town who can read them." He laughed and pinched her cheek.

Judith stared. "Philip, are you as drunk as you sound? *What* has been going on?"

He found his pipe and began filling the bowl. "Ring and tell Angelique to bring me a light. Everything's been going on. Señor Galvez took those men up to Baton Rouge—"

"Ring yourself. What else?"

"—and took the fort from the English garrison, who had been doing nothing for years but lie about and eat their heads off and were probably glad to be relieved—"

She stamped her foot. "Stop biting that pipe and talk plain! Then what happened?"

"—and then," said Philip, perching himself on the bed and jangling the bellcord, "he sent Captain Delavillebeuvre—"

"Captain *what?*"

"Precious, can I help it if that's his name? Galvez sent him up to Natchez, which wasn't fortified worth a farthing, and he announced to the city fathers that the settlements from there to Manchac were now under the authority of Señor Galvez of New Orleans and His Majesty of Spain, and they could either say thank you or start a war—bring me a light, Angelique."

"Yes, Mr. Philip." Angelique went off chuckling.

Judith climbed up on the bed by him. "Go on, for heaven's sake. Is there going to be a war?"

"Of course not. They said yes, thank you, and now we're all in the Spanish province of Louisiana."

Judith sighed. "What was that you said about the church?"

"Locked up, my dear girl. You don't think there will be any Protestant services in a Spanish colony, do you? I wish I could have heard Sylvie Durham's remarks when Alan brought the news. Though after all, it's only fair—when the French ceded this country to England all the priests had to shut up shop." He laughed again as he accepted the lighted stick Angelique brought in. "Thanks. Bring us some Burgundy. We're going to drink the health of the king of Spain."

Judith was still too startled to be sure of her own regard for the king of Spain. "Philip," she ventured, "won't King George do something about this?"

"King George," said Philip, "has been trying for four years to do something about his other American colonies, with very indifferent success. Here's the Burgundy. Let's drink to the day we became Spanish, and the king." He picked up the flask. "October 5, 1779, and King—what do you suppose his name is?"

"Isn't it Philip?"

"No, that was the one who had a war with Queen Elizabeth. I believe it's Charles now, but I really don't know. Angelique, remind me to look up the name of my lawful sovereign."

"Miss Judith," said Angelique, "what is he talking about?"

"He's drunk," said Judith.

Judith wondered what were suitable occupations for Sunday when there was no church. It seemed hardly proper to go about on the Sabbath with the keys and pincushion hanging from her belt and household affairs continuing as usual. Eventually she solved the question by making Sunday the day for her important entertaining. Dining was no sin and it was convenient to have a whole day free for preparations. As far as Judith was concerned this was the only major alteration brought about by the transfer to Spanish rule. Most of the settlers were inclined to accept the union with Spanish Louisiana as a blessing, for Señor Galvez announced early that he had no thought of interfering with property titles or the orderly conduct of trade and since trade was now free of smuggling risks it became brisker. As a tactful gesture the governor sent Irish priests who spoke English into the English-speaking settlements, but he gave quiet orders that nobody was to be coerced into going to mass.

Early the next summer Gervaise came to Ardeith to suggest that Judith go with her on a visit to New Orleans. Now that the political division was obliterated travel was safer, and Gervaise's brother, who was bringing a cargo of blacks up to the Dalroy market soon, would take them back on his boat. Judith was delighted at the prospect. She was eager to see the metropolis of the valley. Philip stilled her tremors about leaving the children, saying Angelique could be trusted to take care of affairs at home.

Judith reflected that she did need a holiday. The summer was dragging heavily, wet and hot, and the dampness brought such a plague of mosquitoes that they had to keep the house in a circle of fire three weeks. The smoke crept in and blackened everything, for it was impossible to live in such heat with closed windows. The maturing indigo brought the annual pestilence of grasshoppers, and though Judith put out what looked like enough arsenic to kill an army, they thrived.

"Isn't there *any* way to kill grasshoppers so they'll stay dead?" she demanded despairingly of Angelique one blazing morning.

Angelique laughed tolerantly. "I reckon their families all come to the funeral, Miss Judith."

Judith pushed her damp hair off her forehead, wondering if it was necessary for the children to make so much noise playing on the gallery. There was a knock and Cicero, the door-boy, put in his head to say there was a woman outside asking for the mistress.

"I don't want to see anybody," said Judith tartly. "It's too hot to be civil. You talk to her, Angelique. If she's begging give her a couple of picayunes from that purse in my room."

Angelique went out, but a moment later she was back.

"Miss Judith, it's Miss Dolores."

"Oh my God." Judith sprang up. "Of course I'll see her. Bring her in."

So Dolores was here again; poor little Dolores to whom she had tried to be kind and had evidently failed—or else why should Dolores have run off last year with her gold-lined goblets and her silver pomade jar? Angelique opened the door and then stepped outside and closed it.

Dolores stood just over the threshold, her hands laced in front of her skirt. She had on a printed muslin dress that had been washed and washed till the flowers on it were vapory blurs. Her hat was old too, and the ribbon that tied it had faded lines where it had been crushed and ironed many times over. There were little beads of perspiration around her lips.

Judith went to her. "Come in, Dolores. Why didn't you tell the door-boy who you were, so you wouldn't have been kept waiting? We bought him after you left last year and he didn't know you."

Dolores smiled her familiar puckery little smile. "You really don't mind that I came, Judith?"

"Of course not. I've wondered so often how you were. Sit down."

Dolores took a chair. She sat a moment playing with the end of her kerchief, then she looked up and asked abruptly,

"Judith, how is my baby?"

"Roger is perfectly fine, Dolores," said Judith, feeling as guilty as if she herself had taken the baby away. "He's hardly been sick at all, except a little bit of trouble cutting his teeth. They take very good care of him."

"I reckon he's walking now?" asked Dolores breathlessly. "And maybe talking?"

"Oh yes, he toddles all around. And he can say a few funny little words."

"Like—father?"

Judith found she couldn't answer. She was suddenly choked up as if there was a wad of cotton in her throat. She put her arms around Dolores, and finally blurted with a break in her voice:

"Dear, I'm so sorry! And I can't do anything. Caleb thinks he's doing right by the baby and I can't help it. But I'm so sorry."

Dolores held to her tight. "You do mean to be good to me, don't you? Sometimes I don't like you but I reckon you always mean to be good. Judith, what do they give Roger to eat?"

"Milk and soft-boiled eggs, and rice-gruel, and things like that."

"Can he hold a spoon yet?"

"No, sometimes he tries, but he spills it."

"Who does he look like?"

Judith still stood holding Dolores' head on her breast. "Mostly like us, honey. He's got the gold Sheramy eyes and his hair is light brown like ours. But I think his nose is going to turn up the way yours does."

"He sure sounds beautiful," murmured Dolores.

Judith sat down, holding both Dolores' hands in hers. She told her everything she could think of about Roger, when he got his first tooth and spoke his first word, how they dressed him and everything she could remember that he had said or done. Dolores listened with her lips parted and her eyes wide. At last she suggested:

"You're right sure they don't ever be mean to him, Judith?"

"Mean to him? I should say not. His father tries to pet him to death."

"You see him a lot?"

"Oh yes. He's here often playing with David and Christopher."

"How big does Roger be now?"

"About so high." Judith measured from the floor.

Dolores dug her teeth into her lip, looking down. "I was think I could forget about him. But I miss him something awful. Every time I see a little boy I wish it was mine. I've got another baby," she added abruptly.

"You have another baby? I'm glad of that," said Judith, and she meant it, though she wondered that Dolores should be so frank about acknowledging it.

"Yes. A little girl. But she don't make it better about Roger, somehow." With the toe of her slipper Dolores followed a crack between the boards of the floor. "Do you think I am very bad because I have another baby?" she asked after a moment.

"Why of course not. It's easy to understand how you'd want one."

"But I didn't want her," said Dolores, laughing a little. She was making pleats in the ruffle around the end of her sleeve. "I didn't know if I should tell you or not, because you will tell Caleb—"

"I won't if you don't want me to."

"It don't matter. He think I am so bad anyway he can't think any worse. He is so damn pious. But I didn't have any place to go and I met a man who was nice to me, and I thought I would stay around awhile and maybe get a chance to go to New Orleans, but—" she laughed shortly. "I was get myself in trouble right off first thing and then I couldn't go any place because I couldn't look out for myself."

"Where is he now?" Judith asked gently.

"Oh, he's still taking care of me. He likes me and I like him too. He gets work pretty regular now there's so much more trade. His name is Thad Upjohn."

Judith thought a moment. "Caleb still wants to take care of you. He has told me two or three times to tell you so if I ever heard from you."

Dolores gave another short little laugh. "Funny, me living right in Dalroy and none of you ever knowing. But rich folks don't come down below the wharfs. I reckon I could live there a hundred years and never have you see me." Her mouth hardened. "You tell Caleb," she said, "I don't want nothing from him nor ever will. I'm all right."

"Very well," said Judith. She did not blame her. Dolores twisted the end of her hat-ribbon a moment without speaking, then she said:

"I don't reckon I'll be going to New Orleans. I'd have a hard time getting along there with a baby and all, and I don't expect Thad would let me go anyway. He makes a lot of fuss over my little girl. Judith, when I told him I was going to have a baby he said we should make a marriage and one of those Irish priests married us. Do you reckon that makes all right?"

"Why certainly," said Judith, though she knew she wasn't speaking the truth. That paper from the English court hadn't given either Dolores or Caleb the privilege of marrying anybody else. It took an Act of Parliament, or something like that, to dissolve a marriage. But maybe since they had been handed over to Spain the marriage laws were in the same sort of jumble as the others and at any rate she wasn't going to take away any scrap of consolation Dolores had managed to find. "It must have been all right," she added reassuringly, "if the priest said it was."

"I didn't tell him I'd been married before," said Dolores artlessly. "But my husband knows about it. He thinks it's all right." Dolores rested her elbows on her knees and leaned forward. "Judith, do you think Caleb would let me see Roger just for a few minutes some day? If I didn't say a single word? Just so I could see how he looks?"

Judith unconsciously doubled her fists. She stood up slowly. "Stay where you are," she said to Dolores as she crossed to the other side of the room and pulled the bellcord. "Angelique," she said tersely when the door opened, "tell Josh to saddle a horse for me and one for you. We're going to Silverwood."

Angelique glanced at Dolores as she closed the door. Dolores got up and came wonderingly to Judith. "What's that for?"

"Honey," said Judith, "I'm going to bring Roger over here so you can play with him awhile. You wait till I come back. I'll get him here if I have to break every bone in Caleb's body to do it."

Dolores put her hands up to her eyes as though ashamed that one of the Sheramys should see her crying. After a silence she looked up and said, "Judith, I'm sorry I took your things."

"It doesn't matter. You can have them."

"I sold them," said Dolores. "We had a hard time at first, and there was a Spanish trader bought them off me."

"I don't mind." Judith put her arm around Dolores' waist. She noticed how carelessly Dolores was corseted now, and remembered how she used to lace in her little figure. "Dolores," she said softly, "I don't blame you for not wanting anything from Caleb, but if you need anything won't you tell me?"

"I don't need anything," said Dolores.

Judith did not insist. She told Cicero to bring some wine and biscuits for Mrs. Upjohn while she was out.

Judith thought grimly she could never again bear a sight so bitter as Dolores' saying goodby to Roger after she had played with him an hour. Dolores could not bear it either. When she was leaving she thanked Judith, but she added in a broken voice, "I can't stand this another time. Just send a nigger down sometimes to tell me how he is."

Judith watched her go and went in to shed tears of pity on her children's heads. When Philip came in she told him she couldn't possibly leave them to go to New Orleans. He retorted that if she didn't get a taste of frivolity soon she'd worry herself into a bad spell of the vapors and what use would she be to her children then?

And New Orleans, once the wrench of parting was over, proved to be delightful. Gervaise's brother, Michel Durand, lived with his family in a house on the Rue Royale. It was built like a hollow square around a courtyard, with the main rooms in front and the slave-quarters behind. Judith found Creole life enchanting—riding in sedan-chairs to call on ladies who sipped coffee behind their lacy balconies and talked clothes and politics in slurry Louisiana French; buying slaves at the market, where the fashionable ladies and gentlemen came to drink coffee and gossip as though it were a club; and dancing at endless balls with young gentlemen who had been to Paris and knew the latest variations of the minuet. She visited the boats that brought merchandise from France and Spain, and got deliciously confused among bales of silk and embroidered shoes, snuffboxes, tobacco cases, flasks of perfume, cases of wine and boxes of glass and china, and fashion dolls proudly decked in the styles sponsored by Marie Antoinette.

Or maybe it was Creoles who made it all so pleasant. She had never seen people who had such gay, casual charm. The young gentlemen flattered her till sometimes she ran to her mirror and enumerated her defects to keep from losing her head entirely. They said her uncertain French was delectable, and they praised her tawny eyes and hair, which did make her stand out among them, for the Creoles were mostly dark. She had her portrait painted by a young artist named Armand Bardou, just back from a Parisian atelier and the rage of the season; he did her head and shoulders against a blue background and went into ecstasies over what he called her Mississippi-colored eyes. It cost her two hundred pounds of tobacco, but though her thrifty conscience pricked her as she wrote the order on the plantation she knew Philip would not mind. He had told her to be extravagant. Life on the plantation was still too primitive to offer much temptation for riotous spending.

They stayed over the New Year. January blew away the fogs that had pearled the streets and the town began to sparkle. Gervaise loved it; this was her home and she fairly worshiped every turn of the levee and every palm in the Place d'Armes, but Judith began to be homesick. She thought how Philip would be dashing over the fields these days, preparing the ground for tobacco and indigo; the oranges were in their full ripeness now, and the children would be making themselves sick sucking the fresh-cut cane. She was, after all, bred to land instead of paving-stones. And she missed Philip achingly. The gallantry of her Creole admirers began to seem pale beside her longing to see him again. She told Gervaise she was ready to go home.

Yes, Gervaise agreed reluctantly, it was time to leave. Going up the river would be easier now than if they waited for the flood of melting snow from the North. Michel was taking another slave cargo up to Dalroy in two or three weeks and they would go then. Judith wrote happily to Philip that she was coming home and sent the letter by the captain of a merchant vessel.

When she came the February glory was over the earth and the air was like velvet and champagne. Judith thought she had never known before how beautiful Ardeith Plantation was or how much she loved it. She told Philip that as he had drunk a toast to the day they were united with New Orleans, she felt like drinking a toast to the day she came home.

CHAPTER ELEVEN

A for Ardeith, and B for baby. He could write those two. "Very nice," said Judith. "Now I'll teach you to make the next one. C. Like this."

David pursed his mouth, gripped the pen in his chubby fingers and made a C and a blot. "Like that, mother?"

"Yes, only try and make it without a blot. There."

"C," said David. "C for what?"

Judith recalled the dame-school alphabet. "C for cherry."

"For what? What's *cherry*?"

"Oh my Lord," said Judith. "This abominable country. A cherry's a fruit, David."

David gave this his consideration. "Like an orange?"

"No, darling. It's little and red. But it doesn't grow here, so we won't bother about it. C is for cotton."

"Oh yes, cotton. C for cotton. What's next?"

"The next is D, which stands for David, but you mayn't try that till you've learned to make C. Now make me a page of A, B, C, very nice and clear."

David bent his sunshiny head over his lesson, working very hard with the tip of his tongue protruding between his lips. Judith's mind ran down the rest of the alphabet. Old Mrs. Cheesewright had taught it to her along with a dozen other little girls, swinging their legs over the edge of a bench too high for them in front of a fire that blistered their faces while the wind came in under the door and froze their backs. E for elbow, of course. David would understand that, and F for flower, and G for girl, though she decided with a wry acquiescence to the objects most familiar to David to tell him G stood for grasshopper. H for house, which was all right; I for ice—how ridiculous. For David it would have to be I for indigo.

She put an arm around him. His golden head touched her cheek. She put her lips to it softly.

"You'll make me blot it," said David.

"No I won't. You're doing it very well. When you've finished you may go out to play."

David worked so hard he was panting. "A for Ardeith," he mumbled. "B for baby. C for cotton."

His little body was so soft under her arm. Strange to know it was going to be hard and strong, and so much bigger than hers that he would be able to pick her up and carry her as readily as Philip had carried her the night she ran away from Lynhaven.

"Oh now look! You made me do it!" cried David. He

pointed to the blot that had jogged off his pen. "I told you to get away."

"I'm sorry, honey. I know it wasn't your fault." She squeezed him to her. "David, you're so little!"

"I'm not so little. I'm bigger than Chris and I come 'most as high as your belt. Oh stop, mother. I don't like being kissed."

He wriggled out of her arms and faced her defiantly, his legs spread far apart.

"Do I have to do any more lesson? I was nearabout to the bottom of the page."

"Yes, you may stop now. We'll learn the next letter tomorrow."

"Arright!" David banged the door behind him. Judith let the paper dry and took it into her room.

She caught sight of herself in the mirror. It was the same mirror Philip had brought to the cabin just before David was born. Judith smiled wryly as she recalled her tears when she had first glimpsed her figure, and wondered if she would feel like crying some more before long. She had been astonished into exasperation to find herself with child again. Christopher would be five years old in June, and after so long a respite she had assumed that heaven had relieved her of further child-bearing. Curling up on the bed, she gave herself up to angry contemplation of the lonesome months ahead when she would be a prisoner in the house, the dragging lassitude and the long fierce battle at the end. She had so much to do, anyway; it was April, time for the thousand tasks demanded by the approach of summer. Judith jerked the bellcord.

"Bring me some coffee," she said when Angelique came in.

Angelique went out quietly. She was oddly quiet these days and Judith wondered if she wasn't quite well, though Angelique had said nothing about it. If Angelique should be sick now that would be absolutely too much. Judith shrugged at her own blooming reflection in the mirror. This was what one got for being so disgustingly healthy, and for being in love with one's husband. She leaned back against the pillows and smiled to herself as she thought about Philip. She did love him so. When she came back from New Orleans after those months of separation she had tumbled into his arms as if she wanted never to be out of them again. She couldn't possibly help that, and neither could he; and she might as well get her mind made up to accept the consequences of being so dearly loved. Be reasonable, she ordered the resentful person in the glass. You aren't going to die. Only sometimes you'd rather. Oh, stop going on like this.

Angelique came in with a cup of coffee. "Is this all you wanted, Miss Judith?"

"Yes, thanks. Will you have the boys bring in a lot of tobacco leaves to dry? We'll be having moths soon and I want to get the blankets put away."

"All right." Angelique went out and closed the door.

Through the window Judith could see Philip. He had stopped his horse and was talking to one of the overseers who stood at his side. Philip was very busy now, setting a gang of Negroes to clearing another field and trying to get the stumps out in time to put in a crop. All his friends marveled at the speed with which he was putting the forest under cultivation, and at the uniform excellence of his harvests. He would be rich if he kept up like this, which meant she would be rich too, for everything he had was hers as well. Not every woman could write an order on her husband's crops whenever she chose without being questioned, and mighty few women were given so many house-slaves when workers in the fields were so sorely needed. Oh, she was fortunate and no mistake, and she ought to be down on her knees thanking the Lord instead of feeling injured. Judith laughed at herself remorsefully and went out on the gallery. Philip waved and she kissed her hand to him. After all, she thought as she watched him out of sight, what really mattered was not slaves and clothes and houses, but being loved; the rest was what the Creoles called lagniappe, something extra. She leaned her head against the post and resolved that this time she was going to behave herself and not whine about having a baby.

The page of David's letters lay on the bureau. Judith wrote in the lower right corner, "David Larne, April 22, 1781," and knelt to hide it in the box in the armoire where she and Philip kept a collection of secret treasures. The box held broken toys and scuffed shoes, a scrap of the silk gauze he had brought her the day he forgot the plaster and the topaz necklace he had dropped into her bosom the day she was washing pots by the river. She took that out sometimes to wear on special occasions. Judith tucked the grubby sheet of paper among the other things and lifted the topaz necklace. She would wear it to supper. It was about time she was getting dressed. She rang, but Angelique did not answer, so she went out to look for her.

Angelique was nowhere visible about the house, and one of the parlormaids said she had gone to her room some time ago. Judith hurried down the hall to Angelique's room. The girl must be ill. She opened the door, "Angelique?" she said.

Angelique was lying on the cot, half dressed. She started up as Judith came in.

"Why, I'm sorry, Miss Judith. I must have gone to sleep."

"But why are you lying down? Don't you feel well?"

"I'm all right." She got up. "I'll get my clothes on and dress you before Mr. Philip comes in."

Judith sat down on the cot. "I think you need a tonic. If you've got spring fever maybe you oughtn't to work for a day or two. Christine can dress me."

Angelique poured some water into her basin and began to wash her face. "I'm really all right, Miss Judith. I had to go out to the kitchen to iron that dress you wanted, and I got all hot and tired by the fire."

Judith rested her elbows on her knees and watched her. If Angelique was sick there was no reason why she shouldn't say so; she was usually well, but Judith had nursed her through one or two minor indispositions before this. Probably, she reflected ruefully, the fact that her own legs had been aching all day made her doubt that anybody could feel quite well. Suddenly she sat up and stared. Angelique had taken out a fresh petticoat and was about to pull it on over her head, standing in her chemise with her arms up.

"Angelique, are you with child?" Judith exclaimed in amazement. "Why on earth didn't you tell me?"

Angelique pulled down the petticoat and began tying the drawstring around her waist. She was looking down. "Well—I thought you might be annoyed with me. I wasn't going to tell you till I had to."

Judith put her chin on her hand and thought a moment. All servants palavered; there wasn't any sense in being shocked.

"I'm not angry, honey," she said. "I own I'm astonished, after your being such a rock of chastity all these years. Who is he?"

"It really doesn't matter," said Angelique, putting on her dress.

"Don't stand up there with that blank look and tell me you don't know!"

"I didn't say that," Angelique returned evenly. "I said I'd rather not tell."

"All right. You don't have to." Judith wondered if Angelique with her golden skin and satiny hair had let herself be seduced by a black boy and was about to bear a dark child she dreaded and was ashamed of. Angelique tied her tignon into a bow over her forehead.

"I'm ready to dress you, Miss Judith."

"Very well. Come into my room."

While she was having her hair combed Judith suggested,

"Angelique, would you like to get married?"

"No, ma'am."

"But you can, you know, if you're fond of him. I'll give you a wedding in the parlor, and a supper afterward for all the house-folk."

"It's very nice of you, Miss Judith, but you needn't bother. Shall I use that bergamot pomade?"

"Yes. But if you change your mind let me know, and I'll give you the wedding." As Angelique put the last pins into her hair Judith turned around. "I'm really glad you're having a baby, Angelique, because I think I'm with child again and you can be my baby's nurse."

"Very well, Miss Judith."

"Don't sound as if it were such a calamity, honey!" Judith patted her hand. "You'll love your baby after it's born. I always think I don't want mine and then the minute I see them it's like looking into heaven. Didn't you tell me you had one that died?"

"Yes ma'am."

"This one will make up for that. And if our children are the same sex I'll give yours to mine as personal servant, and it can grow up in the house. And by the way. Don't tell Mr. Philip I'm with child—I don't want him to know until he's done with the worry of getting a crop into that new piece of ground."

"All right, Miss Judith."

"Bring me a candle," said Judith, "and go to bed. You don't look well at all."

After Angelique had left her Judith stood playing with the combs and jars on the bureau. She wished she had known this before. Angelique had been overworked. And she was behaving queerly. Maybe she ought to be relieved of work altogether until after her delivery. When Philip was ready for supper she detained him in their room to ask what he thought.

"I'm worried about Angelique," she said to him.

Philip pulled down the ruffle at his wrist. "Tell the girls not to use so much starch in my linens, will you? What did you say?"

"I said I'm worried about Angelique."

Philip turned around. "Angelique? Why?"

"Well, after all these years she's got herself with child. She didn't say a word until I noticed it this afternoon and asked her. She looks perfectly awful and she won't tell me anything about it—she's behaving so curiously—"

"Angelique is with child? Are you sure?" Philip took a step forward, into the candlelight; the scar was like a white slash across his face and his eyes reflected the candle-flame in two points as he stared at her.

"Why yes. But what are you—"

He had turned on his heel and was gone out of the room, shutting the door so hard that the latch failed to catch and rattled noisily behind him. Judith got up slowly, catching the post of the bed, and for an instant it was as if the flame swelled until all she could see was the light and the halo around it and Philip's face with the scar, which had never seemed repulsive before. But he was not there; she could hear his footsteps in the hall, then they were gone too, and she put her fists to her temples and pressed as though by doing so she could stop the hammers beating on her head as she cried out:

"Oh Philip! *Philip!*"

She sat down slowly on the edge of the bed and her hands dropped into her lap. For a moment she stayed like that, watching the wavy shadows of the candlelight, and then even the strength to sit up went out of her and she found herself face down, quivering under waves and waves of pain. It brought an anguish that she could not surmount or even fight, the consciousness that what she had just found out was not something that had happened today but months ago, and now she too was with child by Philip because she had believed in him.

She wondered how long it had been going on. For months, certainly, maybe years, and her trust in them both had hidden it from her. Angelique dressed her twice a day and undressed her at night, and Philip would sit and watch while they all three chattered about the house and crops and children, and while she smiled at herself in the mirror their eyes would meet secretly over her head. She could see and feel and hear everything at once; Angelique combing curls on her neck—"Mr. Philip always likes you with roses in your hair, Miss Judith"—Philip's kisses on her shoulders and his arms around her in the dark.

Her forehead rested on the bend of her elbow. She moved her hand down and wrenched off the topaz necklace, breaking the chain, and threw it to the other side of the room. It fell on the floor with a little soft rattle. The flatboat and the dip of the poles in the river, and the sun flaming on the orange trees and she who had never owned a jewel in her life asking him, "Philip, did you come by this honestly?" He had not; nothing he had given her had been come by honestly; he had founded Ardeith Plantation with pirate loot, and now he had cheated her even of his love. He had left her this unborn child of his as permanent evidence that she had believed his lies, and the knowledge that it was alive within her brought a rush of nausea that left her limp and cold.

There was a knock on the door. She jerked up. The knock was repeated and she heard Christine's voice calling:

"Miss Judith! Supper's on table."

"I'm not coming to supper," said Judith. "Go away."

How strange her voice sounded. Clinky, like the sound of a key striking a brass candlestick. She wondered if Christine knew about this. Perhaps Angelique was not the only one. Angelique was the most attractive of them, but she was not the only pretty quadroon in the house. Oh yes, probably they all knew about it and had laughed at her innocence or had been sorry for her. They had talked of it in the kitchen and in the quarters, furtively. "Po' Miss Judith. Wonder if she'll ever find out how Mr. Philip's carryin' on."

"Shut yo' crazy black mouf. You know what you'll get for talkin' too big."

They wouldn't tell her. They were Philip's slaves and they knew too well what punishments there were for slaves who displeased their master. He could do this to her because the very sheltering he had given her made her helpless; she did not own a farthing nor a slave nor a pound of indigo. She bit the flesh of her arm to keep from screaming.

She had not bolted the door. The latch was lifted from outside and Philip came in. Judith raised up again, her hands on each side supporting her as she looked at him. Philip stood there a moment, then he came to the bed and put his hand on her shoulder.

"Judith," he said, "I'm so horribly ashamed and sorry."

She did not reply. She sat there looking at his handsome face with the laughter-crinkles about the eyes and the scar across his cheek, the white linen stock about his throat, the ruffles that went down into his yellow satin waistcoat, his long blue coat, the dark breeches buckled about his well-turned legs, and wondered that she had never known it was possible to hate any human being as much as she hated him. She hated his virile beauty and the strength in the hand that held her shoulder, the fine chiseling of his features, all the details she had loved so much and that made him as irresistible to other women as he had been to her.

"What do you want me to do, Judith?" he asked at length.

"I want you to take your hand off me," said Judith, "and let me alone."

He released her. Judith got up and walked to the bureau at the other side of the room. The candle had melted down to a shapeless mass. She pinched a drip of tallow as she asked him:

"Do you know what you've done to me, Philip?"

He said, "Yes."

"No you don't," she returned in a low voice, still watching the guttering candle. "You don't understand. You never will. It isn't in you."

She was surprised to hear herself speaking so evenly. Temper storms came readily to her when there was nothing of importance to be angry about. She went to the door and put her hand on the latch.

He came after her and took her by the shoulders with both hands, turning her around to face him. "You aren't going yet."

"Yes I am. I'm not going to stay and talk to you."

"But you are," said Philip.

She tried to free herself, but he held her where she was. "Very well," she said wearily. "You're stronger than I am. What is it?"

For a moment he did not answer. His mouth was shut so tight that it was like a line across his face. At last he said, "Judith, I know what you've been thinking of me. I'm not going to let you go till I've told you it's not true."

She gave an exasperated little sigh. "Don't try to tell me it's not your child Angelique is carrying."

"It is," said Philip. "I'm not trying to lie to you."

"It doesn't make any difference," she answered. "I couldn't believe anything you said anyway."

"You've got to believe me," he exclaimed. "You've got to understand that this never happened before and never will again. I'm surer of that now than I was the night I married you. I never could let women alone before. I've told you that. I thought I'd done with that sort of thing. Then you went to New Orleans. You were gone nearly four months."

He stopped. She was looking past him at the darkness beyond the window, where there was a magnolia tree with white flowers like great dim stars.

"Are you listening to me?" he demanded.

"No," said Judith. "I suppose men always think women are going to believe tales like that."

"It's true," said Philip.

She looked around the room where he and she had lived for so long. Nothing about it had changed since this afternoon, only everything looked bigger and darker in the faint light. She had loved it so, and had worked hard to make it attractive. The curtains she had hemmed herself, and she had crocheted the bedspread and only this morning she had arranged the roses on the bureau.

She said, "Philip, will you please let me get out of here?"

He let her go. She opened the door and walked down the passage without looking back. In the hall she saw Angelique, standing there as if she had been waiting. Angelique stepped away from the wall as she passed.

"Miss Judith," she began.

Judith caught her breath. "Go to your room," she said. "Stay there till you're sent for."

"All right," said Angelique quietly.

Judith went on down the hall and opened the door of the room where David and Christopher slept. In the dark she could just make out the outlines of their little figures in the big bed. David slept straight, on his side, with his hands out in front of him. Christopher was cuddled up in the shape of a question-mark. Judith shut the door softly behind her and began taking off her clothes. Letting her dress and stays and petticoats lie on the floor where they had fallen, she slipped into the bed in her chemise and drew the little boys into her arms. They were so soft and sweet. David's fluff of golden hair was like silk under her fingers. She thought how much she loved them, and wondered if they would grow up to hurt her as their father had done.

She shut her eyes, but she could not go to sleep; she turned away from the children and buried her face in the pillow. Her numbness began to pass, leaving her with a flaming sense of fury. She felt a wild desire to make Philip and Angelique suffer as they had made her suffer. Angelique—she had been so good to Angelique to be used like this! Judith began to think of all the things she could have done to Angelique, ordering that she receive twenty lashes for burning her hair with the curling-irons—some women did. She wanted to do it now. How she would love to see Angelique's beautiful slim body tied to the post, quivering under an overseer's whip!

Only now she couldn't do it. Philip would not let her. Philip who had gone to sleep last night with both his arms around her—he would protect Angelique from her, because Angelique was his mistress.

She wished she could shed tears. Her eyes were hot as if she had a fever.

Day was breaking when she finally went to sleep. But the children woke noisily at sunrise. They were surprised to find her with them, and thought there should be some sort of celebration, a pillow-fight or a game, and David got one of the petticoats off the floor and tried to dress up in it, marching up and down in his bare feet with the flounces trailing behind him. Mammy was astonished too, or pretended to be. Judith told her to have Christine bring coffee to her here.

She was aching with sleeplessness, but the children were

too rackety to let her try to sleep again, so she told Christine to bring her fresh clothes and hot water. Christine obeyed timidly, as if frightened. She said Mr. Philip had ridden early into the fields. As she did not see Angelique about the house, Judith supposed she was still in her room. She tried to give David his lesson without much success, for he was restless and she herself too unhappy to care whether he learned his letters or not. He went out to play and Judith told Christine to move her things from the master bedroom into the room where Dolores had stayed. She stood in the window, looking out at the gardens and the fields beyond and the dark border of the forest, with a feeling of empty deadness. Christine brought her dinner on a tray, but she sent back nearly all of it. Most of the day she spent walking from one wall to the other, too tormented to sit still and too tired to do anything. The house was hushed, as if somebody had just died in it. Nobody came near her. From the windows she could see the children playing, and the servants wandering about, talking in undertones. Toward evening she saw Philip riding up and Josh leading away the horse. She put her hands over her eyes, but she only shivered and did not cry. She had not even tears to give him. At last she called Christine and let herself be undressed and put to bed. It was late when she remembered that she had not even gone in to say good night to the children.

When she woke up the sun had risen. There was no bell in this room and she had to go to the door and call Christine to bring her coffee. She did not put on her clothes, for there was nothing she wanted to do. Instead she pulled a dressing-gown around her and began walking again. What a hideous room it was, with its smooth pink walls and stiff walnut-stained bed. Square, like a prison cell, and there was a grasshopper on the floor staring at her. She must remind the girls to put arsenic in the cans under the legs of the beds before the summer influx of ants. The men must bring in some moss, too, for restuffing the mattresses; this one was getting lumpy. Oh, but what for? She didn't care what happened to the house. Somewhere in another room of this house was Angelique, and Philip's child within her—at least she did not have to endure seeing Philip's face on a half-breed child. Angelique could be sold down the river, or up the river, or any place on the face of the earth if only it was out of sight, and her child sold with her before it was born. Anywhere, if only her enticing golden beauty was away from Ardeith, and her slave-child who would look like David.

Judith shuddered, thinking she could have stood anything if only she were not carrying this other child.

The door opened and Philip came in. Judith started.

Philip came over and leaned against the bedpost.

"Judith," he said, "I can't go on like this. I let you alone yesterday."

"Yes," said Judith. She added ironically, "Thank you."

"But you can't keep this up. Staying shut in here."

"Why not?"

She was angry to see how well he looked. Already he was getting his summer tan.

"The household is dazed," he exclaimed. "The servants are

wandering about in a mist, the children aren't half cared for, nobody knows whether there are to be any meals—"

"Oh, can't you stop for five minutes being so damnably physical?" she cried. "You've sent me to hell and all it means to you is that you don't get a good dinner. Maybe I should be grateful to have some slight value to you as a housekeeper!"

Philip regarded her levelly. "Judith, will you in the name of God stop this? I made up my mind yesterday that I was going to leave you alone to work it out. I can't. You see, I love you, whether you know it or not."

"Nice that you told me," said Judith. "I don't know it."

"I never knew it so well," said Philip.

Judith said nothing. She stood playing with the loose sleeve of her dressing-gown.

"Judith," he said at length, "won't you believe me? I've told you what happened between Angelique and me. If you haven't got sense enough to understand it there's nothing else I can tell you. A boatman brought me the letter from you saying you were coming home. I took it to Angelique and let her read it. She couldn't finish for the tears running out of her eyes. I told her I was sorry and that it was over. She broke down then, telling me how she loved you and how overwhelmed she was with her feeling of disloyalty. I said she was not to tell you anything. This was going to be as if it had not happened. She didn't tell me she was with child."

"So I came home," said Judith, "and you told me you loved me better than anything else on earth. That no woman in the world mattered two pins to you but me."

"I meant it."

"And you think nothing else matters. You think when I take myself out of the house you can make love to any pretty woman who happens to be around and I shouldn't care. If you discard her as soon as I'm available I shouldn't mind you discarding me as soon as I'm out of reach. You make me feel like an animal. Oh Philip, is that all it means to you?"

Philip doubled his hands into fists at his sides. "No," he said. "No. Judith, can't you understand?"

"Can't *you* understand?" she cried.

There was a silence. Finally Philip asked, "Is there anything you want me to do?"

"Get Angelique out of the house."

"She's not in the house."

"Where is she?"

"I told her to move to the quarters."

"That's not what I mean! Get her away from Ardeith. Sell her down the river as soon as a trader comes by. Take her to the market tomorrow. Get her *away*!"

Philip stared at her. There was astonishment and incredulity in his expression.

"Judith! Do you know what you're asking?"

"Of course I know. I'm asking that she be put where I won't ever see her again."

"I won't do it," said Philip.

"Oh, you won't?" She almost screamed. She had thought he would acquiesce instantly. This was too much. It was beyond what any woman could bear. "You won't sell her down the river?"

"No," said Philip.

"Are you telling me you're going to keep her? In case I take another trip to New Orleans?"

Philip took a step nearer. "Judith, do you know what those slave-boats are like? You're asking me to murder her."

"I'm not. Plenty of women go down on the slave-boats. I'm asking you to get rid of her. It's so easy for you to say you don't want her again!"

"I don't want her again." Philip folded his arms and stood where he was. "But I'm not going to put her on a slave-boat. You've seen them go by. You know what they are. A woman in her condition—chains on her ankles—"

"Didn't she have chains on her ankles when the boat brought her to Dalroy? She's a nigger, Philip, though I suppose you've forgotten it."

"She's a sensitive decently-bred woman," he retorted, "though I suppose you've forgotten that. She's with child. Judith," he begged her, "you're generous. You've got sympathy and tenderness. I'll do anything in the world for you if it's within reason. But I won't send Angelique down the river."

Judith was breathless with anger. "If slave-boats are no paradise neither is what I've been going through. Get that woman away from here."

"I won't. I'm not a barbarian. A girl like Angelique chained to the wall every night, at the mercy of every African savage on board and every filthy boatman, bearing her child in a slave-camp somewhere in the marshes around New Orleans—why don't you ask me to cut her throat and be done with it?"

Judith twisted her hands together. She sat down and held them still laced tight to her aching forehead.

"Then what are you going to do with her?"

"I'll keep her here till next year. When she's well again she can go down with somebody we know who's making the trip to New Orleans, with instructions that she's not to be sold at all unless as a lady's servant in a respectable house. But I'm not going to sell her now."

"I can't have that child born at Ardeith," said Judith desperately. "I can't stand it, Philip."

"I'm sorry, Judith," he said, gently but inexorably.

"Then go to the Spanish council and get permission to set her free."

"And turn her into a trollop on the docks? There's nothing else for a free quadroon. I certainly won't."

She sprang up. "All right. Keep her here. Tell me I ought to show Christian meekness and put cold presses on her forehead because she doesn't feel quite well. Keep her here indefinitely because you can't find a boat luxurious enough for her to ride in. Keep her as your mistress." Judith took a step backward. "I hope," she added deliberately, "that you have a perfectly wonderful time and that she bears you a child every year and that they're much prettier and cleverer than my children, but it's a shame they'll be niggers and can't get into good society with mine."

Philip walked over to her and slapped her face. He went to the door. As he lifted the latch he said over his shoulder:

"I knew I was going to hit you some day if you didn't learn to keep a decent tongue in your head. I'm glad I've done it."

Judith stood perfectly still. The door shut behind him. She put up her hand to her stinging cheek. She felt it vaguely, as if it belonged to somebody else, for her whole body was tingling with rage that was shaking and blinding her. She dropped down on her knees by a chair and began to sob. They were long deep sobs that trembled through her and left her at last exhausted but unrelieved, aware of nothing but a wordless hate against everything in the world.

After awhile she got to her feet. Her mouth was dry and her tongue felt too big for it. Her head ached violently. All her mind seemed concentrated under the pain in a sharp point of resolution. She dressed and went out of the house, walking fast through the gardens and into the indigo, toward the field-quarters.

She did not often go alone into the fields. The Negroes turned with curiosity as she approached. An overseer took off his hat and nodded.

"Good morning, ma'am. Can we do something for you?"

"No, thank you," said Judith. "I'm only walking down to the quarters."

"Yes ma'am. Hey, you black nigger, can't you keep a straight row? Quit gaping at the missis!"

Judith glanced at the Negroes, naked but for loin-cloths or pantaloons, their sweaty bodies gleaming in the sun. The light ones were Iboes and the black ones Congoes. In a cabin down at the far end of the quarters there was an old Congo woman who knew voudou. She was too old to work, but so wise was she with charms and medicines that even the proud house-Negroes went to consult her for their ailments. Judith turned away from the indigo and stumbled over the rough ground toward the quarters. The old woman who knew so much might know even a way out of her present desperation. She felt soiled and insulted, and she ran toward the cabin of the Congo woman ready to plead on her knees for escape.

CHAPTER TWELVE

Philip did not go in to see her that night, for he was too indignant to want to talk to her again. In the morning he rode out early, glad to be away from the house. But the sun was hot, and in the afternoon he came in again.

Nobody was in front to take his horse. He dismounted and flung the reins over the low branch of a live-oak, annoyed at the inefficiency that became evident as soon as Judith took herself out of the establishment. But when he crossed the front threshold he sensed that something was wrong. The girls were hurrying about in a confused hush, and as he went down the passage he saw Christine running into Judith's room. As she opened the door mammy came out and went quickly down the hall to the back, where David and Christopher were quarreling. She rushed them outdoors with orders to be quiet and not trouble their mother. Philip had started for Judith's room in alarm when he saw Angelique coming down the passage toward him. She should not have been here. He had told her to stay out of the house where Judith might see her.

Angelique came to him quickly and stopped him.

"Oh!" she exclaimed breathlessly, "I'm glad you came in. Maybe you should go to her."

"What's the trouble?" Philip demanded in fright. "Is she ill, Angelique?"

Angelique nodded. She put the back of her hand to her eyes. "I'm afraid she's going to die."

Philip gripped her arms. "Die? Who? Judith? Get out of way, Angelique! Let me in."

"No. Wait a minute till I tell you." She held him back from the door. "That vile old Congo woman. You know the one— you bought her because you were buying all her children—she makes charms for those fools back in the fields—Miss Judith should have known better!" Angelique's voice broke in her throat. She stood with his hands still gripping her, and her fine features distorted with grief. "You didn't know she was going to have a baby. She got some voudou mess from that woman and tried to get rid of it."

For days Philip wandered about the house, helpless and tormented. He gave orders that any slave on the plantation who went to the house of the Congo woman for anything whatever was to be given thirty lashes, but except for this angry gesture he could do nothing but watch Judith and send supplications for her recovery to a deity in whom he had never had much belief. By now he dreaded the sight of Angelique almost as Judith had, though he still could not yield to Judith's tortured pleas that he ship her down the river.

However, he did not think much about Angelique or anything else except whether Judith was going to get well. He did not care if her child came to birth or not, and was neither glad nor sorry when they told him she had not succeeded in putting it out of the way.

Their friends came by in a stream, the women bringing armfuls of roses and calla lilies and well-meant delicacies Judith could not eat. They had heard she was very ill; was there anything they could do? Philip thanked them shortly and said no. He let Gervaise stay awhile, for Judith seemed glad to see her. Gervaise took charge of the house with quiet competence, and gossiped pleasantly of affairs on the bluff, which she always knew before anybody else. She said nothing to indicate that she knew the cause of Judith's illness, and though he found it impossible to believe that she did not he welcomed her tact.

But Judith, who seemed to be blessed with a constitution that could stand almost any amount of abuse, recovered and Gervaise went home. Judith took over her housekeeping again and set the servants to rolling the woolens with tobacco leaves and putting up mosquito bars, but she showed no inclination to move from the room she had been occupying. At first he did not ask her to, for she talked to him as little as possible and eyed him with a smouldering resentment that showed she had not forgiven him. One morning he came into the dining-room where she was giving elaborate instructions to two of the house-girls about starching the curtains. When the girls had gone he said to her:

"You needn't do so much, Judith. It's not necessary, and I don't want you to get sick again."

She sat down by the table where her account-books were. "I'd like to get everything done before it gets to be really deep summer. I'm stronger now than I'll be later on."

He pulled out a chair and sat down opposite her. "Do you feel well?"

"Oh, as well as I've any right to feel. I suppose I'm lucky to be alive." She ruffled the corners of the pages before her. "If you're afraid I'm going to try again not to have this child," she added, "you needn't be. I won't be such a fool twice."

"I wasn't thinking of that." Philip propped his chin on his hands and looked squarely across at her. She did not meet his eyes. "But I'd like to talk to you."

"About what?"

"About how much longer you intend treating me as if I were a not very welcome stranger lodging at Ardeith."

Judith dipped her pen into the ink. "How soon are you going to send that woman down the river?" she asked.

"Are you still thinking of that?" he exclaimed. "I told you I wasn't going to send her down."

"You still mean it?"

"Yes."

She flung her pen on the table, making a blot that ran down

the grain of the wood. "If that child of Angelique's is born at Ardeith I swear I'll never speak to you even as much as this."

"I'll do anything you ask of me but that," Philip returned vehemently. "But I won't put her on a slave-boat now. That's final."

Judith held her head between her fists. Philip set his teeth. It was hard not to yield to her. He had tried to make up his mind to do it. He wanted so desperately to prove to Judith that nothing would be too much for him to do to have her back. But he knew the slave-camps better than she did, and in spite of all he had tried to tell her he could not believe she realized what she was asking. He waited.

Judith did not look up. She sat holding her head as if it ached beyond bearing.

"Philip, don't do this to me!" she exclaimed at last with a sob in her voice. "That child will be nearly white. It will look like you."

She dropped her head on her arms. Philip saw tears staining the frill below her elbow. He stood up.

"Oh, stop talking, can't you?" he said curtly, wondering if she could be enduring much more than he was.

Judith picked up the pen and wrote several words on the page before her. Suddenly she threw the pen down again and pushed back her chair. She went over to the window and looked out. Philip was still standing by the table.

"I'd rather lose every acre of the plantation than see you suffer like this, Judith," he said to her then. "But in fairness to both of us, you're making it too vital."

"You think so?" she asked wonderingly.

"Yes I do. You're breaking up your life, my life, the children's lives, everything we have, because of a passing incident. It wasn't fundamentally important until you made it so."

"No?" Judith fumbled with the latch of the shutter. It rattled loudly in the quiet room. After awhile she went on, her face half turned away from him.

"You still don't know what you did to me. I'm not sure I can make you know. You've been a lie to me all these months since I came home. Oh, I've lived over every minute of it, every time you kissed me, every night I've gone to sleep in your arms with that sense of peace I'll never have again, believing there was nothing else in the world so splendid as what you and I had between us—when all the time I was trusting something that wasn't there. And if that wasn't true, what else is there in the world I can believe in?" She turned around and faced him. "I've built my life on it. And now I've found it was just a vapor in my own imagination. Because I trusted you I let you give me another child. I'm walking around with a living, moving lie inside of me. I tried to kill it because I hated it. I couldn't kill it but I still hate it, and when this child is born I'm still going to hate it because every time I look at it I'll know it's part of the lies you told me."

She stopped.

Philip asked, "Are you quite done?"

"Yes," said Judith.

Philip turned around and went out.

He did not come back for dinner. Judith waited awhile for

him, then ate with the children. She gave David his lesson—
he had reached the letter T now, which stood for Tobacco,
and he could print the whole word. When he had finished she
took her knitting and went to sit by the parlor window where
she could watch David and Christopher playing outside. She
ached with unhappiness. For awhile a spiritual exhaustion
had come over her and she had gone about the house doing
what needed to be done because it was easier to follow an
established routine than to change it, but hardly thinking at
all except to be aware that the glory had gone out of her life.
But trying to find words that would make Philip understand
what had happened had roused her again to the acute pain of
the first days she had known it. She made herself knit. Keeping busy at least prevented her from walking up and down,
striking her fists on each other and wondering why she had
forsaken the stolid virtue of her father's house for *the* undisciplined charm of this.

She could hear the voices of the children and the hum of
insects drowsing in the sun. It was so quiet that when she
heard someone come in by the door behind her she started,
and sprang up in indignant surprise when she saw it was
Angelique.

Angelique shut the door behind her.

"I'd like to talk to you a few minutes, Miss Judith," she said.

Judith had sat down again. Her knitting lay in her lap.

"I'd rather not, Angelique," she answered wearily.

"No, ma'am, I know you wouldn't, but there's something I
want to say." Angelique spoke with calm determination. How

243

heavy she had grown in the past weeks. Judith tried not to look at her.

"Go back to the quarters," she said.

Angelique stood in front of her, her hands linked.

"I will in just a few minutes, Miss Judith. But first I'm going to tell you something, and you can't punish me for not minding because there's nothing you can do to me worse than sending me away on a slave-boat, and I'm to go down the river tomorrow."

"You're going down the river?" Judith repeated in incredulous relief. So he had understood at last.

Angelique went on speaking in a simple, relentless monotone. "Miss Judith, I never meant this to happen. I didn't want it to happen at first. But you know how Mr. Philip is—it's so hard to tell him no to anything—"

Judith wanted to scream. How well she knew it.

"But I wanted to tell you too, Miss Judith, that I was the only one. That's really true. We used to talk about it, the girls here at Ardeith, how the master never paid any mind to anybody but Miss Judith, and it was surprising to some of us because we'd waited on other married people before. I don't mean, just that, but everything about you—we all said we'd never seen a pair that got along together like you and Mr. Philip."

Judith had put her arm along the back of the chair and buried her face in it. Every word she heard was like a reminder of a homeland from which she was an exile. She frantically wished Angelique would stop, but her throat was too choked for her to say so.

"If you've ever had that you know what it is. Colored folks have it too sometimes. I had a husband once. His name was Claude. When they broke up the estate we were sold apart. I think he's on M. Farron's plantation across the river. I don't suppose I'll ever see him again, but I always thought about myself as married to him still. When our baby died he was so good to me. I know you aren't interested in my troubles, but I wanted to tell you because I know how it is when you've got somebody that means that much to you and something breaks it up, and I wanted to ask you please don't let anything break up you and Mr. Philip."

Judith could not lift her head nor force words past the pain in her throat. She heard Angelique go out and close the door, but she stayed with her face hidden against the back of the chair, trembling still before Angelique's assurance.

At length she got up, letting her knitting fall on the floor. She went out of the house and walked down through the indigo fields, past the quarters, and skirted the rice fields toward the levee. She wanted to be alone where she could think, away from the distractions of the house and children. The afternoon sun beat on her as she climbed the levee and looked down at the shining river. Was it true, what Angelique had tried to say, that she could get back what she had lost simply by being willing to take it?

She turned and looked back at the wide, wild kingdom of indigo pressing on the forest. That was Ardeith Plantation, Ardeith of her children and her children's children. Philip had built the plantation. That was what he would leave them. But she would leave them something more, purity of inheritance. Their pride in their line would be based on their faith in her integrity. Civilization had to be a matriarchy.

Two or three flatboats passed under the levee, going down the river toward the docks. Every day they came down, great ugly argosies that had made their dangerous way from Illinois or Pennsylvania, to unload on the wharfs bales of stuff and new settlers as the Dalroy bluff wrenched itself out of the wilderness.

One of them was a slave-boat. She could see the Negroes sunning themselves on deck. Each one had rings on his ankles and chains between. Several Negroes were poling the boat, and a white overseer walked around among them. He carried a whip. Now and then he struck it idly against the wall of the cabin.

Judith sprang to her feet, catching up her skirts so she could run down the levee. She went as fast as she could past the indigo vats and through the fields where the slaves were walking toward the quarters after their day's work. The dark tumbled abruptly out of the sky as she went. She could see lights in the windows of her house.

Philip sat on the gallery steps, pulling up blades of grass with his hands. As she approached he glanced up and looked down again without pausing in his restless pulling at the grass. She noticed he had not changed his garments since coming in from the fields.

"There's a slave-boat docking tonight," he said. "I gave orders for Angelique to be put on it tomorrow."

She had paused by the step. He added, "Are you satisfied?"

Judith put the fingers of one hand tight around the wrist of the other. This was going to be hard to say. She spoke tensely.

"Please forgive me for that, Philip. I mean for saying she had to go. She doesn't have to. No, please don't stop me. I don't want you to give her to a trader. I want something else. I want you to send to M. Farron's plantation—it's somewhere across the river, you can find out where—and buy a man named Claude who used to belong to M. Peyraux in New Orleans. I don't care what he costs. Buy him and bring him here. He's Angelique's husband. Give them a cabin beyond the far indigo fields. Tell her she's got to stay there and not come to the big house. I can't stand having them here. But buy that man as soon as you can find him and give him to Angelique."

She stopped breathlessly. Philip had stood up. He was looking down at her in amazement, trying to see through the dark what there was in her face that matched the rush of her voice.

"My dear girl." He gave a soft little laugh of relief. "Are you trying to tell me you're done tormenting Angelique?"

"Yes. Yes. Will you buy that man, Philip?"

"Of course, if you want me to." He put out his hands and drew her to him. "Don't you know I'd do anything to stop this hell I've been living through?"

She did not answer. They stood by the steps, Philip holding her hands in his. The dark was heavy with scents of magnolias and night-blooming jasmine. She could vaguely see the long draperies of moss hanging from the oaks, and the sparkle of fireflies. As he drew her into his arms she began to understand that to Philip the passing of this crisis meant it was forgotten. But she was wiser now and the dazzle would never again be complete. She let him think it was; she was very tired, though she had not realized how tired she was until she glimpsed the road on which she had just started and saw that it was going to be hard to travel.

PART TWO

CHAPTER THIRTEEN

What a happy lot was his, after all, thought Philip Larne as he leaned back in his carriage. His nineteen years in Louisiana had been bountiful. The forest had gone down before him in magnificent submission. There was no house on the bluff more luxuriously furnished than his, nor any woman more richly dressed than Judith, and his sons were the first in Dalroy to learn fencing from a French master. Not many families even in this prosperous town by the river could witness the inauguration of the new governor in such opulence of velvet and muslins as theirs, or make the journey in a carriage so nobly cushioned against the jolting of the road.

It had been a picturesque ceremony under an array of flags, though half the spectators did not understand enough Spanish to know what was being said. Judith had attempted at first to have her children taught what she referred to as all three of their native languages, but she had given up, owning that it was hard enough to learn good English in a place like this. They had picked up Creole French, and David had sufficient Spanish to read the regulations posted on the church doors. Of what went on inside the churches they knew very little. Religion had become such a confusion of languages and forms that they found it easier to let it alone. Judith had tried to make them pious. She taught them to pray "Jesus, make me gentle, meek and mild like thee," which they dutifully recited and as dutifully forgot, knowing as well as she did that these were not the virtues required for subduing the raw majesty of Louisiana.

Philip smiled at Judith, who sat on the seat opposite devastatingly pretty in a hat with nodding pink plumes, and a muslin gown still crisp in spite of the August heat.

"You're very charming in that outfit," he said to her.

"Thanks. Gervaise says we won't be dressing like this much longer."

"Why not?"

"Well, since they declared a republic in France they're changing everything, even the clothes. Her sister sent her a sketch of a dress that just came in from Paris, and it's amazing—not fluffed out at the sides at all, but long and straight. Greek, she says."

Philip reflected that Judith might look rather well in a Greek dress. She was thirty-four and had four children, but her figure was still as straight as when he saw her first. They had three sons and a daughter, and what gallant children they

were, Philip thought proudly. The two older boys and Roger
Sheramy were riding horseback alongside the carriage. Philip
looked out at them. David was eighteen, a young reflection
of himself, Judith always said, though Philip found it hard
to believe he had ever been so beautiful a youth. David was
golden-headed and blue-eyed, with a round chin and a nose
that might have belonged to an emperor on a Roman coin, and
so tall his mother had to stand on tiptoe to kiss him.

Christopher rode by him, a dark, quiet, austere lad who
reminded Philip of Mark Sheramy. He sometimes thought
it odd that Judith, so unlike her father, should have given so
many of his qualities to her son. Christopher was laconic of
speech and undemonstrative of manner. He said he did not
want to be a planter, though Philip had found it hard to believe
him. Most of the lads on the bluff would have given their eye-
teeth for a share of a plantation like Ardeith.

The third son sat by Judith on the opposite seat, watching
the Dalroy estates as the carriage drove past. He was eleven
years old, and his name was Philip.

Sometimes Philip fancied he loved his namesake best of
all his children; watching the rosy-cheeked youngster across
from him he shivered to remember how near little Philip had
come to being not born at all. He remembered his secret fear
lest this child come into the world with some deformity of
mind or body given him by his mother's reckless agony. But
the baby had appeared yelling with health, and Judith had
named him for his father. Philip was glad of that. He would
not have suggested it just then, but he did want a son named

for himself, and that Judith had wanted it for this one had a tender significance.

Little Philip, blond as David and valiantly pretty in a sky-blue suit with a white lace collar crocheted by his mother, bounced on the seat as he called something to his big brother David, for whom he manifested an adoring worship. David grinned, snapped his riding-crop in the air, and called back:

"Tomorrow I'm going fishing with Roger."

"Will you bring me some new fish for the pond?" Philip demanded.

"Yes, if you'll clean up the weeds around the edge. That pond's a disgrace to the plantation."

"I will. Honest. This very day."

"Phil," said Judith, "don't you think you can possibly sit still until we get home?"

"Yes ma'am, but will you tell the niggers not to bother the fish in my pond?"

"Yes, dear, I'll tell them. Now be quiet."

"I'm hungry," said young Philip. "What's going to be for dinner?"

"There's fig-cake with whipped cream," said Judith, "but you don't get it unless you eat all your rice first."

Philip grinned across at his son. Little Philip grinned back, still restless, though he had subsided obediently.

"Do I get some fig-cake?" demanded Rita, who was six years old; too young to attend the inauguration, Judith said, but Philip thought she would enjoy the parade.

"Yes," said Philip, "if you're good." He put her on his

knee. She was a piquant little girl, with a lot of dark hair in curls down her back.

"And may I come to table with the company?" Rita persisted.

"Yes," said Philip. Judith made a face at him. There was to be a dinner-party at home in honor of the inauguration holiday. Rita was too little to come to table, or so Judith thought, but Philip had been so delighted when she turned out to be a girl that he proceeded from her birth upwards to spoil her. Beginning, Judith said, by giving her a Spanish name that would look heathenish on a parish register, but Philip had retorted that since their children were growing up heathens anyway it was a perfectly suitable name.

Judith said, "Very well then, Rita in the name of the Father, Son and Holy Ghost, and if she grows up to marry a Spanish don from New Orleans don't blame me."

Philip said that would be quite satisfactory. Rita was dowried well enough to marry anybody who struck her fancy. Ninety acres of indigo land, seven slaves and a sum of money for the education of her children—not many young ladies could bring so much to their husbands.

Lord, but it was hot. The horses ridden by the boys kicked up scarcely any dust because of the dampness of the ground. It had rained early in the morning and the earth was still steaming. Rita slapped a mosquito that had lit on her ankle as the carriage jiggled and a boy sprang up from outside, catching hold of the window-opening next to Judith.

"Hey, lady, want to buy some bananas?"

"Oh my Lord!" Judith exclaimed. "Get off, will you? You're going to get your neck broken."

"No ma'am, I ain't. I can hold on good. Want some bananas or some nice fresh figs?"

Rita and little Philip stared as the carriage rattled over the road and the boy clung like a fly, holding with both hands while his basket of fruit dangled from his elbow. He was a dirty little boy in a torn shirt. The coachman riding on top had not seen him and had not slowed the carriage.

Philip was reaching for a coin. "Here. You'd better stop doing this if you want to live to grow up."

"Yes sir," shouted the boy, thrusting two bananas at Philip's hand. "Right off the boat—"

The carriage went over a bump and with a scream he vanished from the side. Judith sprang forward.

"Stop the carriage! We've killed him!"

The children were scrambling to the side to see. Philip leaned out and shouted the order to the coachman. He sprang down, and an instant later the footman lowered the carriage-step so Judith could follow. Philip was indignant; it was nobody's fault, of course—there was no teaching sense to the wild children of the docks—but his carriage had never hurt one of them before. Judith told the children to stay inside while she hurried out to where the boy had fallen in the road.

He was sitting up, holding his knee, from which a trickle of blood ran down over his bare foot and dripped into the ground. His basket had overturned and the figs and bananas were scattered about. Judith bent over him.

"Let me see your knee. Does it hurt much?"

"Not so bad," said the child, though his face was twisting with his effort not to cry. He was a sturdy youngster of about ten. The boys on horseback had come up.

"Need anything?" David asked as he reined his horse.

"Your handkerchief," said Philip, "and yours too," he added to Roger and Christopher. "If we can stop the blood we'll put him into the carriage and ride him home. He shouldn't try to walk."

He began binding up the gash in the boy's leg, giving him another handkerchief to hold to a cut in his face. "I'm sorry I fell off, Mr. Larne," the boy apologized.

"I'm sorry you got hurt. Stay off this leg a few days and you'll be all right. How did you know my name?"

The child winced and grinned. "Oh, I reckon mighty near everybody knows you. You've boughten bananas from me before."

"Have I?" Philip asked smiling. The boy looked up with wondering envy at the three lads on horseback. "You's Roger Sheramy, ain't you?" he asked suddenly, pointing his finger.

Roger Sheramy grinned and nodded. He was about fourteen, and good-looking in his russet coat and high riding-boots. Roger's hair and eyes were tawny like Judith's, but he showed his Spanish blood by the blackness of his eyebrows, which almost met over his nose like his mother's, and his low-bridged nose like hers.

"Yeah," said the young stranger. "I know you too."

David offered to put the injured boy on his horse and get him home that way, but Philip thought riding in the carriage would be easier for him. He lifted Rita to David's horse so the boy could have her place in the carriage, and let them go on to Ardeith. "Where do you live?" he asked when he had helped the boy to a seat.

"Below the wharfs. Rattletrap Square."

Philip gave the order to the coachman. He wished he had sent Judith home. Rattletrap Square was no place for the visiting of a lady.

The boy stared a moment at little Philip's well-cut blue suit, and ran his fingers over the cushioned seat with inquisitive eagerness. "Say," he said suddenly, "you know why I jumped up on your carriage?"

"No, why?" Philip asked.

"Because I'm related to you, kind of. I'm Gideon Upjohn. I wanted to see Miss Judith. My ma talks about her sometimes." His finger pointed to the seat opposite. "Are you her?"

"Yes," said Judith. She leaned forward and put her hand on his uninjured knee. "Gideon, how is your mother?"

"She's arright," said Gideon. He fidgeted. "But she's gonta be plenty mad to see me coming home in y'all's carriage. She told me not to pester you."

"What makes you related to me?" demanded young Philip, who had been staring at Gideon with as much curiosity as Gideon had vouchsafed him.

"We used to know his mother a long time ago," Judith explained. She asked Gideon about his family. At intervals she sent a servant down to give Dolores news of Roger, but the servant always came back to report that Mrs. Upjohn, though she lived poorly, insisted that she needed nothing. Neither Philip nor Judith had seen her in years.

"Ma's arright," Gideon said. "Pa, he's arright too. He works on the Purcell wharfs."

"You have some brothers and sisters, haven't you?" Judith asked.

"Yes'm."

"How are they?"

"Well, Mamie Sue, that's my sister that's older 'n me, she took sick couple of days back."

"What's the trouble?"

"I dunno."

He was nearly as reticent as Dolores had been, though he eyed them with a certain satisfaction, as though proud to have finally gained some attention from the great folk of whom his mother had told him. Philip suspected that he had tumbled off the carriage on purpose. Dolores' stubborn pride, which would have made her hide herself completely from them except for her hunger to hear of Roger, was hardly comprehensible to a boy Gideon's age. Philip remembered his look at Roger Sheramy a little while back.

He caught the seat to keep himself from being jolted off it. The carriage was making a difficult passage along the lanes of the lower town. In the section above the wharfs, where stood the residences of the well-to-do, the roads were cobbled with wooden paving-blocks or stones brought down the river, but down here they were mere puddled spaces dividing the rows of shanties on either side.

Little Philip demanded, "Say, what's all that I smell?"

Judith reached over his head and pulled down the satin curtain that had been drawn back from the window. She had put her handkerchief over her nose. Her face was distorted with horror.

The shanties were so close together it was hard to imagine fresh air blowing between them, except where a house leaned to one side and widened the space between itself and its neighbor. Pigs and chickens wandered around the doors, rooting in piles of garbage nearly black with flies. Barefooted women sat in the doorways smoking pipes, and naked children lay in the mud puddles, splashing water over their bodies to lessen the heat. They stared as the carriage went by. The coachman yelled from his perch, ordering them out of the way of the horses.

"Gideon," Judith gasped at length, "have you lived down here all your life?"

"Sure," said Gideon.

Philip reflected that Gideon probably saw less of his surroundings than they did. He himself was only slightly acquainted with these streets, and he was astonished to observe how congested they were. This, then, was what became of them, those thousands of men and women who poured into Louisiana empty-handed and without the superlative energy needed to wrench fortunes out of the country. He had never given them much thought before.

"Here 'tis," said Gideon. "Third alley from the corner."

Philip called to the coachman and glanced from Gideon to little Philip on the seat facing him. They were about the same age, but Gideon had a precocious self-possession. Little Philip, sheltered and served all his life, was a child such as Gideon had not been for years—not since he had been shoved upon the wharfs to make his own way in the world. The carriage stopped. A group of children, some of them half dressed and the younger ones wearing no clothes at all, stood in the mud and blinked at the unfamiliar sight.

"I'm going in," said Judith. She told the footman to get into the carriage and stay with young Philip, ignoring his protests at being left behind. Two or three dirty children were scrambling over the carriage wheels to finger the design painted on the door. The coachman yelled at them.

"Get off'n dis carriage!" he ordered. "Po' white trash."

Gideon, limping and leaning on the support of Philip's arm, led them down a narrow alley strewn with dead cats and scraps of decaying food. Judith followed, holding up her skirts.

Gideon opened a door. "I reckon my ma's home," he said, "if you all want to see her."

They followed him inside. In spite of the brilliance of the sun without, the room was dim. They heard a woman's voice exclaim, "Gideon, what makes you tied up like that?"

It was a big room, but sickeningly hot and close. At one side was a fireplace where something was cooking in a pot slung over the flames. There were three mattresses on the floor, one of them draped with a mosquito bar hung over wooden supports. Against the wall was a rough pine table, and some stools and packing-boxes stood about. Clothes hung on pegs driven into the walls. There were two windows and the shutters were open, but the house next door blocked off the sun. As his eyes got used to the bad light Philip saw a little girl playing in the corner with a doll made out of a corn-cob, and a woman standing near the pallet. The sick girl was faintly visible under the mosquito bar. Though he had not seen her in so long he reluctantly recognized the standing woman as Dolores.

Dolores let Gideon sit down on the goods-box from which she had risen and came slowly toward her visitors. She was not corseted at all, and her dress was shapeless and of indeterminate color. Her black hair, lined with gray, was pushed out of the way into a straggly knot. Her throat was stringy, and the veins stood out on her hands.

"Hello," she said. "What do you want?"

Philip told her how Gideon had fallen off the carriage and they had brought him home. While he talked his eyes kept going from Dolores to Judith. This morning at the inauguration he had been proud of Judith's elegance, but in this place she looked unreal, like a vision. Her flowered bodice fitted closely about her trim well-laced figure; her hat was white, with four pink plumes and white ribbons tied at one side of her chin; there were black silk lace mitts on her hands, and her petticoat was short enough to show the silver buckles on her shoes.

"Thanks for bringing him home," said Dolores. "I've told him not to jump on moving carriages, but it's hard work selling, and besides—" she shrugged apologetically—"he always likes to get a look near up at folks from Ardeith and Silverwood."

Judith went to her. "May I talk to you a minute, Dolores?"

Dolores hesitated, then walked off with Judith toward a

window. Gideon sat where he was, nursing his hurts. The little girl with the doll stared at them.

Judith was talking to Dolores in a low voice. Philip could not hear what she said, but at length Dolores exclaimed, "No, Judith. No." She moved back, her hands together on her breast. "I don't want for nothing. Thad makes a living on the docks. And as for you," she added sharply to Gideon, "if you go pestering these folks any more I'll set you to loading boats like your pa."

"Yeah," said Gideon. He blurted out, "I just wanted to see how the lady looked."

Philip told her he wanted to pay for the basket of fruit Gideon had lost. She took that, though she hesitated until he assured her that it was the coachman's fault Gideon had fallen. He said it earnestly, though he still believed the child had tumbled down on purpose. These little wharf-rats were too agile to fall off carriages.

The girl on the pallet made a noise in her throat and groaned. "Poor child," murmured Judith. She went to kneel by the pallet and lifted the mosquito bar.

There was an inarticulate retching sound from the pallet.

Philip sprang forward and glanced at the child. He struck the pillow out of Judith's hands and snatched her to her feet.

"Get out of here, Judith!" he cried.

"What is it?" she exclaimed in fright, looking back over her shoulder at the moaning child. "Oh my God—it can't be—"

"Yes it is, said Philip. "Yellow fever." He was dragging her toward the door.

She broke from him and ran. Philip gripped Dolores' arm. "How long has she had it?"

"Two or three days. I reckon you'd better go."

"Is there much fever in this part of town?"

"Quite a lot, all of a sudden."

Judith exclaimed over her shoulder that she would send some necessities, which Dolores must accept for the sake of her child. They rushed out and scrambled into the carriage. Judith ordered little Philip not to touch her.

As the carriage drew up at the steps of Ardeith she gave him decisive instructions.

"Take off every stitch of clothes you've got on and have mammy burn them in the kitchen fire. And take a bath."

"Not my new blue suit!" little Philip protested. "Father, do I have to burn up my new suit?"

"Yes, son, and your shoes too. Hurry, and don't let any of the others come near you till you've put on fresh clothes." They were hurrying indoors.

But after they had scrubbed and sent their garments to be burned, he and Judith began to be ashamed of their fright.

"We were in there only a few minutes," Philip argued. "And there's always some yellow fever in the summer."

Judith had never before been close to a case of yellow fever. She asked Philip what it was like.

"You'll know it if you see it," Philip said with a little shiver. "Bloodshot eyes and flaming red lips and nostrils, and that awful black vomit. But you don't get the fever just by being in the house with it."

Judith felt reassured. She made up a parcel of linens and foodstuffs, and sent them to Rattletrap Square by one of the fieldhands.

Though her parlor was full of guests who had come indoors to escape the mosquitoes plaguing the gallery, Judith lingered in her room, making marks on the heat-softened candle with the end of her comb. Philip came to ask her why she did not come into the parlor.

"I'll be there," she said slowly. "I was thinking."

He told her not to worry any more about Dolores. "You do all you can for her," he said. "It's not your fault she won't take more."

"I'm not worrying about her. I mean not just about Dolores. I was wondering—" she hesitated.

"About what?"

"Philip, did you notice that all the people we saw down in that beastly district this morning were white?"

Philip leaned his elbows on the bureau and looked out of the window. "It's a pretty shameful confession to have to make, isn't it?—but slaves are too valuable to be allowed to live that way."

"I didn't know there was anything so awful in the world," said Judith. "It's not just Dolores—it's all of them. What did they ever do to deserve that?"

"What does anybody do to deserve anything?" asked Philip dryly.

CHAPTER FOURTEEN

But her own life was so full and rich, Judith told herself proudly as she looked down her dinner-table. In spite of the storms that had raged around and within her Ardeith had reached a triumph of serenity, and she herself had created it.

The long windows were open to the floor so that what air there was might cross the room. The pickaninny at the side of the table pulled the fan of turkey feathers with lazy rhythm, while the servants moved about with plates of rice, roasted poultry stuffed with corn-meal and pecans, hot breads and vegetables cooked with spices, figs and peaches and oranges preserved in syrup, lettuces dressed with olive oil, and flasks of imported wine. They talked merrily, for the diners were all good friends—the Purcells with four of their five children, for the oldest girl was married and Gervaise, who was now thirty-six, had been a grandmother four years; the St. Clairs, with two of their crop of blooming daughters; Alan and Sylvie Durham with the two oldest of their children, and Caleb Sheramy with his son. Mark had died four years ago of a swamp-fever, and freed of his dislike for fashionable furbelows, Silverwood was blooming with porcelains and velvets that Roger Sheramy might have as elegant a background as any young gentleman on the bluff. Judith wondered if she should tell Caleb about her visit to Dolores, and decided not to. He had nothing to offer her except material support; that he was willing to give, but Dolores would not take it, and Judith had a grudging respect for her desire to be left in peace.

They sat at table three hours. No wonder they had the habit, which had struck her as so odd at first, for referring to any time after the midday meal as "evening." By the time a dinner of any importance was over it generally was evening. When they left the table the servants brought out the horses of those who had to go furthest. David asked for his.

"May I speak to you a minute, David?" she asked as he went out.

"Why yes," he said, and she followed him to the room across the hall. David waited for her. "What is it, mother?"

She laughed softly, not because there was anything to laugh at but because her pride in him welled up so that she could not help it. "Where are you going?"

He chuckled. "Where do you think?"

"Courting?"

"Don't I look like it?" asked David. He had a gardenia in his coat, and wore his riding-gloves with the embroidered cuffs. Judith tried to believe that all her children had an equal place in her affections, but there were times when she could not help knowing that she loved David best. He was so like Philip that everything she had learned to understand in Philip she could recognize in David without effort, and his place in her heart was already prepared before he grew up. "What did you want to see me about?" he asked.

She put her hands on his shoulders. "May I kiss you, David?"

He laughed and put his arms around her, bending his face down to hers, and kissed her hard. "There."

"Thanks." She was laughing too. "I knew you'd be furious if I started making a fuss over you before the company. Now you may go."

Still laughing at her silliness, David picked up his riding-crop and went out to his horse. Idiot, she thought lovingly. Thinking enough of any girl to ride off to see her in such killing weather. It was after five o'clock, but the heat had not abated. How splendid he looked, riding down the avenue under the oaks. Too impulsive and too volatile, his father said of him sometimes, too fond of girls and fine raiment and too blithely impervious to advice from his elders, but Judith found such faults more lovable than the calm virtues of her second son.

As he rode out of sight she went back into the house and said goodby to her remaining guests. When they had gone she went out to the kitchen to order a simple supper of wine and fruit and biscuits; they could eat no more than that after such a dinner as they had had already. Little Philip was in the back yard clearing up the weeds around his fish-pond. He had started it when David brought some exotic colored fish from the marsh country near the Gulf. Judith came out of the kitchen and sat on the back step to watch him working at the weeds, helped by several little colored boys. Philip was bossing with regal authority.

"Now look ahere. Be careful not to drop anything in the water. And don't you be bothering my fish. Just clean up the edges, and if you work good I'll show y'all the fish my brother David's going to bring me."

"Yassah, Massa Philip."

The little darkies pulled up weeds and slapped mosquitoes busily, following orders with lazy good-humor. Judith noticed with some disapproval that one of them was dressed in the coarse ozenbrig garments of the fields instead of the nankeen and calico worn by the house-boys. She must tell little Philip not to bring boys in from the fields.

The boy in ozenbrig stopped with a handful of weeds and got down on his knees to watch the antics of a bright-colored fish in the water. He reached in with his free hand and poked at it. Judith was about to call and send him back to his proper work when little Philip shouted at him angrily.

"Hey, you! Quit messing around with my fish!"

"Wait a minute, young massa," the boy exclaimed absently. He pushed at the fish with fascinated interest.

Philip rushed up to him. "You'll poke in my pond!" He dealt

a blow with his fist that sent the colored boy tumbling down on the grass. The other children stopped and stared. "Get on back to work," Philip ordered them. "And you, Benny, keep your hands out of my pond."

The boy who had received the blow got up slowly. His hands were doubled at his sides. He took two or three short furious breaths.

"Go on and clean up the weeds," Philip commanded.

The boy leaned down slowly to gather up the handful he had dropped when he fell. Judith got to her feet.

"Phil!" she called.

She had to call twice before he glanced over his shoulder to say "Ma'am?"

"Come here, Phil."

"Wait a minute. Get those little weeds just now coming up. They'll be a yard high pretty soon."

"Come here, Phil," Judith repeated.

He obeyed unwillingly. "What did you want?" he asked as he reached the steps.

She put her hands on his shoulders. "Phil, how many times have I told you not to strike the Negroes?"

Philip looked down. "Well ma'am, I *told* Benny to keep out of the pond! He'll be killing my fish."

"That's got nothing to do with it, Phil. I'm ashamed to think a son of mine would strike a boy who can't fight back."

Philip puckered his mouth crossly.

Judith went on. "If you haven't learned the proper way to treat servants, Phil, you've no right to have them wait on you.

I'm going to send the boys back to the quarters, and you may go to your room and stay there till I tell you to come out."

"Oh mother, don't make me do that! I'll tell Benny I'm sorry. But David won't give me any more fish if I don't clean up the pond. He said so!"

"You may finish pulling up the weeds in the morning, but don't ask any of the boys to help you. Now go indoors."

"Oh lawsy." Philip kicked at a tuft of grass.

"Go in, Phil."

He obeyed, dragging his feet as he went across the gallery. Judith crossed the back lawn to the pond and told the colored children to go back to the quarters. The boy Philip had struck was leaning sullenly against a tree, breaking up a palmetto leaf. As the others ran off she turned to him.

"Is your name Benny?"

He glanced up and made an instinctive little bow to her. "Yassum, missis."

His face was twisted with helpless anger. Judith laid her hand on his arm.

"It was wrong of you to meddle with the fish when Master Philip told you not to, Benny, but I'm sorry he you. He won't do it again."

Benny looked down, still breaking up the dead palmetto fronds. "No'm."

"What are you doing up at the big house anyway?" Judith asked. "Don't you belong in the fields?"

"Yes'm. I was pickin' seeds outen the cotton when young massa come by and said for one of us niggers to come help him do some work up at the big house." He was answering with a stiff resentment. Judith felt a rush of pity for his hurt pride. How brutal children could be!

Benny looked up at her after a moment, lifting a face like pale bronze, with fine-cut, almost aquiline features and large dark eyes with curling lashes. The late sun glinted on the satiny waves of his hair. Judith gripped his arms with a suddenness that was almost fierce. She did not know if it was a single feature of his or the general expression of them all, or something in the cool arrogance of his attitude that had set her heart to pounding. She had resolved bitterly that she was not going to try to find this child. There were dozens of colored children on the plantation, most of whom she hardly ever saw, and he was lost among them. She did not even know if Philip had made any effort to recognize him.

He waited for her to speak with a quiet deference that had no suggestion of servility. She tried to keep herself from speaking. Might it not be better to let him go while she was still unsure?

But she could not help it. "Who—who is your mother, Benny?" she asked tensely at last.

For an instant he did not reply. She saw that her gentleness had turned his anger at little Philip into shame, and he was blinking back tears that he could not bear to let the mistress see. He tried to speak.

"Her name's Angeli—" But the effort of forcing out his voice was too much for him, and he broke from her grasp and wheeled around, covering his eyes with his arm and sobbing against the trunk of the tree.

In her sudden wave of resentment that he should be alive and concrete before her she hardly knew he was crying. She simply saw him, with unthinking detestation. But then, he tried to swallow his tears and when he could not stop them he tried to explain them, and she heard the words struggle out between his sobs.

"I'm—so—sick—of bein'—a nigger!"

With an impulsive movement Judith drew him away from the tree and took him into her arms. He sobbed on her breast. She stood holding him, weak with compassion, for his wrong was so much greater than hers.

After a moment he tried to break out of her arms and leave her, in shame at his tears and his confession, but she kept him back.

"Come sit on the steps with me."

They walked to the gallery edge, her arm around him. The sun was nearly gone. Benny twisted his bare toes through the grass.

"I reckon I went 'n' acted like a baby, Miss Judith," he ventured. "Please ma'am don't tell anybody."

"I won't." They were silent, and she put her arm around him again. After awhile she added, with more effort than it had ever before cost her to say anything, "I'm sorry I can't make you white, Benny."

Her tenderness broke down his reserves. "I'm nearabout white," he blurted. "I'm whiter'n my mammy or my pappy."

"Who is your pappy?" she asked in a low voice.

"Claude. He's one of the indigo men. Only he ain't my sure

enough pappy. They says my sure enough pappy was a man who was really white."

Judith doubled her free hand into a fist in her lap. "They don't tell you who he was?"

"Well ma'am," said Benny with the blunt disregard of childhood, "some says he was the master. I dunno."

"What does your mother tell you?"

"She say it ain't gonta do me no good to know 'causin' some bright-skin niggers is got sold before now for sayin' they was the master's, and my pappy he gimme a frailin' when I say I'm too white to be his'n." Benny sat with his head down and hands dangling between his knees. "But I'm a nigger and I'm too white to be a nigger. It gives me a misery in the heart."

"Yes," said Judith faintly, "I know it does."

Again they were silent. Benny, abashed at having talked so much to a white lady, kicked at the grass, evidently wishing she would give him leave to go back to the quarters. Judith looked away from him toward the darkening sky. There was a great crimson fan over the river where the sun had dropped. Such a beautiful, cruel sky it was, holding in this heat that was still torpid in spite of the twilight. Judith bit hard on her lip, battling again to conquer a resurgence of the fury Benny had done nothing to merit. After awhile, recalling the pity and forgiveness Benny's mother had taught her, she forced it down. She drew his head to her shoulder.

"Benny," she said in a voice so low he could not have heard her if her lips had not been close to his ear, "I want to tell you something before you go back."

"Ma'am?"

"About your misery in the heart. I know what you mean."

"Yassum. Er—I reckon you don't though, Miss Judith."

"Yes I do. Nearly everybody has a misery, Benny."

"You reckon?" He sounded unbelieving.

She held his head on her breast and stroked his silky hair. "Yes, Benny. White folks too."

That was hard for him to comprehend and he said nothing. She went on.

"You'll just have to get used to having a misery in the heart, Benny, because nobody can take it away. You're mighty lucky to find out when you're a boy what it's like because now all the rest of your life you'll understand other folks when they have one."

Benny waited some time before he spoke. She wondered if he knew what she was trying to say. Like all children and a good many adults, he probably thought that since she was immune to his own trouble she was immune to all the rest. At length he asked thoughtfully:

"Is you got a misery in the heart, Miss Judith?"

"Yes."

"What do you do about it, missis?"

"I don't do anything about it. I can't. I just keep it in my heart, the way you'll have to keep yours."

"Huh," said Benny. He lifted his head and looked at her, then back at the big house, that temple of the blessed where radiant white folks lived in unimaginably gorgeous autocracy. He asked incredulously,

"What makes your misery, missis?"

"When it's a really bad one," she said, "you don't like to talk about it."

"Yassum," said Benny. With a sad triumph he added, "Anybody can see what my misery is, though."

Judith took an uneven breath. "They don't have to see how much you mind it."

"Mhm." Benny fingered the muslin of her skirt, examining the clusters of little flowers printed there.

It was nearly dark. Soon the servants would be bringing supper dishes from the kitchen-house.

"You'd better go home now, Benny," Judith said. "Your mother will be wondering where you are. Don't come up to the big house again."

"Yassum." Benny got up. He stood scratching his ankle with the toe of the other foot.

"How is your mother?" Judith asked him in a faint voice that took more strength than a scream.

"She's doin' pretty good."

"She has some other children too?"

"Yassum."

"Tell your mother I asked about her."

"Yassum."

"Good night, Benny."

"Good night, missis."

Judith watched him scamper off toward the fields. She put her arm around the gallery post and laid her forehead on it. In retrospect what she had tried to tell him sounded hollow. As if anybody could get used to a misery in the heart merely by making up his mind to do so. She knew, more strongly than she had known in all these years, that she was not used to hers, and she hoped she would never have to see Benny nor hear of him again.

A Negro man came around the corner of the house. He took off his hat and holding it in both hands he put his one foot behind the other and bowed. "Missis?"

"Yes?" She had started to go in and turned back to him.

"Dat white lady you tole me to take dem sheets and things to—"

"What did she say?"

"She say she ain't got no use for 'em. Her li'l gal's done died."

"Oh," said Judith. How the fever galloped through the bodies of children.

"But I left de things just de same, missis. I thought maybe as how she could find a use for 'em, wrappin' up de li'l gal to be buried and all."

"That's right," said Judith. She went indoors. The passage was dark but from the front rooms she could see the glow of candles.

Little Philip was calling her. The sound startled her into action. Poor child—she had forgotten sending him to his room and now it was dark and he would be wondering if he was to stay there all night supperless and unforgiven. Hurrying into the dining-room she got a candle from the table and went to his door.

"Here I am, Phil. You may come out now."

She opened the door, but the room was big and her candle did not give enough light for her to see him at first. She exclaimed, "Phil, baby, where are you?"

There was a sound from the bed. He was a big boy to be crying because he had been punished. Judith set down the candle and pushed back the mosquito bar. "Phil, if you're sulking I'm ashamed of you!"

He was lying across the bed, his face half hidden in the pillow. Bad boy, he hadn't taken off his shoes and the counterpane was muddy. As she leaned over him he half raised up and made another inarticulate noise in his throat. With a little cry Judith caught him in her arms.

Little Philip's eyes were full of blood. His lips and nostrils were almost purple. He writhed into her arms, clinging to her as if she could protect him, and she felt his face blazing with fever. He murmured thickly, "I kept trying to call you. I reckon you didn't hear me."

Judith felt her heart thumping. She laid his head back on the pillow.

"No, dearest, I didn't hear you. Now lie down like a good boy and I'll take off your clothes. How long since you began feeling sick?"

Whatever it was he said, she did not understand it. She got his clothes off and a bedgown on him, and drew up the sheets, trying to control the spasms of panic that shook her hands. It couldn't be what she thought it was. These things couldn't happen to people who were clean and careful and took pains with their children. When she had covered him she laid her hand on his forehead, thinking that even in this heat her fingers must be cool against such fever as his. At the door she spoke to a servant bringing in a tray of supper dishes, surprised at how level a voice could be above the fear she was feeling.

"Find Mr. Philip and tell him to come here as soon as he can."

Philip came in a moment later. "What's happened, Judith?"

She gestured toward the bed. Philip raised the mosquito bar, saying, "What's the trouble, boy? Eat too much?"

The last word caught in his throat. He sat on the bed and lifted little Philip in his arms. The child's body gave a jerk that ran from his shoulders down to his feet. His father said, "Oh my God."

Little Philip raised his head. He groaned. There was a rumbling noise deep down in his body. He screamed again, and jerked, and there came from his mouth a black discharge that ran over the pillow and sheets in a thick stream. He retched again and vomited again, and sank back in a stupor of exhaustion.

His father stood up. For a moment he did not move. He simply stood there by the bed, and his eyes met Judith's. She felt her face twisting. Little Philip made another retching noise, but nothing came up, and he gave a sharp scream of pain. His father put his hands over his eyes and shuddered. Then he lifted his head and said to Judith:

"Let's get the bed clean. Have them burn up the sheets."

She got fresh linens out of the armoire, moving mechanically without saying anything. Afterwards she remembered Philip's gesture of helpless horror, and thought that was what had first made her understand how awful yellow fever was.

At six o'clock in the morning David came out of the main passage to where his father stood on the gallery.

"I got mother to go to her room," said David. "She—she looks about to collapse, father."

"I'll go to her," Philip said. He had walked out of little Philip's room a quarter of an hour before, because he simply could not bear any longer to see a child of his suffer like that. "David, I won't get down to the fields today. Will you take a look around?"

"Yes sir. Is there anything else I can do?"

"Tell the servants nobody is to leave the plantation for any purpose unless I give the order. And tell them in the kitchen not to serve any food except what's grown on the place. Find mammy before you go out and tell her to keep Rita in the nursery or on the side gallery, and not let her come near your mother or any of the rest of us who've been into Phil's room."

"All right, sir," said David. His voice was low, as though his first sight of the plague had scared him out of his customary self-confidence and he was glad to be told something definite to do. He went inside, and Philip hurried in to Judith. She had been working over little Philip all night, tending him with a rigid calmness and only once or twice hiding her face with a gasp when his screams were too agonized for her to endure.

He opened the door of their room. Judith had thrown herself across the bed and was sobbing into the pillow. Philip sat by her. He took off her shoes and loosened her dress.

"Won't you try to go to sleep, Judith? Christine is taking care of him."

"I can't." She clung to him, shuddering, and hid her face on his breast. "Oh Philip, if he has to die, why must it be so horrible?"

"Dearest, he doesn't have to die!" Philip tried to speak reassuringly and not let her guess how frightened he was. "It's not always fatal. At least half the people who have yellow fever live through it!"

Judith shook her head. "But he won't." She spoke with despairing conviction. "Philip, don't you remember what I did to him?"

"Please, Judith!"

But she could not be comforted. "I killed him in my soul. God waited eleven years so I could see what I was doing. I've thought of it all night."

From further down the hall they could hear faint, tired little cries. Philip shivered and Judith put her hands over her ears. Then she struggled up. "Let me go back to him."

He tried to keep her where she was. She did look, as David had said, on the verge of collapse, and the servants had promised to call if there was any need for her in the sickroom. But she insisted.

"I can hold him up in my arms when the spasms come. Servants are no good—they aren't his mother."

He had to let her go back. Toward afternoon little Philip

fell into a troubled sleep, and Judith went to sleep too, lying on a mattress on the floor. David called his father outside.

There were three cases of fever in the quarters, he said. He had had the Negroes moved to the plantation infirmary and had forbidden the others to go near them. Philip sent Christopher to Silverwood to ask Caleb if Rita could stay there to escape taking the fever by contact.

Christopher returned to say there had been an explosion of plague all along the bluff. Two of the house-servants at Silverwood had been stricken that morning. He had ridden from there to Lynhaven to ask Gervaise if she could keep Rita safe, only to find that Walter Purcell had come in from the wharfs with the dizzying headache and bloodshot eyes that marked the onset of the fever.

It rained that night, and the next day the air was thick and wet. Puddles stood about the soaked ground. Four Negroes collapsed in the indigo fields at noon. Philip hardly heard the report when David brought it to him, for David had come in from the fields with his face flushed nearly crimson. Philip involuntarily grasped his wrist to see if the pulse was faster. David reassured him.

"I'm not sick, father. It's this ghastly wet heat—did you ever see such weather?"

"Never. Have you heard how Walter Purcell is?"

"Worse, I understand. And Mrs. Durham fainted in her garden this morning."

Philip shook his head. David sat down, letting his riding-crop fall on the floor.

"Father, the fields are demoralized. The Negroes are scared to work and scared to stay indoors. Nobody's getting anything done." He seemed to be pleading for courage. But Philip could only say, wearily:

"I don't wonder. It doesn't matter,"

After awhile David went out, as though any sort of movement was a relief from the tension of sitting still. Philip was about to call Judith from little Philip's room and make her rest when she came in of her own accord. She dropped down by the table and held her head on her hands, saying:

"Philip, I can't stand watching him."

He put his arm around her and drew her head back to rest against him. "How is he now?"

"He—he was delirious all night, but now he's quiet—horribly quiet. And he's yellow and splotched and hideous—last week he was so round and rosy! Why don't we take it with him?"

"I don't know," said Philip. "I wonder too."

They said nothing else. There was nothing to say.

David and Christopher came in together. They shut the door softly behind them and stood just in front of it, looking at their parents and then at each other as if each were wishing the other would speak first. Judith stood up slowly and her hands sought Philip's as if she already knew what they had come to tell her.

David said, "He—he's dead, mother."

Philip put his arms around her, but she did not scream or sob. She only said, "Yes, I knew he was going to die."

She was almost rigid in his arms. He motioned David and Christopher to leave them, for he knew a shock first made Judith numb and then brought a fierce reaction. The boys went out. Judith put her hands up to her temples. "Oh please, God, I didn't know what I was doing!"

She went limp against him, a flood of sobs tearing through her. Philip held her, feeling as helpless as a slave tied to the whipping-post.

CHAPTER FIFTEEN

Three days after little Philip died a servant brought a letter from Caleb Sheramy, saying the fever had struck Roger. Too distracted to look for a fresh sheet of paper, Judith wrote across the bottom of the page, "I shall remember you in my prayers," and sent it back.

The next day they heard Walter Purcell was dead. Philip sent David to Lynhaven with a note of sympathy for Gervaise.

When David had delivered the letter he rode to the wharfs to countermand the order for boats that had been engaged to ship the Ardeith produce down the river. The indigo was rotting on the ground for lack of harvesters. Judith had pled with David and Christopher to take Rita and go to a safe place while *they* were still well, but David's questions to boatmen on the docks convinced him there was no safe place. The men said

New Orleans was a charnel-house; the west bank of the river was reeking with pestilence and so were the towns above Baton Rouge. One was as safe here as anywhere else. Everything possible was being done to drive the fever out. On the corners pine and pitch torches burned day and night to destroy the poison in the air, and every ten minutes guns were fired over the river to shake the atmosphere. The taverns near the wharfs were gay and noisy, as though men were trying to drown the rattle of the coffin-laden carts on the road. One of the wagons moved along in front of David, the body-collector walking at the head of the mule. He rapped on the door of each house as he passed.

"Any dead here to be carried off?"

If the answer was yes he dragged the body out and dumped it into a coffin already holding two or three others, shoved down the lid and went on. A little Negro boy sat on a coffin to hold the reins.

David managed to pass the wagon and turned his horse into a better part of town, where well-to-do families lived in houses of cypress or moss-plaster. These people had slaves to make coffins for their dead, and they could order hearses to carry them away, but even these had to wait their turn and the coffins were piled on the galleries, sometimes three or four at a single house. Here and there was a note on a gate, asking that any clergyman who passed would come in and say a prayer with someone who was dying.

David shuddered and felt sick. Smoke from the pitch torches got into his eyes and made them burn. The gardens around the houses were flowering with ironic splendor. David loved growing things, but this mad blooming struck him today as repulsive, almost obscene, as though the plants were laughing at weather that was killing the men and women who tended them. There were a few cases of yellow fever every summer, and he had heard old people speak of a "fever year," but David had never imagined anything like this. He remembered the hopeless sound of his mother's sobs when she cried all night after little Philip died, and wondered if every one of these houses held as much grief as that.

As he slowed his horse again to let a boy cross the street in front of him, a woman ran up from behind and caught the bridle. David stopped with an impatient exclamation.

The woman stood at the head of the horse, panting, "Don't you be David Larne?"

She wore a faded dress from which one sleeve was tearing at the shoulder, and a hat tied with a soiled pink ribbon. It had fallen off her head as she ran after him and hung now on her shoulders, letting him see her streaky black hair. Her eyes were beautiful, soft as black velvet, but her skin had withered and her little dished-in nose had grown rather flat.

"Why yes," he said, "I'm David Larne. What did you want with me?"

"I reckon you've forgot me, ain't you?" she asked him. She was catching her breath. Her dress was open at the throat for coolness, and there were lines of perspiration down her neck. "I'm Dolores."

"Dolores?" David frowned, then his face cleared with astonishment. "My Aunt Dolores?"

"You remember?" she asked with a faint one-sided smile that made a crease down her cheek.

"Of course I do." David smiled back at her, trying to hide his surprise at her present appearance. He got off his horse and stood holding the bridle. "I remember you very well," he added. "You used to play with Chris and me and teach us voudou songs."

Dolores shrugged. "Well, I want to ask you something but I won't be holding you here long. I don't want to embarrass you, honey."

"You aren't embarrassing me," David assured her. Friends of his father's might be surprised to see him standing in the street talking to such a dilapidated woman, he thought sadly, except that in times like these nobody paid much attention to anybody else.

"I heard today Roger is got the plague," said Dolores. "Is it so, David?"

He nodded.

"Is he took bad?"

"I don't know. We only heard it ourselves yesterday, and my father hasn't let mother go there. She's worn out with nursing my youngest brother who died of it."

"Mhm, I know," said Dolores. "Tell her I'm mighty sorry. And tell her I'm sorry I yelled so at that nigger of hers that brought me some things, but I was so distracted with my little girl just dead. David, is there any woman looking after Roger?"

"There's a couple of good nurses at Silverwood."

"Niggers!" said Dolores. "I'm going over there. Thanks, David. That's all I wanted to know."

"Wait!" he exclaimed as she started off. "How are you going to get there? It's a long way."

"I reckon I can walk. I don't be having the fever."

"In this heat? You'll never do it."

"Oh yes I will, honey. I kept off that boy long as I figured he was better off without me. But I reckon if he's got the fever there's nobody can say his mother should stay away and let him die with a pack of slaves minding him. I'll get there."

He was holding her arm. "Get on this horse. Can you ride?"

"I used to could. I guess I haven't forgot. Won't the horse drop dead toting us both, though?"

"Horses aren't as important as people," said David shortly. "Get on."

She sighed. "You're pretty good, David. I'd have thought you'd be ashamed to ride with me." She mounted the horse and smiled at him as he got up in front of her. "You look just like your father."

"That's what everybody says."

"Living image. That's how I could tell it was you."

They rode slowly, without talking much. David wondered what his Uncle Caleb was going to say when he saw Dolores. But it really didn't matter. If the poor woman wanted to nurse her son through the fever not even rock-minded Uncle Caleb could refuse to let her in. He would probably welcome any one who could ease his son's suffering now. David asked about her children. They were well, she said. Her husband could take care of them.

She was silent after that and he did not try to make her

talk. The sun or something was beginning to make his head ache. Ordinarily he paid no attention to the heat—in fact, he liked the summers—but he had never known such weather as this.

At the steps of the Silverwood manor David gave his head a shake to clear his brain. The horse stood drooping with weariness as he and Dolores dismounted.

Dolores stood a moment on the steps. "Funny," she said, more as if speaking to the house than to David, "I used to live here."

David rapped on the door with the butt of his whip. "Where is Mr. Sheramy?" he asked the Negro boy who answered.

"Why howdy, Massa David. He's back in de room wid de young master, sah."

"How is Mr. Roger?" Dolores demanded.

"Ma'am? He mighty sick, ma'am." The boy looked at her curiously, wondering what so bedraggled a woman was doing at the front door with Master David.

"Tell him—" David began, but Dolores interposed,

"Don't tell him anything. He won't throw me out. I reckon," she added with an oblique glance at David, "I know him better than you do, honey child." She started in. "Thanks for bringing me, David," she said over her shoulder.

A door in the hall opened and Caleb came out. He had heard their voices, but they stood with their backs to the sun and for a moment he did not recognize them. Then he said, "Why hello, David." He walked with a stoop, and his face was haggard. Dolores took a step nearer.

She said, "Caleb, don't you know me?"

Caleb stopped. He put out his hand and touched her. He said, "Dolores!" in a strange far-off tone. From the room he had left came the sound of Roger's voice calling him.

"I've come to look after him, Caleb," said Dolores.

He took her hand in his and without saying anything else they went together into Roger's room. For a moment David stood where he was. He could hear Roger groaning and the other two speaking in blurred phrases. He wondered if his Uncle Caleb had loved her. He did not know, but he felt curiously young and inadequate. There was nothing wanted of him at Silverwood. Ahead was the journey home, which seemed long and wearisome before him. His bones ached and his headache was growing harder. He went out and mounted his horse.

How hot it was, though before he was halfway home the clouds had thickened over the sun. He thought yearningly that as soon as he reached Ardeith he would have his boy bring him a cold bath. His throat was burning with thirst. The pain shot through his head till he could scarcely see, and it was hard to hold his seat in the saddle. His hands on the bridle were shaky. Queer what this wet heat could do. It made him ashamed of himself. You'd think he was one of these greenhorn Canadians who'd never felt real sun before.

Here were the orange groves of Ardeith. What a long way it was from the oranges to the house! David made himself straighten up. If his mother saw him exhausted like this she'd think he was sick and she had all she could bear now without getting worried about him. He was perfectly well, of course— or wasn't he? To be sure he was well, only this weather was enough to give anybody headaches. Thank heaven the horse turned of its own accord into the road leading through the flowers to the house. He was dizzy, and saw two oleander bushes where only one was growing; ahead of him the pink house swayed and elongated and shortened as though he were looking at it through a pane of faulty glass. The horse was stopping at the steps. David roused himself with a great effort and got off, and caught at a post of the gallery to keep from falling. He must get inside in a hurry, and get some rest before his mother saw him. In just a minute when his head had cleared and he could walk, he would go in.

She came out on the gallery with his father. He heard her cry out, "David! What's the trouble?" He felt her hands on his face. How cool they were. He tried to answer, but when he let go the post he felt himself falling.

He did not know just what happened after that, but he had a vague sense of lying across the gallery with his head on his mother's lap. There were servants about to carry him indoors. He heard his father say something and then, because her head was bent so close to his, he understood when he heard his mother answer.

"No. No, Philip. Please don't make me do anything. Can't you see I've got no fight left in me?"

In the manor at Silverwood Caleb and Dolores sat facing each other across the bed where Roger lay. Dolores reached over now and then and stroked his forehead with a damp cloth. Caleb could see her in sharp outline by the light of two candles burning steadily in the windless air. How tired she looked, and how old, though she was only about Judith's age. He had made her look like that by driving her away.

He had loved her so desperately in those old days, though he had persuaded himself during these years that he had not. But if they could ever have any peace about that tormented child between them he would tell her he wished he had been more forgiving. Maybe she would not care about knowing. But she loved Roger so; she must be glad to hear that Roger's father wished he could take back his harshness to her. How she worshiped that boy! He would perhaps be dead now but for what she had done for him, twenty times a day washing him clean of the fever discharges, and holding him up in her arms so he could breathe when the spasms came. She had hardly slept at all, and the candlelight showed him the rings of exhaustion under her eyes.

Roger moved uneasily under the sheet and tried to throw it off. Caleb drew it up again.

"Won't you rest a little while, Dolores?" he asked. "I'll stay with him."

She shook her head. "You wouldn't know what to do. I've nursed it before. It gets down below the wharfs a lot, summers."

He went around the foot of the bed to her, and stood with a hand on her shoulder.

"He was so handsome before, wasn't he?" said Dolores without looking up. "I was watch him sometimes, riding on the levee with Judith's boys, all elegant in fine clothes and such a gentleman."

Caleb's hand tightened on her shoulder. "Dolores, I'm sorry I took him away from you."

He spoke stiffly, for he had not known how to say that, or whether she would believe him. For a moment she did not answer. He saw her holding Roger's wrist, feeling for a pulse. When she had found it she said slowly:

"He'd have got the fever just the same, Caleb. Maybe seeing him have it would be worse for me if I'd had him all along."

"Let me fetch you some clean water," said Caleb.

He took the basin and emptied it into the slop-jar and filled it again from the pitcher on the washstand. She took it from him and set it on the table. Roger was tossing and talking in broken words. With a convulsive movement Dolores sprang up and went to the window, hiding her face in the curtain. Her shoulders quivered with voiceless sobs.

Caleb went and put his arms around her.

But she did not want him to hold her, and moved away. It was Roger for whose sake she had come to Silverwood, and not his, and he could not help but know it. Caleb went back to the bed and looked down at his son. He wondered if Roger was going to die.

Dolores pushed back the wisps of her disordered hair. "There's no more water in the pitcher," she said. "Can you get some? I'm burning up with wanting a drink, besides him needing it."

"All right," said Caleb. He picked up the pitcher and went out to the rain-barrels behind the house. There was a light in the kitchen, and two or three servants sitting about, but he did not call on them. Giving what services he could made him feel less futile.

He took the lid off one of the barrels and dipped in the pitcher. The water was fresh, for it had rained that morning and he himself had gone out to cover the barrels as soon as the shower was over so the water might absorb as little as possible of the poison in the air. He set the pitcher down in the hall and went to get a bottle of wine for Dolores. One should be careful about drinking water during a plague.

Caleb reached among the bottles and found a heavy port, nourishing for an exhausted woman. When he went into the dining-room for a glass he stood awhile looking out at the hot, heavy-dewed night, trying to picture her life in that dilapidated neighborhood with that man Upjohn. He remembered bitterly that if he had not sent her away those other children born to her would have been his and not Upjohn's and he would not now be threatened with the loss of the only thing on earth he had to love.

The striking of a clock reminded him how long he had been away from Roger's bedside. He put the bottle under his arm, and holding the glass in one hand and the pitcher of water in the other he tiptoed down the hall.

The room was quiet. That was surprising, for even when he fell asleep Roger groaned and mumbled, and when he was awake Dolores was generally trying to soothe him with soft endearments. Caleb set down the pitcher and lifted the latch noiselessly, but as the door opened he congealed with terror.

Roger's limbs lay perfectly quiet under the tumbled sheet. Dolores was on her knees by the bed, her face buried and her hands clasped over her head. Caleb stood still, feeling as if his heart had come up into his throat and was choking him, and wishing this was true so he could not have to go on living. He set down the bottle and glass and went to her, and put his hand on her shoulder.

"Dolores," he said.

She started back, putting her hand to her mouth. "Hush!"

There were tears on her cheeks, sparkling in the candlelight. He helped her up, his face turned away from the bed, and she stumbled as though it was hard for her to rise. But she caught him with both hands to hold herself up.

"Caleb—" her voice was a thick whisper, and the words were not very clear—"Caleb, the fever's out of him—he's sleeping natural—Oh, God be praised—"

He let her go suddenly, hardly noticing that she swayed and caught the bedpost, for he was bending over the bed with a flood of unbelieving thankfulness rushing over him. He felt Roger's face and hands. They were cool and faintly damp, and though his breathing was faint it was peaceful. Caleb turned around. There was a sob breaking his words when he spoke.

"Oh Dolores, my dear, my darling—he's not dead! He's going to live because of you—I couldn't have saved him."

She was holding herself up by the bedpost, and when he was about to take her in his arms she pushed him back.

"You—you'd better not touch me."

The words were indistinct. In sudden fright he gripped her shoulders and turned her around to face the candles. Her lips were flaming red and swollen and her eyes were bloodshot. She tried to say something else, but this time the words were only low noises in her throat. Her legs gave way under her. Caleb caught her in his arms as she fell.

Christopher walked into the vegetable gardens. One should not venture out into the foul, fever-reeking night air, but he wanted to think, and he couldn't think in the house. It was quite awful in the house. David was wildly delirious, and only a little while ago when his mother had tried to hold him up in her arms to make his breathing easier he had struck at her with such force that the blow had knocked her down. A chair-leg had cut her head and the cut bled badly, so his father made her go to bed.

Christopher sat on a stump and smoked a pipe. His father didn't like him to smoke yet, but it kept off the mosquitoes. He wondered if David was going to die. He was fond of David, but if David should die it would mean more to him than his personal sorrow; it would mean—Christopher faced it grimly—that he himself would be locked in a prison for the rest of his life. Queer to think of this vast plantation as a prison. But could he help it if he was bored to exasperation at dirt-grubbing? This passion for land which David and his father shared, this thrilling to a new acre of forest drawn into the circle of indigo—it was all strange to him. He could not to save his life glance at a field of indigo and tell whether its yield would be scant or plentiful, and what was more, he could not care. But little Philip was dead, and if David died he would be the only son left. He would have to accept the plantation as his inheritance.

He didn't want it, and hellfire and damnation, thought Christopher with black resentment, they didn't have any right to make him take it. His father and David loved growing plants as if they were something human. Christopher could understand that since the crops were their living good indigo was preferable to bad, but the sight of the leaves unfolding and the stalks ripening in midsummer gave him no experience of creation. His father saw the plantation going on long after himself, an enduring expression of the vitality of his house. David saw it that way too, like a crown prince proud of his heritage.

Oh, David—of course David would see it that way. David was so damn perfect. When they were children David had always been bigger and stronger than himself; David learned faster, and when they played games his father would beam with pride at the way David would stir dead leaves in a bowl and pretend it was an indigo vat. When they began going to balls girls couldn't get their eyes off David. He was a magnet when it came to girls. Not that he disliked David, but Christopher couldn't help feeling a bit triumphant now that David instead of himself had taken the fever.

It had all been so simple before David was taken ill. His father, of course, had counted on founding a line of great landowners, but he had been fair enough the day he had called Christopher in and rebuked him for his lack of interest in the plantation. "I know what you're thinking, Chris," Philip said—"that because you're a younger son it's no use for you to cherish a love of the place. Don't worry. I was a younger son myself. No child of mine is going through what I did. There'll be two thousand acres for you, and if you manage that wisely you can add to it by purchase till your holdings are as large as David's."

Christopher blurted, "I don't want to be a planter."

His father was astounded. But once having got out as much as that, Christopher rushed on:

"Nigger-raising and indigo-churning! Watching the sky for rain like it was a sign of the second coming of Christ! I hate it!"

That a son of his should not want land was nearly as incomprehensible to Philip as if he had not wanted food. "But what do you mean to do?" he asked wonderingly.

"I don't know," Christopher owned. "But father, there's lots of men who don't grow crops! Mr. Purcell runs the wharfs, and Mr. Durham builds boats—"

Building boats—that was something exciting, Christopher thought now as he bit the stem of his pipe. Controlling boatyards and arguing with traders. Keeping great ledgers of accounts in colored inks. In a business like that one was master of one's own destiny, not subject to the sun and rain and wind and whatever else the Lord chose to send. There was a career for a man. But if David didn't get well—Christopher blew a puff of smoke toward a mosquito that was plaguing his knee. He'd miss David if he died. That would be bad enough without having his father tie the plantation around his neck, expecting him to be a second David, when he couldn't be a second David because he wasn't born that way. Christopher angrily watched the sky lighten with daybreak. He wasn't going to let any such thing happen to him. He'd show them.

The morning exploded above him, and Christopher went into the house. He got washed up and had the servants give him some breakfast in the kitchen. Calling Josh, he ordered him to saddle a horse, and if anybody asked for him he'd ridden to town. He went to the big moss house where the Durhams lived.

Alan Durham was at home. Christopher asked about Mrs. Durham. She was very much better, and they took him in to pay his respects. She was lying white and querulous on a long sofa with cushions piled around her. He thought her a disagreeable silly woman, but he was polite, and she told him it was very sweet of him to come and inquire. He was glad she was getting well because now Mr. Durham was relieved of anxiety and was able to return his attention to his business. Christopher asked if he didn't need an assistant in expanding his boat-building.

"My father has promised me two thousand acres," said Christopher. "I'll ask him to give me forest. That will be enough timber for thousands of barges."

Alan Durham was astonished. Christopher was only seventeen.

"I can't contract for the land till you're of age," he said. "Of course, if you're really in earnest—"

"Yes sir?"

"I can apprentice you at keeping accounts, assuming that your father consents. You'll have to start pretty low to learn the business. But—" he hesitated—"what makes you think he is going to let one of his sons be an apprentice?"

"If he won't," said Christopher stubbornly, "it's only four years before I'm twenty-one."

"Hm. You're quite sure you won't mind starting as an accountant?"

"Quite sure, Mr. Durham."

Alan Durham fiddled with the window-latch. He smiled faintly. Christopher guessed that it was not every day he had such an offer as two thousand acres of timber. Though he was not sure of the present extent of Ardeith, Christopher knew that before buying any land his father made certain it was as good as there was on the bluff. When those acres were cleared any planter would be only too happy to buy them at a good price.

"All right, Christopher," said Mr. Durham. "I'll take you on now if your father consents; if not, as soon as you're of age. How are you at accounts?"

"Very good, sir." Christopher recalled that arithmetic was the one subject at which he was better than David.

"I see. We'll draw up an apprenticeship contract now, if you like, but remember it's no good unless he signs it. Still, if he doesn't, come back when you're of age and we'll talk it over again."

"Thank you," said Christopher.

That was all he said. He had never had his brother's glibness at words.

CHAPTER SIXTEEN

The fever raced through Dolores and killed her in three days. Caleb suspected she had felt it gripping her long before she fainted in his arms and had held herself up with a furious effort of will until she saw Roger through the crisis. In a flood of self-reproach he tried unsuccessfully to find her other children when a season of cool dry weather ended the plague. But the Upjohns had moved out of the alley where Judith had visited them, and the inhabitants of Rattletrap Square were anonymous except to their immediate neighbors.

When he was sure David was recovering, Christopher went to his father with Alan Durham's contract. Philip read it and his eyes fastened on the date at the end.

"Chris, that wasn't necessary."

"What, sir?"

"If you hate the plantation so much that you tried to escape it when you thought David was dying, I wouldn't have forced you to stay here in any event."

Christopher looked away. It did make him feel rather heartless. After a pause Philip said:

"Being an apprentice won't be much fun."

"I don't think I'll mind," said Christopher.

Philip smiled reluctantly.

"I suppose I ought to be glad you're so sure about what you want to do. So many men don't get their minds made up until it's too late to begin."

He dipped his pen into the ink and wrote under Christopher's signature, "I authorize my son Christopher Larne to fulfill the terms of the above agreement during his minority. Philip Larne."

"I'll have to live in town," said Christopher. "It's too far to ride in every day. Mr. Durham says I can have a room at his house."

"Very well," said Philip.

Judith was angry and hurt when Philip told her Christopher was leaving home. Though David was nearly well she was distraught with what she had been through. The house seemed empty with little Philip gone, and would be emptier still without Christopher. He was a good boy, quiet and dependable, and she would miss him sorely. "But how can he leave us now, Philip?" she exclaimed. "Now, when I need my children so?"

But Philip was more tolerant. "He'll like us better if we let him go," he reminded her. "I'm not particularly pleased with

GWEN BRISTOW

the idea of his being an apprenticed accountant, and I don't think he'll like it, but I'd rather let him try."

"Doesn't this mean he'll never live with us again?" she asked sadly, fingering the keys at her belt.

"I think not," he answered smiling. "He's got to stay there till he's of age whether he wants to or not, and I'll wager by that time he'll be heartily sick of it and glad to get out. But to tell the truth, most of the escapades I got into at his age were because of resentment at not being allowed to do what I wanted, and I'm not going to coerce my children."

She had to yield. But she found it hard to forgive the undisguised eagerness with which Christopher left them.

The house did seem big and quiet. She had not realized how much she had come to depend on the companionship of her children, and she clung to David more closely than ever. Nursing him through the threatening torments of yellow fever had made clear to her how frightful it would be to lose him. Now that he was stronger Philip suggested sometimes that she was over-mothering him. "He's grown, you know," Philip reminded her. "He won't like it."

"Nonsense," said Judith. "He's very fond of me."

"Yes, dear, and I'm glad he is, but that's no reason why you should have interrupted when I started to tell him that as much wine as he and that Durham boy drank last night isn't good for a youngster just up from a wasting illness."

"He doesn't get drunk," said Judith.

"No, but he will if he starts drinking before he's nineteen. And after I've spent my life building up this plantation I don't want to leave it to a young fellow who hasn't any more sense of responsibility than David has now."

"You needn't worry about the plantation," she countered. "David loves every acre of it. I doubt if he'll ever love a woman as much as he loves his land."

Philip smiled. David's zest for the crops filled him with pride, and he was willing to condone a good deal of recklessness in other matters because of it. When David came to them in January with a new plan for Ardeith, Philip was delighted, though the scheme did sound impractical. David announced that he wanted to go to New Orleans. Judith objected—David was still thin, and hardly strong enough for the journey, but he laughed at her.

"Just because you fed me with a spoon last summer doesn't mean you can do it forever, mother." He sat on the dining-table, swinging his legs over the edge, and grinned from her to Philip, who had just come in from the tobacco fields. "Listen. I want to see a fellow named Etienne Bore. His plantation is on the river just above New Orleans. He's been doing things with cane."

"But my dear boy," Judith protested, "anything you want to know about cane you can learn here. Ours will be coming up next month."

"No, wait a minute," Philip interposed. "What has he been doing, David?"

"Well, this man Bore doesn't grow cane for chair-bottoms," David went on eagerly. "Maybe he's crazy but I want to find out. He crushed the juice out of the cane, and found if you boil it just so and cool it just so and refine it just so—" he paused impressively—"it *sugars*, very fine like sand and unbelievably sweet. You can pack it in bricks and ship it."

When Philip frowned incredulously at this idea, David persisted. "Father, can't you see what that means? My Lord, we could ship it to the American states, to Europe, everywhere—if I can find out how it's done, and if you'll give me some land and Negroes to try it—"

"And take Negroes out of good proven crops," said Judith, "to set them boiling cane-juice on the chance that when the stuff cools it will be fit to eat."

But Philip, though he was generally careful about accepting David's impetuous ideas, had listened with interest. "It might be worth trying. We do need a new crop—"

"Instead of indigo?" Judith asked with sudden eagerness, thinking of the summer influx of grasshoppers.

Philip dashed her hopes. "No, instead of tobacco. They've begun growing tobacco in Kentucky, and it's better than Louisiana tobacco. The only reason the Kentuckians haven't ruined our market already is that they have to pay foreign port duties at New Orleans. The Americans are trying to negotiate a treaty giving them free passage of the river, and if they do we can plow our tobacco under and be done with it."

"I'm pretty sure they can't grow cane up there," David urged. "Cane takes lots of sun, and they say it gets awfully cold in Kentucky. May I order a boat, father?"

"Yes, but don't be too confident. Sugar from cane sounds mighty dreamful."

David, however, too exuberant to be subdued by warnings, went off to New Orleans in high spirits. Judith still nourished a secret hope that cane might be made to replace indigo. Though she had lived twenty years surrounded by indigo she still hated it—the grasshoppers pouring into the house gave her shivers of loathing, and the stench of the vats made her ill. The piles of rotting stalks around the vats drew swarms of flies reminding her of the Egyptian plague. Civilization and indigo were simply impossible to cultivate in the same place, she sometimes said despairingly when the effort to keep her house clean in summer wore down her nerves.

One day when David had been gone about a month Philip rode over to call at Lynhaven. The Purcells were still in mourning for their father, and he had not seen much of Gervaise or her children during the winter. As he rode through the gates Gervaise's daughter Emily came running through the garden to meet him. She was the youngest of the Purcell children, a pretty little girl eight or nine years old with a lot of dark hair and a small-featured French face like her mother's.

"Good morning, Miss Emily," Philip called as he dismounted. "How are your folks?"

Emily curtseyed. "My folks are fine, Mr. Larne," she said, and chuckled as she tucked her hand into his. "But they're having an awful row indoors."

"A row?" he repeated.

She nodded, and laughed again softly. "Mother and the boys."

Philip was astonished. He could not imagine Gervaise engaged in anything that might be called a row. He had been walking toward the steps with Emily, but now he paused.

"Maybe I'd better ride on, Miss Emily, and come back later. Just tell your mother we had a letter from David, and he saw your sister Babette in New Orleans. She's doing fine, and so are the children."

"I wish you wouldn't go," Emily protested. "Mother'll want to see you."

But he was about to turn back toward his horse when Gervaise came through one of the long windows to the gallery. She waved and called to him.

"Why, come in, Philip! I thought I heard you talking. How's Judith?"

Philip smothered his surprise as he greeted her and gave her the news about her married daughter. If Gervaise had been quarreling with her sons she didn't look much upset by it. Neither did she look as a woman widowed six months ago ought to look. Gervaise had discarded her mourning, and she was amazingly dressed in a rose-colored gown, with a pink ribbon binding back her hair. Her face was almost impish with some secret merriment.

"It was dear of David to call on Babette," she said. "Now do come in and have a glass of wine with me. Lord knows I need one. My devoted children have been all but ripping me limb from limb." She laughed. "Did Emily tell you?"

"She told me there was a row," returned Philip, laughing back at her.

"Was?" said Gervaise. "Is. Come on in." She caught his arm and pushed back the curtains. Her two older sons were in the parlor glowering. They greeted Philip as if they wished him a thousand miles off. "I'm getting married tomorrow," said Gervaise. "Harry and George are behaving as if I'd announced I was going to rob a counting-house."

She was pouring wine from a decanter on the table. Philip glanced at the two boys. Harry was about David's age and George a couple of years younger.

"Did you tell Mr. Larne the rest of it?" Harry demanded.

"No, precious." Gervaise, still unruffled, handed Philip his glass. "You may do that."

"Mr. Larne," exclaimed George, "maybe you can bring mother to her senses. What do you think of it?"

Philip took the glass and bowed to Gervaise. He was startled, but to save his life he couldn't find her announcement as shocking as they seemed to. "Frankly," he said to her sons, "it's none of my business, and since you ask me, I don't think it's yours."

Gervaise laughed aloud. The young Purcells began talking at once.

"Mr. Larne, he's six years younger than she is—"

"And he hasn't a picayune—"

"And father only died last August—"

"He does nothing but dance and play the clavichord—"

"I think mother is losing her mind!"

Philip began to laugh too. Their fierceness was ridiculous against such a barrier of cool amusement as Gervaise presented. Little Emily, though not understanding the complexities of the situation, giggled as though enjoying the excitement.

"My darlings," said Gervaise, "why don't you tell him the truth? Never mind, I'll do it." She put out a restraining hand. "You see, Philip—"

"Yes ma'am?"

"I'm really marrying a very charming young man. His name is Louis Valcour and he came up from New Orleans last year. Harry wasn't quite right when he said he hadn't a picayune. He has a few. But only a few. And my excellent husband, not wanting me to have to ask Harry's permission every time I went shopping, left me a very good widow's portion, which if I marry goes with me, and they pretend they object to Louis because he plays the clavichord."

She poured herself a glass of wine and stood leaning an elbow on the back of a chair while she drank it. The rose-colored ribbon twinkled in her dark hair. She did look like a bride—not like a young and flustered bride, but like a very self-possessed person who was so sure she was getting what she wanted that she had the quiet joy brides were supposed to have and rarely did. Philip thought of a volatile Creole girl of fourteen handed over to a New England colonial to be a docile wife and housekeeper. Gervaise had not been unhappy. Walter Purcell was upright and conscientious; he had done his duty by her and she had done hers by him, so well that until now Philip had never suspected any passionate yearnings under the compromise Gervaise had made with life. He faced her sons.

"Can't you see what your mother is doing?" he exclaimed. "She's marrying a Creole. Maybe you don't understand it, but if I were you I'd try to."

"Thanks, Philip," said Gervaise. She faced the boys too. "Listen. For twenty-two years I've done what was expected of me. I've been placid, obedient, housewifely, sweet and bored. Now I'm through. I've fallen in love. Yes I have—absurdly or divinely, depending on how you look at it. I'm going to marry Louis Valcour tomorrow. We'll have a house in town and you won't have to speak to him unless you're so minded. But I'm going to do as I please for once in my life."

There was a stubborn silence when she had finished, except that Philip whispered:

"I'm proud of you, Gervaise."

She smiled, as though it was good to have a champion, though she had already been too sure to need one.

Harry and George sighed together. "At least," said Harry with an air of final protest, "we're old enough to take care of ourselves. But what are you going to do about the children?"

"I'm going to put little Walter in school in New Orleans. Emily can stay with you at Lynhaven or live with me, exactly as she pleases."

Philip smiled down at Emily, who sat curled up in a big chair. "What are you going to do, Miss Emily?"

She raised her eyes artlessly. "What do you think?"

"I think, Miss Emily, you'll have more fun living with your mother."

"Then I'll do that."

Gervaise bent and kissed her. "I thought you would."

The ladies of the bluff professed to be scandalized at Gervaise's hasty marriage. Ignoring them as serenely as if they had been rustling leaves in her back yard, Gervaise moved into a little house in town with her Creole husband and for several weeks minded her own business with ironic tranquillity. Her honeymoon over, she invited her chattering friends to a dinner-party.

Everybody came, of course; they said Gervaise was going to have her heart broken by this shameless man who was so eager for her dowry that he had been willing to become a stepgrandfather at the age of thirty-one, and they wanted to see what he looked like. They met a lean, dark Frenchman with a whimsical face and an air of private amusement, who danced beautifully and made no secret of his accomplishments on the clavichord. Judith and Philip liked him at once. They agreed that Gervaise was too shrewd to blunder calamitously with her own life, and they were delighted at her sudden blooming. With them Gervaise was smilingly frank. "It's absurd," she said, "but this should have happened to me twenty years ago, and it would be quite silly of me to pretend that it did."

Mr. Valcour was equally candid about his doings. He had come up from New Orleans with a scant sum of money, all that had been left him by a gambling parent, with the intention of building a warehouse on the Purcell wharfs for the accommodation of traders. After Walter Purcell's death he had called at Lynhaven to complete business arrangements with the heirs, and thus he had met Mr. Purcell's widow, who presented a singularly griefless face under her weeds. He had fallen in love.

"Love!" said Mrs. St. Clair contemptuously, when she discussed the behavior of the Valcours with Judith a week later.

"He adores her," said Judith.

But Mrs. St. Clair, whose daughter was betrothed to Harry Purcell, snorted, "She's robbed her own children for the sake of a fortune-hunter!"

Judith observed that if the young Purcells couldn't live on their income from the wharfs they must be extravagant indeed. She admired the competence with which Louis Valcour was building warehouses with Gervaise's dowry. He prospered exceedingly, and Gervaise gave every evidence of enjoying her lot. She was the first woman on the bluff to appear in gowns made in the startling new fashion of low-cut bodices and sashes tied about the ribs, with skirts straight as bedgowns showing off to advantage every line of a figure more elegant than any woman of thirty-seven had any business displaying. It was not long before the ladies began to whisper that it was perfectly obvious Gervaise wasn't wearing any stays. Judith asked her, and Gervaise retorted, "Certainly I'm not. I'm going to have a baby. Tell them that and see how they like it."

Judith chuckled. Gervaise did not know it, but now that she had a Creole husband and spoke French most of the time, her English was re-acquiring the accent she had worked so hard to be rid of.

CHAPTER SEVENTEEN

David came back from New Orleans eloquent on the possibilities of sugar-cane. He waited impatiently for the crop to mature. Philip was pleased with his enthusiasm, though he privately owned to Judith a certain apprehension lest it wane before the cane was cut.

Judith resented his saying that. The next day she went into the field and reminded David this was his first independent effort and it was important that he prove his earnestness. "I don't believe your father quite trusts you," she warned him.

"Father's mad with me," said David dryly.

"What do you mean?"

"Oh Lord, didn't he tell you?" David stroked a ribbony leaf of cane. "He thinks I made too many bills in New Orleans."

"David!" she exclaimed reproachfully. "I thought you promised not to make any."

"Well, I did—but how was I to know the money he gave me wasn't going to be enough? I had to buy a lot of presents for Mademoiselle Durand—would you want me to go courting a New Orleans lady like poor white trash?"

Judith sighed. David had talked a good deal about the charms of Gervaise's niece. She hoped he wasn't falling in love already. "How much attention did you give Clélie Durand?" she asked.

"Oh mother, don't be silly! She's a nice girl and I liked her, that's all. But father's got no business scolding me for spending a little more than I meant to."

"No," she agreed smiling, "I suppose he hasn't. It was your first holiday in a long time. Do you want me to remind him of that?"

"Will you?" David exclaimed with such unaffected relief that she promised.

When she got back to the house she asked Philip if David had been extravagant in New Orleans.

"Look," said Philip. He put a sheaf of bills on the table before her, and added:

"When he went to buy from the boats he had to do it on credit, for he got rid of most of his cash betting on the cock-fights."

"Cock-fights!" she said laughing. "Is that all? If he never did anything worse than that you ought to thank the Lord."

"But I'm afraid," Philip said seriously, "he doesn't know the value of money, and I told him so. He promised to be more careful, but I don't know how long it will last."

Judith looked thoughtfully at the totals. "Still, I don't see why you're so harsh with him. You can afford this."

"It's not that. He's old enough to learn to keep his promises."

She gave him an oblique glance. "You hadn't learned very much at twenty."

"That's why I know it's important, honey. I was harsh with him, and I'm not sorry."

"He certainly bought clothes enough," she observed, turning over the accounts. "Linen, broadcloth, boots, cravats—but what in the name of heaven do you suppose he wanted with a hundred yards of silk-striped muslin?"

Philip tilted a shoulder and did not answer.

"It's a very intimate sort of present for a lady," Judith murmured. "I'm sure Clélie Durand's father wouldn't let her accept dress-goods from a casual admirer! Philip—"

She stopped with a sense of relief. It wasn't commendable of David to be buying expensive presents for girls who didn't care about the propriety of what they accepted from young gentlemen. But at least it indicated that he had no serious regard for Clélie Durand. She went on:

"Have you been scolding him about that hundred yards of muslin? Funny that a man as sophisticated as you would expect David to be an angel at his age."

There was a pause. "I thought you'd be shocked," said Philip. "That's why I hadn't told you."

"I'm not shocked at all." Judith gathered up the papers in

one hand and tucked her other hand into Philip's. "Oh darling, please pay these and stop scolding him! You're foolish to risk impairing your own credit just to annoy David."

Philip yielded, but he said again that David had to learn responsibility. Judith answered that David was proving his good sense by his attention to the cane. David had set up a contrivance he called a crusher, where he fed his first crop stalk by stalk between two wheels turned by mules. Judith came into the field often, and sat on a pile of fresh-cut canes watching the juice drop down a gutter into a kettle that stood under a flimsy palm-roofed shed. She hoped for David's sake the mess would granulate, though she was doubtful.

But one day just after Christmas David came into the house carrying a big wooden bowl in his arms. He burst into the dining-room where his parents were writing up accounts of the household and plantation, shouting, "Look! Mother, father—look!"

He set the bowl between them and thrust spoons into their hands. "Taste it," he ordered.

Philip and Judith scowled at the stuff before them. It looked like a pile of damp dirty sand. David's face was radiant with boyish triumph. Bravely they plunged in their spoons.

As Judith's tongue twisted over the grains she saw Philip's face clear with astonishment.

"David!" she cried. "It's good!"

"It *is* good!" said Philip.

David hugged them both till their heads bumped. "I told you it would sugar! Now do you believe me?" He sprang up and sat on the table, crumpling the pages on which Judith was writing her sewing-records, and grabbing the spoon from Judith's hand he shoved into his own mouth a pyramid of brown sugar. "It tastes grand," he said with his mouth full. "Father, can I have a big field next year?"

Philip nodded. "You certainly can. This is a crop." His eyes twinkled proudly. "You're a born planter, David."

"Yes sir," returned his son demurely.

David and Judith exchanged a look of secret triumph.

To David the extension of the canefields was more of an adventure than a task. He pushed back the tobacco as lustily as Philip had pushed back the forest. In moments of private candor Philip and Judith admitted to each other that they wished Christopher had been more like him. "Not, of course," said Philip, "that we've any reason to be really disappointed in Christopher."

"No, no," said Judith with a twinge of conscience. "Certainly not."

But they were disappointed. Christopher was dignified and unassuming, a most trustworthy young man, Mr. Durham said. But his parents found it hard to establish any sort of intimacy with him. He was not particularly affectionate, and rarely talked about his plans or asked for advice. Philip had a good deal of respect for Christopher's unwavering confidence in what he wanted to do, and sometimes when David's ebullience amounted to a fault Philip observed thankfully that Christopher would never have a problem or be one, but he could not help a certain dismayed surprise when Christopher did not get tired of accounting.

On the contrary, as soon as he crossed the birthday that made him a man instead of a child, Christopher signed another contract giving him a junior partnership in the business of supplying flatboats to the river-trade, and he kept his nose in an ink-horn. The next year he quietly announced that he was getting married to Alan Durham's daughter Audrey.

Judith owned to Philip that she was uncertain as to whether their uncommunicative son was in love with Audrey or Audrey's share of the boat business. They could not understand Christopher's calm. But neither could they find any objection to Audrey, except that she seemed incapable of enthusiasm. "She'll probably make the most irreproachable housekeeper," said Judith, "and there'll never be a muddy footprint on her gallery."

"That will suit Chris perfectly," said Philip.

Christopher built his bride a compact house of cypress wood with myrtle trees in front, and they settled down correctly and peacefully. Audrey proved as austere as Christopher; her conduct was dutiful and her dinners were faultless and dull. When she gave birth to a daughter the year after her marriage she accepted motherhood with tranquil competence. Judith embroidered a set of dresses for the baby and pouted in private.

"There ought at least to be a fanfare of trumpets about my first grandchild," she exclaimed to Philip. "Audrey behaves as if having children was an everyday affair."

"My darling," said Philip laughing, "it is." He added, more seriously, "Sometimes I can't help wishing, though, that they weren't quite so independent. Building a house and providing for one's first child is pretty expensive and Christopher's income isn't large. But when I offered to help him through he said he didn't like the idea of taking money from his father when he didn't actually need it."

Judith did not reply. If Philip was trying to make an excuse for rebuking her tolerance toward David's spending she wasn't going to give him any opening to do so.

But before long it became impossible to ignore David's extravagance. His yearly allowance was half the sugar profits, and with sugar at two picayunes a pound this was more than his friends generally had. When David got harassed with gambling debts Philip refused to make an increase. David appealed to Judith. It was midsummer. The cane would not ripen before November, and he was ashamed to wait so long to pay his debts of honor. His distress was so evident and his promises so fervid that Judith was touched and wrote an order on the indigo crop. David was almost incoherent with gratitude. "You're wonderful!" he exclaimed. "I'll pay this back the minute I get the sugar made."

He kissed her rapturously and scampered off, calling his boy to saddle his horse. When he got to town he found he had overestimated his indebtedness and with the surplus she had given him he bought her some blue French morocco for party slippers.

Several days later Philip came into the parlor with the cancelled order. He thrust it into her hand.

"What did you buy with this?" he demanded.

Judith was astonished. He rarely questioned her expenditures. "What makes you want to know?"

Philip's face was grim. "Did you think it would go through

without being countersigned? Haven't I told you not to pay David's debts?"

She shrugged and sighed. "Philip, he was half frantic!"

"If he'd stayed frantic awhile it would have been good for him." He came close to her and took her arm. "If you give David one more indigo order after I've told him he can't have it, that's the last order you sign on this plantation."

"Philip!" She jerked from his grasp. "Do you mean after all these years you want me to ask permission every time I buy a yard of ribbon?"

"I mean exactly that," he returned inexorably. "Stop letting David hide behind your skirts. He's got to learn to take care of his property."

"I don't know what's come over you!" Judith cried. "You were the most indulgent father on earth till all of a sudden you began glaring at David like a judge. He's exactly what you were."

"That's another thing. You're not to keep telling him that. At least when I was his age I had to take the consequences of what I did. I didn't have a doting mother to pat me on the head like a mistreated baby."

Judith jingled the keys between her hands. She sat down.

Philip's expression softened. "Now do you promise to behave yourself?" he asked.

"I can't bear seeing him troubled!" she protested with a regretful smile. "He's been so hilarious since he got those debts off his mind. I wish you had seen him this afternoon."

"Where is he?"

"Gone to see a girl. He's got a high hat and a pair of breeches he can hardly sit down in, but he says the newest thing is to have them tight."

After a pause Philip sat down by her and put his hand on her knee. "Judith, it's not your loving David so much that I mind, but your letting it get in the way of your good sense. I wish you wouldn't encourage his philandering."

She laughed. "Can I help it if every girl in Dalroy adores him?"

Philip's eyes met hers. "Can't you help trying to keep him fickle?"

"What do you mean?"

"I mean," said Philip slowly, "that as long as David is surrounded by a lot of women and doesn't single out any one of them you're supreme in his affections, and you're trying so hard to put off the day when you won't matter a picayune to him compared to some empty-headed slip of a girl. Do you really want to make him a mother-ridden old bachelor, Judith?"

Judith was silent awhile, trying to tell herself what Philip said wasn't true. At last she said in a low voice, "Is it—is it very wrong for me to dread losing him?"

"Yes," said Philip.

Judith put both her hands in his. "I—I don't think I ever thought of it quite that way," she said.

Philip smiled and kissed her, and left her there.

David did manage to curtail his fondness for cards that autumn, and he bet only moderately on the cock-fights that had been imported from New Orleans. Judith told Philip he was settling down and Philip, looking over the tall ribbons of the cane, was inclined to agree with her. The Negroes were cutting David's fourth crop and those who were not in the fields were busy enlarging the sugar-mill. There were three sets of crushers now, with stout wooden wheels and long yokes for the mules; and instead of one set of kettles there were six rows of them protected by the thatch of palm-leaves over their wooden shelter. He had the slaves construct another shed nearby for storage of stalks that had been through the mill; for the crushed cane, though it looked so limp and empty, was valuable. When it had dried it became what the Creole planters called bagasse, and bagasse was fuel for the sugar-sheds. No wood but the richest kindling could make so hot a fire as bagasse.

"He's a born planter," Philip said again to Judith, one night in early December, just before they went to sleep.

"I told you he'd be all right," she murmured happily.

"He can hardly bear to be away from the sugar-sheds at grinding time," Philip told her. "Right after supper he went back to watch the fires."

Judith raised up on her elbow, and saw far off in the cane-fields a faint glow that she might have thought was only a reflection of the moon if she had not known the sugar-sheds were there. The fires burned all day and night in grinding time and were never left unguarded. David usually kept watch in the evening and was relieved by the Negroes after midnight. Judith snuggled down under the covers again with a secret thrill. Her men—how nobly they had brought the wilderness under their domain! The fields of Ardeith now stretched so far that it was only on very clear days she could see the border of forest from her bedroom window, like a dark fuzz edging the plantation. And the forest too belonged to Ardeith, miles and miles of it, and it was there they cut their firewood, and there was Christopher's timber. Rita's dowry had been increased to three hundred acres. She remembered with a pang that the increase included part of what would have been little Philip's portion had he lived. But the children who had been spared to her, she reminded herself, were a noble group in whom any mother would take pride. She went to sleep with a feeling of triumphant peace.

She woke up in confused fright. The night-light burned low in its deep glass container. By its fitful flame she could see Philip hurrying into his clothes, and she heard the shrill voices of Negroes in the hall outside.

"What's happened?" she cried.

Philip made a gesture toward the window, hardly pausing in his haste to button his waistcoat. Sitting up in bed Judith saw that what had been the glow of the sugar-fires was a sheet of light. Pillars of smoke went up toward the sky, throwing sparks as they rose, and in front of the fire she could make out hurrying black figures. She gasped and demanded:

"But what is it?"

"That lunatic David left the sugar-fires and they've caught the bagasse," said Philip over his shoulder as he opened the door.

She sprang out of bed and caught him.

"Was David hurt? Where is he?"

"Nobody's seen him," Philip returned with grim haste.

"Let me go, Judith! God knows what that fire will do if it's not checked. Stay in the house."

He rushed out. Judith went to the window, shivering at the sweep of cold air as she pushed the shutters further back and looked out. The bagasse was a raging wall of flame. She sobbed with dismay. That David could have been such a fool! The cornstalks were dry in the fields, and between the plots were spaces overgrown with brown sedges. If the fire got beyond the cleared place where the sugar-mills were, it could destroy the orchards and the indigo vats and perhaps even reach the quarters—it might, if the wind changed to blow sparks in this direction, attack the big house.

She thrust her feet into her shoes and wrapped a cloak around her, holding it together while she ran out to the kitchen to order buckets of coffee. She took them out herself, along with big slabs of bread and meat, and set up supper on a stump as close to the fire as she dared.

The slaves, half dressed and frightened, were working hard under Philip's direction. He had evidently abandoned hope of saving the mills or storehouse, and they were digging a trench around the fire. He saw her pouring coffee for the men and came to her.

"Judith, what are you doing out here? Didn't I tell you to keep away?"

"I'm not going to let you freeze to death," she returned, "or the Negroes either. I brought you a bottle of whiskey."

"Thanks," he said with a grudging smile, and took a drink. She looked toward the fire, burning lower now.

"Is it going to spread, Philip?"

"I don't think so. But the cane is gone, and the crushers, and all the bagasse." In the flaring light his face was sooty. "A couple of the Negroes were pretty badly burned, and another—"

"What?" she asked when he paused.

Philip gestured to the far side of the cleared circle. Judith moved away from the stump to look, and gave a cry.

"Is that man dead?"

He nodded.

Judith gripped both his arms. In spite of the heat of the flame on her face she shivered.

"Philip," she cried, "are you sure David's not hurt?"

"He's nowhere around," Philip rejoined curtly. "He went off—didn't you understand me?—and left the fires burning in this wind."

Judith sat down weakly on the stump, too deeply hurt to shed tears.

Philip turned and called some terse directions to the men. As he did so they heard the frightened neigh of a horse and the sound of running footsteps. David appeared in the ring of light. He ran up to the stump, panting.

"Father, what happened?"

Philip asked him, slowly, "David, where in God's name have you been?"

"Just riding up the road—I never meant to stay so long—the fires were low."

"Never mind," said Philip. "Get over there and help them keep the fire where it is. We'll talk about it in the morning." He turned to Judith. "Honey, won't you go back now? Thanks for the coffee and things, but you'll catch your death of cold with only a bedgown under that cloak."

He spoke so gently that she did not argue with him. She stood up and went back to the house, stumbling over the soft ridges of the fields.

David was vehemently remorseful. He hadn't meant to let anything happen. The Negroes had been told to go to bed and come back an hour after midnight. He was just sitting about, watching the fires burning low under the kettles, and it was cold and pretty lonesome. While he was waiting there Roger Sheramy came up—he had spent the evening in town and seeing the glow of the sugar-sheds had ridden in to see if David was around and if he'd like a drink. "It's mighty cold," said David; "I think I'll ride up the road a little way with you and get warmed up. Everything's all right here."

How could he foretell the wind was going to rise like that, all of a sudden?

He was so penitent that he was astounded not to be immediately forgiven. Hadn't he promised to be more careful after this? What was the use of harping on it?

"Has it occurred to you," asked Philip, "that you endangered the whole plantation and the life of everybody on it?"

"Yes sir, and I said I was sorry! I am sorry."

"I think," said Philip, "a little solitude and leisure to reflect on how sorry you are might be a good thing for you."

"What do you mean, father?"

"I mean that if you'd left a Negro in charge of the fire and he'd gone traipsing off he'd be beaten within an inch of his life and then sent to the guardhouse, and he'd deserve it. If you haven't learned to be more responsible than you'd expect a nigger slave to be—" He got up and walked over to face David. "Son, young gentlemen don't go to the guardhouse for that sort of neglect. But the plantation will do fairly well for a substitute. You'll stay within the limits of Ardeith for six months from today and if you behave yourself I may trust you again."

"Six months!" David gasped.

"Yes."

"What am I going to tell people? That a man of my age can't leave the front yard like a little boy?"

"If you act like a little boy," said Philip as he went out, "your age doesn't make very much difference."

David raged and stormed. It would have been hard to devise a severer punishment. He liked gaming and balls and gatherings in taverns; to be confined for half a year to the house and fields was catastrophic. He was of age, he said, and could do as he pleased.

"Not with my property," said Philip.

David endured imprisonment a week. Then they woke one morning to find that he had vanished.

He had taken nothing with him but a horse and such few garments as might be stuffed into a saddlebag. Through several tormented days and nights Judith tried to tell herself this was only impulsive pique at having been punished and he would come home when his pocket-money gave out. But he did not return, and at the end of the third week she was forced to the anguished conclusion that he had no intention of doing so.

Philip was more grave and stern than she had ever seen him. He had not expected this. But he should have, she flung at him, when she was exhausted with waiting and rushing to the window at every sound of horses' hoofs to see if David had come home. "You treated him like a baby!" she exclaimed. "You might have known he wouldn't stand it."

"Will you be quiet?" Philip said without looking at her. "This isn't easy for me either, you know."

Judith walked up and down the room. Philip stood looking out of the window. "What are you going to do?" she asked at length.

"I'm going down to New Orleans," said Philip briefly.

While he was gone she forced herself to control her nervous suspense with repeated assurance that of course Philip would find him. David hadn't money enough to get very far, and it would be like him to think it amusing to take lodgings in a tavern and live awhile in gayer independence than he had been permitted at home. But Philip returned to say he had found nobody who had seen David. A week later he took a boat up the river as far as Natchez, stopping at every settlement on the way, but again he had to come home alone.

Judith's first emotions of anger and fear subsided into dreadful waiting. Two months passed and then two more. They heard nothing and found nobody who could help them. The rest of the cane was plowed under in the field, because there was no sugar-mill to refine the juice. Philip, as though desperately in need of work to give vent to his anxiety, had the Negroes rebuild the crushers with furious speed.

"Why do you work so hard?" Judith asked him when he came in one night.

"I can't sleep unless I'm tired," said Philip, and she did not question him further. Like him she could not endure idleness, and she got into the habit of taking long rides in the afternoon, trying to make herself tired enough to sleep at night, but though she slept she dreamed of finding David's body on the wharf of some wild river settlement, or his scalp hanging to a wigwam in the Western forest. By spring her hair had begun to get white around the temples.

She wished the canefields were not in such easy sight of the house. The shoots coming up in March were like little knives cutting into her with their reminder of how David had loved the cane.

In August when David had been gone eight months, Christopher offered to take a boat and go North to look for him.

"It's no use," Judith said wearily. "He might be anywhere in the world by now."

Christopher put his hand on her arm. "But he must be somewhere, mother! If he were dead we'd have—"

She almost screamed. "*Please*, Christopher!"

Christopher tried to soothe her, and went away. Judith took her horse and went out to ride in the fields, asking herself despairingly why people wanted to have children anyway. Rita was a dear little girl, but too young for companionship;

of the others one was dead and one a homeless vagabond, and only Christopher to whom she had given less of herself than to the others was an adequate son in whom she could take satisfaction. Her sense of failure was as bitter as her tormenting thoughts of David.

She looked ahead at the green shimmer of the canefields. The cane was not thriving without David. Philip's management was half-hearted, and the stalks drooped as though aware their master had deserted them. But she had not come out here to blame anybody, but to be alone and probe down under the layers of protectiveness one so easily laid over one's faults and make herself recognize as her own doing the fact that David at a man's age still cherished a child's petulance. With a rush of light she realized that she did not want to possess David any more. He was a man and did not need her sheltering; without being aware of it, he was fighting now to be as free of her spiritually as he was physically. She remembered the terrible night when he was born and thought how easy that was compared to the tortured months just past, and knew it was her own fault if she had found this second separation harder than the first.

The sun vanished and the day hung poised in clear white hesitation. After a few minutes the dark dropped abruptly. Overhead the stars began to wink.

Judith turned the horse homeward. By the candlelight from the hall she saw Philip sitting on the front steps. He waved to her.

"Where've you been?"

"Just riding."

He called Josh, who came out and led her horse away. Judith

sat on the step by him. A colored girl put her head out of the front doorway.

"No comp'ny for supper, Miss Judith?"

"No," said Judith. "Just plates for Mr. Philip and Miss Rita and me."

"Funny how she always asks that," said Philip in a low voice.

There was so seldom any company for supper now. This time last year she used to exclaim in exasperation that she never knew how many plates to order. There was hardly an evening when David did not turn up with guests. Judith caught a little short breath, remembering, and Philip reached out and put his hand over hers.

They heard the rumble of a cart beyond the oak trees, and started, for the plantation wagons were not supposed to come in this way. Vaguely they made out the dark lumpy shape of the cart under the trees. "What on earth can that be?" Judith asked.

Philip stood up. They heard a voice. "Hello! That you, father?"

"David!" cried Judith, and she began to tremble so that for a moment she could not go after Philip, who was already running down the avenue. Then, snatching a candle from the table just inside the door she rushed after him, her throat so clogged with tears that she could not call out.

"Hello, both of you!" David was exclaiming as merrily as if he had just come back from a party. "How's everybody?"

Steadying her quivering muscles and wiping the tears from her eyes so she could see, Judith stared. She saw an old and dilapidated cart drawn painfully by an old and dilapidated mule, and on the mule was David, waving and shouting as he came near the house.

In garments so dirty and tattered they might have belonged to a tramp, David nevertheless straddled the decrepit mule with easy gallantry. He had a beard of red-gold curls that made him look like a legendary Viking, and he was sunburned close to the color of an Indian. He grinned as he clambered down, and grasped his father's hand and with his free arm hugged his mother.

"Lord, but it's fine to see you all! Mother, stop crying—I'm perfectly all right."

Judith clung to him, and Philip felt his arms and face as if afraid David might melt under his touch. "Are you really all right, David?"

"Oh, absolutely! I've had a grand time." He took the candle from Judith's hand and hugged her again. "Is that Rita coming down the steps? How she's grown!"

"It's David!" Rita was crying out. "With those whiskers!"

He ran to meet her and swung her into his arms, but after her first welcome she called him a no-count trifling scamp. Rita was only twelve, and not sufficiently overwhelmed with delight to be entirely forgiving. "Everybody's been so worried about you!" she told him crossly. "You ought to be ashamed of yourself."

David laughed and set her down. They were all talking at once, but Rita's voice rose above the rest.

"Anybody'd think the way you're strutting you'd brought back a thousand gold doubloons!"

David pulled her hair. He put his hand on Philip's shoulder and grinned from him to Judith and then down to Rita.

"Honey," he said, "I have."

He held up the candle close to the ramshackle cart. For the first time they noticed that it carried a big ungainly object covered with a piece of canvas. David called greetings to the Negroes who were pouring out of the house and fields to assure themselves that the young master was really back, and turned again to the cart.

"Look," he said portentously.

Philip said, "What have you got there?" And Judith, who did not care, asked, "Dearest boy, where have you been all these months?"

"Oh—nearly everywhere," returned David. "To Savannah, and Charleston, and up the Carolina coast—that's where I found this. The trouble I had getting it back!"

He pulled down the canvas.

They saw an uncouth contrivance of wheels and big things like combs, set on a wooden framework. David stood back like an artist who had just unveiled a masterpiece.

"David, what on earth is that machine?" Philip demanded.

David laughed triumphantly. "They call it a cotton-gin."

He thrust the candle into Rita's hand and gripped both Philip's shoulders as he went on, his words disconnected in his eagerness to say everything at once.

"This is the newest invention—just beginning to be used on a few of the biggest coast plantations. I tell you, it's a miracle. You won't believe it till you see it work. I nearly broke my neck getting it here for cotton time."

"But what is it for, David?" Judith cried.

"It takes the seeds out of cotton. Ten times, twenty times faster than the fastest seed-picker ever born." He was stammering with excitement. "It's so fast you get dizzy with watching. Is the cotton in yet?"

"Some of it," said Philip, laconic with astonishment.

"First thing tomorrow morning we'll put the gin to work—" he clapped Philip on the back—"and we'll have the crop clean in three days!"

Philip began to laugh. Judith did too, almost hysterically, tears still trickling down her cheeks. She should have foreseen some such denouement. David was so utterly his father's son. She might have known he would not come home till he could come in kingly fashion. They started for the house after he had given orders to the Negroes about putting up the gin for the night. Judith walked with her arm linked in David's, too confused with happiness to hear more than an occasional phrase of his zestful monologue.

". . . two or three of these gins and cotton will be twice as profitable as indigo . . . at present prices worth putting half the plantation into cotton . . . simply itching to start it. . . . Lord, but it's fun to be home. . . ."

CHAPTER EIGHTEEN

It was David's cotton-gin that cleared Ardeith of indigo and grasshoppers. He had worked his way to Charleston on a boat that skirted the Florida keys and touched at Havana, where he had heard a good deal about the rising importance of indigo in the countries south of Louisiana. The planters of Guatemala, David told his parents, were putting in enough indigo to dye the world blue. Their competition had already cut prices and was going to cut them further. Cotton was the obvious substitute. This new machine had removed the only drawback to cotton growing on a major scale, and in the United States a hundred pounds of good cotton brought twenty-five American dollars.

Judith did not attempt to puzzle out the value of twenty-five American dollars. The tangle of nations in Louisiana had muddled her ideas of currency to an extent that already over-taxed her arithmetic. But the miracles of the gin were obvious. Planters from end to end of the bluff came to watch the inspiring speed with which the seeds were combed out of the cotton. Judith listened to the talk with a sense of adventure. Between the sugar-mill and the cotton-gin the plantations were on the verge of a revolution. She could feel it not only at Ardeith, but everywhere in the countryside. Indigo, their fundamental product and the source of their living, was suddenly a relic.

The first year of the gins Philip put five hundred acres into cotton. The next year he put in a thousand. The year following he doubled that. Cotton flourished like a weed; ginning was less costly and far cleaner than brewing the indigo dye. And grasshoppers vanished from the parlor floor.

He increased on cane as well, and built a great sugar-house of brick for refining the juice. Nobody talked indigo any more, except a few shiftless folk too stupid or lazy to change crops. Cotton and sugarcane swept new prosperity through the river towns. Louis Valcour built two additional warehouses and then five more, for cotton was bulky and required ample storage space. The Purcells constructed new wharfs at both ends of town to accommodate the increasing river trade. Durham and Larne, flatboat builders, opened another boatyard.

When she heard this Judith turned wonderingly to Philip and confessed:

"I'm simply bewildered!"

Philip chuckled and squeezed her hand with the same

expression he had worn when he first brought her to the moss manor.

"It's progress," he said. "No, more than that—it's fulfilment. It's what we dreamed of when we came down the river."

The face of the countryside was changing so fast that its landmarks disappeared almost overnight. Instead of indigo plantations, broken here and there with tobacco fields, now for miles along the road one saw cotton, and acres of sugarcane waving long green streamers. The indigo vats were gone, and in their place were gins surrounded by storehouses for the unseeded cotton and lines of wagons to take the bales to the wharfs. The tobacco-sheds had made way for ugly brick sugarmills with high chimneys throwing up pillars of smoke day and night in grinding time.

The town was changing too: with increased prosperity new residential streets were branching from the central settlement, and the air clanged with noise of saws and hammers. The wharfs were raucous with commerce. There were new counting-houses, new taverns, new shops for the display of merchandise that people were suddenly able to buy. Docked at the wharfs were more boats than ever, and bigger boats than anybody had ever seen, taking out cotton and bringing in cloth and wine and furniture for the great folk of the bluff.

Everywhere there was a tingle of energy. The river country had lost its serenity of the indigo days. There was nothing assured about cotton, nothing proved by years of experiment. Men who met at the crossroads argued hotly about varieties of seed and the most propitious time to plant. At impromptu gatherings on the corners in town one heard talk of how So-and-So had an improved gin that gobbled up cotton faster than any yet seen, or how Mrs. So-and-So had ordered real silver pitchers for her table. It was glorious, exciting, and sometimes, Judith thought with amusement, a little bit vulgar. But even their clumsiest ostentation had something healthy and likable about it.

Judith fancied she would be left in peace to watch the spectacle, but it was not long before the clamor of progress sounded indoors as well as without.

"We need a new house," said David and Rita.

"But my dears," exclaimed Judith, "what's wrong with this one?" She looked around her pink moss walls, thinking how much she loved them. But of course the children would not understand how intensely she had lived in this house. Rita was talking, with her characteristic clipped terseness. She was fifteen, a slim young person with brown hair and golden-brown eyes like Judith's.

"Nobody's living in moss houses any more. They're primitive. This place," she added crisply, "looks like a nigger cabin."

"With sixteen rooms?" Judith protested.

"But they're such little rooms," said Rita. "And pink walls and everything on one floor. We can't do any really elegant entertaining here."

"They're building houses now of cypress wood," David put in.

Rita laughed shrewdly. "You know what this place makes

me think of, mother? Old pioneers who thought they had something grand."

"Yes, darling," Judith owned, "I'm afraid that's what it is."

"Don't you see what we mean?" David insisted. "Folks notice us. Everybody knows this was the first plantation on the bluff to make sugar, and Ardeith had the first cotton-gin. This house—oh, it's not what's expected of people like the Larnes."

Though she did so with reluctance, Judith had to own he was right. On nearly all the estates around them new dwellings were either being talked of or were already under way. The moss houses had gone out of date as abruptly as indigo.

But though she understood this, Judith listened wistfully to their plans. Hardly any of her dear possessions would be fit for the double-galleried edifice they were designing. Her big dining-table, worn smooth by years of banquets, her cane-bottomed chairs and the woven cane cradle where her babies had slept, even the bed in which all her children but David had been born—they were too old-fashioned for the background of a great planter's family. When the cypress house got under way she walked about lonesomely, touching her furniture and curtains as if they were friends to whom she was saying goodby. "What are we going to do with these things?" she asked.

"Oh, throw them away," said David.

"We may be able to use some of this stuff to furnish the quarters for the house-slaves," said Philip.

"Very well," acquiesced Judith. The spirit with which she and Philip had gone into the wilderness was too strong to be halted, and she was glad of it; her children did not know, and Philip was too ardent to realize, how easy it would have been to go so far and no further and relax among the evidences of what they had already attained. She did not say so to anybody. This was a country whose byword was change, and it had no respect for relics. Everybody was stirring and everything old was being thrown away.

The new manor was painted white. There were two floors, and the front door, which had a handle and knocker of polished brass, led into a straight wide hall uninterrupted by a staircase except for a steep inconspicuous flight at the back for use at night and in bad weather. The floors were joined by two staircases that started from either side of the front door and rose like the arms of a V to the gallery above. Outside staircases were the most modern idea for hot climates, where one spent so much time on the porch anyway that it was inconvenient to have to go indoors every time one wanted to go upstairs.

The upper and lower halls ran from the front door to the back for the sake of air-currents, and the rooms to either side were large, high and many-windowed. They had starched white curtains and mirrors in gilded frames and on the walls candle-sconces of glass or polished tin, with circular reflectors to throw the light. In the parlor hung the portrait of Judith made in New Orleans when she was twenty-two, and a portrait of Philip painted several years later by a French artist who had spent a winter in Dalroy. Though the slaves had made most of the furniture, in the parlors were heavy pedestal tables from France, and a cushioned French sofa or two. There was also a clavichord bought from a nobleman who had escaped the Terror with a few household goods, the sale of which was enabling him to drink himself to death among the barbarians. It was very frail and fancy, half the inlay had dropped out, and clavichords were going out of date anyway, but Rita loved it, and played tunes on it assiduously.

Philip said, "For heaven's sake, Judith, let her enjoy herself; she's already older than you were when you married, and we won't keep her forever." Judith sighed and agreed with him. Certainly Rita did look picturesque at the keyboard, and the young gentlemen of the neighborhood listened soulfully without being disturbed by the fact that the vicissitudes of transportation from Paris to Louisiana made the melodies somewhat off key.

At the back of the house were the sewing and weaving rooms, for though they now bought most of their dress-goods Judith was too careful a housewife to trust readymade sheets and blankets. Across the hall were the storerooms and wine-closets, a row of important doors whose keys clinked from her girdle. The kitchen was brick, to be safe from fire dangers, and the rain-jars at the back were of earthenware pottery painted in bright colors. The quarters for the house-slaves were separate from the main house and joined to it by a covered passage. They too had galleries where the servants could sit when they were done with their day's work. "It sho ain't eve'ybody what belongs in a house like this," the servants told one another, and they bragged to those from other families that at Ardeith the house-folk lived nearly as high and mighty as the missis.

Upstairs were the bedrooms, eight of them besides the chambers of the bodyservants, for such a manor as this must be always ready for guests. Adjoining David's chamber was another room with cushioned chairs and a needlework table and footstools with embroidered covers, for the young master might be expected to bring home a wife any time now and she would want a sitting-room of her own.

"This house is so perfectly sumptuous," Rita said to her mother, "I almost hate to think of getting married and leaving it."

"You won't be getting married yet awhile," Judith said hastily.

"Why not? I'm sixteen." Rita rubbed her eyes. She and David had been up late the night before at a ball Gervaise had given for her daughter Emily, and Rita had only just wandered into the dining-room for breakfast.

Judith smiled regretfully as she poured Rita's belated coffee. One of the kitchen-maids brought in a hot waffle. When she had gone out Rita asked:

"Mother, am I going to have a good dowry?"

"Certainly, if you marry a nice young man."

"I might marry a rather poor one," Rita said soberly. She had a way of keeping her thoughts to herself, and Judith wondered if this suggestion of candor was indicative. Rita added, "I think I ought to get married before David does. I'd feel like an old maid with another young lady in the house who had more authority in it than I had. And David—"

"What about David?"

"He's been following Emily Purcell around at every ball we've been to lately. I'm sure he's in love with her, for I've never seen him pay any girl such steady attention. Don't you think it would be nice?"

"Why yes." Judith reached for the coffee-pot and poured a cup for herself, recalling how she had dreaded such an announcement before David ran away. Today she was merely glad he was attracted to so desirable a girl as Gervaise's daughter. What a fool I've been in my lifetime, she thought ironically as she added to Rita:

"Emily seems a nice girl, but very quiet. Do you know her well?"

"I don't reckon anybody does. She doesn't get very intimate. But she knows how to dress and she will entertain beautifully. I think she's quite suitable." Rita giggled across her waffle. "I'm glad," she added, "I won't have Martha St. Clair for a sister-in-law."

Judith began to laugh. Roger Sheramy had married the youngest of the St. Clair girls only a few months before, and though Martha was exceptionally pretty she had many of the qualities of a spoilt baby. "Don't say that outside the house," Judith warned. "Roger's your cousin."

"Yes ma'am. But you know, Emily's not very pretty but I don't believe she's ever shed as many tears in her life as Martha sheds every week. And Martha's got nothing to cry about. Cousin Roger spoils her to death. Mother."

"Yes?"

"May I go riding this afternoon with Mr. Carl Heriot?"

"Why yes. Take Melissa with you. And don't stay out after sunset. You may bring Mr. Heriot to supper if you like."

"Yes'm. And I wish you'd get Melissa a new riding-skirt. I hate to see a young lady all frocked up followed by a shabby maid. It spoils the effect."

"Why don't you give her the green one you had last spring?"

"That's a good idea. I think I will." Rita put down her knife and fork and started out. At the doorway she turned to ask, "Mother, when I get married and go to my own house, may I take my clavichord?"

"Of course, honey. Nobody plays it but you."

"Thank you, ma'am." Rita went off, and Judith smiled thoughtfully as she looked after her. If Carl Heriot was the rather poor young man Rita had in mind Judith could not see any great objection, except her reluctance to have Rita undertake marriage so young. The Heriots were a Tory family who had fled to West Florida early in the American rebellion, when a party of rebels showed their disapproval of Tories by burning the Heriot homestead in Pennsylvania. They had not managed to bring much property with them, though what they did bring had been invested in forest lands, and they now dealt in timber and firewood. Carl's mother was fond of detailing the glories of their past, but Carl himself was a sensible young fellow who did not appear to be over-conscious of being an injured aristocrat. He might, Judith concluded, do very well as a husband. That afternoon as she watched Rita ride off toward the levee with him, followed by her black chaperone resplendent in Rita's discarded riding-habit, Judith told Philip she thought they made an exceptionally pretty couple.

"I'm glad you think so," Philip said. "Carl and I had a talk while he was waiting for Rita to come down. He asked permission to pay his addresses."

Judith smilingly rolled the corner of the curtain like a lamplighter. "Are you sure he hasn't already done it?"

"I suspected he had. He seemed pretty sure she'd be willing to receive them."

"I hope you asked about his prospects."

"Oh yes. He was very frank. Carl's a younger son, you know, and there's not a great deal to be divided anyway. He was quite engaging when he told me he'd always had an idea that what they lost by being Tories had been exaggerated in his mother's recollection. But Rita's dowry will be enough for them to start on. What are you thinking of?"

"David."

"And Emily Purcell? I'm sure of it. He asked me this morning if a young gentleman wanted permission to court a young lady with a stepfather, should he ask her stepfather or her oldest brother or her mother. I told him her mother, though he'll probably have to arrange about the dowry with Harry Purcell. I'm glad. It's time David was getting married."

"Oh dear," sighed Judith. "Two weddings—with everything else!"

Philip laughed. "At least we don't have time to get rusty," he said.

Judith felt breathless. They had entered a new century and now wrote dates beginning with eighteen instead of seventeen, and it seemed as though everything had altered with the almanac. Rumors began to rustle that Spain was to return Louisiana to France, and the Creoles were eager to believe it. Though they had been for so many years technically Spanish, they were still largely French in blood and tradition and heard proudly of the conquests of Napoleon. "It will be divine," said Gervaise when they met on the wharfs one December day. "Louis is always complaining that he never could learn Spanish."

Philip grinned. "But if we're returned to France we won't be able to ignore decrees that don't suit our convenience by saying we couldn't read them."

Gervaise smiled coolly at Philip, and then at Judith, who was riding alongside him. "Monsieur, madame," she said, "you were brought up in the English colonies. You don't understand that we would put up with a few annoyances to see the Bourbon lilies in the square."

"It wouldn't be the lilies this time, ma'am," Philip reminded her. "It would be the tricolor. We live in an age of revolutions."

"Oh dear," murmured Gervaise. "I reckon I'm getting old. Louis was shocked only this morning when that impudent Emily said to him, 'But who cares if we turn French? Who cares what we are?' She is so young she thinks nothing that happened before she was born was of any possible importance."

Philip was laughing. "Shall we marry David and Emily under crossed flags?"

"My dear Philip, have you no manners? They haven't signed any betrothal-papers yet." She laughed back at him. "Now I really must go. I've been buying a new house-boy for two weeks and I've got to haggle some more about the price. I've got him down to a hundred pounds of cotton, but I won't give more than ninety and the trader won't believe me."

"Shall we see you at dinner tomorrow?" Judith asked as Gervaise beckoned her maid.

"Certainly." She kissed her hand. "Que le bon Dieu vous bénisse!"

Philip and Judith rode off to the stalls where traders were displaying silks and muslins. Rita had demanded a trousseau fit for a princess. Her betrothal to Carl Heriot was to be formally announced the next day at a dinner-party, and Judith was too busy to be much concerned about pending political changes.

The next morning, however, when she was on her way out to the kitchen to supervise the stuffing of the turkeys, she heard David say something about the supposed transfer to France and asked him what he thought about it. David reined his horse, for he was riding into town.

"I don't think anything about it," he said. "If they're going to hand us about without asking our opinion they've got no right to expect us to stand up and cheer every time they do it."

He laughed and rode off, and Judith laughed too, thinking his nonchalance was typical of what most of them felt. She shivered, and reminded herself there must be a fire in every room of the house before the guests arrived.

When they did begin to come, she was so occupied with greeting them and admiring Rita, who curtseyed and received congratulations with only the proper shade of girlish fluttering, that she paid very little attention to what anybody said. But when she finally paused by the punch-table to catch her breath over a glass she sensed an eager shrillness of talk that was hardly to be accounted for by Rita's approaching bridal. "What's all the excitement?" she asked Louis Valcour.

He paused with his wineglass halfway to his lips, astonished. "My dear Mrs. Larne, haven't you heard?"

"Heard what?"

"A boat arrived this noon with the news. The transfer to France was only a formality. Louisiana has been sold to the United States of America."

"Good heavens!" said Judith, and nearly spilt her punch. "Do you mean we're Americans now?"

Gervaise approached and held out her hand. "What do you suppose we'll be next? Dutch?"

"With yet another language to learn?" objected David, who had come up with Emily very slim and adoring at his elbow. "At least the Americans speak English."

Judith sighed. "Seriously, how long do you suppose this will last?"

"What? The American dominance?" asked Louis. "Not very long, if our history's any criterion."

"Sold," said David with a shrug. "Not even ceded."

Rita approached them with Carl. Carl was saying, "Just wait till my mother hears of this!"

"How much were we worth?" Judith asked.

"Fifteen million dollars," said Louis Valcour.

"And how much is that?"

"Madame," he returned, "I haven't the remotest idea. But it sounds like a stupendous sum."

"Where's Christopher?" Rita demanded. "He always understands about money. Cicero," she said to one of the servants, "go find Mr. Christopher and bring him here at once. Tell him it's a matter of business. That," she added twinkling to the others, "always makes him run."

"At any rate," murmured Judith, "it's something to live in a country worth fifteen million dollars."

When Christopher appeared, Rita asked, "Who is the president of the United States, and how much is fifteen million dollars?"

"His name is Thomas Jefferson," said Christopher promptly, "and fifteen million dollars is four hundred and thirty-three tons of silver."

"Holy angels," murmured Gervaise. "How under heaven do you know so much?"

"The boat brought copies of the Congressional debates," Christopher responded smiling. "The Congressmen raised a big row about it. They said Louisiana couldn't possibly be worth so much. No country on earth could. One pious old speechmaker from New England said he would advocate that the older Anglo-Saxon states secede and make their own government rather than be overwhelmed by foreigners and heathens from the Mississippi valley."

"It's all fantastic," murmured Judith, and Rita said, "I'm still puzzled."

"Look," said Christopher. He took a coin out of his pocket. "This is a picayune. It's worth approximately half an American dime. Their monetary system is very simple—ten dimes to the dollar. That's all."

"Two picayunes to a dime, ten dimes to a dollar, fifteen million dollars—Oh Lord," said Rita, "I can't count that far. I don't blame them for not wanting to pay it."

"Carl!" said a sharp voice, and Carl Heriot turned to see his mother approaching them. "What's this nonsense about Louisiana's having been sold to the Americans?"

Carl smothered a chuckle. He was a merry-faced young man with a freckled nose and a lock of hair that no amount of brushing would keep from standing straight up on the crown of his head. "It's true, ma'am," he answered. "We were just talking about it."

"And after all I've been through!" said Mrs. Heriot. "We might just as well have stayed in Pennsylvania."

Judith linked her arm in that of Rita's prospective mother-in-law. "It probably won't make much difference. Just some new parades. I don't think you'll mind it."

But after the guests had gone that evening, and she was changing into a simpler gown for supper, she asked Philip if he thought there was anybody in Louisiana who really liked the idea of being American. "There are the Spanish," she said, "who would rather be Spanish; there are the French who'd rather be French; and there are lots of people like the Heriots—"

"And people like ourselves," said Philip, "who are so used to being nothing at all that we don't care. However, Chris says it will be good for trade on the river. The Americans are supposed to be very enterprising."

"Carl wants to be married immediately," said Judith irrelevantly, "but Rita wants to put it off till April so she can wear real orange blossoms."

"Tell her," said Philip, "April will do very well, because Emily is trying to induce David to wait till June so she can carry calla lilies. Let's go to supper."

Rita had her wish about the orange blossoms, and she was married in the parlor of the Ardeith manor under an arch of white roses. One of the newly opened residence streets ran across the Heriot property, and Carl built her a house there, not large but invitingly gracious, set in a broad garden. Rita said, "It can be a really superb estate when we get it all planted," which meant when the timber and firewood business improved sufficiently for her to afford a landscape artist. Judith was glad Carl and Rita had such confidence in their future; building a little house on a vast piece of ground was gratifyingly indicative of the spirit that seemed to animate everybody of their generation.

Two months after Rita's wedding came David's. He and Emily spent their honeymoon in New Orleans, and one day in July he brought her home.

Judith put bowls of roses in their chamber and big dishes of gardenias on the tables in Emily's sitting-room. How quiet the house was, she thought as she arranged the flowers. The weeks of David's honeymoon had been the first time she and Philip had been alone together since they lived in the log cabin. When she thought of how different Emily's homecoming would be from hers it gave her a curious, inexplicable feeling that was somehow pride and somehow sadness.

She looked out to make sure everything was ready that Emily might receive the welcome due a bride. They were all in front, the house-folk and field-slaves and overseers, for it was a holiday on the plantation. How many of them there were—three or four hundred Negroes and ten overseers with their families, waiting before the big house to pay respects to the young lord and lady who would one day rule them all.

Judith caught sight of a carriage approaching on the road and went hurriedly to the upper gallery and down the stairs. On the gallery below was Philip, with Caleb Sheramy and Roger and Roger's wife Martha, and Rita and her husband, and Christopher with Audrey. "They are coming," Judith said to Philip.

He went to the steps and pulled the rope of the great plantation bell. The bell rang so rarely that it had a sound of oracular authority. It was there for great occasions or dire emergencies, and when it rang it meant that every soul on the plantation must drop his tools where he stood and come to the big house.

The bell clanged, and Martha covered her ears. "What a noise!" she exclaimed. "Like the crack of doom."

The slaves, who had been lounging on the grass, scrambled to their feet. The family on the porch stood up. The band of musicians in the parlor began to play softly. Judith went to the steps and waited opposite Philip.

The carriage turned into the avenue and stopped. The coachman, grand in black coat and high hat, grinned at the fieldhands from haughty distance. The footman sprang down and opened the door. David got out, sweeping his hat toward the slaves as they began to cheer. Emily put her hand into his and followed.

For an instant she stood there, looking with a faint, half-abashed little smile at the slaves and the big house, as though hardly sure all this could be for her. She was slim and apple-breasted, in a sheer blue gown that fell straight and narrow to her feet, girdled high with a chain of rosebuds on a velvet ribbon. Below her little puffed sleeves her arms were covered with long gloves of white lace. The brim of her hat was drawn close to her cheeks on each side by wide blue ribbons that tied under her chin. She regarded them all with wide dark eyes, pleased and yet very shy, and her hand still held David's as though but for him she would have run away. David was looking at Emily with such proud adoration that he hardly seemed aware of the others except as audience for what he had brought home. "Aren't they sweet?" Philip said suddenly to Judith.

"He loves her very much," said Judith softly.

Behind her she heard Carl Heriot murmur to Rita, "She's scared to death."

"Don't be silly," Rita retorted. "So was I. And I'm not usually bashful." The house-girls to whom had been given the honor tossed flowers for Emily to walk on. The others began to exclaim, "Evenin', young miss! Evenin', young massa!"

Emily smiled and looked up at David. He tucked her hand under his arm, and as they began to walk toward the house other Negroes behind the curtseying house-folk shouted "Marriage gif'!"

Emily began to laugh. David dropped her arm and felt in his pockets. Emily cupped her hands, and when he had filled them with coins she flung her bride's largesse to the slaves. They cheered and scrambled. The footman brought a bag of coins from the carriage and David held it open so Emily could dip in her hands for more.

The slaves tumbled down and got up, shouting, "Happy days foh de missis! Happy days and plenty chirren!" Judith laughed softly as David and Emily made their slow progress to the house. When they reached the steps Philip went down and took Emily's hands in his and kissed her. "Welcome to Ardeith, daughter."

Emily said, "Thank you, father."

She turned to Judith. Judith put her arms around her. "We wish you every happiness, my dear."

"And for you," said Emily.

Judith took up the keys hanging from her girdle and detached two of them from the chain. "Your rooms, Emily."

Emily accepted them smiling. She went to the others, to have her cheek kissed by the ladies and her hand by the gentlemen, and Judith put her arms around David. In the garden the slaves were singing. Judith whispered, "She's a darling, David. You're going to be very happy."

David glanced after her. "I know it. But thanks."

They reached the front door. Philip and Judith held it open, but David and Emily paused outside the threshold. Emily shook her head. Judith smiled as she went in first. How properly the child was doing everything. Nobody could say Gervaise had brought up an ill-bred daughter. From within the hall she glanced back at them. Emily turned her face up to David's. She looked so happy and trustful that her somewhat irregular little features were beautiful for a moment as she put her arms around his neck and he carried her over the threshold.

CHAPTER NINETEEN

The boss said there would be no more work on the wharfs this afternoon. The cotton boat would be loaded tomorrow right around sunup, and them as wanted jobs was to be on hand bright and early.

Gideon Upjohn sat on an empty wheelbarrow to rest. He was disappointed, for he had counted on loading that cotton boat today and having work tomorrow on the sugar boat. Now they'd probably load the two boats at once and a man couldn't work at but one of them.

Damn them merchandise boats from downriver, he thought sullenly. Cluttering up the wharfs so there wasn't no room for the cotton. Looked like them fancy-pants on the bluff would buy enough wine and shoes and mirrors to get satisfied sometime.

Maybe he'd better look see how Esther was coming along. If she'd sold all her fruit by now they could take a stroll through the park. Do her good. Esther sure had a bad time, working like a mule and her old man taking all her money to buy corn liquor so he could lie around drunk. Gideon skirted cotton-bales and hogsheads, pushed his way among the men bringing crates to the Valcour warehouses, and went down as far as the slave-market. There were a lot of high-class ladies and gentlemen around the slave-market, bowing and curtseying and kissing hands and smirking like they were already dead and reading on their own tombstones how good they were. Gideon stuffed his hands into his pockets and got past them, closer to the riverfront, where some stevedores were lying around. He saw Esther walking about with her basket. She was so slim and nice, with yellow hair that had a soft shine like daffodils even though she said she didn't have time to comb out the braids except on Sunday nights, she was so tired. Must be awfully hard on a girl, walking these hot docks all day long.

As he went toward her one of the men to whom she had offered her fruit leered and stroked her neck. Esther jerked back, and he tried to put his arm around her. Gideon rushed at them and shoved the man so hard he tumbled down.

"You goddamn grasshopper," he cried, "you keep your hands off'n this here lady!"

The others laughed as the fallen stevedore blinked up at Gideon. He was too drunk even to fight. Gideon took Esther's arm. "You come on with me, honey."

Esther hugged her basket, looking like a scared rabbit. He

led her away from the group to an empty goods-box near the stalls of the traders.

"You sit down here a little bit," said Gideon gently.

She looked up, her eyes deeper blue than ever under tears. "There wa'n't no need of you doing that, Gideon. Not that it wa'n't mighty fine of you."

"I ain't gonta let nobody treat you like a dock-woman," Gideon retorted hotly. He sat on the box by her.

Esther looked down, running her bare toe along a crack in the board floor of the wharf. "You might have got hurt," she said in a low voice. "And I'm used to looking out when men pester me. I mean—" Her voice trailed off with a little choke. She reached for the basket standing at her feet, but her throat choked again and she burst into tears. Gideon put his arm around her and patted her shoulder.

"Don't you go crying now, sugar," he begged her awkwardly. "It ain't no use."

"Oh, I know it." Esther dried her eyes on her sleeve and swallowed hard. "Only sometimes—" She put her forehead on her hands. "Only sometimes I go crazy, like, every damn day selling, and keeping off men, and two or three picayunes all you can make if you sell every banana you've got."

"Sure, honey, I know." Gideon sat forward and looked at the wharf-boards. After awhile he blurted, "Esther, you got to get off these here docks."

"God knows I wish I could." But she shook her head hopelessly.

"Honest, Esther," he persisted, "it ain't right. A nice girl peddling. You know where you'll wind up."

"No I won't."

"Yes you will. There ain't a woman can hold out. "Specially one like you that ain't tough. Some night your pa'll beat you one lick too many and you'll run down here and any drunk sailor'll look better to you than going home—"

Esther sat back and gripped the sides of the box with both hands. "Why don't you hush up, Gideon? You know ma ain't fitten to work, and she's gotta eat."

"And your pa's gotta drink too, I reckon."

Esther sighed helplessly. "Gideon Upjohn, you drive me outen my head. Ma says he can't help drinking. Him with his peg-leg and can't work good and all. He worked all right when I was little, sure enough he did. But them keelboats jammed and he got his leg took off—oh, my Lord." She sighed again, and she looked so tired and so powerless against the universe that Gideon was filled with rage. There had been six children in Esther's family, but two of them had died as babies and three more in the fever year, and now Esther who was the youngest had been left to hold everything on her thin little shoulders.

"Them Durhams hadn't ought to sent keels up the river in high water," said Gideon.

"Ah, sure, but they pays extra for boatmen in flood-time, and I reckon pa figured it would be all right." Esther did not even speak resentfully.

But Gideon was less cowed. He said, "Men's all the time getting killed or having their bones broke trying to go up in high water. They ought to send niggers."

Esther shrugged without trying to answer. Gideon spoke desperately.

"Esther, sugar, won't you get married to me and let me get you off these docks?"

"Oh Gideon," she said in a despairing voice, "don't start that again! By the time I'd had two or three babies and you were having to pay some woman to look after them while I had another one—and pa yelling his head off seeing alligators climb the wall—and ma sick and needing somebody to make gruel—"

Gideon's hands unconsciously doubled. Esther was so right, but he exclaimed, "Honey girl, you's just plumb outen your mind. I been crazy about you so long."

She patted his hand gently. "There ain't many like you, Gideon. But I ain't got no right making you take over my troubles. You better just go on looking out for yourself."

"Hell," said Gideon. "Why can't I look out for you too? I'm strong and I work hard and I don't go running to the bar every time I get money in my pocket like some. Why can't I get enough to look out for my girl and her po' old ma and young uns too if they gets born? I ought to!"

"Yeah," said Esther. She looked around at the boats. "Tell that to them that owns the wharfs."

They were silent. "I reckon I better be getting rid of this here," said Esther after awhile. She reached again for her basket.

"I'll tote it for you," said Gideon.

They walked around, toward the stalls where rich folks were examining the goods brought by the trading ships. A carriage stopped above the wharf and a footman opened the door. He bowed as a gentleman got out, followed by a young lady in long fluttering skirts and a ribboned hat. Behind her came a maid in a tignon, who held a parasol over the lady's head. As they passed Gideon and Esther the lady remarked:

"I hope they've brought some nice Irish linens."

She was a soft-voiced lady, very blonde and lovely, but Gideon did not notice her very much. He was looking with eyes that were cold and angry at her husband's high silk hat and fine-tucked linen shirt and long tight trousers. They met some friends, and the lady held out her hand to be kissed. She bought something at a stall and handed the parcel to her maid.

Gideon turned suddenly. "Esther."

"Huh?"

"You see that air fellow buying leather? He's got his wife with him in a yellow dress and the nigger woman holding the parasol over her."

"Yeah, why?"

"You know who that is?"

"Ain't it them Sheramys from Silverwood?"

"Yeah. What'd you say if I told you that air fancy-pants was my brother?"

"Huh?" She gave him an incredulous scowl.

"Ain't it funny?" said Gideon. "Him strutting around in a tall hat and got mo' niggers 'n he can count and buying his wife enough pretties to sink a ship—ain't it too funny? Couldn't you just bust laughing?"

"You better lemme get rid of this here fruit before you start any yarns," said Esther practically. Gideon made her rest on a goods-box near the stalls while he hawked the fruit for her. When at last the basket was empty he came back and gave her the money. It was getting late, and the crowd about the stalls was thinning. Gideon and Esther walked arm in arm to the park above the wharfs, and he told her about his relationship to Roger Sheramy.

"Lawsy me," said Esther, marveling. "But Gideon—how come he don't pay you no mind?"

"I expect he don't even know I'm living, honey."

"But don't you reckon, if you went around to Silverwood nice and proper like, and told him who you were—"

"Huh," said Gideon. "Them snippy niggers'd throw me off the place. And he wouldn't believe me. I'd be just one more wharf-rat to him, claiming kin."

"Well, well, well," said Esther. "I expect you're right. But it's queer, knowing."

Gideon stroked the dust with his toes, making five marks in a line. Esther added:

"I better be getting home. Time I was cooking supper."

They walked out of the park. The shops gave place to taverns and these to lodging-houses. The street got narrow and smelly, and noisy with children yelling and women quarreling indoors. Gideon held Esther's arm and guided her close to the houses. They turned into an alley. As they neared the door of the house where she lived Esther started and drew back against him.

"Oh my God, Gideon, listen to that!"

"Just some drunks having a fight, sugar. I'll get you home safe."

Her hand tightened on his arm. "It sounds like pa. If he's home again—"

Before he could answer she broke from him and pushed open the door. He came after her, and by the light of the cooking-fire he saw Esther's mother crouched behind a chair that she held as a barricade, pleading with Esther's father as he stormed about, his peg-leg thumping on the floor. The room had the smell of cheap stale whiskey. The man's clothes were filthy and there were streaks of tobacco-juice down his shirt.

"Where's Esther?" he was shouting. "I got to have some money. Brat—break every bone in her body—"

As Gideon sprang at him Esther screamed. "Please get out and leave us alone! He'll kill you with that peg-leg!"

The man was raving drunk, but with a fierce twist he jabbed the peg at Gideon's knee, knocking him down. Gideon heard Esther scream again and saw her father twisting her wrist. Her hand unclasped and the coins she had earned that day clinked on the floor. As Gideon pulled himself to his feet the man staggered out. Esther said, "Wait, ma," and ran to Gideon.

"Is you hurt bad?" she panted.

He supported himself against the wall, shaking his head. There was blood creeping from a cut in Esther's forehead.

"I can walk in a minute," said Gideon. "You better look out for your ma. I reckon she's fainted."

Esther retreated slowly and knelt by her mother. Gideon moved his leg to see if he could walk. He got to the side of the room where Esther sat on the floor with her mother's head in her lap. Gideon held himself up with the overturned chair.

"Can't you bring her to?" he asked.

Esther looked up at him. She shook her head. After a moment she answered:

"Ma'd all the time get blue and not breathe right when pa tried to beat me. I reckon this time done for her."

"Oh lawsy me," said Gideon tenderly. He sat down on the floor by Esther. She had covered her face with her hands, and tears trickled through her fingers, reddened with blood from the cut in her forehead.

"You don't know how I feel, Gideon," she murmured. "Ma was all the time sick, but she was mighty sweet to me. And I reckon you don't understand about pa. She was in love with him, I swear to God she was, and she said he was all right till he got his leg off—"

Her voice broke. Gideon put his arms around her and held her tight. Her mother's body slid off her knees to the floor. She cried on his breast. He could hear people screaming and talking in the other rooms of the house. It was nearly dark, and the cooking-fire made only a vague glow in the shadows. At last Esther said:

"I wonder what I'm gonta do now."

That roused him. "Don't you know?" he demanded. "If you don't I'm just before telling you. You's gonta get married to me first thing in the morning and I'm gonta look out for you and if that drunk pa of yourn ever bothers you again he's gonta get killed."

Her face was still hidden against him. "He treated me right when I was a little thing," she whispered.

"Well, he don't no more. Ain't you gonta marry me, Esther?"

She nodded. "I reckon I ain't no count by myself. Oh, you *are* so good!" she exclaimed, and put her arms around him.

Gideon took her home with him that night, to his sister's, where he had lived since his father died. His sister's husband had a good job as watchman in one of the Valcour warehouses, and they had three rooms, so that Lulie and her husband had a bedroom all to themselves. That night Esther slept in the room with Gideon and the children. The next day he got a body-collector to come for Esther's mother and they put her into a grave in the public burying-ground.

Esther said it wasn't right for them to get married the day after her mother died, but Lulie said that was better than Esther's sleeping in the same room with Gideon when they weren't married. Lulie's little girls slept in the room with Gideon but then they were children and besides they were related to him. So Esther and Gideon were married, and they rented a room in another alley. Lulie hated to have Gideon move, for he had paid for lodging with her and that helped out, but she could see he and Esther would want a room of their own.

Esther was a good wife. She worked hard and took good care of him. Every morning she cooked him a fine break-fast and packed him dinner of corn-pone and fried eggs and sometimes an orange, and she wasn't all sloppy like some women. No sir, Esther was clean, and she scrubbed the floor till you could mighty near eat your dinner off it. She washed his clothes regular, and he had a clean shirt two days a week, ironed and mended, and what was more they always had a sheet to their bed, not lying on the bare mattress like some. Gideon didn't know how he'd ever got along without Esther. Lulie was a good woman and did the best she knew how, but Lulie was always having children and she'd get careless. Not that you could blame her, she said it seemed like there was all the time a baby between her and the washtub and scrubbing gave her such pains in the back. But it was nice having Esther, young and well and sweet.

When he came in of an evening she would make him lie on the bed with his head in her lap and she would run her hand over his forehead and tell him how good he was, and how fine for her not to have to tramp the docks any more, and he'd feel less tired. Then she'd bring a pan of water and wash his feet and get them cooled after working all day, and make him rest while she dished up supper. It would be a good supper too, cornbread crisp and hot and not soggy like some women's cornbread, and molasses, and generally stew-meat. You most generally could hardly eat stew-meat; that was what the butcher shaved off the bones after he'd cut the chops and steaks for rich people, but she was smart about boiling it with bay-leaf till it tasted like something. "You got to have meat in your belly if you tote cottonbales," Esther said, and she was right too. When she had washed up the pans and covered the fire they'd take a stroll along the bluff where the streets were wide and quiet, or maybe if he'd been lucky at getting work they'd go see a cock-fight, or call in some neighbors and play cards. Or if it was bad weather they'd just sit and talk to each other, and she'd tell him how much happier she was now than she'd ever been and all on account of him.

Oh, they were doing fine, they were, and he loved Esther more all the time. She got nicer, and began to drop the way of tough talking she'd picked up on the docks. There were some words it was all right for men to use but not women, and when he told her so she wouldn't be mad, she'd just say, "I'm powerful sorry, honey—you know what it's like on the docks, and pa." He wondered where her pa was. Not that it mattered, long as he kept away from Esther.

Even after she told him she was standing behind a baby and didn't feel so peart, Esther got the cooking done all right and kept the place tidy. The baby turned out to be a little girl, and Gideon named her Gardenia for the flowers that smelled so sweet in the park in summertime. It was fun sometimes having the baby around, but sometimes it was bad, like when Gardy had colic in the night and kept him awake, and a man had to have his sleep if he was going to do a job of work. Sometimes of a morning if the baby had been wakeful Esther would be too tired and bothered with it to fix him much breakfast and he'd get cross though he tried not to. By the time he got to the docks he'd be groggy in the head from no sleep.

Days like that, he'd get plumb worn out by dark and it wasn't as nice going home as it used to be. The room wasn't so neat, for the baby's clothes were hanging around to dry and everything was messed up. Not that Esther was lazy, but with Gardy crawling around and pulling things out of place she couldn't be forever picking up and doing the cooking and washing too. She didn't scold him, not even when she needed a new wash-pot and he couldn't get it for her because he'd got tired staying around hearing the baby squall and had spent all his money at a cock-fight. He told her he was sorry, but she just gave him a funny look and said, "Don't you go feeling bad, honey. I know how it is."

But that night he woke up and she was crying. He thought maybe the baby was sick again, but little Gardy was in the bed on the other side of Esther sleeping like nothing could wake her but the last trump. Gideon put his arms around Esther, saying, "Don't be so upset, sugar. I know it's hard, washing without no good pot, but I'll get you one."

"It ain't the wash-pot," said Esther. "It's—it's—well, everything. I knowed it would be thisaway. Before long you'll wish you ain't never set eyes on me."

"Ah, go on," said Gideon. "You know I'm crazy about you. Go to sleep and you'll feel better."

Esther said, "No." She sat up. "I'll go to sleep but I won't feel better. I'll quit whining but I won't feel better."

"Whatever is the matter with you?" he exclaimed. "You keep me awake like this and then you wonder why I'm fuzzy-headed in the morning."

"I'm behind a baby again," said Esther.

"Oh Jesus," said Gideon. "And her just weaned?" Then he felt ashamed of himself, and he added, "Say, that don't matter. Anybody to hear you talk would think you weren't married or something disgraceful."

"Oh, all right," said Esther, and lay down again. When they got up the next morning she fixed the baby's milk and boiled his hominy without saying anything else about it, but she had a look that made him think of somebody that was seeing forty years all at once instead of just one day at a time.

Pretty soon he knew she had been wiser than he, for the water was extra high that spring. Men on the docks dreaded high-water years like the plague. The river got full to bursting and the current was so fast men couldn't control the boats, and mighty few traders would risk cargoes. There would be days and days when Gideon got hardly any work at all. Esther dragged herself around the stalls, trying to find one where they would give an onion with the rice, but the grocers said with trade held up they couldn't afford to be giving lagniappe. Some nights they had no supper at all.

He might have asked Cass, Lulie's husband, for help, though he'd hate to, but Cass was just getting half wages now. Mr. Valcour had put the free laborers on half-time work. When Cass asked how they were doing Gideon stuck out his chest and said: "Oh, we're doing fine, fine," because he couldn't bear to have folks know anything else of him. It was shame more than hunger that hurt him. There were always bad times now and then when you didn't expect to have everything, but to see his own wife big with child pulling herself around and looking like death, and his own little girl getting thin, that made a man feel terrible.

"If I was you and could walk," said Esther, "I'd go to them Sheramys and tell them how it is with us."

"Hush your mouth," said Gideon. "I swear they wouldn't do nothing."

"But why not?" she demanded. "Holy heaven, they still buys things. I see them folks, coming down in painted carriages, scolding because ain't no boat brought up fancy shoes from New Orleans. They got to have shoes in warm weather even. And that Roger Sheramy own brother to you."

"Christ almighty," said Gideon, "the water'll be down by June."

"Sure," said Esther, "and me being delivered before May."

"I swear to you, Esther," he argued, "them folks on the bluff don't know what it's like for us when the river's high. My ma lived at Silverwood and she knew. She said when you've got plenty you always got something else to worry about."

"I don't know what folks worry about when they've got plenty," said Esther wearily.

She nearly died when the second baby was born. Lulie came in and nursed her, and the neighbor women, though they had little enough for their own families, brought rice or pieces of fruit to help Esther get her strength back. The baby was so little and wizened Gideon marveled that he lived at all, for Esther didn't have any milk. But three other women in the alley who were nursing young babies took turns feeding him at first so he wouldn't starve. Times like this made you understand how good people were, Gideon thought sometimes; if it wasn't for bad years and trouble you never would know.

GWEN BRISTOW

He managed to get some carpentry work. The Purcells were taking advantage of the slow trade to repair the wharf-sheds. It was hard, for he wasn't used to carpentering and didn't know much about it. But he thought he was right lucky to be having any work at all when there were so many that didn't. It seemed the river wouldn't ever go down, for instead of getting to a peak and breaking out over the plantations it stayed mighty near on a level, not making any really bad floods but too swift for traffic. There never had been such a hard spring for the dock people.

Gideon began to wonder if he could go on at all, working till his back nearabout broke and never getting enough for what his folks needed. Yet tramping the docks was easier than going home, for the room was hot and smelt always of stale cooking and diapers drying, with baby John whining on the bed and little Gardy toddling around all dirty from falling in the mud around the door, and Esther so cross he hardly dared speak to her. Not that he blamed her; God knew it was as hard for her as for him or maybe harder. But he went sure enough crazy one night when he came in and found Esther's pa was back.

He hadn't meant to do anything, but when he found the old man there Gideon's head started to spin. The baby was crying on the bed and Gardy was screaming with terror as the old man shook Esther by the shoulders and shouted that he knew she had a husband making good money and she had to give him some for whiskey. As Gideon opened the door Gardy ran to him for protection and tripped over the old man's foot. The

372

old man kicked at her. Gideon grabbed Esther's meat-knife from the table and stuck it into the old man's throat.

When his head cleared and he looked down at the old man with his face in a puddle of blood on the floor Gideon could not be sorry he had killed him.

But the door was open, and a woman in the alley outside was yelling with horror. She ran to the next door, and in a minute or two the room was full of people. The woman cried out that the two men had been having a fight and the young one had killed the old one. They took Gideon off to the calaboose.

Esther was sure they would let him go when she told the law-men how it happened. Meanwhile she got a neighbor to keep the children and she went back to peddling fruit on the docks.

When they stood Gideon up before the judges she found there was hardly anybody at the court that could even talk plain. They jabbered English and French and Spanish all at once. Gideon had learned Spanish from his mother and Esther had picked up some French on the docks, but the law-men didn't use words she and Gideon knew. There was one judge who didn't know a word of English and another who didn't know any Spanish and there were clerks who kept translating and retranslating until she was so befuddled in the head she didn't know what any of them were talking about. They wanted Gideon to sign a paper and by that time all he could do was shake his head in bewilderment and try to make them understand he didn't know how to write his name.

The next thing she knew a long-nosed man was announcing that the person of Gideon Upjohn was re-consigned to the guardhouse and he was to be hanged for the crime of murder. Three men said that in three languages and it was the only statement of the day Esther understood clearly. She cried out and rushed to Gideon, throwing her arms around him and sobbing.

But a man pulled her away, saying, "Now, now, lady, don't take it so hard."

Gideon exclaimed, "Say, look ahere, ain't I told you—" But they told him to be quiet and took him off.

Esther dragged herself home. She sat down on the floor and gathered up her children, but she had hardly strength left to cry over them. While she sat there the rent-man came in. He had to have the rent; it was three days behind now, he said.

"I ain't got a copper," Esther told him dully. It was as if all the feeling inside of her was dead.

The man told her he couldn't wait any more. If she didn't have the rent she'd have to move out in the morning. Bright and early he'd be around and if she wasn't out he'd set her and her young uns in the street.

The children were crying for their supper. Esther found some hominy grits in the bottom of a bag and boiled it for them. She got into bed and pulled the children into her arms. So their pa was going to be hanged and they were going to be put into the street. No they weren't either, Esther said to herself with a blazing resolution. Nobody was going to do such things to her man and her young uns while she was up and around. Gideon could say what he pleased. Tomorrow she was going to Silverwood and they'd have to kill her to keep her from saying to Mr. Sheramy what she wanted to say.

In the morning she got up early. She put her belongings into a bundle and carried it and the children to Lulie's. When Esther told her she didn't have a place to stay Lulie said she'd keep the children today. Esther let her think she was going to the calaboose to say goodby again to Gideon.

She started walking the road that led across the bluff to the plantations. The day got scorchingly hot as the sun went higher. Esther had dressed herself as neatly as she could and put on her shoes, but when carriages passed the horses' hoofs kicked up clouds of dust and before she had gone a mile she was dirty all over. The heat made her head itch and tingle under her sunbonnet.

The plantation country was strange to her, and she called to a Negro turning a wagon into a road through the cotton-fields. "Where is Silverwood?" she asked.

He pointed with his mule-whip. "Up de road."

"Far?"

"Right far piece, I reckon."

Esther held her hands together tight. "You ain't by chance going there, is you? So you could give me a ride?"

"I sho ain't, white 'oman. I got my work to tend to. I ain't got no time to be totin' folks around."

He struck at the mules, and the wagon lumbered on. Esther sat down on the ground. Her legs ached so she wondered if she could get up again and keep going, but she managed at last to do it.

The road curved past more fields of cotton and a seemingly endless stretch of cane. Then there was a patch of wood and more fields. She asked another Negro she met on the road and he told her these fields belonged to Silverwood, and the next big white house was the manor.

The manor was set away back from the road behind trees and flower-gardens. Esther walked around the gardens to the back door. The house-slaves were working around or taking their ease on the steps of the quarters. Esther went up the back steps and knocked.

"I want to see Mr. Sheramy," she said to the door-boy who answered.

The door-boy looked at her sweaty face and sticky hands and the dust around her skirt. "He out in de field," he returned. "What you want wid him?"

"I want to see him," said Esther. She moved a step back and held to the gallery rail. She was so tired her legs were shaking.

Two or three Negroes lounging about the kitchen-house door surveyed her with indifference. "De missis don't 'low no beggin'," said one of them.

Esther wheeled around. "You shut up, you black nigger," she cried. "I want to see Mr. Roger Sheramy and you can't make me move till I do see him." She whirled back to the door-boy. "If he's in the field where's the old master? His father?"

The door-boy shrugged. "Ole massa Caleb, he done been dead dese two years. What de matter wid you, 'oman?"

"There's nothing the matter with me except I'm so wore out from walking I can't hardly stand up," Esther exclaimed.

"I want to see Mr. Roger Sheramy because I'm married to his brother and he's gonta be hanged if Mr. Sheramy don't do something. I've got to—"

"You get outen my sight," said the door-boy. "You married to de massa's brudder! He ain't got no brudder. He swat yo' backsides. Get out. Trash!"

"Damn your black hide," cried Esther.

At that moment the back door opened and there stood the lady Esther had seen with Mr. Roger Sheramy on the wharfs. Esther instinctively thought anybody who was so pretty must be sweet too. The lady was small and frail-looking, with a fluff of golden curls bound by a fillet of blue ribbon. Her gown was made of cool white muslin, and a ruffle stood crisply around her shoulders. She led a little boy by the hand.

"Lem," she exclaimed, "what on earth is all this noise? Haven't I told you darkies not to quarrel?"

Her eyes fell on Esther, standing against the gallery rail with her sunbonnet askew and her face distorted with anger. "Who is this woman, Lem?" she asked.

The door-boy shrugged. "Miss Martha, she just came and pounded on de do'. I 'spect she's plumb crazy. She says her husband's gonta get hanged—"

Miss Martha glanced at Esther. "What was it you wanted?" she asked with remote condescension.

Esther started forward. "Please ma'am, ain't you Mrs. Sheramy?"

"Yes, I'm Mrs. Sheramy. What are you doing here?"

"I got to see you," pled Esther. "Please ma'am, let me see

you! I done told this nigger and he said it was a lie. It ain't no lie. I'm named Upjohn and my husband is brother to your husband and they're gonta hang him—"

The lady's mouth tightened. Her eyes tightened too. Her hand holding the little boy's tightened. She said:

"Come inside."

Esther followed her. Mrs. Sheramy opened the door of a big cool room with white curtains and pictures on the walls. She pulled an embroidered cord and a Negro woman came in.

"Mammy, take Master Cyril to the nursery," said Mrs. Sheramy. "And don't let any one disturb me until I ring again."

His mammy led the child out. The lady sat down in a big chair by a table on which there was a bowl of flowers. "Now what are you talking about?" she asked.

Esther dropped into a chair. She hadn't been told to sit down but she was too tired to stand up any more. Her clothes felt sticky and her tongue was thick with thirst. She told her story. It was blundering and disconnected. The words came out before she had time to form them. Mrs. Sheramy listened, her chin on her hand.

"I don't know whether you're lying on purpose or simply out of your mind," she said at last, and her words were slow and cool and distant.

"I ain't neither one!" Esther cried desperately. "Please ma'am, ain't your husband ever told you his ma married a man on the docks?"

Mrs. Sheramy gave an adjustment to one of the roses in the bowl. "My husband never knew much about his mother," she said after a moment. "There was some vague yarn about her having taken up with a man on the docks. But I have no way of knowing whether or not your husband is her child—and even if he were, I don't know what you want of me."

"I want you to help me," said Esther weakly.

"But my good woman, how can I?" Mrs. Sheramy smiled gently. "I'm sorry for you, but you say your husband killed a man and was legally condemned to execution. There's nothing I can do about it. It's deplorable that you and your children should be left unprovided for—here." She opened a drawer in the table and took out a purse. "This will help you until you can find work."

Esther stood up slowly. Her hands clenched. "I think," she said, "you are the meanest woman I ever saw."

Mrs. Sheramy came to her and put the purse into her hand. "You'd better go," she said soothingly.

"I won't go." Esther threw the purse on the floor. "I don't want none of your money. My husband can make a living for me and my young uns if he gets out of jail. I want you to go down and tell them judges he knifed my pa 'causin' pa was drunk and kicked my little girl."

Mrs. Sheramy sighed. "But if that's true, Mrs. Upjohn, why didn't you tell them?"

"I tried to. But I couldn't make 'em understand no ways. They was all jabbering at once and half guinea-talk anyhow. They'd listen to folks like you!"

"But I didn't see the murder. I couldn't testify," said Mrs. Sheramy patiently, as if explaining something to a child. She picked up the purse. "You'd better take this and go, Mrs. Upjohn. Screaming like this won't do you any good."

"I ain't going," said Esther. "I'm gonta stay and tell Mr. Sheramy his self. I ain't going no place."

"Oh yes you are," said Mrs. Sheramy, and even through her exhaustion Esther wondered that any one could speak with such sweet gentleness when you could see she was burning up with rage. "And I'm afraid," Mrs. Sheramy added evenly, "that if you continue to shout and make a scene I shall have to ask the servants to take you out. Now will you go quietly, or shall I ring?"

She put her hand on the bellcord. Esther felt her own hands making vague movements in front of her. Mrs. Sheramy's pretty, pitiless face seemed to get further away and then very close, then Esther felt a strange lightness in her head and she knew she was falling but she couldn't help it.

When she opened her eyes she was lying on a soft clean bed with a blue counterpane. Standing at the foot of the bed was Mr. Roger Sheramy, and his wife was sitting nearby. Mr. Sheramy looked a little bit like Gideon. He had the same whimsical dished-in nose and the same heavy eyebrows growing almost together.

"So then what did you do, Martha?" he was asking.

"Why, I started to pull the bellcord, and she fainted."

Mr. Sheramy's hand tightened on the bedpost. "Martha," he said slowly, "I didn't know you had it in you."

"Good heavens, Roger!" she exclaimed. "That tale has been scandal enough already—are you going to take in any illiterate convict who claims to be related to you? You'll have them in droves at the back door."

He sighed, and after a moment he glanced at Esther. "I think she's coming to. Will you have one of the girls bring some brandy?"

He sat down by the bed. Esther looked up at him in speechless gratitude.

Roger was in a good deal of a quandary. Esther's story, recounted to him when she had been fed and rested, sounded entirely true. Caleb had never told him very much about his mother. Roger thought now that perhaps if his father had really wanted to find her other children after she died he might have been able to do so. Though in one detail Martha might be right—if the story was given public credence there'd be no end to the paupers and convicts who would demand his bounty on the ground of possible relationship—still Esther roused his natural sense of justice. Whether or not Gideon Upjohn was the son of Dolores, if he had killed a man under the circumstances Esther described he didn't deserve to be hanged for it. Roger told Martha so when he found her in tears that afternoon.

"There's no reason for your being so distressed," he said to her, "just because I want to help a man in trouble."

Martha's tears trembled on her lashes as she looked up at

him. One of her ringlets had escaped the ribbon and lay like golden floss on her forehead. "Roger, darling," she murmured, "it's not myself I'm distressed about. It's Cyril."

"Cyril?" he repeated, puzzled.

Martha sat on his knee and put her arms around him. "Of course, dearest. Don't you see what will happen if you acknowledge any relationship with people like that? That woman's filthy brats yelling 'Hello, cousin!' every time they see Cyril on the wharfs! And you know what a scandal gossipy women can make out of it once it gets started. Oh, don't do that to him! Our darling baby that we love so much—please don't, Roger!"

She laid her cheek on his and held him tight. When she wept he was always helpless, and he felt unable to cope with her now. But he tried to.

"Martha, you're asking me to be quite heartless. Do you really want to let a man be hanged when he doesn't deserve it, without even trying to get a fair hearing for him?"

"But you aren't responsible for anything that's happened to him," she pled, lifting her head again. He felt one of her tears trickle down his cheek. "And neither am I—"

"I wonder," said Roger thoughtfully. "Did Mrs. Upjohn tell you she'd been evicted for non-payment of rent?"

"Yes, and I offered her money."

"Well—doesn't your family own that property below the wharfs?"

"I believe so. That was part of the original St. Clair grant from the king. But is it my fault some people can't pay rent?"

"No, honey, it's not your fault. But if I'm a landowner who helps make the laws I ought to be interested in seeing that they're administered fairly. Besides, Gideon Upjohn is very likely to be my half-brother, and if I don't help him out of this I'll never have any peace of mind again."

"Suppose that man is your half-brother," urged Martha. "You aren't responsible for that. And you *are* responsible for your own child. Do you want Cyril to have a family skeleton tied to his heels everywhere he goes? I couldn't *bear* it, Roger!" She put her hands to her eyes and began to sob again, softly and helplessly.

At last Roger left her. In desperation he sent the carriage to Ardeith. The coachman bore a note to his Aunt Judith, asking her to come to Silverwood at once. He had to talk to somebody who knew more about his mother than he did.

Judith appeared just before dark, followed by a maid carrying a parcel. "That," she said to Roger, "is a bedgown. I'm not going back along that lonesome road at midnight. Now what's the trouble, child? Your letter was half illegible and entirely frantic."

Roger laughed with relief. He was so glad to see her. He knew she had small respect for Martha and in less drastic circumstances he would have hesitated asking her to settle one of their disputes, but Judith was at least definite in her thinking, and would understand his conviction that he must help the Upjohns in spite of Martha's tears.

"It's like this, ma'am," he began, when they had gone into

the parlor. "I'm not exactly frantic, but I do need advice. You knew my mother."

"Oh," said Judith. "I was sure this had to come up again. What's happened, Roger?"

Roger told her about Esther's coming to Silverwood.

"I see," said Judith finally. "You want me to suggest a compromise that will be just to Gideon and yet pacify Martha."

"Exactly. Aunt Judith, is Gideon Upjohn my brother?"

"Yes," said Judith. After a moment she asked, "Where is the wife?"

"Here. She wasn't fit to be sent home today. I talked to her. All she wants is a chance to live in peace, and in spite of Martha it seems to me the least I can do is give it to her."

Judith watched a feather of smoke above the candle. "Then Roger, why don't you do it? I know you don't want to quarrel with Martha. I won't pretend I ever got along very well with her, but I won't pretend either that I think it's any sin for a man to be in love with his wife. Get a smart lawyer and have Gideon Upjohn tried again. And if anybody wants to know why you did it, say the poor fellow's wife came begging at your door and you heard her story and took pity on her. The name Upjohn doesn't mean anything to the parlor gossips Martha is so afraid of."

"Fine!" Roger exclaimed gratefully. "Thank you, Aunt Judith. Martha can't possibly object to that."

The next morning, after she had talked to Esther Upjohn, Judith went down below the wharfs and paid a year's rent on decent lodgings for Esther and her children. Roger engaged a notable lawyer who obtained Gideon's release. Before the case was over Roger considered that he had been an extremely generous and chivalrous young man. He had not laid eyes on Gideon Upjohn, but he had spent a great deal of money on the lawyer. Not many men would have done as much, Martha said, and this, Judith admitted, was quite true.

Martha said it lying pale and pretty against her pillows, for the morning after Roger decided to defend Gideon she woke feeling so weak that she could not possibly get up, and she remained an invalid throughout the proceedings. Roger worried, for Martha was ordinarily as healthy as a colt. But Martha, languidly inhaling the perfume of roses lying in the curve of her arm—for the perfume of roses eased her nausea a little—murmured that with what she was going through it was hardly surprising that her health had broken down. When she got no better physicians were summoned from New Orleans. They said it was a strangely prolonged case of the nervous vapors, and recommended that she be bled.

The day she was to be bled Roger summoned Judith to be with her, and Judith, in a state of exasperation, brought Emily along. Emily had never had the vapors, and though she was less pretty than Martha she was considerably easier to have around.

Judith sat by Martha and held her hand, and after it was over and Martha lay in an exhausted sleep, ravishingly white and lovely, Judith left Roger to sit by the bedside and went out to the parlor where Emily was waiting.

"Here's a glass of sherry," said Emily. "You probably need it. How is she?"

"Thanks, darling. I do need it. Oh, she groaned quite pitifully."

"I don't doubt it," said Emily. "Let's go home."

"Do you think she's likely to need us again?"

Emily shrugged. "I think she'll sleep all night. And after this Cousin Roger won't dare own the existence of his lowly relations."

CHAPTER TWENTY

Generally Philip and David shared responsibility for the plantation, Philip supervising the cotton and David the cane. Emily was as enthusiastic about the sugar as David. Even after she had children to occupy her attention Emily rode into the fields often, and could discuss the possibilities of the harvests as competently as he. Judith admired her for this. David would have tired easily of a woman who confined her conversation to clothes and babies, and she was glad Emily had sense enough to know it.

About the time of David's marriage Philip had bought a tract of sugar land west of the river and shipped a boatload of Negroes across to work it. David and Emily sat on the steps talking about the crop on this land one evening when Judith brought her knitting out to the gallery.

"I was telling David he should send a white overseer across the river," Emily said when Judith joined them. "The Negroes aren't likely to do much work without supervision."

"I thought the same thing at first," David put in, "but they seem to be turning out pretty good crops. Father wanted to try out a Negro overseer, and he sent the best sugar man we've got as head of the gang."

"Did he? Who?" asked Emily.

"Fellow named Benny. He's young, but he's smart as a whip. His mother used to work in the big house when I was a little boy, till father put her in charge of the day-nursery in the fields. Benny's nearly white, and he's got a lot more sense than the average slave."

Emily nodded thoughtfully. "If the other Negroes respect him enough to mind him, it may be a good idea."

"It seems to be working all right," David told her.

Judith went back into the house. In her own room she stood drumming her fingers on the mirror. So that was what Benny was doing. She had not mentioned Benny in years, and had not seen him since the afternoon little Philip was stricken with yellow fever. But when she heard David speak his name she knew she had not forgotten and that she still resented him. Evidently Philip had bought that extra sugar land for Benny's sake, and she told herself she ought to be glad the problem presented by his existence had been solved so nimbly. But she was not; she could not be glad of anything that reminded her of the agonizing period preceding Benny's birth. However, she added grimly, if the years had left her undisciplined within they had at least taught her to hold her tongue. And she did hold it. She did not speak of Benny, not even when David mentioned him one night a year later while they sat at supper.

"Father, there's something I've been meaning to tell you about that cane-patch across the river."

"What's wrong with it?" Philip asked.

"Nothing's wrong with the cane—yet," said David. "But that fellow Benny we sent across as overseer—we're going to have to bring him to this side."

"What's he been doing?" Emily asked, when Philip said nothing. Judith did not look up. She made herself sip her wine quietly, and buttered a biscuit.

"He's making trouble," said David shortly. "Benny's smart, but he's nearly white and that sort always seems to get obstreperous in the fields. He's started a lot of fool talk over there about how the Negroes do all the work and get nothing for it, and he's making them discontented."

"Good heavens," said Emily. "And everybody says the Negroes at Ardeith are pampered like children."

"Ours have always been contented," David answered, "but it just takes one big-talker like that Benny to start rebellion. If he can't learn to keep quiet I'm in favor of selling him—then he might learn what it means to belong to a master who doesn't indulge his Negroes."

Judith had split her biscuit and buttered it too thickly. She scraped off the surplus, and heard Philip ask:

"What's he telling them?"

"Something about their being free and getting land of their own in the West. A lot of nonsense, but dangerous."

Emily laughed a little. "Will you pass me the marmalade, David? You'd think an intelligent Negro would have more sense than that. Doesn't he know anything about the laws relating to freedmen?"

"Of course not," returned David. "Negroes think being free means they'd be white. Benny's been a slave all his life and thinks such things as food and shelter are free as sunshine. What do you think of selling him off the place, father?"

"I don't want to sell him, David," said Philip tersely. "But I'll attend to him. How's the cane on this side?"

But David would not be put off the subject. "But look here, father. I don't want Benny in the cane, this side or the other. If I'm to be responsible for the sugar I've got a right to have workers I can control. If you want to put Benny in the cotton that's none of my business, but he's never been a cotton hand."

Philip was silent.

"You know," said Emily after a pause, "if I were running a plantation I'd either sell bright-skin Negroes to townspeople or make house-folk of them. They're almost never any good in the fields. They put on so many airs. Always pretending to be related to the big house—"

"That will do, Emily," Philip exclaimed. "There's no sense in making a speech. I'll attend to him."

It was the first time he had ever spoken sharply to her. Emily stopped and colored. David was too well-bred to rebuke his father in the presence of other people, but he glanced at him indignantly, and Emily said:

"I—I'm sorry, sir. I didn't mean to be meddling."

Philip put his hand on hers. "Forgive me, honey. But it's been pretty hot today, and I'm tired."

Judith managed to get through supper, and she tried not to think about Benny. He was none of her business, she told herself over and over, and she had no right to object to Philip's attempt to be just to him. Philip was quite right to keep him at Ardeith where he was sure Benny would receive good treatment instead of selling him to an unknown master who might or might not be kind. She wished he could be set free, but this was an easy escape that she knew Philip would not take. The condition of freed Negroes was pitiable and nobody could pretend otherwise; hedged about with all sorts of legal restrictions, they were in worse state than the poorest of the poor whites. She said nothing about Benny to Philip, and knew he was grateful for her silence. But she could not help thinking of him. David did not know who he was—half the bright-skins on any plantation claimed to be related to their owners, and if Benny knew his origin and spoke of it David would regard it as more big-talk. But David was still concerned about him. Judith heard him say so to Emily.

"What did your father do about that bright-skin in the sugar?" Emily asked one day.

"He put him in the oranges for the present. But that's not

full-time work, and he'll have to go into the cotton. Father won't take my word for it that Benny's a born troublemaker. If I were master of the plantation I'd get him off it in double-quick time."

Judith went out, and got rid of her tense nerves by scolding the girls for not polishing the brass knocker on the front door. She was glad David talked politics at dinner instead of plantation affairs.

She was glad too that politics were assuming unusual interest, because she could fill up her mind with the state of the country and so crowd Benny out of it. For a long time the residents of the Dalroy bluff had virtually ignored their political affiliations, taking them as something changeable but uncontrollable like the weather, but now they were in a state of uncertainty that hampered their development. Dalroy was growing fast. All the Louisiana country was filling up with population since the purchase by the United States, but Dalroy was in the subdivision that had been West Florida. The province at one time, when it was under English rule, had been completely separated from the rest of Louisiana, and whether or not West Florida was part of the Louisiana Purchase nobody seemed to have decided. She asked David to explain it to her.

"It's rather funny," he said. "The Americans assume that we're American, but the Spanish governor is still here. And meanwhile we obey whatever American laws we like and whatever Spanish laws we like and nobody seems to pay much attention."

He was so casual that Judith was amazed when the men of

the bluff suddenly decided they were going to do something about it.

It was a day in late summer. Judith sat on the gallery embroidering a dress for Emily's little boy Sebastian when Emily came down the staircase by the front door. "Please ma'am," she exclaimed, "are all those gentlemen going to be here for dinner?"

Judith turned around. "What gentlemen, Emily?"

"I saw them from upstairs." Emily gestured toward the front, and Judith caught sight of Philip and David riding into the avenue followed by about twenty others. She gasped. On pleasant days she generally ordered dinner for ten, for Philip and David were likely to bring in two or three guests apiece, but she had not prepared a banquet.

"I can have the girls scramble eggs," she said to Emily, "but I wish they'd told me they were planning a party."

"It doesn't look like a party," objected Emily. "They aren't bringing any ladies."

Judith went to the steps to greet the guests. There were the three young Purcells, and Louis Valcour, Roger Sheramy, Christopher and several men of the Durham family, Carl Heriot and his two brothers, and several more. "Can you feed us?" Philip called as he dismounted.

"Yes," she called back, "if you aren't particular about what you get." She could not help laughing in spite of her annoyance. Philip's expression was scampish like that of a little boy about to raid the pantry. Leaving them to pay their respects to Emily she drew Philip to the staircase, demanding, "Will you please tell me what you're up to now?"

Philip grinned upon her. "We're just before displacing the Spanish governor."

"Philip, for heaven's sake! How are you going to do it?"

He laughed and snapped his riding-crop. "We're going to meet in the public square at dark, several hundred of us, and go to the palace and order him out." He chuckled at the others. Philip's hair was nearly white, but except for that he looked hardly older than David.

"But isn't that sort of thing dangerous?" Emily was protesting. "Isn't there an armed guard at the palace?"

"Why don't you let the American government put out the Spanish officials?" Judith exclaimed.

"The American government," said David, "has had seven years to do it, and they've never paid us any mind. So we're doing it ourselves. Louisiana has been organized as a territory and before long it will be asking admission into the Union, and we're part of Louisiana. Yet there's that Spanish guard eating up our taxes, and the Americans either don't know the Spanish are still here or don't care. So—" He drew a document from inside his coat. "We've drawn up a declaration of independence for West Florida."

Judith sat down weakly on a step. "I never heard of anything so absurd in my whole life."

"Why absurd?" demanded Roger Sheramy. "By tomorrow morning either we'll be locked up or you'll be living in the nation of West Florida."

"And then watch the Americans notice us," finished Philip.

She caught sight of Emily's dismayed face. Judith frightened too, but she had lived with Philip and David longer than Emily had and knew the impossibility of stopping either of them when they had set out on some such wild scheme as this. So she only sighed, murmuring, "Try to keep your heads on your shoulders," and went in to order dinner.

They ate hurriedly, all talking at once with such gusto that she found it hard to learn anything. Emily was quiet, as though no longer disturbed by revolutionary dangers, but toward dark as the men rode off to meet their friends at the square, Judith saw her drop tears on Sebastian's head as she kissed him good night. Emily let him go off with his mammy, but as they went out she exclaimed:

"I'm scared! Anything might happen to them!"

Judith took her hand gently. "The Spanish governor really hasn't any right to be here, honey."

"I don't see," said Emily faintly, "how you can be so calm."

"I was wondering how you could be."

"Oh dear," said Emily, "I was shaking inside. But I hated to get panicky in front of David."

"I wish I had been as wise as you when I was your age," Judith said smiling.

Emily did not seem to hear. She laughed shortly. "David thinks I'm so self-possessed. When he went off he said it was good to have a wife who wasn't frightened—Martha Sheramy was half drowned in a cascade of tears."

"Oh—Martha," said Judith. "She looks so pretty when she cries."

"I don't," said Emily shortly. "But I'm still scared they're going to be shot."

She took up some crochet and went to sit by the candle. After a while she looked up to add, "It's very sweet of you not to pet me. I hate to be fussed over."

It was late, but neither of them suggested going to bed. Emily went to see how Sebastian was and came back to report that he was sleeping in peaceful oblivion of the affairs of nations. Judith brought her embroidery to the candle. More concerned about the attack on the palace than she had confessed to Emily, she was too restless to sleep. For a long time they worked silently. It was nearly midnight when Emily dropped her work into her lap and sat up abruptly.

"What's that?"

"I didn't hear anything," said Judith. But she stuck her needle into the muslin and listened.

"There it is—it sounds like somebody shouting a long way off." Emily went to the window.

Judith followed her, remembering that she was older and must set an example of courage. "But my dear, if there was a battle it would be in town. They can't possibly be fighting all the way out here!"

Emily had pulled back the curtain. Her hand caught Judith's shoulder. Judith gave a gasp.

Far off in the fields, so far that they were tiny as stars, were moving torches. They were not advancing in a line, but in a confused huddle, and there was the faint sound of angry voices. Emily put her hand to her throat with a cry.

"That's not soldiers!"

Jerking the curtains together Judith stepped back from

the window. Her scalp felt prickly and the palms of her hands were suddenly wet.

"It's Negroes," she said.

Emily pressed backward, her hands spread out against the wall and her whole body quivering with fear.

"*Benny!*"

The syllables slid into an inarticulate cry as she rushed out of the room and up the back stairs to the nursery.

Judith pulled the bellcord and heard the bell jangle in the silence of the house-quarters. With a furious effort she made herself stop trembling and forced her thoughts into clarity. They were miles from any other residence. A slave uprising at Ardeith could happen and nobody need know it until she and Emily and Emily's children were found murdered when the men returned in the morning. They had never seriously considered any such possibility. The Negroes at Ardeith were well trained, well treated and to all appearances happy. But one malcontent like Benny could stir up rebellion in a hundred others who would never of their own accord have dreamed of such a thing. Evidently he had done so. They were a mob, crazy and undisciplined, yelling for the chance to plunder the big house while the masters were away.

She was about to ring again when Christine ran in, her eyes heavy with sleep. "What's the trouble, Miss Judith? I went to sleep waitin' to get you ready for bed."

"What do you know about a disturbance among our people?" Judith demanded.

Christine's eyes popped. "Ma'am?"

Judith drew aside the curtain.

"Oh my lawsy, those dirty field-niggers!" Christine burst into tears and fell on her knees, her hands clasped in supplication. "Miss Judith, I swear before God us house-folk haven't done a thing! We don't get mixed up with them—you know we don't—I swear to Lord God Almighty, may he turn my bones to water—"

"All right, get up and quit slobbering." Judith spoke almost fiercely. "If you mean what you say wake the others in the house-quarters and have them get horses. And if you don't want to get killed be quick about it. You know the fieldhands think the house-folk live as mighty as the master and they'd kill you as soon as us. Hurry." She wheeled to face Emily, who came in leading Sebastian by the hand, followed by mammy in her bedgown with the little girl. "Emily, give those children to mammy. She'll take care of them as well as you can. Do as I tell you!" she ordered as Emily hugged the children defensively to her. "And here's the key to the gun-room. Get a gun for yourself and bring one to me."

She went out to the gallery. The rebellious slaves were rushing upon the house, nearly here now. Judith pulled the rope of the plantation bell. It clanged commandingly. That would rouse the overseers, and any Negroes who had spurned Benny's yarns of glory.

Emily brought her the guns. "Did you lock the gun-room?" asked Judith.

"Of course."

"Good. If they got in there we'd be massacred. There can't

be very many of them armed now. Here. You've shot birds and squirrels. Keep your hand steady. Don't shoot to kill unless you have to."

Emily gave her children a last terrified embrace and mounted a horse. The house-servants were rushing out in various stages of undress. Judith hurried back indoors to get guns for Josh and Cicero, and a few others of the oldest and most faithful. She sprang upon a horse and they rode to meet the fieldhands.

Their leader had evidently tried to make the Negroes advance quietly upon the house, but at sight of the house-folk armed and mounted the last vestige of their discipline fled and they rushed ahead wildly. There were not more than a hundred of them, riding work-mules and carrying sticks and torches made of lightwood. Only a few had guns, for except those belonging to the overseers no firearms were permitted in the fields, but Judith saw with horror that many of them brandished machetes, the murderous short-handled cane-knives, with blades wide at the top and narrow toward the bottom and saw-teeth on both edges pointing down toward the handle. Machetes were distributed in the morning by the overseers and locked up in the sugar-house at night; she wondered whose carelessness had permitted them to break into a sugar-house, then she remembered with a blaze of fury that Benny had been a sugar-overseer with machetes under his care. She saw him on a horse at the head of the yelling mob. A torch showed her his face and she knew him because he looked like Philip.

She heard a shot and then another, and saw half-dressed overseers riding upon the Negroes, and colored women running up from everywhere, shrieking.

"Drop those machetes!" yelled a man's voice, and the overseers' guns cracked. Several of the Negroes fell, dropping their knives, but she hardly saw them. She was conscious only that Benny was riding toward her, very close, and he had a machete tied around his neck and a gun in his hand.

"Get that white nigger!" one of the overseers shouted. "He's heading them!"

Judith raised her gun. Her hand was quite steady. She took aim and fired.

He reeled back for an instant, recovered and struck at his horse. Judith fired again. He fell to the ground. "Look out, ole miss!" somebody cried behind her, but she was hardly aware of danger. She forced her horse into the seething black mob, catching the bridle in the bend of her elbow as she reloaded her gun, and as she passed the spot where Benny lay huddled she leaned over and fired into his body again.

A sharp fire blazed in her knee where it was crooked over the saddle and she saw the flash of a lightwood torch along the teeth of a machete. With the butt of her gun she knocked it aside before it could fall again. For an instant she sat rigid, hardly aware of the terrified neighings and jerkings of the horse under her, for it was as though the pain in her knee had pierced what had been simply a blank determination and she could not think of anything except what she had just done.

Her mind felt curiously numb, in odd contrast to the live

agony in her body. The shots and yells around her seemed very far away. She felt a hand over hers on the bridle and in the darkness heard somebody say:

"Ole miss done got hurt—she's liable to faint dis minute."

It was old Josh who had come down the river with Philip. She recognized his voice and knew she was being snatched off the horse. That was the last she knew that night.

The next thing she got was the sense that the whole lower half of her was afire with pain and there was cold water on her face. She made an involuntary little moaning noise in her throat and heard David say, "Don't try to move, mother. You'll be all right."

She looked around. It was early morning and she was in her own room. There were big spots of blood on the bed-linens. David was there, and Philip, and Emily leaned over the bed stroking Judith's forehead with cloths dipped in cold water. Judith asked, "Are the children safe?"

"Yes dear," said Philip gently. He put his hand on hers. "But don't try to talk yet."

He was sitting on the edge of the bed. Judith turned her head suddenly away from him and put her arm over her eyes, remembering that she had killed his son and put a last vindictive shot into Benny's body when he was dying on the ground. She heard herself make another sound like a groan. Emily's voice said:

"She must be in the most dreadful agony, David! Do you think she could stand a sleeping-draught?"

"Not yet, I'm afraid," said David. He knelt by the bed. "Mother, please try to stand it. You've been so brave and we're all so proud of you!"

"Oh, can't you be quiet?" Judith cried.

For awhile after that everything was confused again. She saw them that day through pain and blazes of fever, but the next day her head was clearer. Emily was nursing her with an almost reverent gratitude, and David would hardly leave her. They told her over and over that it was her courage that had saved the house and their children, when she held back the rebellious slaves till the overseers and loyal Negroes could get there, and when she killed Benny his followers were thrown into panic. Her other children and her friends poured in with congratulations long before she was well enough to see them. The story of her bravery was being talked of everywhere; how it had grown in the telling she was not sure, but she found herself a heroine. Oh no, there had been no serious damage, they said—a few of the Negroes had been killed and several overseers hurt, and they had ruined some of the cotton by riding over it, but the leaders were in the guardhouse and the rest were penitent. It was all Benny's doing, he with his handsome tales had got them crazy for a while. But she had killed Benny, though she had reached an age when a lady should have no more to do than see to her house and be waited on by her grandchildren; she had ridden at him and killed him as valiantly as a soldier.

Judith listened bitterly. When she could bear it no longer and begged them to stop talking and let her alone, they said she was splendidly modest.

But she lay awake and thought for hours when Emily, knitting by her bed, thought she was asleep but would not leave her lest she awake and want something. She tried to analyze what had happened to her that night to wipe her clean of all the wisdom and self-control she thought she had learned, and tried to think whether or not it had been absolutely necessary to kill Benny. Yes, probably if she had not done so somebody else would have. But she asked herself over and over as she lay there, if she had killed him to save David's children or because she hated him, and she did not know. To the end of her life she did not know. She felt a weight of shame heavier than any burden of grief or anger she had ever known.

For the first few days it was so heavy that she could not bring herself to ask where Philip was. He had been there when she first regained consciousness, but since then she had not seen him. Finally she could bear it no longer and she asked David why he had not come to her.

"Father's a little bit ill," David said, and she fancied he hesitated a fraction of a second before he answered. "He caught cold at the palace the other night—we never should have let him come with us, at his age."

"Did you get rid of the governor?" Judith asked, for the sake of something to say.

"Oh yes. He's going back to Spain. We'll be admitted to the Union as part of the state of Louisiana." He bent over her. "Don't worry about father."

"Very well," said Judith. But she was thinking, a cold. A little cold. Enough to keep him away from me. Enough to let me understand that he alone of them all knows I haven't any charity or forgiveness in me.

She had asked them to leave her alone at night. She was free of fever now, and slept more comfortably if she wasn't being watched over. After the others had gone to bed Judith lay awake. If she could have done so she would have gone to find Philip, but her leg was in splints. She thought of how she and Philip had loved each other for thirty-six years. And now he would not forgive her because he knew that secretly she had not forgiven him.

Oh, he might have been more gentle, she cried silently into the dark. He might have known that sometimes one is as helpless in the grip of passion as in that of a human enemy. Remembered now, that last shot was not needful, but at that minute it was inevitable. Philip might have understood that.

She heard the latch lift at the door, and started indignantly. This everlasting devotion—why need they come creeping upon her in the middle of the night?

"Judith?" said a low voice. It was Philip's, and yet somehow strange.

She raised up. "Philip? Philip!"

By the flicker of the night-light she saw him latch the door. He was wrapped in a dressing-gown and had a woollen scarf about his throat. Kneeling by the bed he took her into his arms, and for a moment she held him with such thankfulness that she did not notice how his face was burning against her. But at last she exclaimed:

"Philip, you're ill! You're on fire with fever!"

"Yes, I know," he whispered. "Those children keep me so supervised I can't move, and I had to slip out like a prisoner. I hope I didn't wake you."

"No, I wasn't asleep. But you're really ill!"

She was sobbing. He felt her tears, and asked, "But honey, didn't they tell you I was ill? I think I've been out of my head. How are you?"

"I'm all right. Nothing but a cracked knee. You shouldn't be out of bed, Philip. Come lie down here and I'll cover you up."

He drew himself up by the bedpost. His movements were unsteady, and he almost fell on the bed by her. Judith painfully edged herself over to give him room. He took her in his arms, but his embrace was weak. She asked:

"Can you go to sleep, dearest?"

"No," he said, "I want to talk to you. I did leave you alone the first day, before the fever got me quite helpless. I'm sorry. I can't seem to say it very well. But I'm sorry."

"Then," she asked faintly, "you do forgive me for killing him?"

"There was nothing else to do, was there?"

"No—but did they tell you I fired again when he was on the ground dying?"

"Yes, I know that."

"And you forgive me for that, too?"

"I didn't at first." His voice was weak and the words were not very clear. "It's all right. None of it seems to matter very much."

She drew his head on her shoulder, telling him not to talk

any more. Philip lay by her quietly. Judith wondered if really good people could ever know what it meant, this peace that came with the knowledge that there was one human being who knew your innermost sins and secrecies and loved you in spite of them.

Suddenly she sat up, and her shattered knee responded with a wrench. "Philip!" she cried. "*Philip!*" When he did not answer she felt his hands and face and body; they were not cold, but not as hot as they had been. She called and shook him, but he did not respond. At last she heard David at the door.

"Mother, what is it?" he demanded as he came in. "Is that father? What's he doing out of his room?"

He called Emily, and knelt by Philip. Judith drew herself away from them with terror that made her stiff and speechless. But when David raised his head and looked at her she found that she was asking:

"Is he—dead, David?"

David nodded, and then suddenly he covered his face with his hands and dropped his head on the counterpane, like a child. Judith watched, too stunned to speak to him or touch him, and at last she sank down and gripped her pillow with both arms and buried her face in it.

After a long time she heard Emily say:

"David, this is killing your mother. We—maybe we should have told her he was dying."

David came to her and she felt him slip his arms around her. She yielded, and began to sob quietly on his breast, but her tears were neither comforting nor cleansing. She was conscious of nothing but a bleak emptiness, and of years and years ahead when she would be old in a young world with nobody to talk to.

They laid out Philip's body in state on the gallery. Judith lay on a couch at one side, while the Ardeith folk came to pay their respects.

They gathered around the house, some of them standing still with lowered heads, some of them wailing, or singing strange reverent hymns that blent religion with voudou and grief.

Her children and her children's children were grouped behind her. They were very attentive. Little Sebastian held the bottle of fragrant water, which he doused on a handkerchief for her to ease her tears. She managed to thank him. She was not shedding any tears. All she could think was that this ceremony was another way in which she was retreating into loneliness.

Words began to form in her mind. "He was their master. He was their father. They loved him, of course. But he was my husband. We were together. Don't they understand? Can't they imagine what it means to be together for thirty-six years and then not to be together any more? Oh, Philip, Philip, Philip!"

But he was dead. He was quite stiff and cold, on a dais draped with white satin and piled with white flowers.

David went to the step and clanged the bell. There was a hush. He began to speak.

"One minute before you come to the steps. We do not want you to be disturbed as to the future, either our people or our overseers. No one will be discharged or sold. Ardeith Plantation will go on as if the old master were still here. Now in single file, please."

He stepped back and stood by the bier. The overseers first, with their wives and children, came up the steps. They were in black and held their hats in their hands. First they paused by the couch where Judith lay.

"You've sure got our sympathy, ma'am."

"One thing you can be sure of, Mrs. Larne, we were mighty proud to be working for him."

"Thank you," said Judith.

They filed by the bier, pausing and shaking their heads. The chief overseer went to David and held out his hand.

"And to you, sir—well, everything we'd ever have done for him."

They shook hands. "I'm certain of it," David said. "Thank you very much."

"Well sir—you know, there being a little trouble with the niggers—it won't happen again. They're all the sorriest kind, sir. Just that white nigger that made trouble."

"Yes, I understand. I've never doubted your loyalty."

"Thank you, sir. Mighty good of you to say so."

Then came the Negroes. They passed Judith first. The men put one foot behind the other and holding their hats in both hands bowed with reverence. The women and children curtseyed.

"Miss Judith, we's powerful sorry, ma'am."

"He was a good man, ole massa."

"Us niggers sho praised de Lawd we belonged to him."

"He gone right straight to glory, sittin' on a golden throne."

"Bet dey had jubilee in heabn when he come."

They filed by, laying on Philip's body flowers from their own gardens, till the dais was nearly covered with roses and lilies and purple water-hyacinths from the bayous.

At last it was over. They wheeled her indoors, for she was not strong enough for the journey to the churchyard. Judith lay in the parlor, Christine there lest she wanted anything. She knew what they would do. They would take him to St. Margaret's, which had been a log chapel when she and Philip were young and was now a church of gray stones brought down the river. They had dug him a grave in the Larne plot by the grave of little Philip, dug seventeen years ago. There was a stone on little Philip's grave, with his name and the dates of his birth and death, and underneath a verse from Scripture. "Is it well with the child? It is well." She remembered how bitter her heart had been when she ordered that gravestone.

There would be another stone on Philip's grave. She could see it in her mind. "Philip Larne. Born in the colony of South Carolina, June 6, 1744. Died at Ardeith Plantation, Louisiana, September 23, 1810. No man liveth unto himself, and no man dieth unto himself. . . ."

Why did she want to put that? Why not "Blessed are the

dead who die in the Lord" or one of those other unemphatic texts gone trite from repetition? She did not know, except that the other was so true of Philip.

The household began to arrange itself without him. David held a conference with the cotton overseers. He had never had charge of the cotton, and they would be good enough to bring their records as soon as possible for his information. They could start picking in the most advanced fields. And better look to the gins, to see that they were in good condition.

Everything closed up over the gap Philip had left. Nobody missed him, fundamentally. In no life was there vacancy but in hers.

They did not tell her, but gradually she came to know that her knee would never heal completely. It would not hurt any more, but it was twisted. She would be lame for the rest of her life, and she would never mount a horse again.

It was not important. Nothing was important, except that she was so lonely. David and Emily were deferential. The children never spoke to her without curtseying first. She was a great lady full of years and honor, with a gold-headed cane and a cap of finest lace over her white hair.

One day in the fall she rang her bell, and told Christine to bring young miss to her.

Emily came to the door. Judith sat in a big chair, her cane at her side.

"Yes, mother?"

"Come in, my dear." As Emily advanced into the room Judith unfastened her girdle and held out her hand. "The keys, Emily."

Emily's hands closed over the bunch. Unconsciously her eyes widened, as though seeing further horizons; she straightened up and looked taller.

"Thank you, mother."

She was a good girl; she would never remind her husband's mother how useless she was, nor suggest that she had outlived her authority.

"I hope I'll care for the house as well as you did, mother."

"I'm sure you will," said Judith. "And Emily, I'll have my things moved out of the master bedroom this afternoon. If it's quite convenient, I'll turn the back study downstairs into a bedroom. The stairs are rather hard on my knee."

"Of course," said Emily. "And wouldn't you like the sitting-room next door? You'll want one of your own."

"Thank you, dear. You're very generous."

Emily glanced at the keys in her hand. She detached two of them and handed them back. "Then these are yours."

"Oh yes. My own rooms. Thank you, Emily."

When Emily had left her she still sat by the window, looking out at the flowers and the cotton beyond, thinking how strange it was that the vigorous little farmer's girl she had been when she came down the river should have helped create this culture of tradition and gentle ceremony, whose strength lay in the fact that everybody knew what to expect from everybody else. Even now, though she had had so vital a hand in its making, she was not sure how all this had come about.

411

The afternoon was so quiet that she could hear the Negroes singing in the cotton.

I'll lay mah hand
Whar de cotton fields stand,
Hallelujah, Lawd Jesus,
I was bawn on dis land!

Hard to remember that she had first seen those fields as a jungle. Yet all this had happened in her lifetime. She had lived so swiftly. And now that was over. She had seen this incredible transition, had been herself part of it, and she had reached the time when nothing else was demanded of her.

Judith laced her hands over the head of her cane and felt a surprising release. Except for her lame knee her health was good, and she would probably live for years—years in which she could enjoy the civilization she had until now been so busy making. She would never have to live frantically again. She would never know such joys as she had known, but never again have to suffer as she had suffered. It was good to feel this relief from intensity. Her children and grandchildren would repeat her experiences and she would be there if they needed her, rich with wisdom because she had traveled their road before, a wisdom free alike of ecstasy and pain, and easily given because she had been relieved of that young sense of the universe circling around herself.

Judith smiled in her quiet triumph, marveling that not until she gave up the keys had she understood that in doing so she had paid the cost of peace.

ABOUT THE AUTHOR

Gwen Bristow (1903–1980), the author of seven bestselling historical novels that bring to life momentous events in American history, such as the siege of Charleston during the American Revolution (*Celia Garth*) and the great California gold rush (*Calico Palace*), was born in South Carolina, where the Bristow family had settled in the seventeenth century. After graduating from Judson College in Alabama and attending the Columbia School of Journalism, Bristow worked as a reporter for New Orleans' *Times-Picayune* from 1925 to 1934. Through her husband, screenwriter Bruce Manning, she developed an interest in longer forms of writing—novels and screenplays.

After Bristow moved to Hollywood, her literary career took off with the publication of *Deep Summer*, the first novel in a trilogy of Louisiana-set historical novels, which also includes *The Handsome Road* and *This Side of Glory*. Bristow continued to write about the American South and explored the settling of the American West in her bestselling novels *Jubilee Trail*, which was made into a film in 1954, and in her only work of nonfiction, *Golden Dreams*. Her novel *Tomorrow Is Forever* also became a film, starring Claudette Colbert, Orson Welles, and Natalie Wood, in 1946.

PLANTATION TRILOGY

FROM OPEN ROAD MEDIA

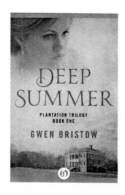

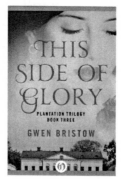

Available wherever ebooks are sold

OPEN ROAD

INTEGRATED MEDIA

Open Road Integrated Media is a digital publisher and multimedia content company. Open Road creates connections between authors and their audiences by marketing its ebooks through a new proprietary online platform, which uses premium video content and social media.

CPSIA information can be obtained
at www.ICGtesting.com
Printed in the USA
LVOW08s1039210517
535323LV00002B/416/P